THE BERKELEY PIT

an historical novel

THE BERKELEY PIT

an historical novel

DOROTHY BRYANT

For Mary Dolven

Dorothy Bryant

CLARK CITY PRESS

All inquiries should be addressed to:
Clark City Press
Post Office Box 1358
Livingston, Montana 59047
(406)222-7412

Cover design by Russell Chatham and Cody Redmon.
Cover photograph by Cody Redmon.
Photograph of the author by Robert Bryant.
Production by Millicent Hampton, with techinical assistance from
Cody Redmon.

First Edition
Library of Congress Control Number: 2007933299
ISBN: 978-0-944439-61-6 [Cloth]

Also by Dorothy Bryant

FICTION

Ella Price's Journal
The Kin of Ata Are Waiting For You
Miss Giardino
Prisoners
The Garden of Eros
Killing Wonder
A Day in San Francisco
Confessions of Madame Psyche
The Test
Anita, Anita

NON-FICTION

Writing a Novel
Myths to Lie By (essays, reviews, stories)

PLAYS

Dear Master
Tea with Mrs. Hardy
The Panel
Posing for Gauguin
The Trial of Cornelia Connelly
Sad But Glorious Days
Eros in Love

The major characters in this book are fictitious,
but the major events really happened.

A Note from the Publisher

During its first incarnation in the late eighties, Clark City Press received many unsolicited manuscripts every month, more than we could possibly deal with. A few of the staff looked at what they could, but what they did read was undistinguished at best, and went downhill from there to the unspeakable. Nevertheless, I was always of the opinion that valuable things got by us unnoticed.

Dormant for eight years from a manufacturing standpoint, when the phoenix awoke and started getting to its feet in 2001, Clark City Press had a staff of one, and only after six years of operation did that recently increase to two. Commensurately, the number of volunteer manuscripts coming in has been small. So, when two chapters of *The Berkeley Pit* showed up in the mail, I had time to take them home to read, hardly suspecting my long held contention that unsolicited did not necessarily mean poor, was about to be spectacularly proven correct.

Reading these chapters was like being stung on the point of the nose by an especially large bumblebee. I couldn't believe it, and my initial response was an almost twisted sense of denial that this could be. Nothing this tight and powerful could possibly simply appear in the mail. But there was not a shadow of a doubt in my mind, that the serving I had just tasted was quite out of the ordinary, and I couldn't get to the phone fast enough to order the whole pudding. When it came I devoured it in one long incredulous sitting.

When the shock subsided, and was replaced by astonishment, I reasoned that I must have barely glimpsed the tip of an iceberg, because novels of this depth and clarity simply do not spring from the hands of amateurs. I was grateful such an extraordinary work had been sent to us, and wondered how and why, until in her beautifully hand written letter, Dorothy Bryant explained that while visiting Montana a decade or so ago, doing family research at the archives in Butte, she had become acquainted with Edwin Dobb. Long familiar with our reputation for publishing carefully and beautifully, it was he who encouraged her to send the finished novel to us. We already had confidence in Dobb through his columns in *Harpers*, and had included one of his essays in a book we published called *The River We Carry With Us.*

I needed to get back on the phone to find out who this remarkable writer was. The call began with my sheepish admission that I had no idea who she was, which she seemed to take in stride. During that first conversation, Dorothy educated me to the fact that she had been writing professionally for thirty-five years, during which time she had published eleven novels, and three books of non-fiction. Five of her seven plays had been produced. The iceberg then, was more formidable than I could have imagined. As to her age, she allowed it was older than mine, which is sixty-seven, and we let it go at that.

Before long a box arrived filled with books, some work still in manuscript form, and a biographical sketch. I started reading, and by the end of the first novel, *Ella Price's Journal,* the hook, having been nicely positioned by *The Berkeley Pit*, became firmly set. By the end of the second one, *Miss Giardino*, an honest, graceful, mesmerizing novel that seemed to leach over into the realm of poetry, I found myself obsessed.

Since Dorothy had seemingly reinvented the form

three times, I now wondered what might be in store for me as I picked up *The Kin of Ata Are Waiting For You*. Nothing could have prepared me for that experience, which was so uniquely ethereal, that any attempt at describing it simply disappears in its shadow. To state the obvious, in no way whatsoever did this fourth book mimic the other three. Four for four.

Now I was holding the thickest of all the books, *Confessions of Madame Psyche*, and by now knew better than to even try speculating as to the direction of the coming journey. I didn't care, I only wanted to go where Dorothy took me because now I was hopelessly in love with her in the same way I have been with Käthe Kollwitz for more than forty years. Only the great novels bear you helplessly and inevitably along, causing you to lose yourself completely in an alternate reality. By the end of this stunning volume, I was as overwhelmed as I have been in this lifetime. Walking to my library, I pulled out *Grapes of Wrath* and *My Antonia*, placed them on either side of *Madame Psyche*, and put them back at the end of a shelf, even though all were now out of alphabetical order.

The quality of the work aside, it struck me as rather amazing that *The Berkeley Pit* came to us on the heels of our having published three other strong and important titles built around Butte, Montana: *Mile High, Mile Deep*, *Birds of a Feather,* and *Motherlode*, all of this one-hundred-percent serendipitous. It did however make me into something of a minor Butte scholar, which enabled me to understand the depth of research that went into this novel named after the infamous pit mine in Butte.

It helps to know that Dorothy's parents immigrated from northern Italy to Butte early in the twentieth century. Unlike others who went to an early grave in that mining city, Dorothy's family managed to move on to the dream of California, and the lush farms and orchards of the Santa Clara Valley. Dorothy then, is a native Californian, who has spent her life in the San Francisco Bay Area.

The setting for *The Berkeley Pit* is Berkeley, California from the 1960s through the 1980s. I was living in California during the sixties, was present at many of the real events which frame the novel, and had known several of the non-fictional characters like Robert Scheer and Eldridge Cleaver. I went to Peace and Freedom Party meetings, peace marches, sit-ins, Black Panther rallies, and Peoples Park riots, so I was well-positioned to appreciate the extraordinary accuracy of the book's events, locales and characters. In addition, I found the fictional supporting players to be beautifully constructed to represent familiar types like Jake Steadman, the everyman bookseller, Marsha Franklin, the everywoman dilettante, and Lisa Lyon, the quintessential manipulator of the system.

The very air during the sixties was electric with hope throughout the country, and Berkeley was one of its primary transformers. I was there then, but I was also there fifteen years later trying to step around the drug addled flotsam blocking the door to Cody's bookstore, and to witness first hand Dorothy's description of a society which had become co-opted and corrupted by insensitive, crude, and often mean users bitterly lashing out, its idealism lost along with its ability to recapture even a ghost of its early glory.

The story is narrated by a junior college writing teacher. Her sometime-student, Harry, is the subject. Reluctant at first to tell his story, she has decided that if she doesn't, no one ever will. Her narrative alternates with passages from Harry's manuscript, in which he describes growing up in Butte, detailing how his family got there from

Italy. In this novel within a novel, Dorothy assumes the voice of a conflicted young man, something just as difficult as a male writer speaking in a feminine voice. This she does with complete authority. The complex form of *The Berkeley Pit,* in common with all good writing, calls no unnecessary attention to itself, but rather serves the higher purpose of simply being an appropriate vessel for the story.

Essentially a tumultuous book, it nevertheless ends on a plaintive note not unlike Nicolai Rimsky-Korsakoff's masterpiece *Shaherazade,* wherein the closing movement is characterized by a deliberate lack of crescendo calculated to mitigate the chaos and grief, leaving us with a profound sense of longing tempered by serenity.

Produced in the autumn of a brilliant and noble career, this novel is by turns sympathetic, generous, often deliciously witty, intuitive, understanding and, perhaps most of all, compassionate; in all respects a luminous example of mature literary authorship by one of our most genuine national treasures. Discovering Dorothy Bryant was a revelation, something perhaps like having never known Franz Schubert lived, and then accidentally hearing the "Ava Maria." My life has been enriched and changed forever.

Russell Chatham
Livingston, Montana

To Pat Cody

whose warmth, intelligence,
integrity, and commitment
exemplify the best of Berkeley

On the day the twin towers came down, I hardly left my television set. Over and over again, I watched the plane make its graceful turn and plow a fiery furrow through the second tower. Over and over again, I watched each tower slide down upon itself. Over and over again, I watched New Yorkers running ahead of clouds of crashing debris pursuing them through the streets. And over and over again, I saw Harry running, his head snapping back and forth in quick glances over his shoulder to see how fast the cloud was gaining on him.

By the end of the day, of course, I realized the man caught on film was too short and too young to be Harry, who is over fifty by now. I'd had another of my "sightings" of Harry, tricks of memory and imagination that have haunted me for over a decade. I imagine that I see Harry in the photo of a crowd on the back page of a newspaper or on the television news—watching a building burning, or standing by the side of a derailed train in Arizona or Madrid. In my first look at a video of a rescue of lost hikers in the woods, I scan a face that looks like Harry's. I even listen carefully for the names of miners buried in accidents in Utah or Bolivia. Of course, it is never Harry, but I never stop seeing something of Harry in every scene of disaster.

Harry's own disaster was minor, local, generally forgotten. Few people knew or remember Harry at all. He was forgotten twice: when he left Berkeley in 1969 and again when he left even more dramatically in 1989. Only I have tangible reminders of him—in my garage: a box of his classroom papers, his attempts at a novel, a few letters. Still, I'm probably the wrong person to write Harry's story. I suppose these repeated "sightings" of him are simply my unconscious reminders to myself that if I don't write it, no one else will.

I knew Harry for only two or three years spread over a twenty year period; no, not as a lover, not even as a close friend. I was his teacher during the late sixties, and I tried to be his friend during the late eighties. When we first met, Harry was about twenty, and I was thirty-six—older, really, because I already had a fifteen-year-old daughter. Harry and I stood on opposite sides of the great divide in those days—age thirty.

Some people I knew in the sixties, despite being over thirty, did throw themselves into the scene and have given first-hand accounts of their experiences in dozens of memoirs and histories. This is not one of those memoirs because I was not one of those who dove in, but only dipped a toe in now and then. In 1959, I assigned Thoreau's "Civil Disobedience" to a high school English class in San Francisco, but I didn't go along to Mississippi with three of them in the following years. In 1960, I demonstrated as police hosed protesters against the un-American Activities Committee down the marble steps of City Hall rotunda, but I carried my protest sign outside the building, across the street, at a safe distance from the fracas. In 1961, I signed yet another petition against atomic bomb testing, but I didn't travel to test sites to join sit-ins. I gave a few dollars to people who sat in at hotels and car dealerships demanding jobs for blacks, but I didn't join those sit-ins either. And in 1962, when Pat Cody stopped me on the street with a petition titled "Out of Vietnam," I had to ask her "what is Vietnam?"

2

My husband and I had come out west from Chicago in 1950. The climate was good for our sinuses but didn't save our marriage. By the time our daughter was in school, her father had gone back to a suburb near Chicago, and Carol and I were on our own. I did substitute teaching in every public high school in San Francisco, and six private ones, while I worked on an MA at San Francisco State. By the early sixties I was ready to apply for a job at a community (then called "junior") college.

The best offer came from Oakland City College. I could have stayed in the city and commuted over the Bay Bridge, but I believed in living near the students I taught. So in 1964 Carol and I crossed San Francisco Bay, too late for the shop-in protest at the grocery store near the UC campus, but just in time for the start of the Free Speech Movement. As usual, I stood on the outer edge of the action on Sproul Plaza as Mario Savio stood on the surrounded police car and shouted, "—then you've got to put your body upon the gears, you've got to make it stop." And the following year Carol and I walked side by side in the first big march against the Vietnam War, one of the few things we still did together during her perilously defiant teenage years.

We rented a two-bedroom cottage in South Berkeley, next door to our landlady, Mrs. Temple (to this day I have never dared to call her by her first name), a dignified, ageless woman with definite opinions. Always neatly, even elegantly dressed when she stepped out her door, whether to welcome her church ladies or her grandchildren, or to put out her garbage can. When we moved in, Carol promptly wrote her exasperated father and dismayed grandparents that everyone else on our block was black, but that was not quite true. There was one very old Japanese-American lady who had returned to her house after the World War

II internment camps closed, one white woman whose black husband had left her, two Filipino families—and always one or two houses being briefly rented and wrecked by shifting hordes of white self-proclaimed hippies.

Mrs. Temple endured and ignored them. She had endured worse after her husband died, getting her three children through the university and out to the suburbs now opening to them (one daughter out of the country, married to an Italian architect.) They nagged her to follow them, but she ignored them too. She had her neighbors, her church, and her friends at the university food service. She had just retired, but still did occasional catering for special university occasions.

Our house on Milton Street was about a mile south of Berkeley High School, where Carol went to school, and about a mile north of Oakland City College, in what used to be an old high school building on what was then called Grove Street, where I taught English. The student body at the college was becoming darker and more demanding. The faculty—white and a few blacks—was split over plans to build a new campus with a new name—Merritt College—up on a hill where it was less likely that young men like Huey Newton and Bobby Seale would wander in.

Both Newton and Seale were briefly enrolled in my composition class, Newton for only about five weeks, until he was arrested and sent to jail for knifing a man at a party. He came back to the college a few months later but never bothered with an English class again. He'd met Free Speech Movement protesters in jail and now he and Seale spent most of their time selling Mao's *Little Red Book* on the UC campus, using profits to build (and, some said, arm) the organization they named the Black Panthers. I followed their beginnings as "cop-watchers" with sympathy. I'd met

Jessica Mitford and heard stories from her less famous husband, lawyer Bob Treuhaft, a veteran fighter against the long-standing tradition of Oakland police beating and robbing black men as they came out of a bar after cashing their paychecks. Even Mrs. Temple was nervous about going to Oakland after dark—ever since the third time she had spotted an Oakland Police car trailing her car until she crossed the Berkeley line. And I could never forget the 1965 anti-war march with the line of Oakland Police standing on the Oakland border, watching silently as young thugs threw rocks and swung clubs, while we all tried to cover our heads and turn back.

My other students never became famous like the founders of the Black Panther Party, though one or two, like forty-ish Marsha Franklin, were connected to prominent men. Marsha, whose husband taught Classics at UC, held a better degree in literature than I did and was, she said, just looking for someone who would take her writing seriously. Another half-dozen women her age were invisibly entering a classroom for the first time since high school, marriage, and children. They were far outnumbered (and shunned) by the young, clustered on either side of age twenty, about half black or brown, with a trickle of Asian immigrants and American veterans like Harry, already returning from the war zone whose name we'd hardly learned.

In those days, the two-year public colleges in California were free, and poor people, theoretically, could take courses that paralleled the university, then transfer. Or they could prepare for the parallel courses with remedial courses, if they needed them. Most did. And most thrashed about the college—confused, angry, and afraid of failure— then dropped out, a few to find jobs, most to find only more confusion, until they dropped back in again for another try.

5

They came and went, and I often felt like a false obstacle set between them and a promise of some undefined better life.

But that's their story, not Harry's.

In January of 1967, on the first day of my 2 o'clock remedial comp class, I started as usual, printing large block letters on the blackboard:

ENGLISH 101

R. CARSON

I passed out a list of books and requirements, then gave the first assignment, the writing sample. "I'd like you to spend the rest of the hour writing something. There's no grade, no right or wrong subject, no right or wrong form." I tried to smile reassuringly as they froze. "Just get something down. Write a poem, if you like." Their frowns only deepened, the most frightened ones turning angry. "I only want to know where you are, what kind of help you need. Write about why you're here, where you've been. Where you want to go from here. You can summarize your life or just tell about one incident that was important. No special length. Just give me enough so I have an idea of how you handle words. When you're through, you can give me your paper and leave. And before our next meeting, read 'The Lottery' by Shirley Jackson."

Predictably, one young man packed up immediately and left. The rest settled in with furrowed brows. I sat down and began reading papers from my previous class, every now and then nodding as someone put a paper on my desk and left. By the end of the hour, two people were still

6

writing, but when I stood, they handed me their papers—one of them with a shrug of despair, the other with a slight, uneasy smile of satisfaction.

That night I sat down and shuffled through the papers. I stopped at the first student who had ever taken me up on my casual suggestion to write a poem. That poem was my introduction to Harry.

Harry Lynch
Eng. 101
R. Carson

The Berkeley Pit

Say I was born in that pit
    a mile high
    a mile wide
    a mile deep
eating its way into the city
where nothing grows

Say I grew
    in a crouch
    ducking rocks flying at
    widows walls
    groaning
    cracking
    splitting
Sinking into the maw of the city
that devours itself

Say that father son unholy ghost were

crucified
and no messiah came
Say all prayers and curses were silenced
Swallowed with them down those
   gagged
   drowned
   throats.

Which one was Harry Lynch? Not one of the diehards who were still there at the end of the hour—I'd glanced at them and their papers. Had he dashed this off and left after a few minutes? Maybe. But it had the look of being thought through, written before, rewritten, memorized, at most tweaked a bit during the class hour. An aspiring poet? Definitely a reader, rare in a remedial class—he had used the word "maw" and he'd tried to imitate the style of some twentieth century poets. Literate, bright, maybe talented—but worrisome.

Berkeley—a deep pit? a city devouring itself? More than one bright schizophrenic had enrolled in my classes, turning in vivid descriptions of the nightmare world he inhabited part of the time. After a few weeks, if I was lucky, he or she would drop out. I was careful not to show my sympathy for these mental invalids. A friend of mine had been shot by one he'd befriended—yes, back in those days when guns on campus were almost unheard of, even in Oakland. My friend survived, but was often depressed and ill, as if infected by the disease of the student who'd shot him (and then killed himself). "Be careful, keep a distance when they reach out," he would tell me. "When the furies seize them, they go after the people closest to them." So I wrote coolly on Harry's paper, "Vivid images, but I don't quite get these metaphors."

On Friday I handed the papers back, taking a sharp look at the tall, pale twenty-year old who claimed Harry Lynch's paper. I read one of the others aloud. It was riddled with spelling errors and the verb reversals of black English, but gave a clear and direct description of the student's trip through the Southwest on his motorbike. "This writer says what he means, directly and simply, and that's good writing. Some corrections in spelling, some standard English verbs, and this could be worth an A." I could see that, as usual, they didn't believe me—they knew better, knew that good writing was pretentious, intimidating, genteel.

I asked what they thought of "The Lottery." Silence. I pushed and prodded and out-waited their silence, until they let spill a few grumbles: the story was some kind of trick on them. I prodded some more. Why did the author want to trick us? Silence. Finally Marsha came to the rescue, suggesting tentatively that maybe the author wanted to shock, not trick us. A young girl disagreed with Marsha, two young men started arguing with the girl, and the argument slowly, miraculously evolved into a discussion of scapegoating. Not bad for the first day. But I was sweating and exhausted by the end of the hour, as usual. I sent them out with an Orwell essay to read, and orders to clean up the mechanical errors I'd marked on their papers. "Use your handbook. If you need help, my office hours are right after this class. Oh, and don't forget, Eldridge Cleaver is speaking at three o'clock. In the auditorium. Extra credit for a page of opinion on what he says."

I had hardly sat down in my office when Harry appeared in the open doorway. He was well over six feet tall, with tan, thin hair, and pink cheeks pitted with acne scars. His blue eyes were round and soft, with an uncertain look that contradicted the glare he tried to create by narrowing them. His jaw was square, but his lips were full and soft. The muscular arms hanging from the short sleeves of his blue T-shirt ended in hands that seemed disproportionately small, with thick, stubby fingers. His thighs strained against his slim jeans, not fat but not strongly muscular. Like some very tall men, he seemed not quite put together—merely assembled from large, uncoordinated parts.

"It's not a metaphor."

I motioned him to step inside and sit in the chair at the side of my desk. He sat, unfolding his long legs until it seemed they could stretch to the bookshelf wall behind me. Well, it was a narrow cubbyhole of an office; it didn't take a giant to fill it.

"Your poem, you mean?"

He nodded, looking down at me with narrowed eyes and pulling a creased sheet of paper out of his pocket. Obviously he had crumpled it up, intending to throw it away, then had changed his mind.

I smoothed out the sheet of paper. "Let's start with the title, 'The Berkeley Pit.' You created a metaphor when you described Berkeley as a pit where nothing grows. And you'd have to prove, to me at least, that this metaphor really helps me to see Berkeley more clearly."

A relieved smile nearly erased his frown, widening his big eyes, loosening his jaw. "Oh, no, not Berkeley, not the city of Berkeley. The Berkeley Pit is in Montana. It's a real pit."

"Montana?" My image of Montana was a vision of wide highways running through forests, of rushing streams, leaping fish, wild bears.

"Butte, Montana. Mining. Mostly copper. Called it

10

'the richest hill on earth' until the veins thinned out, then they started pit mining."

I looked at the poem again. "Explain it to me, line by line."

He turned slightly, shifting his legs into a tangle as he leaned his elbow on my desk and bent his head over the poem. "'Born in the pit'—ever see a pit mine?"

"Like the diamond mines in Africa? Just the famous photographs, huge craters with men running up and down those long spindly ladders."

Harry nodded. "Except in Butte, it's trucks, big as a house, on a spiral road on the sides of the pit, hauling the rock they blast out, round and round, up the side of the pit, out to the smelters. They started pit mining when I was about eight, in 1955. Blasted through old underground mines, dug out whole neighborhoods that were built over those mines. Meaderville, where I was born, that was the Italian section. We lost the house when I was about four-teen. Mine hill, where the first underground mines were sunk, is about a mile high in elevation. The Berkeley Pit must be about a mile wide by now. Not a mile deep yet. That was stretching it a little, but I liked the sound of it. And it's almost true; the underground mines, some of them, went down a mile."

"Here's a metaphor," I told him. "'—eats its way through the city where nothing grows.' You compare the pit to an animal, biting into the earth."

"Oh, right!" His face lit up in discovery, like the proverbial man who discovered he had been speaking prose.

"'—city where nothing grows'?"

"A hundred years of smelter smoke and dust, waste runoff. The soil is a funny, orange, chemical color. At sunrise

11

it's kind of pretty up on mine hill, looking up from the flats. But nothing will grow in that soil, not for over a century." He nodded, then looked pleasantly surprised. "That's a metaphor too. As the underground mines closed, a lot of men were laid off—not many jobs in pit mining, negative growth, people leaving if they can, the smart ones. All my life the population has been going down. Nothing grows."

"You've been working on this for a while, haven't you?"

"And that's cheating." His eyes narrowed again and glared fiercely, fearfully at me. He looked ready to heave himself up out of the chair and flee. I quickly pointed to a line of the poem. "Oh, I think I get this line now. They blasted with dynamite to dig the pit?"

He nodded. "The gravel would fly past, sometimes you were ducking big rocks. You'd see windows break and cracks run up the walls. That was supposed to drive us out if we refused to take a settlement and clear out before they started. But Nonnarina wouldn't go. My great-grandmother. Oh, here's another eating metaphor, 'the maw of the city that devours itself.' That's not good, to repeat the same image?"

"It's fine. A short poem should probably stick to one image. And you have to be consistent about punctuation. Some poets don't use any. Some do, and they follow the rules. Check your handbook. And here's something I don't get, 'widows walls'?"

"Miners die young. Bunch of old widows left in Butte."

"Then it's possessive. And plural. Apostrophe after the s. Or, if you don't want to use punctuation, just take out the s—'widow walls'—though that might make it a bit obscure, it's up to you."

12

"Widow walls," he murmured thoughtfully, nodding provisionally.

"And it's 'sank,' not 'sunk.'" Harry nodded and scribbled the correction. "And what about the last verse? The religious references—the trinity—God swallowed by the pit?"

He leaned over the paper, finger on one line, then another. "No. 'Father, son, unholy ghost,' that means my great-grandfather, my grandfather, and my father. He's the unholy ghost, my father, never really knew him, mine accident when I was about four. My great-grandfather too. My grandfather went slower, the Con."

I must have look puzzled.

"Miner's consumption, silicosis, lung disease." His head was bent over the poem as if to hide his feelings, the way his casual tone of voice did. He looked up and smiled. "Nonnarina wouldn't like that; 'father, son, unholy ghost'— sacrilegious."

"And the gagged, drowned throats?"

"When they shut down an underground mine, they turn off the pumps, and the shaft fills up with ground water." He had straightened up in the chair and put his feet on the floor, his right heel slightly raised. His leg began twitching, his right knee vibrating nervously.

"Is it your first poem?"

He nodded. He was blushing bright red.

"How long have you lived in the Bay Area?"

He shrugged. "Haven't lived here. I've been in the Navy since I was sixteen."

"The Navy takes men that young?"

"I lied. I was almost seventeen, that's legal with parents' permission. My mother jumped at it. I had to get out of Butte. I spent three years on the USS Hawklotte out

13

of San Diego. Mostly back and forth to Vietnam, bringing troops out, bringing wounded and dead and nut cases back. Then they sent me up here. Oakland Navy Base, clerk-typist, sitting at a desk without much to do. So I thought I'd sign up for a class or two. Just to kill time."

"How much high school did you finish?"

"Not much more than year." He looked worried. "But they said you don't need a high school diploma to come here."

"That's right," I nodded, to reassure him. "You do a lot of reading."

"On board ship, time on my hands. About four hours of work in the radar room—they gave me a test and put me in there as assistant to an assistant. After my shift, nothing to do but drinking, dope. I got bored with that. I went through the library on the ship. Then, whenever we put into San Diego, I'd buy a box full of used books for the next trip." He smiled unself-consciously, almost forgetting to be nervous. "There was this lady in a second-hand book shop. She'd keep copies of almost new books she thought I'd like." The blush spread over his face again as he averted his eyes. I concluded that they'd shared more than books when he was in port. (How quaint it seems now—that he blushed.) He went on quickly, the blush fading. "And an old guy on the ship. He'd been in the Navy since the Korean War. He went for the classics, the old writers. He wrote poetry, was always reading to me, his poems, or poets he liked. A lonely guy. Drank a lot. He dropped dead, heart attack, just as we docked after my last run. And I got sent up here."

We sat in silence for a few seconds, in respect for the lonely guy who drank and wrote poetry. "I guess I did cheat on this, not writing it on the spot."

I shrugged and shook my head. "I'm not concerned about

14

that. I just wonder if maybe you ought to be in English 1A."

He looked panicky. "I was flunking English when I dropped out of high school."

"That was four years ago. You've done a lot of reading, and—look, I don't have a 1A this semester, but there's one that meets the same hour as my remedial class. I can get you into that one."

He went on shaking his head. "I wish you'd do something else for me." He swallowed hard, and his knee began to vibrate again, so violently that he stood up and moved toward the doorway. "Let me into your creative writing class."

"It's not really my class. I'm just filling in this term for the poet who teaches it. He's on sabbatical. It's our first and only creative writing class, a mixture of poetry and fiction."

"That's fine by me."

"All right. I'll be glad to have you. But you should take English 1A too, so that if you want to transfer to the university—"

This time he was shaking his head almost violently. "I really need the basic grammar, all that stuff. And I'm not going to the university," he said, as if the idea were too preposterous to consider. "When I get my discharge, I have to get a job. There's a big vocational program here, right?"

I nodded. The important thing was to keep him here until he was sure what he wanted to do, what he could do. I was already sure that he underestimated his potential. "The creative writing class meets on Tuesdays and Thursdays at three. Show up and I'll add you to the list."

"Thanks." He turned to leave.

I handed the sheet of paper back to him. "Why is it called the Berkeley Pit?"

"They started the blasting at the site of the old Berkeley Mine."

"And how did that mine get its name?"

He shrugged. "All I know is that it was one of the early mines they sunk—sank. Before Nonnarina came, before 1900, they were digging hundreds of mines, one next to the other, all kinds of crazy names: the Neversweat, the Little Sister, the Morning After, the Alice—whatever came into a guy's head when he started drilling."

"I assign a sort of mini-research essay at the end of the semester. A few pages, just to learn how to use the library. That could be an interesting subject—how the Berkeley Pit got its name. I wonder if there's some connection with the City of Berkeley. It's spelled the same way."

He looked worried again, nodded nervously, and left.

I went from my office straight to the auditorium. The climate had changed since Martin Luther King had been considered a controversial speaker. Now, even if we could have gotten King, someone more aggressive like Malcolm X—three years dead—seemed more likely to bring out an audience. Stokeley Carmichael demanded an impossible fee, and H. Rap Brown hadn't answered calls and letters. We were ready to settle for our own Huey Newton, but what had made him suddenly prominent was that he was in jail again, awaiting trial on a murder charge. Bobby Seale's inarticulate passion couldn't hold an audience. That left Eldridge Cleaver, just out on parole and newly titled the Black Panther Minister of Information. He was scheduled to speak at a Free Huey rally in Los Angeles, but had been persuaded (because of Huey Newton's connection to the college) to stop briefly on his way to the airport.

He'd talk only a few minutes, but we probably wouldn't be able to get him at all when his book came out in a couple of months. *Soul on Ice* was a collection of articles he'd published in *Ramparts*, a new, slick, radical magazine bankrolled by a rich San Franciscan. I'd read only Cleaver's first *Ramparts* article, an attack on James Baldwin, who was not the only one of my heroes rejected in the new Black Power mood: Langston Hughes demeaned blacks; ditto for Richard Wright, who then deserted them for Europe; Ralph Ellison was elitist, an "oreo" (brown on the outside, white inside). I seemed always to be slipping to a fall-back position in getting my students—black and white—to read. If my students would read Cleaver's book when it came out, I would settle for that, no matter how I felt about what he wrote. Only that they read something.

When I reached the door to the auditorium, I was stopped by a very young, very nervous black student. "This is a Black Power speaker. No white people."

"I think you're mistaken," I said with a bland smile. "The Black Panthers welcome white allies—at least that's what Huey said the last time I heard him." He frowned angrily at me, then uncertainly. No point in shaming him into the need to prove anything; I turned and walked down the hall to another entry, where the black "guard," one of my students, smiled and opened the door for me.

The auditorium, as usual, was only half full; those students most likely to stay for a not-required speaker often had jobs they rushed out to after classes. There were more males than females, and more whites than blacks despite the confused "guard" who'd tried to keep me out. As I looked across the hall, I thought I recognized Harry Lynch standing against the far wall. Also along the walls stood about

17

two dozen Black Panthers in their black leather jackets, powder-blue shirts, black berets, and, as always, very dark glasses masking their eyes. Their erect, menacing posture seemed an improvement over the studied slouches I saw on street corners outside.

Cleaver came out onto the stage. I'd seen him before, but always found it fascinating to watch him walk to the podium, slowly, with sensual insolence in every step. Sexy. Was it only the defensive pose of the almost life-long convict, always on guard, always in danger? He was as tall as Harry, and rail-thin, all muscle, graceful as a dancer. His beard was longer than it had been in the photo on the cover of *Ramparts*, but his hair was still clipped tight to his well-shaped head.

Cleaver began abruptly in a rich, low-pitched voice. "It's very hard to know where to start—in the middle, on the side, the front, the top, the bottom. Because our situation today, from whatever angle you look at it, it's just a lot of bullshit going on. I'm told that when I speak at a college, I shouldn't use four letter words, that cursing a state-supported institution, that's like cursing my own freely elected government. Well, I say, fuck the government, fuck the president, fuck the racist pigs, dig it?"

The brief outbreak of nervous laughter, then applause seemed to energize him. His voice gained resonance, quickly mounting in spikes of rage.

"America the Beautiful has been unmasked as America the ugly, America the hideous, the horrible, the murderer of mankind, in fact the number one obstacle to human progress on the face of the earth today, the successor to Nazi Germany!"

Louder applause. Smiles. Whether or not the audience understood or agreed with Cleaver's words, they were

18

entranced by his reckless attacks. I'd heard them before, the very same words, at Kezar Stadium in San Francisco, at a Free Huey rally in a Berkeley park. He never got much beyond these general condemnations, but I hoped he'd conclude, as usual, that "fuck the system doesn't mean drop out, take drugs and alcohol!"

Obviously he never prepared a speech, but, like a great improviser, tickled some sensitive spot in his audience, inducing a kind of intoxication that grew as it passed back and forth between him and his audience. At moments, with little more than a gesture and a curse, he evoked a roar of excitement.

The verbal limits of this virtuoso performance gave credence to rumors that his forthcoming *Soul on Ice* had been written mostly by Beverly Axelrod, the lawyer who'd won him parole, then massaged into shape by editors at *Ramparts*.

I had known Beverly slightly in San Francisco, when she was married to a teacher at a high school where I substituted for a whole term. She was five or six years older than I, intense, impatient. On the half dozen occasions when I'd met her, she was bored, dismissive of teachers in general. (I didn't blame her—we were a dull lot.) Her love affair with Cleaver—not unique among the white women lawyers now defending black convicts—broke up her marriage. Soon after she won his parole, Cleaver left her for a younger woman from a middle-class black family, and Beverly, said my sources on *Ramparts*, was quietly broken-hearted. I had heard that she no longer practiced prison law.

"—and I'm tired of having my door kicked down and other people have security and use it to enforce oppression! Don't just kick down my door, let all doors be kicked down!" Shouts and applause filled the auditorium as Cleaver glanced at his watch, then left the stage and strode down the center aisle, surrounded by erect Black Panthers, eyes roving suspiciously over the audience.

I was out of the auditorium by five o'clock, and I almost obeyed my reflex to hurry home. But Carol had gone off to UC Davis and suddenly—there was no sacred dinner hour, no responsible parental presence to maintain. Nevertheless I felt like a truant from Real Life, a would-be adolescent, as I drove north to Berkeley and headed for The Med.

The Mediterraneum Caffé on Telegraph Avenue was, and still is, a bare, cavernous room, its walls covered by huge painted images of Grecian masks and Roman pillars, dimmed by layers of smoky grime. Toward the back, an open metal stairway rises to an airless mezzanine with a few, usually empty tables, and a toilet I used once in 1965, then took care to avoid. In 1967, the main floor was crowded with large round and small square marble-topped tables jammed together, hardly leaving room for small, hard chairs. A counter lined one wall, espresso machines hissing, tended by three or four burly, scowling men who barked orders and passed out coffee and pastries to patrons who often formed a line all the way to the door. Only four blocks from the campus along shop-lined Telegraph, near the best bookstores and "art" movie house in the Bay Area, the Med drew a mixed clientele: students, faculty, clergy from the immediate area; workers, teachers, writers, activists, and drifters from everywhere.

Weekday mornings, from seven until almost two,

it was quiet. A few people sat at tables writing or reading manuscripts. Professors, priests, staff from nearby stores, carpenters came by, usually for take-out and only a few words with someone seated at a table. After two o'clock came students and teachers, social workers and salesmen from all over, unwinding for an hour, sipping, smoking, arguing politics and poetry. After seven, half the tables were held down by solitary students, studying. Later in the evening, large groups would drift into the now smoke-dim room after a lecture at the university, or a movie at the makeshift Telegraph Repertory (folding chairs in a dingy room at the top of a long dark stairway above a market), or a then-rare author's reading at Cody's Books—and the Med became quite lively again until it closed at midnight.

At all hours, day and night, there were young activists passing out leaflets, and a few old regulars, mostly men, loners who seemed to live at the Med, the way old alcoholics live at their local bar—former or perennial university students, former writers who had long ago published a well-received excerpt from a novel still unfinished, or artists who had been written up many years ago as promising.

I came into the shadowy cavern out of the late afternoon sun and stood for a moment between the espresso machines hissing at my left and the rumble of voices raised in an argument to my right. Blinking as my eyes got used to the dim light, I saw Jake waving at me from one of the larger round tables.

Jake Steadman and I had met in San Francisco in the fifties when both of us were long-term substitute teachers at Commerce High School just before it closed. Jake was the best and the worst teacher I had ever met. When I heard deafening noise through the wall between our classrooms, it might mean Jake was late again. Or he might be there, but absorbed in explaining a line of poetry to one student while the other thirty rioted. He devised the most creative and imaginative assignments (which I adapted freely) but usually lost the papers the students turned in. He must have been forty then, still darkly handsome, and all the girls were in love with him. His only passion was for his young son, whose latest photo he would pull out at every opportunity.

Not surprisingly Jake lasted only two months at Commerce High. I lost contact with him, hearing vague reports that his wife had put up some money to set him up in a used bookstore in Berkeley. Jake had rented space just outside Sather Gate, on the corner of Telegraph. It was absorbed into Sproul Plaza when the university campus spread southward. From there Jake moved down to the new campus border at Bancroft, where his rent kept jumping up, and up again. Just before I moved to Berkeley, he moved again. The shop-in (to force hiring black) at the grocery store on the corner of Telegraph and Haste had been the last straw. The supermarket chain abandoned it to build a new, bigger store somewhere else. The old pre-war, obsolete, sprawling building went up for sale, and, in the briefly uncertain market created by the Free Speech Movement protests, Jake's wife bought it, turned it over to Jake, and divorced him. Jake bought out the stock of one of the sleepy old bookstores that, one by one, were selling out to be replaced by better managed stores like Moe's or Shakespeare & Company. Then Jake took his own huge, eccentric collection of books out of storage and added them, along with almost anything you brought in to him, provided you would accept exchange credit instead of cash. Entering Steadman's Used Books was like entering a time-warp to find a dreamy or crotchety man like the ones who, back in the old low-rent days of the Great Depression, sat all day surrounded by piles of books that sold slowly, if at all.

By the time I moved to Berkeley, Jake was no longer wiry and dramatic. In his early fifties, he looked suddenly much older—pudgy and bald and worn. He had taken to smoking a cigar, and when he squinted against the smoke, he looked like a shrewd old poker player. The first time I entered his store, I looked around the dusty cavern, with its overflowing shelves and piles of books on the floor, thinking the musty disorder had been caused by his recent move. But the disorder never changed—except for the rising piles of books—during all the years Jake owned the store.

When I needed a new book, I went to the gleaming, brand-new, glass-walled Cody's Books across the street, where Pat Cody labored in a back office and Fred Cody bustled around the main floor, smiling and arguing politics with students and politicians. But when I wanted a quiet hangout, I went to Steadman's Used Books, where Jake would look up from a book through a cloud of stinking cigar smoke and say, "You know, of course, that George Gissing's novels make Hardy's look lame."

I waited in line at the counter, bought a cappuccino, and went to sit at Jake's table. I think that was the day I first met his son Aaron, who sat there along with four or five other high school students. They had just come from Sproul Plaza, where they had watched a few students burn their draft cards. "You should have seen all the television cameras! More reporters than card burners. All to see a few bits of paper get burned up. What does that mean?"

"Nothing," insisted a light-brown boy with Asian

eyes. "All those guys had student deferments anyway."

"I heard someone is trying to pass a law," insisted a freckled redhead.

"Someone's always passing another law. But the main thing is—it drives the military crazy, even if it doesn't mean anything," said Aaron.

"But then it does mean something!"

"Means shit!"

Jake sat quietly, benignly, almost cheerful among the shouting group of young people, of whom his son was clearly the center. Aaron was about fifteen, with pale skin, black wavy hair, and black long-lashed eyes. He was already taller than Jake and more dramatically handsome than Jake had been when he was younger. Jake introduced us, and Aaron gave me a dazzling smile as he shook my hand. The argument went on. Like Jake, I listened while I sipped my coffee, interested in what kids said to each other when they didn't notice us. Then suddenly, the whole group stopped talking and rose. "We're going up to the record store on Channing. They're supposed to get another shipment of *Sergeant Pepper's Lonely Hearts' Club Band.* If we don't get there fast, they'll sell out again."

"Don't forget we're having dinner?" Jake asked uncertainly.

Aaron nodded. "I'll be at the store by seven. But after dinner, I have to go right home. Homework. Mom'll kill me if I put it off again."

Jake watched as Aaron moved toward the door. As he opened it, I thought I glimpsed a familiar figure outside. My new student, Harry? The sun was setting behind him, and I couldn't see him clearly. Whoever it was stood for a moment in the doorway, then backed away and disappeared.

"Free Huey! Buy a badge, give a donation!" A young

white girl hovered over us waving FREE HUEY badges. Jake only stared at her for a second, then clamped his teeth down on his cigar. I gave her a dollar. She took it without a glance at me, dropped a badge on the table, and moved on. "Free Huey!"

"You going to wear that at the college?" I shook my head. "Why not?"

"I don't think—as a teacher—"

"You going to wear it right now?" I shook my head again. "Why not?"

"Well—due process. He has to go on trial. I'd wear one that said 'Fair Trial for Huey' but—" We both laughed. As a rousing slogan, my version lacked something.

"But you didn't have the nerve to refuse her." I shrugged. "You think he killed that cop?"

I shrugged again "I'm not sure."

"Huey was in your English Class?"

"Briefly."

"What'd you think of him?"

I searched for the right words. "Very bright, intense. Very capable."

"Capable of what?"

"I'm not sure."

"Is there anything you *are* sure of?"

"Yes." I stood up. "I have to go home and read papers."

The next day Harry appeared in the Creative Writing class, where I was following the format designed by my absent colleague. I was glad to see him sit down next to Marsha Franklin, who, in a motherly way, showed him her syllabus, pointing to the assignment we were discussing that day: "a short dialogue that reveals character." I read aloud a few of the dialogues turned in, made some of the usual "show, don't tell" comments about several lines and praised some good ones. Then I assigned the next exercise: a description of a room. I ended with the usual alternative assignment. "Although this is a beginning class, some of you have been writing for a while. If you have something else you've been working on, a poem, a story, part of a novel, anything—you can turn that in instead of the assignment, or along with it, if you like." Harry stayed after class, lingering near the doorway as the other students walked through it. He was looking at me uncertainly, as if he wanted to speak.

"What did you think of Eldridge Cleaver? I did see you at his lecture, didn't I?"

"Yeah. Fantastic."

"You brought me a paper on his speech for extra credit?"

"Well, no. I tried, but it's hard to say just what he said—it's what he is, not what he said, what he came out of. He was in prison. I nearly ended up in—" Harry stopped short, took a breath. "But it didn't break him. He broke it! He got strong in prison, writing, telling it like it is. And that could get him put back into prison again—you heard how the police are always harassing him. But he just keeps telling it like it is. I wish I had his guts." Harry dropped a book, picked it up awkwardly, bumped against the door jam. True, poor Harry was nothing like the man who inspired him. Even if Cleaver's menacing grace was just a public pose learned in prison, it had assurance. Poor Harry lacked any control over the potential strength of his large body. He seemed to be writhing with indecision as he leaned on the door jamb.

"Do you have a question, Harry?"

"No. I—I started something."

26

"Another poem?" Silence. "Want me to take a look at it?"

"It's no good."

I laughed, gently and, I hoped, reassuringly. "Bring it in."

"I did." He leaned his body away from the door jamb, took a step toward me, handed me a couple of pages of manuscript, then turned to flee, bumping into the other side of the door.

"Wait." I looked at my watch. "I have an hour if you do. There's no other class in here this hour. Sit down and let's take a look."

Harry Lynch
Eng. 222--Creative Writing

Invaders

Maco Duci F carved on
An ancient stone half-sunk
    in a foothill of the Alps
Grave of a dead general
Marching north from Rome?
    retreating back to Rome?
One step ahead of
Barbarians
Sweeping through the hollow
From west, east, north, south.
Warlords overrun the cowering people
Taking the sheep, the corn, the women,
Killing the men, killing each other

Lord Langero from the east
Stands on the body of

the warlord from the west
On this highest point
Of this mound of a foothill
Downslope of the Alps
Marked by the Roman stone.

"I give you my name
I promise you peace,
    shelter from invaders
You will build here, where I stand
    My castle.
    You promise me
    Half
    Of your lambs, your corn, your grapes
    And the first night with
      every virgin bride
    I promise you justice
    I cut off the hand of the thief,
      the head of the rebel.
    Now bow down.
    I keep all my promises."

But forever come the new invaders
Burgundians
Humbert the Whitehanded, the most fierce
And the strongest, most sly
Romans of the Cross
And the castle of the Lords Langero
    slowly crumbled
Until nothing remained but the name.
The crossed Romans stood on the rubble
Of the castle on the highest point of the
      footprint climbing the Alps
    "Build the temple here
    To your new Lord
    Lord of the Cross."
The King of Savoy rode up from Turin

"Yes, build the temple to the
   Lord of the Cross
But bow to me."

Another century, two
The people of Langero bowed and built
And paid tribute
   no longer to the Lord,
   now to the King
   and the Church.
They knew that nothing would ever change.

Suddenly
Came the greatest invader
Roaring down from the north
Over the iron road
Blasted through the Alps
Surveyed Langero, stopped, chose, planted
A dark satanic mill
To enslave the people
And to witness the birth of
Honor.

I read through the poem three times as Harry sat next to me, his eyelids lowered, his feet shuffling as if at any moment he might turn and run.

"It's—more difficult, but interesting," I said, trying to calm him down.

He groaned and shook his head.

"More obscure. Historical? Let's see. The Alps—"a footprint—?"

"Langero, the town where Nonnarina was born. My great-grandmother. Onorina Carlo. The town she came from—"

"You researched this in the library?"

"Langero isn't in the history books. Not even on most maps."

"Sit down, Harry. Talk me through it."

He sat, and his right knee immediately starting its nervous spasms. "The stone is the oldest thing there. Nobody knows who left it. Maybe the Romans."

"That would put it at more than 2000 years ago? And the next invader is the warlord, Langero?"

"One of them. There's some doubt about his name. Malangero? Laberangero? Anyway he stayed long enough so the town took his name, Langero. His castle was built near the stone. The highest point in the village is called Castello, just a small mound of rubble left. The laws, the tribute he took. That's supposed to be in some of the church archives in the Langero."

I nodded. "The feudal phase, brutal, but I guess it was the only way to get protection from the other warlords?"

Harry suddenly laughed, looking a bit more relaxed. "Did you ever see those books about Italian hill towns? I got one out of the library. Langero's not in it, but it must have looked like those—all these 'quaint walled cities' wrapped around a castle? One gangster protecting his turf and serfs against all the other gangs rolling in."

I pointed to a line. "What's this? Romans of the Cross? Christians?"

"Missionaries. Coming up from Rome from about 600 on? I'm not sure about that. Took another thousand years, but eventually they got the people to build this big church. Right where the old castle had been, even used some of the stones from the castle. I guess that says something. The church isn't all that old—late seventeen hundreds."

"You've seen it? You've been to Italy?"

"No. Nonnarina told me about it, showed me a picture of her and my great-grandfather in front of it when they got married. Pillars and a bell tower, all that." Harry was silent for a moment. "I don't know what ever happened to that picture."

"Where did you get the history? Humbert? The King of Savoy?"

"Nonnarina had an old book. A little thin book, written out, not printed. In Italian. She wrote it when she was a little girl. Wrote down what some teacher told her about town history—and a priest, who was trying to write something about the village church. Maybe her parents filled in some stuff. The ink was all faded and brown, the paper shredding. She gave it to me when I was a little kid. She was hoping someday I'd learn to read Italian."

"You didn't speak Italian?"

Harry shook his head. "She spoke the dialect, Piedmontese, wrote Italian. They're different. I could understand the dialect when I was little, but I forgot everything when—I didn't care about learning to read Italian until it was too late."

"It's never too late."

"I mean too late for her to know. When I was little, she would sometimes read a little from the book and try to translate it—her English was pretty good. Every other sentence, she'd stop, fill in something, tell me something she hadn't written down." He shook his head again. "I wish I'd bothered to write it down. She died when I was about fifteen." For a few seconds he was silent, far away, but at least his knee had stopped twitching. "I took her little book with me when I went into the Navy. Never even looked at it. Just wanted—something—"

"A keepsake."

He nodded. "The only thing I wanted from Butte. Second time I shipped out, a new chief petty officer came on board. Old guy, close to retirement. He'd been in Italy in World War II, learned Italian. We had time on our hands when we were at sea. So he read it to me, sentence by sentence, translating, and I wrote it down in English. Words he couldn't figure out, he'd make a guess at them."

I picked up the second page of his poem again. "I think I get the image of the last verse. The last invader is the railroad, the tunnel through the Alps—when?"

"About 1880. The year Nonnarina was born. You got that? 'Finding Honor'?"

I shook my head.

"That's her name. Onorina means Honor. Everyone called her Rina for short. My mother and I called her Nonnarina. Nonna means grandma."

"And your quotation from Blake? 'Dark satanic mills'?"

"The railroads brought machinery, factories. Langero became a factory town. Textiles."

"Did she work in the factories?"

"She and everybody else from age ten. Even after she married my great-grandfather, even after my grandfather was born. But she never used to talk to me about that. Mostly she talked to me about her mother. She really missed her mother. She'd tell how her mother planted vegetables and kept chickens so they'd have something to eat besides polenta. A lot of people didn't. Not even enough polenta, hungry, and the whole family working twelve hours a day in the factory. I don't know how to tell that."

We sat in silence for a few seconds. Then Harry suddenly snatched the poem from me and began to crumple it up.

32

"Don't do that, Harry!"

"It's no good. It doesn't work!"

I took the crumpled sheets from him. "Don't ever throw anything away. Give yourself a chance to learn something from it. Ask yourself, what did you learn by writing this?"

He let out a disgusted grunt. "That you can't cover two thousand years in a twenty-line poem. Anyway I can't."

I nodded encouragingly. "So?" Harry looked blank. "William Faulkner said something funny once. He said that all writers start out wanting to be poets, and when they fail at that, they try short stories, and when they fail at that, they write a novel." Harry looked at me blankly. "Harry, I think you're trying to write a novel. About your great-grandmother."

"A novel." At first he look frightened, then attentive, as if he were listening to some faintly voiced message. "A novel?"

I nodded. "Why don't you just keep going—in prose—describing her childhood in Langero. Didn't she tell you anything about it?"

He shook his head. "I have no idea how to show that, how to write about that. Can I research that time in factories? What they looked like? Is that in books?"

"Harry." I was suddenly inspired, excited. "You're in luck. *The Organizer!*"

"The what?"

"It's a movie. Italian. Marcello Mastroianni. Set in Turin about that time. About a strike in a factory. I'll bet they used actual settings. It's on that schedule I passed out the first day. The university film series? You kept it?" He shook his head. "Harry! Have you even been on the Cal campus?" He shrugged.

"Harry!" It was time for my standard sermon. "Listen, you're living near a great university. Just because you're not enrolled there, that doesn't mean it doesn't belong to you. The campus is open to you—films, library, public lectures, lots of them free. Use it. Now, get a *Daily Cal* and check that film schedule. I think *The Organizer* plays two more nights. Tonight. That's an assignment. It's been a couple of years since I saw it, and it's worth seeing again. Maybe I'll see you there. Then we can talk more about your novel."

That night was mild, and I decided to walk up to the campus. By the time I got into Wheeler Hall, the lights were down and the credits already on the screen. I sat down in the first empty seat I could feel my way to. At this second viewing, I watched the movie as if I were Harry, looking for technical, visual details of the factory machinery, the building, the roads walked by the workers from factory to home. The bare, crowded rooms of the family—the simple, telling detail of the boy rising in the dark and breaking the layer of ice on the water in his wash basin—not the usual American image of Italy. The interior factory scenes looked usable, but the exterior scenes were more urban, not like the old hillside village Harry had described. He would need some other sources to fill that in, maybe those books he'd found on Italian hill towns? Then I forgot Harry and just sank into the movie.

The lights went up. I stood, turned to look around, and saw Harry sitting only a couple of rows behind me.

"What did you think?"

He nodded slowly. We walked out together, down through Sather Gate and across Sproul Plaza. We were almost at the opening to Telegraph Avenue before he started talking. "That could have been the factory where Nonnarina worked."

I nodded. "Looked authentic."

"And the kid, the little kid at the end, after the strike fails, and he has to go into the factory—?" I nodded. "That little kid would have been just the age of my grandfather, Nonno Joe, Nonnarina's son. He was born there after my great-grandfather left for America. Never even saw his father until he was ten years old and his father sent for them. Sent second-class tickets, not steerage. Nonnarina always made a point of saying that." Harry turned and glanced down at me, his eyes wide. "It came to me, just as the movie was ending. I remember Nonno Joe telling me that Nonnarina was seasick all the way across the ocean. He thought she was dying, and he tried to tell people. But no one in second-class understood Italian, so he dragged them to see his mother lying on her bunk, and they just nodded and smiled, and he thought, these Americans, they must be monsters." Harry laughed. "Poor little kid. It's hard to think of my grandfather as a scared little kid. But I could almost see him in that movie, really see him." Harry breathed a regretful sigh. "I couldn't see him back when I was that age and he tried to tell me."

"Those interior factory scenes might be useful— visual details."

Harry was silent as we crossed Bancroft and started down Telegraph. The street was well lit and lively, restaurants full of people, all ages and types. On the sidewalk, huddles of youngsters, whites skimpily dressed in faded, ragged Levi's, blacks in clean, newly pressed tight pants, whites with long hair cascading from head bands circling their heads, blacks with modest but growing afros. Hard to remember how rebellious simple hair length seemed then, when the Beatles' ear-lobe length hair was still being condemned as indecent, even, in some mysterious way, dangerous.

We passed a white girl in a long, shapeless dress cut from a faded Indian bedspread, sandals, and an old army jacket. Her dull brown hair was long and straight, her face unpainted. In those days of painted, crimped, pinched, Barbie Doll movie stars—who set the standard not only of beauty, of but true womanly propriety—her determinedly plain look was both rebellious and quaint. The girl was passing out flyers for the Sunday Be-In at Golden Gate Park. Harry absentmindedly took one. She thrust one at me, then took another look at me, frowned, and pulled it back. "You're too old." As she turned away, Harry gave me an anxious look, so I shrugged and said, "She's right."

"You know," said Harry. "I almost wish I hadn't seen that movie. Every time I sit down to write, I'll just see that movie in front of me, those characters."

"I'm sorry. I thought it would help."

"I wish I knew more about that time. Like I know Butte. You know, she left one factory town to come to a worse one."

"Maybe you should move ahead and tell that part."

"When she comes to America?"

"If that's the part you think you can do. Fill in the holes later." I pulled another literary reference out of my didactic reserves. "That's the way Fitzgerald worked."

Harry only looked more worried, mumbling, "Yeah, but that's Fitzgerald."

36

I shrugged. "He wasn't 'Fitzgerald' when he started—just another guy like you who wanted to write." I was stretching the truth, of course. Fitzgerald had come from a privileged background, like most writers. Not even Jack London, despite his pretense of poverty, had had a background as poor as Harry's, as "culturally deprived," as we used to say before the phrase was banned as demeaning to poor minorities. Harry's deprivation, though not as severe, more closely resembled that of a writer like Richard Wright. Maybe that was why he had been so impressed by Eldridge Cleaver.

We stopped in front of the Med. "I skipped dinner. A glass of steamed milk sounds good. The Med okay with you?"

He looked toward the crowded tables dimly showing through the steamed-up windows and shrugged. "Never been inside."

"Oh, I thought I saw you at the door a few days ago. Looking around, not seeing anyone you knew, leaving. I do that sometimes."

"You saw me?" I nodded. "I was just curious. Didn't expect to see anyone I know. Don't know anyone at the university."

"Neither do most of the people who hang out here." I stepped forward and swung the door open, as if there was no doubt Harry would follow me in. He did.

I led him to the counter, where I ordered steamed milk/Orgeat. Harry, after a confused look at the list of espresso drinks, said he'd have the same.

Sometimes it's hard to remember that in those days, outside of North Beach in San Francisco, no one in the Bay Area was likely to have confronted such a list except at the Med, probably the only coffee house in Berkeley. We turned and looked at the tables, jammed full, mostly students studying alone. I knew I wouldn't see Jake, who worked the night shift alone at the store, refusing to hire anyone to take it on. Nor Fred and Pat Cody—if not at work in the store, they'd be at a meeting or at home with their four kids.

"Someone you know there?" Harry pointed toward a large brown hand waving at me, then pointing to a couple of chairs on either side of him.

I looked, then nodded, not very happily. "Bill." I waved back at one of the old regulars who "lived" there. I led Harry around chairs jutting out at all angles, all filled with people unable to move them an inch even if they'd noticed us. We sat down with Bill between us. "Hi, Ruth, haven't seen you in here lately."

"Harry, this is Bill Jackson. Bill and I were in a writing class years ago at San Francisco State."

Bill nodded at Harry. "Yeah, until I understood that a black poet like me was more than a racist like Murray Morris could handle."

I had long ago given up trying to contradict Bill's version of what went wrong. Murray Morris was only one of many writing teachers who'd seen great promise in the tall, light brown, handsome Bill, who seldom completed a class, and always left embittered and angry. In those days Bill had read in North Beach clubs with poets like Alan Ginsberg, had worked at City Lights Books (until he quarreled with Ferlinghetti), had left his black wife and dated only white women, including me, briefly, had taken hundreds of classes, on both sides of the Bay, but no degree, and seemed to end every relationship, every job, every class, with a quarrel and a grievance that sounded perfectly plausible. I'd begun to back off carefully from him during our first night together, after his third phone call within one hour to his lawyer, to check on the status of suits he'd brought—against a publisher, against a private school where he'd substituted briefly, against a landlord who'd refused to rent to him. He was paranoid, but was that surprising? Those were the days on the brink of the Civil Rights explosions, when, even if Bill had completed a degree, there wasn't much he could have done with it. I tried to keep our relationship friendly but distant, remaining one of the few friends he hadn't accused of betrayal—yet.

He earned a fair living working as an electrician, and when he was not working, he sat in The Med, where there were always new people showing up, young white students admiring his poetry, his ability to recite lines of famous poets endlessly, his amazing good looks, his references to famous people, whom, it seemed, he knew intimately, and scorned. Bill had recently begun passing out business cards captioned "Photographer."

"I just finished my best poem," Bill said. "Want to hear it?" We both nodded, of course, and, against the din around us, Bill leaned across the table and recited. He began each verse with, "What is Africa to me?" The question was addressed to a different person for each verse: a white man, a black woman, a child, a young black militant, an old black grandmother, a history scholar. At first the question sounded dismissive, then confused, then plaintive, then defiant, then despairing, then—

A laugh exploded behind me. "No, he don't know what is Africa to him." Another laugh. Harry was looking over my shoulder with a gaping mouth and wide eyes. I turned and looked. It was Eldridge Cleaver. I recognized Robert Scheer (one of the editors at *Ramparts*) and Jerry Rubin with him (Rubin was the one who was laughing). I hadn't noticed them sitting in the back corner. Heads turned and silence followed Cleaver's sinuous twisting and weaving around chairs and tables as he moved toward the door. Harry was mesmerized. Cleaver didn't raise his voice, didn't look toward Bill, but in the sudden, brief silence, we heard every word. "Africa ain't nothing to him because he scooped it all out of himself and poured in vanilla. Even got that voice sounds like he swallowed an Englishman and Martin Luther Coon. He's one of those old 'kneegroes,' lived on his knees so long if he ever had stood up once for his manhood, he'd fall dead. Let's get back to the city, get some fresh cool foggy air." They were out the door, and only Rubin's high pitched laughter came back through it.

Most of the people who watched and heard didn't even know who or what Cleaver was talking about, hadn't heard Bill's poem. After several nodded, "Yeah, that was Eldridge Cleaver," to their table mates, they quickly went to other talk. But Harry's eyes had followed his hero all the way to the door, and now they came back to Bill with a bored dismissal that made Bill drop his eyes, and suddenly look much older than his fifty-or-so years.

It wasn't fair. It had been Bill who'd sat me down and played me records of late Mable Mercer and early Malcolm X. Bill who'd kept reminding white liberals like me of the doors closed to him, even as he'd nudged his way into relations with us, speaking like us, reading what we read. He'd blazed the trail for this new generation who strutted down his path in dashikis or Black Panther leather. They— mocking his elegant intonation but adopting their own ghetto affectations—had no use for men like Bill. Neither did the new-left young whites. No wonder Bill had begun to fly into paranoid rages.

To change the subject, I asked Bill, "How's the photography going?"

Bill mumbled, "Been shooting mudflat sculpture, in color."

"Mudflat—? Oh, you mean that dump art, out on the tidelands by the freeway? Have you seen it, Harry?" Harry looked blank. "There are new ones every day. A whole airplane, last time I drove to the City—all assembled from trash." I realized that although my enthusiasm was real, it sounded false. I was trying too hard. "No one knows who started it. But now the art teacher at the college has started taking his class out there—against the law, of course, trespassing, but—"

"Hi, Ruth. Room for one more?"

I was glad to see Angel, who nodded and smiled vaguely at Bill, snatching a chair from a nearby table as someone vacated it.

"Harry Lynch, my student at Oakland City. Harry, this is Angel—Peter Derby. Angel does a talk show on KPFA." I didn't have to explain why Peter Derby was called Angel. His long golden hair curled like a shining halo around his pink, cherubic face. His clear blue eyes were always benign, gentle. When something was said or done that made him really angry, he only looked a bit puzzled, as if he didn't understand the feeling that possessed him like a toothache, and couldn't understand why anyone would have wanted to provoke that feeling.

"Oh, yeah! I think I heard you—in the morning? I just discovered KPFA."

"So does Ruth," Angel added graciously.

"You on the radio too?" Harry was impressed.

I shrugged. "Once a month. Like dozens of other volunteers, coming and going."

Ever since its beginning, around the time I moved to San Francisco, KPFA had resembled an active volcano,

41

boiling with inner tensions that erupted every five years or so, spewing out some angry people, then settling again into simmering conflict. Just after one of these eruptions, the year before, Pat Cody introduced me to Angel, who introduced me to the head of Drama and Literature, in need of replacements who knew literature, and could do the Morning Reading once or twice a month. Angel was one of the few who were paid a pittance for their work. The rest of his meager living he made by working part-time shifts at four or five bookstores.

"Have you heard? Mohammed Ali refused to be drafted," Angel said to Bill. "This will get black people against the war."

I was dubious. "Most of my black students despise Martin Luther King for 'detouring from civil rights' to oppose 'that white man's war.'" It seemed that Bill agreed with me—explosively.

"Where black men are doing most of the dying! Angel, you just don't get it! Every time that punch-drunk cretin thumbs his nose at white people, he throws black people into paroxysms of delight—which doesn't mean they'll come out against the war. They'll love Ali that much more, but they'll let him sink." With that, Bill got up and left.

Angel looked at me in confusion. "Did I say something?"

I shook my head. "Something upset him—before you came in."

Angel nodded, no less confused, but sympathetic—toward Bill, toward me, toward everyone. Angel always wore a Make Love Not War button on his T shirt. Women often took him up on it, then dumped him, except for the very needy ones. Still in his mid-twenties, he'd already been married twice to strong, bright, unstable women who'd soon left him. He carried a torch for each of them, and for other women who wandered in and out of his life. He reeked of pot and beer most of the time but always seemed alert. After closing Cody's or Moe's at eleven, he might go out dancing till daylight, then show up fresh and ready for his morning interview show on KPFA.

"Don't usually see you in here at night," Angel said.

"Mastroianni film at Wheeler," I explained.

"The one about the factory? That's a great film."

"For Harry, it's like a family portrait. His family came from that part of Italy."

Angel turned to Harry. "You don't look Italian."

"My father was Irish, but dark. I look just like my Italian grandfather. Northern Italian. All blue-eyed blondes, some redheads too."

Angel smiled and nodded. "Until I saw that film I thought it was all Anna Magnani stomping grapes under the sun. So you're at Oakland City—I mean, Merritt." The name had just been changed. "Live in Oakland?"

Harry hesitated, and his nervous knee began its trembling again. "Alameda."

"Oh, I thought that was all Navy."

Harry hesitated, then blurted out aggressively, "Okay, I'm in a barracks at the Navy base. I'm still in the Navy. Military. Okay?"

Angel shrugged, murmured, "Okay," nodded, made a soothing smile.

"I didn't go to Vietnam and kill anybody. I just brought guys over there, and brought some back in body bags. Okay?"

Angel nodded again. "I guess you run up against a lot of anti-war feeling."

Harry shrugged.

"Not much at Merritt," I said. "For a lot of my students, getting the skills to qualify for the military is a big step up."

"But here," said Harry, "if I was to walk in here in uniform, I'd probably get killed."

Angel smiled and lowered his voice. "Beware rabid pacifists." Perfect. As usual, Angel dissolved the tension. We laughed, and Harry's throbbing knee slowed down a bit.

Chairs were scraping the floor around us, people leaving. It was getting late, and the Med was thinning out. It was almost possible to have a quiet conversation.

"So what was it like?" asked Angel. "What's this war all about?"

"I never did find out, never met anyone else who did."

"When do you ship out again?"

Harry shook his head. "I went in when you could still join for a definite hitch, three years. It's up now. They can't extend it unless we're at war—a declared war."

"Not signing up again?"

Harry shook his head.

"Can they draft you?"

Harry shrugged his uncertainty.

"Well, not if you get a student deferment," Angel said.

Harry shrugged again. "I'd have to take more classes. I don't know if I can afford that. I have to move off the base soon, find a cheap place to live. Need a job too."

"You're not going back to Butte?" I asked.

"I'm never going back to Butte," he said, with quiet, flat conviction.

"Cheap place to live? Done. Right around the corner on Haste. One of those big old houses. Our commune. Jennifer

and I moved in there a year ago and—well, Jennifer's gone."
Angel looked sadly amused, as if his inability to keep a
woman were a confusing but innocent practical joke on him.
"We have one empty room, a tiny one off the kitchen, like
a closet, used to be the maid's room in the grand old days,
I guess." Angel laughed. "The house is a wreck, but your
share of the rent would be cheap. You could stay in that
room until someone moves out of one of the bigger ones. Or
until the university tears the place down. They own that
block. They're always trying to throw us out and level the
whole block. Anyway, you're welcome."

"You don't even know me," said Harry.

Angel laughed again. "I don't know half the people
in the place. Or even how many we are. It changes. Danny's
supposed to be in charge, but he's pretty busy, so—"

"Dan Lyon?" I asked.

Angel nodded, looking surprised. "You know
Danny?"

"Not really. I know his ex-wife."

"Which one?"

"Lisa."

At the anti-war march in 1965, I had found myself
walking beside a woman who had appeared at Merritt with
a group of local poets reading from their work. I'd bought
a copy of her slim, self-published collection, and she'd been
pleased enough to remember me. Lisa was a thin, inter-
esting-looking woman about my age. She too had brought
along her daughter, a bit younger than Carol. Together,
we four had skirted the march, walking a bit faster than
the flow, to the front, near the sound truck, where Allen
Ginsberg, dressed in white cotton, chanted and *OMM*'d in
the midst of a dozen boys and two or three girls, leaning
over the wooden planks built up to form high sides around

the truck bed.

Suddenly Lisa's daughter had begun waving her hand and shouting, "Daddy! Look, there's daddy!" She pointed to a tall man who alternated between shouting into a bullhorn, waving a clenched fist at the police, pointing the crowds forward toward them, then stopping to toss his head dramatically, throwing back the thick black hair that fell over his face. As he began shouting again, one of the march leaders jumped up into the truck and wrenched the bullhorn away from him, speaking into it. "Ignore that. We're not going forward. We're turning off here. Oakland police barrier. We don't want anyone to get hurt." The man with the black hair struggled to get the bullhorn back again until the leader pushed him off the truck. "Daddy! Daddy!" But he had turned away, and Lisa said, "Daddy doesn't hear you, sweetie. My husband," she murmured to me, her teeth clenched. "But not for long, if I can help it. I've already filed." Then she changed the subject. After that night I often recognized Daniel Lyon, passing out leaflets, shouting at street rallies, or standing silently on the side of a platform while someone else introduced Abbie Hoffman or Eldridge Cleaver.

"Isn't Danny amazing!" Angel wasn't asking a question. "Brilliant. Studied law, art. He got that other lawyer, you know, the one who paints murals, to show him how to paint one on an outside wall of our house, the wall facing toward the university. Like Dan wants to defy the university, dare them to tear down our walls. He's the one who started the junk art out on the mudflats." (I didn't interrupt to say that Dan Lyon was only one of a dozen people who claimed to have started the mudflat art.)

Angel was describing the commune to Harry again. "I don't know, you might not be able to deal with it. I wake up in the morning, and there's another stranger in the kitchen—often a lovely stranger some guy brought home night before. People move in and out, and—" Angel looked at me and laughed. My face must have shown that I was remembering the one time he had brought me into that smelly warren. "—and sometimes they leave a mess. Eduardo—he's our neat-freak—calls a meeting, and we talk about our commune rules, and some people follow them for a while." Angel gave me a gentle look that was as close as he ever came to a reproach. "It *is* worth the trouble. We're part of a social experiment. It's a new way of life, more loving, more cooperative. Dan says it's the only hope for the future. And we're lucky to be in on the creation, even if things are a little rough. You have to be able to live with differences— surprises—and not freak out."

Harry smiled. "I lived on board ship with some pretty weird guys."

"Why don't you come around tomorrow? Or—" Angel looked at his watch. "I'm going back there now. Early show tomorrow, and I haven't finished reading the book. Want to come with me, take a look?"

We all three got up and went out into the dark. "Want to come along, Ruth?"

"I'll pass this time. See you tomorrow, Harry."

They walked north up Telegraph toward Haste, and I headed south, feeling a bit pleased with myself. If Harry was edging closer to the university (as I was beginning to think he should), Peter "Angel" Derby seemed like a decent guide for him. Angel was a caring man, a responsible activist, judging from his broadcasts on KPFA, who'd taken care to finish his graduate work at the university while pursuing his alternative lifestyle. A good example for Harry, I thought, at the time.

Harry moved into the commune on Haste while he was being discharged from the Navy into uncertain status as a possible but unlikely draftee. He soon asked me about classes that would parallel university requirements, and I sent him to a counselor who helped him map out a plan. I showed him how to get privileges at the university library—going there frequently would get him used to being on the campus.

He stayed in my composition course (as well as the creative writing class), and, at the end of his first term, he turned in the mini-research paper I had assigned.

Harry Lynch
English 116
Research Paper
May 25, 1967

The Berkeley Pit

How did a pit mine in Butte, Montana get the same name as a university town in California?

In the 1860s Frederick Billings stood with other rich men looking at the property of the new University of California, which would soon move from its then-location in Oakland.[1] Billings recited the last three verses of a poem written by Bishop George Berkeley in 1752, "Verses on the Prospect of Planting Arts and Learning in America."

There shall be sung another golden age,
   The rise of empire and of arts,

The good and great inspiring epic rage,
 The wisest heads and noblest hearts.

Not such as Europe breeds in her decay;
 Such as she bred when fresh and young,
When heavenly flame did animate her clay,
 By future poets shall be sung.

Westward the course of empire takes its way;
 The four first Acts already past,
A fifth shall close the Drama with the day;
 Time's noblest offspring is the last.[2]

Billings said that the new university location should be given the poet's name, Berkeley.[3] Did that poet's name also get put on a mile-wide pit dug into the mining center, the heart of Butte, Montana? Is there any documented connection? No, but the connection is there, hidden in the history of Butte and Berkeley.

Mining started in Butte, Montana in 1862.[4] First it was gold, then silver and copper about 1870. George Hearst, Lloyd Tevis, James Haggen, and Marcus Daly formed a mining syndicate in 1875.[5] Copper was needed for new inventions: telephone, 1876; electric light, 1879. Workers came from Europe: first Cornish, then Irish, then Italian.[6] A smelter was built by Charles Meader, an independent mine operator. The area around the smelter, called Meaderville, became the Italian settlement. The big mine owners owned everything: the mines, the land over them, the railroad, the newspapers, the lawmakers, the judges.[7]

In 1891 Hearst died, and his family sold out. With some of her profits Phoebe Hearst built the School of Mines and the Hearst Gym on the UC Berkeley campus. She made other donations to the University of California (money that could have gone into safer working conditions, health care, pensions, widow's benefits for miners).

Daly, Clark, Heinze, known as the "Copper Kings," fought each other for control until Standard Oil forced them all out. By 1901 Standard Oil's Anaconda Company controlled the hundreds of mines on "the richest hill on earth." From then on, money flowed east. There were daily injuries of miners, weekly at least one fatal accident. No statistics were kept on slow death from silicosis. No health care, no disability payment, no death benefits, no pensions. (Bloody battles to organize unions is a topic for another, longer paper.)

In 1915 Standard Oil dropped Anaconda.

In 1918 Butte reached its peak population, 90,000.[8] That year Anaconda bought the Guggenheim pit mine in Chuquicamata, Chile, began to alternate operations between the two countries, playing one mine off against the other. Well-known miners' saying: "The Company never had a strike it didn't want."

In the 1930s Great Depression the population of Butte dropped to 30,000, one quarter of the people on welfare. During World War II miners' pay was held under wage control, and more men left to work in shipyards on the west coast. Butte never recovered population or production. The last attempt at underground mining (1952) used "block caving" but failed.

The Greater Butte Project (proposed in 1947) started in 1955. Aim: moving the town down to the "flats," start pit mining on the hill, at the site of one of the oldest copper mines, the Berkeley Mine.[9] Many people fought the destruction of homes and historic buildings on Mine Hill—land technically owned by the Company. Unions went on strike. (ongoing strike now, 1967).[10] Last residents forced out of Meaderville and other old neighborhoods by 1964. The Berkeley

Pit continues to grow.

No sources document a connection between the Berkeley Pit and the City of Berkeley. Nevertheless, there are clues:

1. The spelling is the same.

2. The largest town in Montana is Billings, named for Frederick Billings.

3. Frederick Billings owned railroads, timberlands, lumber mills in Montana—all essential to mining.

4. Frederick Billings knew George Hearst and his wife Phoebe.

5. Frederick Billings must have visited Butte frequently for business reasons.

6. Mines in Butte were named casually, by anybody who might be there when digging started. All kinds of names—like Little Ida, Orphan Girl, Rubber Neck, Venus, Wake Up Bill, and so on and on, hundreds of them.

Further research may prove that the Berkeley Mine—later becoming the Berkeley Pit—was named casually during a business visit by the same man who named the City of Berkeley in the same casual way.

(Footnotes)
[1]The Story Of Berkeley, Ed. Gerrard York
[2]Samul's Treasury Of English Verse
[3]The Story Of Berkeley
[4]Mining In Montana By Janet Forrard
[5]The Copper Kings By Aaron Garwood
[6]Copper Camp, Wpa Project, 1943
[7]Montana, An Uncommon Land, By K. Ross Toole
[8]Montana And The Great War By Everett Pace
[9]The Montana Standard, February 1955
[10]The Montana Standard
[11]Frederick Billings By Josh Anders

"I'd like to give you an "A" on this paper, Harry, but I can't."

Harry stood in the doorway of my office, grinning at me.

"You tried to include too much for such a short paper. Your opinion of Hearst's business ethics is off the subject—" Then I added hastily, "—though, given your family history, I can see—on the other hand, you did a tremendous amount of research—which was the purpose of this paper, to learn to use the library." Harry nodded. "So the only real problem is that your footnotes are sloppy. Details like that are a nuisance, but you have to do them. Just open the handbook and follow the form. I don't mean learn it. Just follow it each time, like following the dots." Harry went on nodding. "But you certainly earned an A in the course."

"I really want to thank you."

"For what, Harry?"

"When I got into these books on early mining days, it was like someone turned the light on. Stuff that Nonnarina told me—or tried to tell me—it all started coming back. I'm working on my novel. It's just pouring out."

"Good. I look forward to reading it."

On the last day of class in January 1968, I was almost too distracted to notice when Harry handed me another, thicker manuscript. I put it into my old briefcase—already fat with final exam essays—then sat for a moment in a numbed silence. It was the day of the Tet Offensive. The North Vietnamese invasion of the south had verified the most horrific, hysterical accusations we'd heard at demonstrations.

Harry seemed to read my mind. "So all that crap

about 'impending victory' was a big lie." I nodded. "I'm glad I'm off that ship for good. The body bags aren't the worst—if you've never seen a burn case—"

"Stop!" I almost shouted. "Sorry. Let's not talk about it." I picked up my loaded briefcase. "Are you going to Marsha's party?" Marsha Franklin had passed out invitations to an anti-war fund-raiser at her home, including maps of the Berkeley hills.

Harry shrugged. "I couldn't find a ride." I wasn't surprised. I doubted that many of my students, even those with cars, would feel comfortable climbing up to what was foreign territory to them, or, if familiar, a place where their mothers cleaned houses.

"You can ride with me." Harry hesitated. "Come on," I said briskly, and casually led him to my car, just as I had led him through the door into the Med.

Marsha Franklin had entered my writing class the year before, with everything that most of my older women students lacked (and everything that most of my young students would never have): a good university degree, a husband who was a full professor at the university, a son at Stanford, a daughter at Mills, and a large and gracious old house on one of the wooded roads that snaked up the eastern hills of Berkeley. Marsha had even published a couple of poems twenty-five years before, while she was still in college. She had signed up for my remedial comp class by mistake, but stayed, "glad to have a woman prof for a change," turned in stories and poems instead of the elementary assignments, and offered help to some of the students, her age and younger, who really needed it. At forty-six, she was almost as pretty as she must have been at twenty—petite, delicate, with a round, innocent face framed by blonde hair becomingly streaked with silver. Yet, if Marsha was more fortunate and accomplished than my other students of her age, she seemed more bitter and frustrated than any of them.

She had poured these feelings freely into the journal I required from all my students. I usually just riffled through the pages to make sure a page a day had been covered (or let a student who worried about privacy riffle through in my presence). Marsha wrote more than the required page a day, in fact, covered page after page with memories and feelings, most of them negative, and clearly wanted me to read them. I read enough to learn that she hated being a "diplomatic cookie-baker for faculty parties"; that her husband, had "made me stop writing," because he needed "a weak echo of his thoughts, his ambitions, his needs, his plans." And that her coming to take a class at Merritt College "is my divorce from his smothering demands—he'd make sure a real divorce would be a divorce into poverty for me." Then there were the worries about her children. Her older son was failing, dropping out of Stanford, and she suspected her daughter was on drugs. Her younger son was skipping his classes at Berkeley High and refusing even to think about going to any university.

After she got some of those feelings off her chest, the writing evened out a bit, and she began to devote the journal to notes and descriptions, bits of overheard dialogue, exercises to get her back into the habit of observing, thinking as a poet. She had signed up again when I took over as substitute for the creative writing class. She invited me to coffee, though not at the Med, which she passed through only for take-out when she was on her way to meet her husband on campus. Then we began meeting for lunch at a little Chinese restaurant near KPFA after I did my monthly reading. We never mentioned any of the personal outpourings of her journal. We talked about her writing, which she said she could not discuss at home or anywhere else in her world as a faculty wife.

When she asked if it was okay to pass out invitations to her party, she explained its intent was "to pass the hat and get support for some local clergy who had been indicted for 'counseling men to evade the draft.' But nobody has to give money. Some of these kids might just want to hear the speakers." When I said I thought it was okay, she smiled and added, "Ivan is furious."

"Your husband supports the war?"

She had laughed. "No. It's probably just that the party is my idea, that's what he hates. And he doesn't like Father Mike."

"Who?"

"You'll meet him at the party."

As we drove up Grove, I asked Harry how things were going at the "commune" on Haste.

"Okay, I guess. I'm not there much but to sleep. Can't study, no space, no quiet. No problem. I go to the library. Come home, there's always a party or a meeting all night."

As we began to climb up Cedar Street, we fell silent, and I concentrated on the twists and turns up the curving, rutted roads that dead-ended into each other as they rose up the hill. I laughed apologetically as I doubled back on my second false turn. "We should have brought the map. I always get lost driving up here." Harry nodded absently and concentrated on the views of the Bay and San Francisco flashing at us through the gaps between trees lining the roads. Finally I recognized the Franklin driveway, a steep, unmarked decline already jammed with cars. I parked on Grizzly Peak Boulevard, and we walked back to the opening of the driveway, then steeply downward among the cars for over a hundred feet, to the sprawling redwood shingled house.

As we stepped through the slightly open doorway into a thick, noisy crowd, Harry began to look panicky. People were clustered in a dozen groups scattered through the wood-paneled living and dining rooms. There were scraps of conversation about the Tet Offensive, but more talk related to university affairs. I didn't see anyone I knew, but didn't expect to.

One group circled around a man who seemed to be expounding a theory of Berkeley. "A city? No, a string of islands, isolated from one another, sometimes unaware each of the other, yet often in blind conflict." Islands? someone asked skeptically, and he started counting on his fingers. "The university, of course, like a citadel, all but walled off from the city. The churches, business, industries, public schools, private schools. Each residential neighborhood makes a world: hills, flats—northside whites, southside blacks, Hispanics west. Spotted with a network of petty crime families all over the flats—some of them go back three generations. So do the cops, who know them all, and, of course, they're on an island separate from the firemen. Waves of transients—students and visiting professors, hippies, seekers, crazies, political agitators—pour through them as through a fog or a gathering of invisible ghosts—or the way European invaders hit all the South Sea islands, hardly noticing the indigenous tribes."

"Looks like you're ready to start another book, Joe. Got a title?"

"How do you like *The Berkeley Archipelago*?"

Harry wore a frozen, angry frown obviously meant

to mask his confusion at being brought to this "island" so foreign to him.

"Harry! I'm so glad you could come!" Marsha pointed Harry in the direction of some young students, then took my arm and began to steer me toward a tall, hefty man with a ruddy complexion and a white Van Dyck beard, who was walking around with a bottle of white wine in one hand and three glasses in the other, held by the stems between curled fingers. "Ruth, this is my husband, Ivan." Compared to tiny Marsha, her husband seemed a giant, literally overshadowing her.

Someone called Marsha away, and I was left with her husband, who managed to pour me a glass of white wine, still keeping the other glasses wrapped in the fingers of one hand. "Your readings on KPFA are superb," he said, in a deep voice and a drawling accent I couldn't place. I remembered Marsha telling me he had spent much of his childhood living in parts of Europe where his father taught Portuguese/Brazilian literature.

"You've heard me?"

"When your broadcast happens to coincide with my office hours. You know what I like about you? You're absent. Your voice has no character of its own. It doesn't get between me and the story. It's like clear water, distilled water, tasteless, empty of any mineral properties or—" He went on with what I assumed was a compliment, but wasn't sure. Soon I was lost, as I remembered having been lost in some college classes where an amiable professor rambled on and on, leaving his captive audience far behind.

Suddenly he fixed me sternly with a hard glance, and said, "But that review of *The Graduate* was a trifle moralistic, you know. Yes, Marsha brought that rag home." He began to analyze my review published in a short-lived little arts and film magazine, losing me again. Then he suddenly stopped in mid-sentence, greeted a passing man and went off to refill wine glasses. Whatever his relation to Marsha, whatever his feeling about the purpose of the party, whatever his speech mannerisms, Ivan Franklin played the host like a harmless, friendly, absent-minded teddy bear. Even his pompous criticisms were friendly, too innocently well-meant to offend me.

I stood there gulping at my glass of wine, as if it might dull the assault of voices and laughter blending into meaningless, irritating, wearying noise. I drifted toward the kitchen, a little island of quiet. Glancing through the doorway, I saw a black woman in a silvery cocktail dress, a towel wrapped around her waist. "Mrs. Temple?"

She looked up from the plate of crackers she was arranging. "Oh, Ruth. Hello." Back to the plate.

"Are you catering this? I thought you'd retired."

She shook her head. "Just came in here to get out of all that noise."

"Lillybee, what are you doing back here?" Marsha was behind me, starting to jingle a small bell. "I'm just about to start the program."

Lillybee? Short for Lillian? It was the first time I'd heard Mrs. Temple's first name.

"Okay, Marzypan, just a minute. I'm coming."

Marzypan? For Marsha, obviously.

"Father Mike is going to speak."

As Marsha moved away, tinkling her little bell, I saw a look of distaste flash across Mrs. Temple's face. She saw me watching her and said, "You go ahead."

I was in no hurry either. The little bell was still tinkling over the din of a dozen conversations. I picked up a knife and began slicing cheese, putting it on the plate of crackers.

"So, Marsha takes your class at the City College?"

"Yes. She's a good writer."

"She says you're a pretty good teacher too."

"Have you known Marsha a long time?"

"Oh, my, yes, longer than any living soul but her mother—since I was Lillybee and she was Marzipan, but just to each other. I was her baby-sitter when I was in high school. Right in this house. Her father was a professor too. Wonderful man, got me the job at the university—back when they didn't hire black people. Got a scholarship for my son. Too bad he and Ivan split on politics."

"Politics?"

"Oh, way back, when Ivan and Marsha just married. That loyalty oath? The old professor had tenure, refused to sign, but Ivan signed it, not to lose his job. That was a bad time. Broke up friendships. Almost broke up this family." She shook her head. "I wasn't taking sides. Talked about the kids, theirs and mine, nothing else. Then the old professor died, and we all got into politics together, those that signed and those that didn't. And me too."

"Politics?"

"About ten years ago. Ran most of those businessmen off the City Council, those Republicans who used to do nothing but keep their taxes down, keep colored in their place. We did it together, Marsha and Ivan working on the hill vote for blacks like Sweeney, Rumford. Me and my church folks working on South Berkeley for Kent and some of their hill candidates, good people, university people who took an interest in Berkeley back then, all parts of Berkeley, in those days. Ancient history. But we had fun, before those new people run us out. White and black. Call themselves radicals. 'Progressives.' Huh. Don't know the first thing about Berkeley. Don't care. Just came in here to mess around for a while, then leave the mess for us to clean up."

"Well," I said, "I guess that's what the Black Panthers are trying to do."

Mrs. Temple froze and looked up from the plate, wiping her hands on the towel around her waist. She opened her mouth, then closed it again.

"I mean—" I said, uncertainly. "—trying to form coalitions like—"

Mrs. Temple gave an almost imperceptible shrug and removed the towel. "Sounds quiet out there now. You want to go hear that priest."

"Aren't you coming?"

She poured herself a glass of water and drank it down. "I heard him already."

I went back into the living room, where Marsha had climbed up on a stool and stood jingling the small bell, then stopped. She smiled, and, like a little girl shyly forcing herself to speak to the grownups, began to talk about the purpose of the party, to raise funds to defend six priests and ministers—"none of them Quakers, which might have been safer," who had offered draft counseling and were charged with "conspiracy to encourage draft evasion." Marsha's mouth trembled in her apologetic smile, and I glanced across the room at her husband, who was beaming, smiling, still filling the nearest glasses. If he was furious, as she'd said, he certainly was putting on a good act. "I want to introduce Father Mike Ruga, who can give a clear explanation of what this means." Marsha stepped down as we applauded.

Father Ruga was an extraordinarily handsome man, with wavy black hair, a strong jaw, and intense eyes. "It means that the warmongers want to put a chill on the faith community, which has a double responsibility—to resist the war and to turn around our superiors, whom, of course, we are defying!" Father Mike had a strong, musical voice, and he spoke with gusto as he described the charges, the schedule of hearings, the possible trial dates. "With enough support, I think we'll never come to trial." Polite applause. Then he introduced the other ministers and rabbis who had been charged, and we applauded each one. As Marsha walked through the crowd with an elegant glass bowl—into which we all put cash or a check—people began shifting around, opening a gap through which I saw Harry, smiling happily, next to Angel, who stood behind a table of books offered for sale.

By the time the fund-raising talk ended, I was standing near a window. It took a few minutes for me to realize I was standing next to Pat Cody. Pat was pale, with straight, short blonde hair, conventional, forgettable clothes, and matter-of-fact, deceptively bland eyes behind unfashionably framed glasses. She had a quiet, still way of blending into the background, like an alert deer. In those days she blended into the background at Cody's Books too, managing the books, keeping the store afloat writing articles on economics, raising their four children.

"How do you know Marsha?" I asked her.

"Anti-nuclear vigils. We used to stand together every Sunday in front of City Hall. She would show up late—after church—and our kids would run around us for a few minutes."

The party had become noisy again. Loud music began pouring from a record player. Pat looked at her watch. "I rode up with Angel. He's representing Cody's Books tonight—proceeds to the cause." She sighed. "Looks like he'll be here late."

"I'm ready to go," I said. "I'll drop you off. Harry can go home with Angel."

We waved at Harry and Angel, making exit signals, while they nodded cheerfully. Harry was being pulled to the middle of the room to dance with a beautiful, very thin girl, Marsha's daughter?

Pat and I climbed up the driveway and down the road, stumbling over roots and rocks. Pat pulled out a pocket flashlight. "I always bring this up here. These people think street lights and clear numbers on the houses ruin the scenery."

We found my car and started down the hill.

"Where's Fred, at the store?"

She shook her head. Fred was at a meeting called by young activists to organize response to the latest war news. Pat sighed, then laughed. "He's trying to cool off some hot heads who'd like to shut down the classes of some of these folks."

When I got home, I made a cup of tea, then sat wishing I had an excuse to delay facing the pile of exams. Oh, yes, I did have an excuse in my briefcase. I could spend a few minutes dipping into Harry's attempt at his novel. I intended to read only a few pages, but I read it straight through.

Three weeks, Onorina lying on her bunk, retching and moaning. The hold of the ship smelling like vomit. Ten-year-old Tato, wandering the decks alone, climbs down into the cabin, looks at her and cries, "Don't die, Mamma, don't die." She can't raise her head, can't tell him she wants to die.

The ship docks. Alive but weak, she pins the paper to her coat.

Onorina Carlo Cardone

Train

Butte, Montana

Onorina and Tato hold hands, not to lose each other. Hours and hours in the noisy building bigger than the church in Langero, bigger than the whole village. A line, another line. Each time they reach the head of the line, a new confusion, a new shame. People gabbling questions she can't understand, translators speaking bad Italian with ugly Sicilian accents or worse American accents. Men in white coats poking, peering at her like an animal. Just as she thinks it will never end, they are pushed through a door, onto a barge, and, half an hour later, pushed off onto the land. America. Noisy crowds of people rushing one way and another. She tightens her grip on Tato's hand and walks into the crowds, looks for respectable women, points to her sign, another woman, another. Finally one of them smiles, says something in English, then in French, then in stiff, formal, blessed Italian. The woman shows Rina how to buy train tickets, sits with Rina and Tato all the way to Philadelphia. Then kisses Tato on the forehead, shakes Rina's hand, waves, "Buona fortuna," and is gone, into another crowd.

Rina sits beside a window, watching America pass. Tato runs up and down the aisle, finds a French boy, a Greek girl to play with. Rina can eat a little now, even the disgusting American bread. America passes. Chicago—twisting tracks through miles of railroad yards. After Chicago—a single track, empty land, yellow grass on both sides. The third night, thunder and lightning enough to split the earth, no hollows to hide in like Langero, only flat, open land and lightening searching to strike whatever stands.

The tenth night a thousand cows blocking the track, not like cows in Langero, longer horns and legs. Every morning a shanty railroad station. Rina makes herself leave the train at each stop, walks up and down, up and down, past surly, spitting white men slouching against cracked-paint wooden walls, and long-braided Indians mumbling over whiskey bottles. Rina's eyes straight ahead, Tato's hand in hers, until it is time to board the train again. An ache settles into her bones.

The train begins to climb up from the flat plains of grass. Up to trees. Thick forest. Rina and Tato doze, wake up to see snow. Thinning trees. Low scrub. Higher and higher. Darkness comes again. They doze.

Someone shaking her shoulder. Rina opens her eyes. The conductor. "Butte," he says, "ten minutes," holding his hands flat out so she can count his ten fingers. She nods, arranges her hair, puts on her hat, her best hat, now dusty and crushed, rubs her handkerchief over Tato's face, smears the dirt, spits on the handkerchief and keeps rubbing until Tato cries.

Through the window, light shining behind the mountain. Sunrise? At four in the morning? A forest fire? Burning wood never smelled so bad. Never made such unholy light, such black smoke, white smoke. The train stops at the station, dingy and ugly as the others, but bigger. A wooden sign swinging in the cold wind: BUTTE. Faces of men standing on the platform, there he is, Francesco. He does not carry a lantern, does not need one. He and the train station, everything, lit up by the strange light behind and above. "Tua pappa," she says to Tato. Tato sees a man like the other men at the other train stations, a stranger, a rough American.

Rina steps down from the train, and the stranger grabs her, hugs her hard. He smells of sweat and wine and sulfur. He rubs Tato's head. Rina pretends not to notice Tato pulling away. Francesco is a stranger to her too. His mustache longer. His eyes red and tired. The twist of his mouth, hard, coarse, that is new. For eight years Rina had refused to come to America. Till her mother, the mother she never wanted to leave, said, "Your place is with your husband." This man? Is this man still her husband?

The trunks come off the train onto a cart. They all three push the cart uphill, toward the strange light. Toward the noise. The rotten smell. Rina hears the crunch of their feet in the snow. Then the sound is drowned out by thumps and clangs, metal on metal.

Dim street lights. Brighter lights from windows of low wooden shacks, from windows of high buildings like great brick barns. Lights on everywhere. Shops open. Does America never sleep? Rough laughter spilling out of some buildings, then men spilling out, stumbling, fighting, singing, shouting. Now Rina can see the hill, source of the light and noise and smells. Tall black skeleton towers, like thin iron birds with mean little round heads looking down from the sky. All around them lights flash, sparks fly out like showers of stars. All at once, a blast of red flame shoots up into the sky, higher than the little round heads of the black skeleton birds, disappearing in white smoke, shooting up again.

They turn right, still pushing upward toward four giant smoke stacks, tops invisible in the clouds of thick, gray smoke pouring from them, drifting, sinking down over the hill. Tato starts to cough. "You get used to the smelters," Francesco says. "They say the arsenic in the smoke is good for the skin, makes it soft and white. Makes the Butte women good-looking." He says this with a look and a tone that Rina does not like. He laughs, then coughs, coughs. Rina decides, wherever he learned to talk that way, he won't talk that way in her home. If she can make a home in this place.

They climb the icy road. On either side of them the snow is blackened by dark chunks, stones, ooze. "Slag." Francesco pronounces the ugly English word with authority. "Waste from the smelters." Some of the slag makes little hills, and some is pressed into blocks, stacked and falling over into the road.

"Where do they put it?" Rina asks, speaking for the first time.

Francesco shrugs. It just piles up, near the mines, the houses, everywhere. He leads them past one of the giant iron birds, close enough so they can see the thick metal cable running down through the middle of the skeleton. "Head frame. Some say gallus frame," he says. "Some call them gallows frames." That ugly laugh again. "Because too many men die down there." He describes how he is jammed into a cage and lowered, plunged down into a mine by the cable that spins out from the head of the iron bird. He points to each head frame as they pass, naming the mine it marks: "Leonard. Black Rock. Berkeley. Minnie Healy, Colusa. I work all of them." Tato stumbles. "Almost there. Meaderville. Grosso, Zermani, Calvetti—you know them. They all live here. All the Italians, mostly Piedmontesi, a few Genovesi."

A whistle screams, and Rina almost screams with it. "Just the end of a shift," Francesco explains. "That's the Leonard Mine. You can tell by the whistle. All different. Every mine whistle has a different tone. After a while, you know every shift change, every mine. Three shifts, twenty-four hours a day. When I first came, it was two shifts, twelve hours. But to stay down there twelve hours—" He stops and shakes his head. Small, dark shapes seep out from under the tall head frames, like dark eggs laid by the skeleton birds, slowly rolling away. Men going down the snow slope. Most of them rush toward the shacks nearest to the mines, almost next to the black head frames, saloons where lights flicker, doors open and close, sucking men in.

Finally they reach a two-story wooden house where a woman greets them in Piedmontese. This is Netti, a distant cousin of Francesco, born in Cirié. Rina is almost too tired to speak. Netti leads her upstairs to a tiny room hardly wide enough for a narrow bed. Somehow, a cot for Tato has been squeezed in against the wall. Francesco leaves—he's on the next shift at the Judy Mine. Rina and Tato fall on their beds in their clothes, sleeping and waking and sleeping again between thumps, crashes, fire showers outside, and men tramping around inside the boarding house.

Rina wakes up, hears kitchen noise. Tato still sleeping, a pained frown on his little face, like a bad dream. She finds her way down the stairs, along the hall to the kitchen. Netti points out the window to the outhouse, to tubs where she can wash, even lends her a towel, and, when she comes back in, sits her down with a cup of coffee. "I don't usually take families. Single men are less trouble." Netti chatters on, softly, kindly, in soothing Piedmontese, all about her three children, about her husband killed in a mine accident, about her rules for her boarders. "This is a decent house. Francesco had no worry about bringing you here." Rina sees a clock on the wall. Ten o'clock? Night? "Morning" But it's still dark. Netti shrugs. "A lot of time we don't see the sun. Street lights burn all day. It's the smelter smoke." Netti keeps stirring a pot on the stove. "You get used to it." And the noise, day and night? "It's only quiet when there's a lay-off or a strike. You learn to thank God for the noise," she says, crossing herself. Rina gets up to help Netti set the table.

Netti serves three meals a day, three dinners for miners coming off each of the three shifts. Stew.

The same stew warmed over and over. For an Italian, Netti is a lousy cook. Most of her ten boarders eat at the saloon. Netti doesn't care. They have to pay, eat or not. Rina decides then and there, silently, that if her family pays for meals, they eat them, and Francesco doesn't buy his dinner in a saloon. But how can they eat this *pachok*?

Every night after Francesco and Tato fall asleep, Rina cries. Prays and cries. During the day, she keeps busy.

She takes over the cooking for Netti, and dinner becomes edible. That means taking over the shopping, buying from the wagons that come into Butte every week, produce from a few Chinese out in Bear Gulley, meat and milk from a few Italians who farm up in Brown's Gulch. She finds her way to little Italian shops in Meaderville where she can find mortadella and prosciutto, and imported parmesan. The shopkeepers like Rina, because she knows good food. She asks where she can buy seed so that in the spring she can plant a little kitchen garden, with fresh herbs too, like her mother's garden back home in Langero. Shopkeepers laugh. No one sells seeds. Waste of money—when the snow melts, it will uncover dead dirt, killed by the smelter smoke, the chemicals used in the mines, the waste spilled out of the mines. Nothing grows in Butte.

Except in one place. A mile downhill, on the flats, what used to be the garbage dump, where Indians squatted and scavenged. Now there is Columbia Gardens, twenty acres of trees and lawns and flowers, grown in good dirt carted in and renewed every year. A lake with little boats, an oriental dance pavilion where the young people dance every Saturday night, watched by police who stop the fights between the Irish and the Poles and Serbs they call bohunks, between the Cornish and the Italians they call wops.

Columbia Gardens was a gift to the people of Butte from one of the old Copper Kings, the only thing any of them ever gave back to Butte before they all left for New York, sucking the profits after them.

On the Fourth of July, Rina, Francesco, and Tato take a basket of food on the new trolley car down to Columbia Gardens. Tato runs and yells and rolls in the grass, an animal suddenly returned to nature. Francesco and Rina dance in the Pavilion, once, twice. Then Francesco is too breathless to dance. He buys a bottle of grappa (alcohol is forbidden at Columbia Gardens but always sneaked in by someone). After a few drinks he joins some men who are going back up mine hill to a saloon. Rina and Tato end up going back to Netti's boarding house on the trolley alone. When Francesco staggers in late, she says nothing. She blames herself for leaving her husband alone for eight years in this terrible place. She will be patient. She will bring back the Francesco she married.

Rina sees ten lunch pails lined up on the shelves in Netti's kitchen, sees the boarders buying Cornish pasties from a peddler on their way to the mines. She learns to make pasties and to pack the three-tiered lunch pail: dessert at the top; pasty in the middle; tea on the bottom. If not too deep underground, a miner can build a little cooking fire, heating up the tea that steams and warms the pasty without ruining the dessert. Soon she is preparing seven lunch pails a day for the boarders, then ten, then seventeen, for other men who have heard about her meatier pasties, her light crust. She does laundry too, as cheap as the Chinaman, and cleaner, does Netti's laundry too, for the use of her water and tubs.

She sends Tato to school clean and well fed every morning. He comes back bloody and dirty in the afternoon. The Irish boys outnumber everyone else five to one, and they gang up on greenhorns who speak with an accent. "No, Mamma, please don't go to the school. That'll only make it worse. And don't call me Tato."

"Si, you are growing up, Giuseppe."

"No, my name is Joe. Call me Joe."

Francesco still comes home at least an hour after the blast of the whistle, smelling of hard liquor, coughing. At night in bed, he pokes into her, then pulls out in time to avoid a baby, coughs even harder. Rina tries to hold him in, begs him to give her another baby before she is too old. A little girl would cheer her up. No. At night she still dreams of home, still wakes up crying. Francesco never hears her, or pretends not to hear.

He gives her what he earns, what's left after the saloon. But during the next lay-off, he takes what she has earned and spends it in the saloon, while she tries to keep them in food. When that lay-off ends, and he goes back down the mine, she starts to hide her earnings in a can under a floorboard of their bedroom. She tells him she has spent it all on food and clothing, especially shoes for Joe, who is growing so fast. Joe seldom comes home from school bloody now. He is fluent in English, no accent, a real American, has friends, even one or two Irish.

Francesco still drinks too much. Rina begins to walk up to the mine at the end of his shift on payday. Other wives are there too, for the same reason, to coax their husbands past the saloons, get them home with their pay still in their pockets. The women huddle in small groups, each group speaking a different language, all talking about the same things—their children, their neighbors, how to cook a traditional dish when you don't have the right Polish or Lebanese ingredients. And they talk about the work of their husbands. Rina learns more about the deep hole where Francesco works. She knows that the cable running through the gallus frame lowers the men into the mines. Now she hears that it drops the cage down the shaft at thirty miles, forty miles an hour, plunging a thousand feet, two thousand. She learns about "widow-makers," the electric drills that bore into the walls of the shafts, filling the air with silicon dust that cuts and destroys the lungs. Already Rina knows who is coming into the boarding house before she can see him; each man has his own cough, like a signature. She learns what gives Francesco headaches that drive him to fury—nitro-smoke from the blasting. And the noise from the drills roaring and screaming in the low tunnels. The other women complain that their men are going deaf from the noise. Yes, that would explain Francesco's indifference to her complaints—some of it. She learns that horses live their whole lives down in the shaft, dropping their manure in the tunnels. The men too, make manure, and drop food and snuff and spit chewing tobacco. The smell down there must be—Rina cannot even imagine the rotting garbage and urine and shit of hundreds of men and animals, all piling up in the tunnels.

Standing under the head frame of the Alice Mine, Rina recognizes, for the first time, someone from Langero. It is little Sara, the pathetic, pale and skinny daughter of Angela, a coarse girl with a bad reputation. Sara was born only a month after Angela managed to marry "Ghitarra," the wandering street boy who made her pregnant. Rina's mother often fed Sara, who was either forgotten or, if noticed, beaten by her worthless parents. "Ghitarra" earned a few pennies and his nickname by wandering through villages as a street musician, until a labor contractor put him on a boat for America. Angela and Sara had left Langero before Rina and Tato. Angela bragged that they were going to California, where her husband had bought a big cattle ranch. Yet here they are, little Sara more starved and scared than ever.

The first cage comes up, jammed with men like bound sticks of sooty wood. Sara's father "Ghitarra" is one of them. He shoves his lunch pail at the shivering little girl, to carry for him as she stumbles down the hill six or eight paces behind him. It is a ritual greeting of many children to their fathers—a privilege for a favored child. Not for Sara. She is frightened, forced to make a ritual show of love for her unloving father.

More men pour out of the narrow cages, stumble, blink, shiver, made blind and dumb by the sudden return to topside. Peeling away from each other in silence. Maybe they can't understand each other. Francesco says the Company purposely makes up crews of ten who speak six or eight different languages, while an Irishmen shouts orders in English. Dangerous, but it slows down union organizing among the men. Not that the Irish gang boss wants Italians or Serbs or Swedes or Lebanese in his union. The Company likes that too, likes the way the Irish hate the bohunks and the wops, everyone hates the chinks and the blacks—not even allowed in the mines, let alone the union.

Francesco is in the next cage. As soon as he hits the cold air, he is lost in a cloud of steam made by condensation of his own sweat. No wonder most men go right into the nearest saloon. No wonder families build their shacks between the head frames, as close as they can get. Men walking twenty minutes from the mine to home have died of pneumonia. Some of the women are holding blankets. After the first time Rina sees Francesco merge into a cloud that rises from his body, she too carries a blanket to throw over him for the walk home. And he comes with her willingly. But on the days when she cannot go to meet him at the head frame, he comes home two hours later, smelling of liquor, surly and impatient. She does not complain. No use to complain of anything. Except a baby. A little girl. One more child before she is too old. Francesco refuses, mounts her nearly every night, or in pale dawn after a night shift, but always pulls out in time.

One night Francesco comes home very late, very drunk, robbed of his week's pay. Rina loses her patience. They owe the butcher, and Joe is out of his shoes again, and "you go to the saloon!" In a fury of shame, he hits her, knocks her down. Then Joe is on him, screaming and crying, and hurting Francesco, who is too drunk to resist even a ten-year-old boy. The other boarders turn away. Silence. Francesco cries. He begs forgiveness. Rina says nothing, puts him to bed. During the night Francesco wakes and apologizes again. Rina forgives him. They touch. They look to make sure Joe is sleeping soundly. Francesco lets his seed pour into Rina. Her monthly bleeding stops. Her midnight crying stops. There is new life in her body.

It is too early to buy a baptismal dress, even if they could afford one. When the baby is born, Rina will probably borrow one from a neighbor. But she can look. Between the laundry and the cooking, she can take a walk to the fancy shops and tall office buildings west of Meaderville, in Uptown Butte, which she has hardly seen. She can window shop and dream for an hour.

Between Meaderville and Uptown is Dublin Gulch, where the lowest Irish women and their hordes of dirty children watch her pass, yelling curses at her, even throwing rocks. These poorest of the Irish, the shiftless, swear their filthy words, yet they speak also for the other Irish who are not so low and poor. They speak even for the priest at Saint Patrick's, who tells Rina that Italians are not welcome there. "There's an Italian priest in Butte now." East of Meaderville, in

McQueen, Holy Savior Church, where the Austrians go. "They don't mind Italians." Some of the Austrians even speak Piedmontese, coming from towns just over the border from Langero.

Rina gets through Dublin Gulch unhurt and is suddenly Uptown. Grand ladies shop there. Netti has told her that the grandest of all, dressed in the most elegant of imported fashions, are prostitutes, courtesans too high-priced for most miners. They and the less beautiful ladies, the respectable ladies, walk in and out of tall brick buildings, pretending not to notice each other. But they all notice Rina. They all give her cold stares, no matter that she wears her good dark dress, her respectable hat, her black gloves, kept fresh and clean for church. "Greasy Italian" mumbled by someone nearby—she knows enough English now to understand, but when she turns, she can't tell who said it.

Only one block south, the row of Jewish merchants welcomes her, standing outside their shops, calling to her as to everyone, joking, enticing, begging her to come in. She understands their gestures, not much of their strange English—gets a bit more of the Yiddish they sprinkle in, like pieces of the German dialect spoken by some of the Austrians. One of the men confuses her enough to get her into his shop, lowers the price on a suit of long underwear for Francesco, once, twice, three times, until she feel obliged to buy it, doesn't know why, doesn't know whether or not she has been cheated. Better go back to Meaderville. Avoid Dublin Gulch. She turns downhill. A mistake. She is on Mercury street, Chinese running back and forth carrying mysterious baskets, painted, fringed, half-naked women lounging in windows or on front porches, smoking, laughing, waiting for men who come at all hours, day or night. Like the miners, the prostitutes work round-the-clock shifts. Rina never tells Francesco that she blundered into Mercury Street, that she even knows of its existence. Does Joe? They must get away to California. A little prune ranch out in the country. She prays for California, seldom leaving Meaderville anymore. Men are always coming to Butte, sending for their families, leaving Butte, going on to California. Some day, soon, if she can just save the money.

Men hear of her cooking and pay her to let them come to dinner. She charges them a quarter, gives three cents to Netti for each man who eats. One of the few married men brings his wife, and that night the dinner table is almost like a family. One young man brings along a Cornish miner, who sits silently, not understanding a word, but devouring Rina's good food. She makes more and more pasties for men who pick them up on their way to a mine. Her cooking is becoming known beyond Meaderville.

Her first pains come after Joe leaves for school. Francesco must take a shift at any mine where they take Italians. She nods, "just come home right after." She finishes the second bake before she tells Netti, who helps her up to her room and sits with her. The pains go on and on, her water breaks, but no baby. Blood. It won't stop. Still no baby. Netti goes looking for a doctor. By the time she finds one who will come to Meaderville, Rina has pushed out the baby alone and lies there, blood soaking everything. The doctor is Irish, and drunk. He reaches into Rina, stitching her with needle and thread, like a gutted chicken. He giggles drunkenly as Rina screams. The bleeding stops. Netti cleans up the blood, the afterbirth, washes the baby. A beautiful little girl. Rina calls the baby Loretta, after her mother.

Joe comes home from school, sees the baby, bursts into tears. "The last layoff we didn't have enough to eat, and you go out and buy a baby!"

Francesco comes home and pours free wine for all the boarders. Rina can hear them joking, laughing until late that night. Rina sleeps, wakes to feed the baby, sleeps, drinks and eats whatever Netti can bring her, thanks Netti, blesses Netti, who shrugs, "Women have to help women." Every day Francesco brings home beer from the saloon—beer gives strength, makes milk. After a few days Rina is on her feet, weak, but able to care for the baby. The doctor comes to pull out the stitches. Still drunk, still giggling at her screams. In two weeks she is cooking again.

Two years, three years, and Loretta is a beautiful child, blonde and blue-eyed like Joe, like Rina when she was a girl, before her hair thickened and darkened. Rina cooks and washes for more miners, saving and hiding her earnings. She organizes Saturday night parties at Grosso's, the candy store adjoining Grosso's saloon, where Francesco proudly perches Loretta on the bar. Gradually Francesco and some of the men are enticed into the candy store. They help the children clear the floor for dancing. Francesco begins to play his accordion again. He no longer sings, has no breath for singing. But he drinks less, brings home more of his wages to Rina.

That year, the next year, during the brief summers, they go to more picnics at Columbia Gardens. Francesco stays with them, and does not drink. It is Joe who runs off with his friends, shouting, playing tricks on girls, pretending to hate them. Loretta celebrates her fourth birthday at Columbia Gardens on the monthly Children's Day, when picking the rare, precious flowers is permitted. She takes a bouquet of seven pansies home with her and sleeps with them, inhales their live odor, until they dry and crumble.

War begins in Europe. All at once there are plenty of shifts, most mines hiring Italians too.

Francesco is finally bold enough to take out citizenship papers—before he could get a shift only because he was an alien, not covered under Montana's new Workman's Compensation law. The Irish start off in support of Germany against their old enemy England, but Italy stands with England and France from the start, so Butte Italians are more accepted now. But at Holy Savior Church, among the Austrians, Italians are now hated enemies. They must build themselves a new church.

More work in the mines, but more accidents than ever. Repeated, staccato shrieks of a whistle scream panic and death at least twice a week. Rina knows the whistles now. Minnie Healy—no, Francesco is at the Judy Mine tonight. Orphan Girl? No, Francesco is down the Hangover Mine today. She heaves a sigh of relief, crosses herself, then makes pot after pot of soup to bring to the families of men injured or killed in an unlucky mine. Wet-drilling is now the law, but too late for Francesco. His lungs are so bad he can barely finish a shift. There are fewer fights between Irish and Italians, more between the Union Irish and the radical "Wobblies" coming into Butte to organize everyone kept out of the Irish-run Union. A bomb goes off in the union hall. The old Irish Union men accuse the Wobblies, but everyone knows it's the Irish Oranges bombing the Irish Greens. Francesco tries to keep clear of all of them, works his shift, brings home his wages.

He is ordered to see a company doctor, which means the Company wants to lay him off before an official diagnosis qualifies him for Workers Comp. Rina brings out and shows Francesco all the money she has secretly saved, almost enough for train fare to San Francisco. Francesco nods, even smiles. Their dream can still come true. Calvetti and Marchetti and Zermani all found cheap land south of San Francisco.

Five acres of prunes in the Santa Clara Valley. They cultivate their orchard, sell their fruit, eat their own vegetables and chickens and rabbits, hunt quail to stew for polenta, take the train to the beach to pry abalone off the rocks. They work in the canneries: peaches, then apricots, then pears—or is it pears first? If Francesco can put off the Company doctor just another few months, they'll have enough money for land in California.

That very day, America declares war on Germany. For the first time Francesco is put on steady, at the Speculator Mine. Francesco skips his appointment with the Company doctor, works every day, comes home with all his pay, talking about five acres of prunes, all at sea level where he could breathe freely, and never, never any snow. His lungs will heal. Two months wages will do it.

Almost two months later, on June 8, a whistle shrieks, Rina listens, freezes. Yes, the Speculator whistle. She leaves the soup on the stove, the pasties and bread in the oven, the tubs of soaking laundry. By the time she gets outside, other whistles are shrieking, a chorus of panic. People are running past the house, running up toward the Speculator, no, the Granite Mine, no, both. As she struggles uphill, carrying Loretta, she becomes part of a crowd. Coming from below are more sirens, ambulance, fire trucks all rushing uphill. Loretta is too heavy. Rina puts her down, holds her hand tightly, pulls her along. Loretta falls, is pulled to her feet and dragged on, not crying, not fussing as she usually would.

Joe is already there. Loretta throws her arms around her brother, hugging Joe, afraid of her mother, as if Rina herself is giving off shrieking panic whistles, sirens, shouts. They stand together in the growing crowd around the head frame, held back by police.

A groan rises from the crowd, like one voice. Smoke.

Smoke curls up through the middle of the head frame, billows out. Fire down in the mine. The firemen stand there, helpless as the women. A cage comes up. A few miners stumble out, dragging a few more. The cage goes down again and again, only six men come up, then four, then two, then five—one of them Sara's no-good father, Ghitarra. They are rushed downhill in screaming ambulances. The cage goes down again, deeper, longer, comes up empty. Only a few men were in the upper tunnels. The rest, two or three hundred, are below, some a mile down.

The crowd stands there until dark. The only news is cruel, ironic—the fire had spread through the new ventilator system from the Speculator Mine to the Granite Mine. A Company man appears, come down from the sixth floor offices in the big Hennessy Building. He stands and watches, helpless as all the others. Nuns appear with coffee and sandwiches. Six priests, the rabbi, even the black preacher who washes dishes on weekdays at the Butte Hotel and three Chinese with tea and almond cookies—though they have none of their own down there. No one asks the firemen why they stand there doing nothing. Everyone knows they can't go down until the fire burns itself out.

In early June the nights are still cold. Loretta shivers, dozes, cries in Joe's arms. "Take her home, Mamma. Nothing to do here. Go home. I'll stay and wait for Pappa. I'll bring him home." Rina carries Loretta home, feeds her from the top part of the soup pot still unburned. Cleans the scorched pasties out of the blackened oven. Stands over the wash tubs all night, scrubbing. Waiting.

The next day Rina climbs up to the head frame and stands in the shifting crowd, sends Joe home to sleep. One day. Two days. Climbing back and forth, keeping the vigil with the other families, the changing shifts of firemen. At the end of the third day, the first firemen finally go down. At each level, when they leave the cage and go to the ladders, they have to free and push down the hanging bodies of horses, legs tangled in the rungs, horses that tried to climb the ladders to escape the fire.

The first bodies are loaded into cages and sent up, pulled out by men on top, some of them sons or brothers or fathers of the dead. The hearse from Duggin's Funeral Home stands by. Another cage, another, another, a longer wait each time a cage goes down. A scrap of paper is found in the shirt pocket of one of the bodies, a few words scrawled. "Ruth sell everything take kids to California."

Francesco's body is never found. Nobody is sure how many are down there somewhere. There are twenty funerals a day, church bells tolling all over Butte. All of Meaderville comes to Francesco's wake, rosary, funeral—the body conspicuously absent—mostly for Rina's sake, some of them after burying their own dead. After the funeral mass they come to Netti's boarding house for the best food Rina can prepare. Francesco's funeral takes half of the money she had saved for California.

The rest goes for Loretta's funeral a few months later, when she becomes the first child in Butte to die in the flu epidemic sweeping across the world as the Great War comes to an end.

The Company Investigation of the Speculator fire blames sabotage. One of the German miners must have been a spy, a suicide saboteur. The German widows protest. The Company falls back on the usual reason: some miners violated some safety rule, which they do not name. For that reason, as usual, families are denied compensation.

The coroner's office investigates; coroner's report disappears.

The following week Harry and I sat in the Med in the dim morning light; the place was nearly deserted. We were still between terms, but I had telephoned Harry at Steadman's to tell him I had read his first chapter and loved it. We arranged to meet and go over it in detail.

"It's a great story. I couldn't put it down."

"But—?" Harry's knee had started working again, apprehensively.

"I liked your use of present tense."

"But—say it—not enough dialogue. I know what you're going to say. No real scenes where people say and do things."

"Harry, you're too hard on yourself. You'll have to rewrite, of course. But you may want to just keep going, pour it all out and then rewrite. The important thing is that this story comes out of your guts. A great start! You just have to keep feeling your way along. I can hardly wait to learn what happens to Rina. What a remarkable woman, a real hero."

"She was."

"Where did you get this part of her story, from your parents?"

"From her. From Nonnarina, when I was little, hanging around the restaurant, listening to her, listening to some of the old folks." Harry laughed. "Some of it I wasn't supposed to hear, her and the other old ladies talking about sex and childbirth. But in the kitchen, they'd forget me, the kid in the corner with his nose in a book."

"Restaurant? She went to work in a restaurant?"

"Her restaurant. That's the next part of the story. Netti wanted to get out of Butte—like everyone always wanted to get out of Butte, especially after the Speculator Mine fire. It was the worst hard rock mining accident in America. Should I put that in?"

"Put everything in. You can decide what to take out when you rewrite."

"Netti sold the house to Nonnarina cheap, no down payment, carried the mortgage. There were already a lot of miners coming to eat Nonnarina's cooking. So she kicked the boarders out of the downstairs rooms, put in big tables, served family style, did just what she had been doing, but more of it. She put a sign outside—Casa Della Rina. Same sign was still up there when I was a kid. She tried to get Nonno Joe to work with her, but he quit school and went down into the mines. The Company had promised jobs to the sons of the men who were killed. Yeah, ironic, the only thing they gave the families—a guarantee of the same killing job. But good money for a kid. Minimum age sixteen. Nonno Joe was only fifteen, but he lied, and they let him. He was going to save money, he said, even help Nonnarina. But he ended up spending most of his pay, just like the other miners, coming up out of those shafts and heading for the nearest drink. Prohibition came, and that helped."

I nodded. "It shut down the saloons."

Harry laughed. "No, it had no effect at all on the saloons. Prohibition was called the Widow's Compensation. A lot of them fed their families making rotgut and selling it—men came to Butte from all over to buy it." He laughed again. "I heard Nonnarina talking once with a woman about how the town sewers used to get clogged up with mash and grapes."

"So she became a bootlegger."

"No, no! Never. She had a legitimate business, Casa Della Rina. Only illegal thing she did was to serve wine with dinner, made a little more money that way. But it was always good wine. She chose the grapes herself when the trainloads came in, knew the best Italian wine makers, paid the cops off in good wine. Everyone trusted Nonnarina, respected her."

"And her restaurant was a success?"

"Best known restaurant in Meaderville, after the Rocky Mountain Café. People liked her food, liked her rules. Rules for good behavior. That was an ugly time in Butte, strikes, riots, men knifed right in front of their homes. Famous Wobbly organizer dragged out of his hotel and lynched. That's when Nonnarina made the rule—no politics in Casa Della Rina. People from all sides came to eat, but she was strict. "Lasciate fuori i politici, o andate fuori!" Leave the politics outside or get out. Someone painted it on the wall in Italian and in English. That was still the rule when I was a kid. People respected her for it, but I'd have heard more about what was going on if she hadn't made that rule. I guess I can get that from the library."

"Didn't Dashiell Hammet write a novel about the twenties in Butte?"

Harry nodded. "*Red Harvest*. I read it on board ship." He laughed. "He called Butte 'Poisonville' in the book. But his book is just another tough-guy whodunnit. After the opening, there's nothing about a real mining town, about the miners." He shook his head. "Well, what do I know? I never worked down there." He smiled. "Nonnarina used to tell my mother she'd kill both of us if Mom let me go down." Harry fell silent. His eyelids drooped. I had been noticing that his clothes were a bit rumpled. Since moving into Angel's communal house, he probably was getting less sleep.

"You rode back with Angel after Marsha's party?" He nodded. "Things going well at—?" I tilted my head in the direction of Haste Street.

Harry smiled. "Probably like that boarding house in Butte when Nonnarina first came—a lot of noise, people in and out all day, all night. But instead of the smell of sulfur, the smell of pot. The first time I smelled pot—on board ship—I thought of Nonno Joe. He never smoked regular tobacco, but in that last year before he died, every morning when he got up, he smoked a medicinal cigarette, prescribed by the doctor. It smelled like pot. I like to think it really was—really gave him some kind of relief." Harry was looking dreamily somewhere above my head. Then he raised his hand and waved at someone behind me.

It was Angel, nodding as he sat beside Harry. "They're gone. All clear." Angel turned to me, smiling. "Campus cops, three of them this time. The university keeps trying to serve us an eviction notice, which they really can't do without getting some name to fill in, someone to serve. So we disappear when they come. Danny Lyon says that'll put them off a little longer. They tacked more notices on the door before they left. We tore them down. Next phase will be the use of force, Danny says. He—oh, here he comes now. Danny, over here."

Daniel Lyon, leaning on the counter waiting for his coffee, waved his hand in our direction without bothering to turn around. His hair had grown to a dark, oily cascade down the middle of his back. He usually tied it into a pony tail, but today it was loose, held off his face with a red bandanna folded into a head band. His t-shirt and jeans were fashionably faded and streaked with dirt. He brought to our table, along with a tall latté, a strong smell of sweat I remembered coming from the poorest children at school during my depression childhood, when baths were harder to come by. Now that smell was as much a political statement as worn Levi's. He sat down with a satisfied grin at Harry and a curt nod at me. "Next time the fucking bulldozers."

Angel nodded. "I'm surprised we held them off this long. They're going to build their new dormitories come hell or high water."

"It's not dormitories they want," Daniel was saying. "It's us. To get rid of us. Do you know who's come and stayed a night or two during the past two years?" He began dropping the names prominent at demonstrations of those years. "We're a headquarters," he said, rather grandly, "like Castro's mountain hideout, a stop-over visited by revolutionaries from—"

"And by a lot of guys who just want sex and drugs," Angel laughed.

"They're revolutionaries too! We have to channel all that renegade spirit—so when the pigs come to get us, we'll fight back. I know two lawyers who'll arrange bail. I'll do our defense in court. It's a great opportunity. So, now the next step is to lay down in front of the bulldozers." He smiled with a kind of cheerful rage.

Angel gulped audibly, smiling at himself. "Danny, I'm a confirmed coward. I'll stand by with my tape recorder and put it all on the air."

Daniel sneered, then shrugged. "That's something. Everybody has a role to play." He turned to Harry. "What about you?"

Harry hesitated, then mumbled, "I don't think I want to be noticed by the police."

"Oh, your family," Daniel sneered.

Harry flushed. "No. I—I just got off probation."

Contempt changed to interest, even respect, as Daniel waited for details. When it was clear that Harry would offer none, Daniel gulped down his latté and stood. "Gotta go. The rally—about the draft deferments being canceled for grad students? Best thing could have happened." Daniel licked the milk off his upper lip. "The next Vietnam protest is going to be a blood bath!"

"I'll go along," said Angel. "Just one stop to get my tape recorder. "Who's speaking?"

Daniel shrugged. "We invited David Harris. Joan Baez. Eldridge Cleaver. None of them answered. I listed their names on the flyers anyway, to get people there. If none of them show up, I'll speak. Hell, I'll speak anyway."

After they left, Harry and I sat in silence, finishing our coffee. Then he said, "I want to thank you for introducing me to Angel. Now I'm meeting a lot of people."

I had been thinking the same thing, but not quite so optimistically. "I'm glad things are going well. Just don't—well, this is none of my business, but—don't get so involved that you neglect your classes. People like Angel and Daniel—lots of the activists Daniel named—they have choices, contacts that you don't have. And you mentioned being in trouble with the law?"

"That's why I went into the Navy. It was the service and probation or jail. I've stayed out of trouble, and I'm clear now, I think, but—"

I nodded. "You're right to be cautious. A police file, even a minor, juvenile record, is the kind of thing used against dissenters."

"And it works. Makes me gutless. You saw the way Daniel looked at me."

"Don't be so hard on yourself. Daniel doesn't practice law because he has a trust fund from his grandmother."

86

Harry looked at me incredulously. I nodded. Lisa had told me that she tried to maintain good relations with Daniel to squeeze out a bit of money for her daughter from time to time. "And Angel has a graduate degree in Library Science. He's been offered good jobs, but he doesn't want to leave Berkeley now. I know this is none of my business, but—" I wasn't sure if this was the right time to point out the gap of class and privilege between Harry and his new friends. I wanted to plant in Harry the conviction that he was their equal, yet to warn him that they stood on a firm base he lacked. "They've got a few advantages you want to pick up before—" How to keep him in touch with his reality, yet not discourage him? "Your struggle is complicated by—"

"By my struggle to pay my share of the rent, eat, buy textbooks, study until I get meal tickets they don't need. That's what you mean."

"We can do something about the books. There's a fund at the college. See me the first day of classes."

"I need some part-time work too. Got any work around your house?"

"The garden. Just hacking back some bushes for now, a couple of days' work, that's all until spring. You're hired. I think Marsha already has a gardener, but you could ask. What about the shops here?"

"I've tried a dozen stores and restaurants on Telegraph. They all hire students from the university. Angel's trying to get me a few hours at Moe's Books, or even at Cody's Books, but I have to wait. Everyone wants to work at Cody's—even Mario Savio is going to take some shifts. So why would they bother to hire somebody like me?"

"Have you tried Steadman's? Right up the street?"

"I went in there once, but the old guy at the counter just shook his head, didn't even look up."

I stood. "Let's try again."

We took a last gulp from our cups, then left, walking the few steps to Steadman's Used Books. Jake was sitting alone behind the counter, almost hidden behind disorderly piles of books on either side of the old cash register. I saw the rising spiral of his cigar smoke before I made him out.

"Hi, Jake."

He looked up, glancing over the lowest pile of books, then used both arms to push two piles of books aside. One of the piles collapsed, spilling books onto the floor at our feet. Harry bent to pick them up, then stood holding them, not sure where to put them.

"This is my student, Harry Lynch. He's writing a novel about his family in Butte, Montana."

Jake raised his eyebrows. Then he stood up and took the books Harry was still holding, putting them back on what he seemed to recognize as the appropriate pile. "What period in Butte? Current?"

"From about 1900 up to now."

"I've got an old copy of *Perch of the Devil*. You know it?" Harry shook his head. "Gertrude Atherton. California writer, pretty much forgotten now. Butte in the early 1900s. Let's see, it must be in here." Jake got up and turned to a locked glass cabinet where he kept rare books. He squinted at the glass, hesitated, looked puzzled. "Did I sell it to that collector? Well, it's got a few pages of good description, that's about all. There's another writer, much better, wrote in the thirties, grew up in Butte—what's his name? Brinig, that's it, Myron Brinig, *Wide Open Town*. You know him?" Harry shook his head again. "A Jew. Obviously homosexual, just hints here and there. Forgotten, of course. I got in a copy of his *Singerman*, Jewish family saga. I sold it to the UC Library, good price. Don't know any post-war Butte writers, no fiction. You've got a wide open field. But check Brinig out at the library, he's good on the early Butte Irish too."

"Harry's really more Italian than Irish, in spite of his name."

"Miners in your family?"

Harry only nodded, so I spoke up. "Three generations. Two killed in mine accidents, one by silicosis."

Jake nodded, unsurprised, and began to talk about labor history in mining towns. There seemed to be no limit to the subjects and places Jake knew something about. Maybe he should have been a research librarian. No, he was too disorderly. He had landed just about in the place where he ought to be.

I heard a slight noise behind me and turned. Lisa Lyon had come from behind the shelves in the back of the store. I didn't know how long she'd been standing there, holding a dozen dusty books, listening to us. There was a smudge on her forehead and on the burlap-sack blouse she wore over a long Mexican skirt, probably more acquisitions from thrift stores that, assembled on her thin body, were magically, uniquely exotic. Her face lit up in a smile as I recognized her. I glanced at the books she held. "Looks like you found a lot of things."

"These? I'm just helping Jake out a little." She smiled at Jake, her eyes resting on him for only an extra second, enough to let me know they had become lovers. (Later, privately, Lisa told me she had moved in with Jake, subletting her little cottage and making a small profit over her low rent.)

"I brought Harry in because he needs some part-time work. What do you think?" I was speaking to Jake, but smiling at Lisa. She instantly caught my eye and nodded.

"I think he's a godsend! Jake, I can't haul these

boxes of books around. My back is already sore." She gave both Jake and Harry a trembling, flirtatious smile, which somehow included me as well in a plea for my approval. Lisa always seemed desperately unsure of herself, fearful, overwhelmed, and looking to everyone else for guidance.

It was settled with Jake that Harry would come in a few hours a week to help Lisa sort and shelve and clear out junk books. I couldn't take credit for that. It was Lisa. Surely, Jake was in love. Otherwise he probably would have refused to let his dusty disorder be disturbed. I only hoped the affair lasted until Jake got used to having Harry around or until Harry found more steady work.

As the 1968 spring term started, I saw less of Harry. He was taking my English 1A class along with a full load of other classes and working part-time for Jake. On Saturdays he took the long bus ride up to Marsha's house to do some rough hacking-back her gardener wouldn't do, and once or twice a month he dug around my garden.

The year had started hopefully after President Johnson announced he would not run again. Triumphant anti-war students scrambled to support a candidate who would end the war. Then dreams of peace became nightmares with the shooting of Martin Luther King. The memorial at Mrs. Temple's church was one of several I attended. Marsha was there too. She and Mrs. Temple held hands, and we all cried.

All over the country riots erupted. For the next couple of days we expected the same here, especially after Eldridge Cleaver's shoot-out with Oakland police. Cleaver said that police had pursued and harassed a car full of innocent Panthers going to a picnic. The rumor around the college was closer to the police version: that Cleaver had driven out hunting for police, calling for "blood" to avenge the death of King (whom he no longer called Martin Luther Coon). Every day brought some new crisis or threat or rumor of threat. The week after Cleaver was arrested, one of our black instructors went to the office of the white president of the college and had laid out a dozen bullets on his desk. I had no idea what that gesture meant and didn't ask—best not to spread the story and see it bloat up to another explosive rumor.

Tension and grief frayed everyone's nerves. I expected to get some relief in the dusty quiet of Steadman's Used Books, but I was wrong. Even before I opened the door, I could hear Harry and Jake yelling at each other from behind separate shelves where each was working. The subject was two new books—Cleaver's *Soul on Ice* (which had just been published and named the *New York Times* "book of the year.") and Styron's *Confessions of Nat Turner*. I gathered that Harry was defending Cleaver's book and attacking Styron's.

"Let me get this straight," Jake said. "You say Styron's Nat Turner is just another stereotype, the black man who wants to fuck a white woman."

"Right."

"Just the old racist lies again."

"Right."

"Then Cleaver writes about raping a few dozen white women as a protest against white racism, and you can buy that."

"Right." Harry's voice was fainter.

"Then he dedicates his book to his lover, his lawyer, a white woman he dumps as soon as she gets him out. And you can buy that."

Silence.

"Because he's black."

"No, because—" Silence.

"Did you read Styron's book?" Silence. "I didn't think so!"

"What does Styron know about being a black slave, or even about being black?"

Jake had seen me. "Didn't you say Harry was writing about his great-grandmother?" Back to Harry. "What do you know about being a female immigrant from Italy half a century before you were born!" Back to me. "Tell me again how you felt about Cleaver's attack on James Baldwin? Calling him a sick queer?"

Jake had hit a sore point with me. But I thought Harry needed an ally. I shrugged. "Young writer attacking the father figure. Baldwin did the same thing to Richard Wright."

But Harry didn't need my help. "If all Eldridge wanted was to become Number One Angry Black Writer, he could have done that and been safe! Instead, he joined the Black Panthers and put himself right back in the sights of every cop's gun!"

Impressed, I nodded, but Jake was unrelenting.

"I don't know what's wrong with you, Harry! Hanging out with Angel melt your brain? Maybe he can't tell the difference between a revolutionary and a thug, but you've been poor, you've had to survive the thugs, you ought to know—"

"Whatever Cleaver was, now he is—"

"What is he?"

"A—a survivor!"

"Oh, and you want him to survive? Did it ever occur to you that all those white radicals egging him on are having the time of their lives? Risk free? They're not the ones who are going to get shot the next time he—"

To my great relief the door opened behind me. It was Father Mike, wearing a clerical collar above his gray sweatshirt and jeans. Since seeing him at Marsha's party, I'd become more conscious of him on Telegraph Avenue, but we hadn't met. "I'm Mike Ruga." He put out his hand and smiled.

I took his hand and smiled back. "Ruth Carson."

"Jake, I could hear you out on the street. Can I get into this argument?"

Jake grunted. "Argument's over."

"Good," said Father Mike. "I got enough arguments going on. The bishop had me on the carpet again."

Not only was Father Mike still in trouble for draft counseling and writing anti-war articles in a liberal Catholic paper, he also had declared "sanctuary" at Saint Michael's Chapel, without consulting his superiors. It wasn't clear what he meant by "sanctuary"—something like the draft counseling and legal advice he was already giving. But the word, printed in headlines in the the *San Francisco Chronicle,* conjured up images of medieval church doors bolted against a tyrant's battering ram.

Harry came out from behind a shelf. "What will the Bishop do to you?"

Father Mike grinned. "Oh, hi, Harry. He already did it. Put another priest over me at Saint Michael's. I'll be doing 'outreach.' "

"Demoted, eh?"

"Yep. Just the demotion I've been praying for. Peace work. Street ministry. My new boss is going to let me start a soup kitchen in the basement. Like Jesus said, 'feed my sheep.' Volunteers accepted."

Harry instantly raised his hand, and Father Mike

acknowledged him with a nod and some gesture like a blessing. "I just came in to post these, okay, on your window?" He posted one flyer inviting volunteers to help start the soup kitchen and another one announcing a rally and teach-in during the first week in June.

The rally turned into a candle-light memorial service for Robert Kennedy. Mrs. Temple (who had taken the assassination of this second Kennedy much harder than I had) came along, and Carol too, since the term at UC Davis had ended. The service—with the usual speakers drawn from clergy and political activists—took place outdoors on the UC campus, on the slope near the music building. The crowd was smaller and older than usual because most students had already left for the summer. A woman went from one person to another with a clipboard, trying to register people for the new Peace and Freedom Party. Father Mike had his clipboard, signing up volunteers for the soup kitchen. A half dozen people were distributing flyers from organizations with names like "Socialist Anarchist Brigade" (or was it vice versa?), groups that sprang up, then disappeared. Dan Lyon was passing out flyers from one of these groups calling for a rally on Telegraph Avenue in support of striking students in France.

When I got home, I pinned mine up on the wall, but two weeks later, when the day came for the rally in front of Cody's, I was in San Francisco playing tour guide to cousins from Chicago. That was how I missed the first riot on Telegraph Avenue, hearing about the beginning of it from Harry, who had fled to my house when police began making arrests. Some accounts blamed police over-reaction, some blamed provocation by the crowd blocking the street. Whatever the cause, Cody's Books suffered serious damage when a canister of tear gas was "accidentally" thrown by police through a plate glass window (Harry raged at how an officer had stopped him from running in to remove it). The store was closed for a day or two.

As soon as Cody's Books opened again, I walked up to Telegraph, and into the store, holding a handkerchief over my face. The smell of tear gas clung to everything. I picked up a book by a black writer I hadn't read yet. Opening it was like fanning the chemical smell into my eyes. I blinked and bought it. Dozens of loyal customers were doing the same thing, clearing out the books, one by one, so that Pat and Fred would not be stuck with an unsaleable inventory. The book I bought was *The Man Who Cried I Am,* written by one of the black writers leading an attack on Styron. Its final chapter was in the form of a fictitious government plan to put activists in concentration camps. (It was a sign of the times that this chapter was copied and passed around as an actual document for the next five years, while the smelly book sat on the desk in my office in my futile attempt to persuade students, including Harry, that the government plot was fiction. "Well, they're probably cooking up another just as bad!" I shrugged. Probably.)

As the spring term ended Harry was celebrating the release of Cleaver on bail. Cleaver was so famous now—as a writer, as principal speaker for the Free Huey campaign— that university students had invited him to teach a class on campus in the fall. The center of conflict was now there, along with Harry's attention. Jake could not say he was being misled by Dan Lyon, not at the moment. Lyon had gone off to the Democratic National Convention in Chicago.

I was at a dinner at Marsha's house when the Chicago riots erupted. We were about a dozen people, all university couples except for me, a visiting English poet, and the Codys. (Fred had met the poet when he was doing graduate work in England, and Pat was an occasional contributor to a health journal edited by one of the professors.) Fred looked exhausted and worried, his tall, heavy frame slouching, his eyes heavy from lack of sleep, still not recovered from negotiating efforts to keep another, and another, and another Telegraph Avenue rally peaceful.

I remember I was talking to a Professor Bernard Person, near retirement after thirty years of "trying to teach students to write their native language!" when someone turned on the television set, showing five or six seconds of police and demonstrators in violent, bloody struggle. Then the face of Walter Cronkite filled the screen. He was standing on the floor of the Democratic Convention, his usually bland composure shaken, looking into the camera and declaring, "The Chicago police are behaving like thugs."

"Which is just what those clowns hoped to accomplish!" thundered Ivan.

Fred opened his mouth to answer him, but Marsha cut him off with, "We're ready to eat, I think," as she turned off the television.

Ivan ignored her. Like an old Biblical prophet looking down on his stunned followers, he shouted, "They're worse than plain criminals! Attacking the university. Then going to Chicago, dressed like freaks—Jerry Rubin and all his friends—screaming and throwing fire bombs at the police. Well, they got the attention they wanted. On every TV

96

channel, all over the country. And you know what they're going to accomplish? They're going to give the election to Nixon. We already have a grade-B actor for governor. Now we're going to get a paranoid crook for president!"

We moved to our chairs around the long table near windows that looked over the bay to San Francisco.

"Look at that sunset, not a bit of fog tonight," said Marsha. Everyone but her husband turned obediently toward the windows. Fred fell into sullen silence. We all went home early.

The next morning I got a call from Bernard Person, the professor who'd agonized with me about teaching Freshman English. He'd been approached by a textbook publisher to compile a new anthology of essays for Freshman comp. Was I interested in collaborating on it? We made a date to meet and plan.

As soon as I hung up, the phone rang again. This time it was Angel. "I'm covering the nominating convention of the Peace and Freedom Party for KPFA. And a friend of mine is starting an underground paper—"

"Another one?"

"—*Freedom Weekly*. He wants me to cover it for the paper. But, Ruth, I'll have my hands full, and anyway, I can't write. I thought maybe you—it's only three days, this weekend, in Richmond, only ten miles away—and your classes don't start till next month."

"I can't, Angel. I have an appointment on Friday, and another project that is going to take all my time outside of teaching."

"Can you think of anyone else?"

"What about Harry?"

"Can he write?"

"Better all the time. And being asked to do it—to be in print—would inspire him to do his best."

"Why not? Harry's a smart guy. Thanks, Ruth."

The first issue of *Freedom Weekly* featured Harry's article announcing the Peace and Freedom Party nominations for the November 1968 national elections: for president, Eldridge Cleaver; vice-president, Jerry Rubin; for State Assembly, Huey Newton and Bobby Seale (both still in jail). Under a huge photo of Eldridge Cleaver, his acceptance speech was printed in full.

Or not quite in full?

When Harry proudly handed me a copy of the paper across the counter at Steadman's, he complained that his editor had deleted most of the obscenities. He had also dropped the comment that got the biggest cheer from the audience: "If elected, the first thing I'll do is probably burn down the White House!"

Then Harry told me a bit more of the drama that had been cut from the article he had turned in. "It was on Saturday, the second day. They had finally settled on the agenda, but were still bogged down on the platform. I was down by the stage with Angel when we heard all this noise in the back. In marched about twenty Black Panthers, rifles and all—unloaded, Angel says. They marched down the aisle and lined up in front of the stage, facing the audience. Then one of them jumps up on the stage, grabs the microphone and demands 'suspension of the agenda for a statement by the Black Panther Party Minister of Information!' Eldridge

Cleaver climbed up on the stage. Everybody cheered. Then everything happened fast."

"They nominated Cleaver and the others?"

Harry nodded happily. "By acclamation."

Jake called out from behind a set of shelves. "I thought Cleaver was still below the Constitutional age to run for president." Harry looked surprised, then sullenly indifferent. Jake's silence, from behind the shelf where he was working, filled the store.

I asked Harry, "Nobody mentioned that?" He shook his head. "Nobody objected to their—?" I was going to say "takeover" but, the way Harry was looking at me, I decided not to put it so strongly. "—to this change?"

Harry shrugged. "A couple of the black delegates near me walked out." Harry laughed. "Cleaver watched them and said, 'Any black man who's a Peace and Freedom Party delegate has to be a freak anyway.' "

"Did you put that in your article?"

Harry shook his head. "It was just a joke."

"What do you think he meant?"

"It was just a joke!" Harry's voice hardened defensively.

"Sounds like the whole process became a joke."

"It's no joke. It's—it's a—" Harry turned away. He seemed to be making a big effort to contain his anger at me. Best to let it go.

"I'm glad to see you in print, Harry. You made a very good start." Harry grunted and picked up a boxful of books.

The Panthers and the Peace and Freedom party were not the only ones who weren't playing by the rules. Two or three weeks later, Huey Newton was convicted of "voluntary

manslaughter" instead of murder. The next morning Mrs.
Temple told me that some of her church members, awakened
during the night by gunfire, had seen an Oakland police
car speed away from Black Panther Headquarters, only a
few blocks from us. That afternoon I walked up to Shattuck
Avenue to look at the shabby storefront, its windows plas-
tered with election slogans and posters: Newton seated on
a rattan chair holding a spear (staged and photographed
at Beverly's house, using her African art as props); a giant
head of Cleaver, his eyes shrouded by dark glasses, mouth
open in accusation. It was obvious that the shotgun blasts
had been aimed at that mouth. As for the figure of Newton,
the entire body, from the center outward, was in shreds and
shards, riddled with bullets.

This symbolic execution expressed what began
happening every week or two. Shoot-outs between police
and Panthers spread across the country, with casualties
about the same on both sides, and each side accusing the
other of shooting first.

By the time the fall term started, Harry was writing
regularly for the *Freedom Weekly*. He covered most major
crises on the university campus: the UC Faculty Senate's
vote against the regents' ban on Cleaver's lectures (Marsha
told me that Ivan fumed and cursed Cleaver but voted
against the ban); meetings of student groups; demonstrations on Telegraph; picketing and sit-ins. Harry wrote
almost nothing about Merritt College. Nor did any of the
major media, who reprinted over and over the same photos
of the same few Black Panthers waving guns. Black Panther
presence at Merritt was sparse, except in the form of rumors,

a stew always threatening to boil over, wild rumors rising in steam and disappearing before they could be verified, followed by the rise of new rumors.

One of the wildest rumors concerned Harry's hero. It was whispered to me on November 5th, election day (when Ivan Franklin's grim prediction—Nixon's victory—came true). I was in my office later than usual, when a head poked through the slightly open doorway. It was Brentley, a handsome young black student who'd been in and out of my English class for a couple of years. I'd helped him get out of some trouble when he got into a minor scrape with the police. (He'd done a couple of stupid, not really criminal, things. All I did was to get advice from Mrs. Temple's police officer nephew on where to send a character reference.) Brentley was friendly with several Black Panthers. He had often veiled his eyes with dark glasses, but never quite adopted the uniform nor joined the party. Lately he had been turning in good work and had stopped wearing the dark glasses, exposing his soft, intelligent brown eyes to us all.

"Still here?"

I looked at my watch. "You're right. I'd better get out of here. I still have to vote." He looked uneasy, made no move. I gestured toward a chair. Brentley put his head out the door, turning it this way and that, then quietly closed the door before he sat down. Oh, no, I thought, don't tell me he's in trouble again.

"Two weeks from now," he said quietly. "Maybe Monday. Maybe Tuesday—I'll let you know ahead of time. You stay home. You're sick. Don't come in to teach."

"Why?"

"I can't tell you."

"Then I'll be here, Brentley. You can't tell me to do

101

something and not tell me why."

"If I tell you, you have to promise not to tell anyone."

"I can't promise that. If you're trying to keep me out of some kind of danger, we have to warn everyone."

He sat silently for a full minute. "Maybe it won't happen."

"What won't happen?"

One more deep breath. "Eldridge. There's a court order for him to go back to prison? Parole violation? Possession of firearms?"

I nodded. "Later this month."

Another long silence. "He's going to take over the college, call on all Panthers, all other volunteers. Anyone off the street. Come up and shoot it out with the police. From the tower?" Brentley tilted his head in the direction of the ornamental tower connecting the two wings of the building.

"He's going to—what?" A laugh rose in my throat, but then stuck there.

"He's got a stash of weapons. Some already smuggled in. Food. Dope. Supplies for a siege. He says if he goes to prison, the guards'll kill him there. He won't go. He'd rather die fighting."

"He can't be serious. Calling kids in off the streets to join him? The police will shoot them." Brentley nodded. "You're absolutely sure this comes from Cleaver? Not one of those undercover agents the Panthers say are always spreading false rumors?"

Brentley nodded again. "Sure."

"If there's a chance this is true, I have to report it. You know I have to."

Silence. Then, "Not yet. A couple of people are going to visit Huey in jail, try to get him to pass down an order against it." Brentley stood up, opened the door. "Or at least tell Eldridge to schedule it for a weekend—when no one will be here."

Brentley put his head through the narrow opening, looked both ways up and down the hall, then turned back to me. "For God's sake, don't let anyone know I told you." And he was gone.

The days passed, and nothing happened. Brentley avoided me, not even attending my class. I badly needed advice, but should I mention this and make trouble for Brentley? Add another impossible rumor to the dozens that swirled around us for a day or a week, then died? Two weeks passed. Three. Then morning headlines announced that Cleaver had jumped bail and disappeared. (I took a deep breath, then went back to bed with a giant migraine)

In retrospect, Cleaver's disappearance seems to have marked the beginning of the slow unraveling of the Black Panther Party, except for the short-lived Panther Breakfast Program for Oakland children. I told Mrs. Temple I was happy to see Black Panthers turning away from gun-toting toward education and food programs. She eyed me coolly. "Happy? Ask Mr. Edington—member of my church?—ask him if he's happy. Five or six of them come by his dry-cleaning shop, every Friday, like clock-work, for 'contributions for the breakfast program.' First time, he didn't give. That night his window got broken. Now he gives."

Carol and I spent Christmas, as usual, in Chicago with my parents. We got home, exhausted, on December thirty-first, collapsed in front of the TV set, and opened a bottle of champagne. We bade farewell to 1968, the year so many hopes had died in violence, and drank to better times in 1969, as the television news flashed another rerun of Richard Nixon promising "an honorable peace in Vietnam."

The next day I went to Merritt College to do some work before classes began again. In my mail box, I found a thick manila envelope with a note from Harry.

I hope you don't mind storing this somewhere. I'm not asking you to read it. It's just notes for the rest of my novel—dates, characters—you know, like you told me to sketch out.

Things have gotten kind of hairy at the commune, and I don't want to risk losing it. Just throw it in a corner somewhere safe, and I'll pick it up when things settle down.

I got my grades. Thanks for the A in English 1a. I'm signed up for your 1b. I can't fit in Professor Salceda's creative writing class, so I hope I can just keep bringing you parts of the novel when I have something worth reading.

Harry

I took Harry at his word, putting the envelope on a shelf in my office and forgetting it. Years later I brought it home to store with the other things Harry left behind. I went through it only recently, when I decided to write this account. Harry had made headings, year by year, starting from the year his great-grandfather was killed. Under these dates he was in the process of listing events—world wide, local—along with incidents involving his family, which he underlined.

I regret that I didn't at least skim through these

104

notes when he gave them to me. If I had, perhaps I'd have
better understood how he reacted to the events of 1969.

1917
- Meaderville Dam breaks again, tons of tailings,
  sludge fills streets, houses
- US declares war on Germany
- Governor orders brothels closed—prostitutes
  spread throughout Butte
- Montana's Jeanette Rankin, first woman
  in Congress, votes against war
- Bolshevik revolution takes over Russia
- W.E.B. Dubois leads 15,000 blacks to protest
  race violence in New York
- 10% of Butte men join the army (high percent,
  no draft, many protesters)
- Granite Mt/Speculator Mine fire kills 168
    Nonno Francesco killed in Speculator
    Joe, 15, quits school, goes to work in mines
    Sara works as live-in maid after school—better
    than staying home and being beaten by her
    father
- Miners' strike "equals treason" National Guard
  occupies Butte
- IWW organizer Frank Little dragged from hotel,
  beaten,hanged
- Rustling cards screen out union organizers
  from mines
- 1/3 of population leaves Butte

1918
- Great War ends
- Flu epidemic kills millions worldwide
    Flu kills Loretta, age seven
- Butte St. Patrick's Day parade outlawed because

of rioting
- Montana Sedition Act (pushed by Anaconda)
  used against IWW
- Federal Sedition Act, proposed by Montana
  senator, passed by Congress
    Nonnarina opens Casa Della Rina
    Joe's best friend is Mike Lynch, son of Irish
    woman who cursed Rina when she walked
    through Dublin Gulch

1919
- Versailles Treaty, League of Nations
- Sinn Fein proclaims Irish Republic
  —war with Brit—Butte
- Irish celebrate
- 19th Amendment—woman suffrage—Butte women
  have voted since 1914
- Butte miner's strike protests wage cut,
  rustling cards, 7,000 men idle, no gains
- Hundreds leave Butte every day
    Joe, 17, dances with Sara, 15, at Columbia Gardens.
    Sara's father "Ghitarra" drags her out, beats her.
    Rina: "stay away from that no-good family"

1920
- Prohibition goes into effect
- No effect on Butte, new saloon song about how
  anti-alcohol crusader Carrie Nation beaten,
  run out by local whores 10 years ago
- Butte widows make gin and wine
- Women admitted to bars,
    Sara's mother Angela seen in bar where women
    "work" upstairs
- First radio broadcast
- Company guards shoot picketing miners, 1 dead,
  16 wounded
- Mining of zinc and manganese begins

106

- St. Helena Church built in Meaderville for Italians
  Joe starts going to St Helena Church where he can see Sara
- Office jobs open up for women
  Sara lands after-school office job as bookkeeper, father goes every payday to take her money before she goes home to live-in maid's job
- Rapid snow melt floods Butte
- IWW strike, 11,000 miners idle, riot and shooting at Neversweat Mine
- IWW banned from mines

1921
- National guard leaves Butte after 4-year occupation
- Mines shut down for 9 months
- Anarchists Sacco and Vanzetti murder trial
  Irish boys attack Joe "wop anarchist," Mike Lynch defends Joe

1922
- Chong Sing, Mon Sen, Leong Mon killed in Butte (Tong Wars—Chinese Vs Chinese)
  Sara's mother disappears, rumor: in a brothel in Billings
  Sara's 2 brothers put in orphanage by father

1923
- Anaconda buys Chuquicomata Mine in Chile (from Guggenheim)
- Federal agents raid another still in Brown's Gulch, north of Butte
  Rina hires Sara to keep the books for Casa Della Rina, refuses to let her father into restaurant when he comes for her pay
  Sara's brothers, age 15, 16, run away from orphanage, live on street with support from Sara,

*Father arrested, violent when he learns she gives
them part of her pay*
Rina wants to fire Sara, but feels sorry for her

- Newspapers mention Hitler in Germany, Mussolini
  in Italy
- "Stiletto," age 25, first appears in Butte, eats
  at Casa Della Rina every night. Rumors: from New
  York, Mafia assassin

1925
- Hearst builds castle in California
- One Butte miner dies every week in accidents
    Sara's father put in mental asylum
    Joe laid off when company doctor finds a spot in lung
    *Joe makes good (illegal) wine for Casa Della
    Rina, other restaurants*
    *Stiletto offers Joe big money to ship to eastern
    bootleggers, Rina throws him out of restaurant.
    He comes back, offers Rina 50/50 split on girls
    he'll install in her upstairs rooms. Rina reports
    him to police. Nothing happens. Stiletto buys
    land on the flats, builds a casino. Still eats every
    night at Casa Della Rina. Rina won't serve him,
    sends black dishwasher to serve him.*

1927
- Municipal airport in Butte
- Worst snowstorm since 1908 hits Butte
    Sara's brothers leave for Idaho
    *Stiletto disappears, reappears, disappears, reap-
    pears*
    Rumors: married to Mafia Princess in New York
    Opens another casino on the flats

1929
- Anaconda buys Columbia Gardens from estate of
  "Copper King" Clark

Rina learns Joe and Sara are secretly meeting, fires Sara
Stiletto offers Sara bookkeeping job in his casino. No choice, she takes it, keeps looking. Sara turns 18 (legal age to marry without parents' consent.) Joe takes her out of Stiletto's casino, right to the church, marries her. Rina: 'How can I write and tell my mother you married into THAT family?' Then gives a wedding dinner for all of Meaderville.

- Stock market crash

  Maria born exactly 9 months after wedding day
  Stiletto sends gold spoon, baptismal gift, Sara returns it
  Rina insists Joe, Sara, Maria live at Casa Della Rina. Rehires Sara as bookkeeper. From the start, Rina ignores Sara, takes over Maria.

1930
- 4 million unemployed
- For the first time in history, more leaving USA than coming
- Sliced bread invented 1931
- Pipe brings natural gas to Butte
- 8 million unemployed in USA
- Jehovah's Witnesses founded, appear in Butte, leave

1932
- Roosevelt elected president
- 84% miners unemployed, most mines closed down
- Giant hailstorm in Butte rips off roofs, kills birds

  All windows at Casa Della Rina broken by hail. Glazier repairs window free (no one knows for years that Stiletto secretly pays glazier, then leaves again for New York.)

1933
- Prohibition repealed (no effect on Butte)
- Temp in Butte drops to 52 below zero in February
  Stiletto returns, opens fifth casino—catering to millionaire hunters

1934
- Polio epidemic—Butte children under 18 quarantined
- 4-month strike 6,500 miners—unions recognized
- Italy invades Ethiopia
  Nonnarina's mother dies in Italy, Nonnarina spends one day in bed

1935
- 25% Butte families on relief
  Joe stops making wine, too short of breath to work
  Maria age 6, starts school, Stiletto sends art supplies, orchestra instruments to Maria's school

1936
- Silver Bow Creek floods Meaderville
  Casa Della Rina closed one month for repairs and cleanup
- Spanish Civil War begins
- Two sons of Butte Jewish merchants, one Cornish miner, one German, go to Spain to fight against Franco

1937
- Butte High School built
- Butte Ski Jump—WPA project
- Population of cemeteries outnumber living people in Butte

1938
- Hitler annexes Austria
- Germany and Italy pass anti-Jewish laws
- Evel Knievel born in Butte

1939
- Hitler invades Poland = World War II
- 17% unemployment USA
- First commercial transatlantic flight
- 200 experimental television sets made in USA
  Maria makes her First Communion, Stiletto sends gold locket

1940
- First Social Security checks sent out
  No benefits to Rina as widow

1941
- Japanese attack Pearl Harbor, USA enters war
  Letters to Rina from Italy stop
- WPA installs first sewer system in Walkerville
- Statue of "Copper King" Daly, rammed weekly by autos, is moved to Montana Tech campus
- California sends Italian aliens to concentration camp in Butte, released after 8 months
  Rina sends some food to prison camp. No reaction in Butte, even from Irish. No one takes Italians seriously as enemies "Italians can't fight."

1942
- First Montana state welfare payments for silicosis
  Joe—(laid off before official diagnosis)—gets nothing, offered a job bartending for Mike Lynch, takes it. Rina furious.
  Mike Lynch's son Ed, 17, expelled from high school last year for constant fighting, goes into Navy. Back of the bar is covered with photos of

Ed in navy uniform.
Stiletto sends a piano to Casa Della Rina for
Maria's 13th birthday. Rina says it must go back,
Maria threatens to run away, Sara cries, Maria
screams, piano stays

1943
- Unemployment ends—army, west coast shipyards, mines all open
- Manganese mined for war weapons
- WPA leaves Butte
- Mussolini quits, assassinated, Italy surrenders
  Nonnarina writes to her family, no answer
  Maria, 14, dances 3 times with Stiletto at Columbia
  Gardens, fights back when Rina and Sara drag
  her away

1944
- D Day invasion of France

1945
- President Roosevelt dies in his 4th term
- Atom bombs dropped on Hiroshima, Nagasaki
- War ends
  Nonnarina gets first letter from Italy in 5 years;
  her sister is dead
- World copper reserve 100 million tons = layoffs, mines close down
- Penicillin, first cure for syphilis
  Ed Lynch comes back, out of Navy, pins medals
  over his father's bar, goes to Columbia Gardens
  dance, cuts in on Stiletto and dances all night
  with Maria. More fights than ever after a few
  drinks. Joe quits working in Lynch's Bar.
  Maria, 16, quits school, seen daily with Ed

1946
- Strike in Butte mines
- Strike in Chile mine

> *Stiletto offers chef job to Rina at his best casino. Refused.*
> *Stiletto offers bookkeeping job to Maria. Rina says no. Maria takes the job.*
> *Ed Lynch hangs out at Stiletto's casino when Maria is working, gambles, never loses.*

1947
- Last underground mine sunk in Butte
  —Kelley Mine

> *Ed Lynch one of few hired at Kelley Mine—rumor: Stiletto arranged it*

- Mayor announces Greater Butte Project—Plan: turn mine hill into pit mine, move the town down to the flats. Promise: pit mining means jobs for another 50 years.
- Protests get nowhere—all land on mine hill belongs to company
- Taft-Hartley Act weakens unions
- 400 houses built down on the flats

> *Maria marries Ed Lynch Rumor: huge cash wedding gift from Stiletto*
> *Maria gives birth, two months after wedding, boy named Enrico after Rina's father. Ed calls him Henry, later Harry. Rumor: Ed is not the father. Rina, Sara, Maria, Ed, and baby Harry all live at Casa Della Rina. Ed and Maria fight. Maria goes back to work at Stiletto's casino, Ed gambles, drinks, tells horror stories of how many he killed to win his medals. Sara is as afraid of Ed as she was of her father. Rina cares only about Enrico/ Harry, often left with her. Sara is busy nursing Joe, too short of breath to leave the house.*

1948
- Chile uses Permanent Defense of Democracy Act
  to jail labor leaders
- 35 Butte miners killed in accidents
  Ed Lynch crushed between elevator and shaft at
  Kelley mine, no compensation, accident blamed
  on his violation of safety rules
  Nonnarina refused offer from Anaconda to help
  move Casa Della Rina to flats
  Nonno Joe bedridden
  Maria moves to a house owned by Stiletto, near
  casino where she works, leaves Harry with Rina,
  comes to him on her days off.
- Gandhi assassinated
- State of Israel proclaimed
- Apartheid in South Africa
- USA blacklisting communists, suspected or former,
  loyalty oaths

1949
- Communist revolution in China
- Anaconda official jailed for selling defective
  material to US gov in World War II
- Anaconda raises land rent on mine hill from $1 per
  month to $100 per month
  Anaconda offers Rina relocation money. Rina
  refuses to move

1950
- Korean War
  Christmas Eve, Maria and Nonnarina pull Harry
  on a sled up to the Speculator Mine Head Frame,
  strung with lights like all remaining head frames.
  This is the first time Harry (age 3) remembers
  going to Midnight Mass. First a stop for prayers
  for Nonno Francesco, "in Heaven" Also buried
  a mile down here ("So Heaven is a mile under

the Speculator Mine head frame?"), Nonna Sara never comes along, not welcome, still ignored by Rina.

1952

· Civic Center sports complex built on Butte flats
  Enrico age 5, starts school, tells Nonnarina to call him Harry

1953

· First TV station in Montana transmitting from Butte

1954

· Brown v. Board of Education verdict launches civil rights movement
· Little effect on small black population of Butte, already in schools, but still segregated housing and jobs, like the Chinese.
· Travona, Butte's oldest mine closes
  Nonno Joe dies
  Nonnarina refuses to move off mine hill, Company lowers amount offered to help relocate. "Take it or offer goes down again."
  Sara goes to Idaho to live with one of her brothers.
  Stiletto buys Maria a house near his new casino. Maria tries to take Harry "No, I won't leave Nonnarina."
  Maria begs Nonnarina to move: "No"
  Maria: "All right, I'll stay here too" But spends most nights on the flats, "working late."

1955

· Anaconda starts pit mining at Berkeley Mine in Meaderville
· Anaconda annual profit highest ever
· Butte population 33,000, 1/3 what it was when

Nonnarina came from Italy
- Most Meaderville restaurants, casinos closing, moving down to the flats
  Nonnarina refuses to move

1956

Casa Della Rina closed 3-4 days a month to repair damage caused by blasting
- Bobby Knievel hired at Berkeley Pit, drives tractor like a stunt motorcycle, cuts main power lines. Fired.

  Harry's favorite teacher (third grade), from NY, hired one year ago, fired: "suspected communist" Harry doesn't understand what a communist is, just something bad, dangerous, sneaky -- Miss Segal beautiful and kind and gave him books. "That's how they suck you in," says the priest. Harry never goes to church again.

1957

- TV news: Beatnik poet on trial in San Francisco for obscene poem "Howl"

  Harry can't find a copy of it (banned at Butte Library)
- TV news: black kids trying to go into school in Little Rock, Arkansas, mobs of white kids screaming, spitting at them.

  Harry watches with best friend Walter Boyd, who also lives with his great-grandmother Ooma, Crow Indian, second cousin of White Man Runs Him, scout for Custer. They live in an old shack on land owned by Stiletto, between two casinos, where Harry hangs out waiting for his mother to get off work. Walter says, "They didn't waste spit on my Crow ancestors, just killed them."
- Frank Scalice, Albert Anastasia (Mafia) shot dead in NY.

*Stiletto does not leave Butte for the whole year—
first time he stayed so long without a trip to NY.
Rumor: target in Mafia war. Maria hardly comes
to Casa Della Rina, "working late."*

1958
- US unemployment 5.1 million
- Indian demonstration at Custer Park, wooden
  marker for Lame White Man placed near memorial
  to Custer's soldiers.
      *Harry (age 11) and Walter Boyd (14) hitch-hike
      to Custer Park, dance in ceremonial ring as
      marker is placed. Get home very late that night.
      Maria, Nonnarina worried, furious. The next
      week, Stiletto evicts Walter's great-grandmother,
      tears down shack. Harry and Walter swear it
      won't break up their friendship, but they don't see
      each other much, especially after Walter becomes
      basketball star, scholarship winner.*

1959
- Cuban revolution, Castro
- Strike at Berkeley Pit, six months. Anaconda
  increased production in Chile, laid off more Butte
  workers, broke the backs of the Butte unions. "The
  Company never had a strike it didn't want."
- Franklin School in Meaderville closed—earthquake
  damage. Soon catches fire, like all buildings abandoned on mine hill.

1960
- FDA approves contraceptive pill
- On TV: San Francisco City Hall riots drive out
  House un-American Activities Committee
      *Harry recognizes Miss Segal, fired-hosed on steps
      of rotunda*
- Anaconda tried for pollution charges, threatens

closure, loss of 7,000 jobs, wins

Harry hit by flying rocks from blasting near Casa Della Rina. Maria insists he move down to her house on the flats. Harry won't leave without Nonnarina. Nonnarina refuses. "Sixty years we say YES to the Company while it kills my husband, my son, your father. Now I say NO! NO." Casa Della Rina closed 12 days in October for blasting damage

- Vietnam: 900 American "advisors"
- Edward Kennedy comes to Butte to campaign for brother John

1961

- Sputnik, Russian astronaut Gargarin

  Harry's 9th grade science class at Butte High suddenly gets intense. "The Russians beat us!"

- Bay of Pigs fiasco, attempt to invade Cuba
- Berlin Wall started
- 215,000 tons of rock a day trucked out from the Pit
- Few businesses left on Mine Hill

  Casa Della Rina open 3 days a week, few customers. Maria begs Nonnarina to accept high paying supervision of Stiletto's best restaurant. No. Nonnarina turns 80. "I'm not dead yet. I die here, where I built something. You finish school, Enrico, go to college, go to California like we always said we would." But when Harry says he'll take her with him, she refuses. "My daughter, my husband, my son are here, in this ground. When I die, I want to rest with them."

1962

- Vietnam: 11,300 Americans
- Cuban missile crisis ends
- Butte declared a national historic landmark

  Maria, Stiletto gone from Butte one weekend

every month. Business trip.

- Eichmann hanged, (few Jews left in Butte, synagogue closed)

     "Jews are smart. They got educated, got out. You go too, Enrico."
     Casa Della Rina stands almost alone, but still has a few customers who drive up the pitted, blasted roads. Harry (15) is always patching new cracks in the walls, ceiling

1963

- President Kennedy assassinated
- Washington DC march— MLKing "I have a dream—"

     Pit blasting opens old mine shaft under Casa Della Rina, back portion of house falls into crater, rest of house tilts on the edge.
     Nonnarina agrees to move out immediately
     Nonnarina dies
     Harry drops out of school, lives with his mother on the flats
     Bobby Knievel hires Harry as helper

1964

- 23,000 Americans in Vietnam
- TV: Berkeley Free Speech Movement on UC Campus, Mario Savio in front of Sproul Hall, "stop the machine"
  32 hours on top of police car, surrounded by crowds to keep police away
- Strike threatened in Butte. Anaconda shuts down, loss of 5,000 jobs, strikers give up

     Harry arrested 4:30 a.m., police waiting as he climbs down from roof. Tried and convicted— burglary. Because still under 18, jail term or probation with military service. Joins the navy. Old folks say, "Just like his father."

During the first month of 1969, the unruly Butte motorcyclist Harry called "Bobby" was as much in the news as were the anti-war protesters. Unlike them, Evel Knievel, wearing a stars-and-stripes suit, made pro-military speeches before performing his daring motorcycle stunts. The film clip of his disastrous, near-fatal attempt to jump over the fountains outside Caesar's Palace in Las Vegas was played over and over again on the TV news, between excerpts from President Nixon's speeches promising an honorable and victorious end to the Vietnam War. The ironic juxtaposition was not lost on anti-war art students. Posters went on sale instantly.

Dan Lyon carried one when he approached our table at the Med one rainy day. "Last one left!" he said, holding out a poster for sale, and nudging aside Bill Jackson, who had been passing around his color photos of the whimsical mud-flat sculpture. On the painted poster, Evel Knievel's suit had been exaggerated to make his figure an animated American flag; the fountains at Caesar's Palace spouted blood; the flying motorcycle—dropping bombs—plunged head first into the bloody spray; around the fountain, blood-spattered bodies of Asian children lay scattered on the ground. As Daniel gloated over his brisk sales, Bill Jackson gathered up his photos and left. Pat Cody, having bought one of Bill's photos, and having already exceeded her rare twenty minutes at the Med, gulped down her coffee, stood up, and bought Dan's last poster, saying, "I know the girl who did this. Not her best, but she'll be an important artist one day." (Pat was right.)

"Back to the store?" Angel asked.

"Free Clinic," she explained. "Do you have any idea what the gonorrhea rate is on the Avenue?"

I pretended not to notice the look exchanged by Angel and Harry—a hint that they knew the problem first hand? We went back to the subject of crashing motorcycles, military stalemates, the latest, disputed figures of casualties on both sides, and whether the Third World Liberation Front strike for Ethnic Studies would shut down the university before classes even got started. Dan poked Harry in the ribs. "So, do you think your hometown's great and only hero is finished?"

Harry shook his head. "They just rearranged the plates and pins that are holding him together. He already announced another jump."

"Oh, I didn't hear about that," Angel said.

Jake snorted. "Not the sport you'd be following avidly. Or is Angel actually a Hell's Angel?" We all laughed. It was hard to imagine Angel riding down the street with any motorcycle club. Jake turned to Harry. "You knew him in Butte?"

Harry hesitated, then nodded.

"A friend of yours?" Daniel pursued, smelling something interesting in Harry's reserve.

Harry shook his head. "He's about ten years older than me."

"But you knew him?" Daniel's question—and his expectant silence—were insistent.

Harry shrugged, clearly uncomfortable. "Bobby Knievel. That's his name. A great all-around athlete. He was good at any sport he tried."

"But—" Angel prodded gently.

"No good on a team. Fought with the coach, the players. He had to go solo, wouldn't share it with anyone."

"But that's good for some sports, like boxing, swimming."

"Skiing," Harry nodded. "He was a championship skier, then started his motorcycle jumps, then spent a couple of years in the Army."

"So you know a lot about him. Come on, Harry, tell us."

Harry hesitated, then shrugged. "When he came back from the Army, he was already pretty well known, but not making any money. Bobby could never hold down a regular job, and motorcycles cost money, especially when you start modifying them. He needed money, so—so he stole it. Working solo, as usual. One night I was out late, walking around, waiting for my mother outside the casino where she worked. I looked down this alley behind some shops, and I saw him, coming down off the roof of a jewelry store. And he saw me too." Harry paused, took a breath. "A couple of days later he stopped me on the street, bought me a beer—"

"How old were you?" I asked.

"Almost sixteen." Harry laughed. "Getting served a drink in Butte was never a problem, at any age." Harry was more relaxed now, getting into his story. "Bobby said he'd heard I was smarter than the kids who ran after him, and knew how to keep my mouth shut. He needed some help. Was I interested? I told him, sure."

"Why?" asked Angel. "Were you afraid to refuse?"

Harry shook his head.

Daniel leaped in. "He was poor!"

But Harry shook his head again. "Not really poor—not for Butte. No, I was—pretty mad about—pretty mixed up—I had dropped out of school, and—anyway. Bobby'd check out offices with money or salable goods. I'd sneak out of the house nights my mother was working, and meet him. We'd go up about three or four A.M. and cut a hole through the roof. He'd drop in, take the stuff, climb out, pay me right then—he always had some cash along for me—and take off. My job was to clean up after him and patch the roof. By the time anyone knew something was missing, we were both long gone."

"Never got caught?" Daniel was looking at Harry with new respect.

"Not for about a year. Bobby never did. Maybe he paid off the cops, I was never sure about that. Gradually I started to think some people knew, and I should quit. But I didn't. One night I was finishing up alone, and suddenly the cops were there. They said someone saw me and called them. They didn't even ask who I was working for. That's why I think they knew. So it was jail or the military and probation. Stay clean for three years, and you stay out of prison. Anyway, they gave me a break. Because of my age. Because of my mother, maybe because of—she had a friend—"

"On the police force?"

Harry shook his head. "But I think he's the one tipped off the cops. To get me out of Butte before I got into real trouble. Maybe as a favor to my mother. Or because he—" Harry had stopped smiling and his knee had begun to twitch. It was time to change the subject.

Angel, tactful as ever, stepped in. "So, Danny, you see the heavy equipment parked on Haste? They say the bulldozers are going to roll tomorrow."

"Over my dead body," Dan growled, smiling. "What about you?"

Angel shook his head. "I lined up another place to stay. What about you, Harry?"

Harry hesitated, then he said softly, not looking at me. "I'm with Danny."

123

Three days later the university demolished the last row of houses on the block behind Telegraph Avenue. The house where Harry, Angel, and Dan Lyon had been living was virtually empty by that time except for a handful who had barricaded themselves in. Despite Dan Lyon's yelling and rock-throwing, and lying down, and being dragged away by police—the bulldozers rolled. Within a couple of hours, the last five houses were piles of debris.

Harry showed up at my house that night, breathless and furious, raving as if he were drunk or drugged, but there was no smell of liquor or any sign of drugs that I could recognize. "They killed Nonnarina the same way! I've been there, I know, that's the way they do it, there and here, those rotten, fucking killers! This time we're not going to let them do it! This time it's going to be different! This time—"

I sat him down and gave him a small glass of brandy and a big glass of water. "Tell me what happened, Harry."

"You know what happened. Go up there and look."

"The university tore down some old houses on university property."

"Yeah! That's all!" The look he gave me was full of generalized, anguished hatred. "Yeah. Their property, everything belongs to them?" He gulped down the brandy.

"What did you say about your Nonnarina? Who killed her?"

"The same people, the Company, the ones who own everything, different names, but the same." He took a gulp of water, coughed, laughed—whatever word could describe the furious bark that came out of his mouth. "Sometimes even the names are the same—Hearst—walk through

Sather Gate and ask yourself how that got paid for!" He shook his head. "You don't get it." He lurched out of the chair and stood.

"Tell me about Nonnarina. I thought she was in her eighties when she died. Being that old it was only natural that—"

He fell back into the chair. "In her eighties and strong. She could have lived another ten years. Twenty. If they'd just left her—but, no, they had to take everything— all her life she lost and lost and made do and lost again. She lost her home, her country, so she made a new one, made it on a dead mountain. Lost her family in Italy, so she made a new one here. Lost her husband—even before he was killed, she lost him when he went down the mines, it changed him. Lost her son even before the con killed him—married to a girl she was ashamed to have in her house. Lost her grand-daughter to a drunk who beat her up, then to an old crook, in that order or vice versa. Shit, I'm not sure, not even sure which one was my father." He choked and coughed and I poured more brandy.

"She must have been proud of you, Harry. She had you, Harry."

"What good was I to Nonnarina? After fifty years of her making something out of nothing, they wanted even that nothing, that dead hill. Dig it out, blast it out, blast you out!" Harry gulped down the brandy, took the bottle, and filled his glass. "And for the first time, she said NO. So they kept on blasting, opening the Pit right under her, and she kept saying NO, until—"

Harry was sobbing, and I didn't know whether the brandy and the emotion it released was good or bad for him. I didn't know what to do, except wait.

He quieted down. "Then Casa Della Rina tipped and

started sliding into the pit. The back of the house broke off. The kitchen, my room, all my clothes and stuff. My mother picked me up at school, took me down to her house, near the casino where she worked. She told me Nonnarina had given in, agreed to leave the hill, the next day, just wanted to pack up a few mementos that night. She'd be ready to go in the morning. I could skip school the next day. I could ride up there with my mother and help Nonnarina bring all her stuff down to my mother's house.

"It was December, twelve below zero, two feet of snow covering the hill. The fire department had put the Christmas lights up on the old head frames. Early the next morning, we left before it was light. The Christmas lights were still lit up on the head frames. But Casa Della Rina was dark. We went in, called her. Went all through the house. She wasn't there. Maybe she rode down with someone else? But who else was there? One or two neighbors packing up, clearing out. Three or four saloons. A couple of boarding houses for some pit workers. They weren't working because of the snow. My mother got on the phone, calling around. I went outside, walked east, uphill.

"I knew where to look. She was there all right. At the old Speculator Mine where we used to go every Christmas Eve, and she'd talk to Nonno Francesco, and then we'd go on to midnight mass. She was there, a lump under six inches of snow, sitting, leaning against the old head frame, like it was a summer day and she was just waiting for him to finish his shift and come up.

"I pushed the snow off her face. I thought she was smiling at me. But when the medics got there, they said, no, it was just rigor mortis setting in."

I didn't know what to say, so, of course, I touched his shoulder and then said something stupid. "I'm so sorry,

126

Harry. I understand how you—"

"No!" He shrugged off my hand and stood up. "No, you don't understand. You can't understand because you're not a loser. I am. I come from a whole family of losers, a whole town of losers, in a world of losers, where if you fight back, if you say NO, they kill you. Even if you say yes, they kill you!"

"You're right, Harry, I'm one of the lucky ones. But I have to believe that we could change your luck, that—"

"Change my luck? Right! But this is it—can't you get that?—the first time, right now, right here, where a lot of people are getting together and saying NO! Whether it's the war or civil rights or free speech or the old wreck of a house they're living in—there's a chance, just a chance, that people together can say NO and that NO will change everything. Everything! There's no way I walk away from this." He started for the door.

"Where are you going?"

"Rally." He swung the door open.

"Where will you sleep tonight? You could stay in Carol's room." No answer. He was gone.

Harry missed the next two days of classes at Merritt. I tried to reach him at Steadman's Used Books, but Jake said he hadn't come in. When he showed up again in class, he was carrying a loaded duffel bag and looked as if he'd slept in his clothes. There was a bruise on the side of his left eye. I stood in the doorway to stop him from running out when the class ended. "If you're determined to sleep outside, you can do that in my back yard. It's safer." He didn't answer me, just pushed past me. But late that night I heard him walking up the gravel driveway alongside the house. The next morning, when I went out to offer him a cup of coffee, he was gone. But after class that day, he said he'd appreciate camping in my back yard until he could find a place.

The block behind the row of little shops on the east side of Telegraph was cleared within a week. Then the land stood empty, except for the parked cars quickly filling it up during the day. With the first rain, it turned into a tire-rutted mud hole. Bits of trash floated between the parked cars, and, when the puddles dried, the dust and trash was churned up by cars pulling in and out. It seemed that Dan Lyon had been right—the university had no immediate plans for the land, had acted solely to get rid of the activists and drifters squatting in the old houses.

Dan and Angel had moved into girlfriends' apartments. Harry spent most nights in my back yard. I gave him the key to a leaky shed near the back fence, where there was a toilet and sink, but no shower or stove. An old table and chair stood among other junk Carol and I had stored there and covered with plastic against the dampness. "Most of this can go to the dump," I told Harry, who cleaned the place out, making room for his sleeping bag. He refused to use my shower or my kitchen. He would shower at the Merritt gym and eat at Father Mike's Kitchen, which now served a free meal every evening. "I'll only be here a couple of weeks." Harry seemed more reserved with me than before. Perhaps he was embarrassed at having cried and spilled out such painful memories.

Harry looked in vain for something he could afford. Rents were climbing, as more and more people came to Berkeley, some escaping even higher rents in San Francisco, some attracted by media coverage of marches and riots. Restless young men roamed Telegraph Avenue and spilled out into neighborhoods, especially ours, where rundown houses owned by suburban heirs of their black parents wore forlorn signs, For Sale Owner Will Finance. (Mrs. Temple had explained to me that South Berkeley was "red-lined," designated too poor by banks who withheld financing. That was why my rent had been so low. That was why so many houses were being rented to hordes of transients. That was why she was willing to carry the loan if I wanted to buy my little cottage. "I'm getting too old to deal with plumbers and roofers." I had taken her up on it and had begun 1969 as a home owner).

Harry tried moving into one group rental, but on the first day caught another occupant trying to steal his old portable typewriter. He moved out again. The second one he tried erupted in a pre-dawn knife fight when one tenant tried to steal another's guitar containing his drug stash. These people were not the mellow hippies or dedicated politicals of Angel's commune.

I began to think it might be a good idea for me to have a man—especially a big man like Harry on the premises. "You'd be doing me a favor." In return for housing in the shed, I told him, he could do a little more gardening work for me. Mrs. Temple hired him too. He repaired the roof of the shed. He ran an extension cord from my house, and I found am extra space heater he could use. In those days, electricity was cheap, and the increase in my utility bill was insignificant, worth the convenience of having Harry around—though I saw little of him, except in my English 1B class and at Jake's bookstore, where he worked three night shifts. Sometimes I saw him sitting alone at the Med, surrounded by stacks of library books. When he was not studying at the Med, he was usually with Daniel Lyon or with Angel, heatedly discussing the latest crisis.

He usually waved and beckoned when I walked in,

but I rarely joined them or Bill Jackson, who was always alone now. A few minutes of his sad face was all I could take. Usually I preferred bringing take-out coffee to Steadman's Books (I was one of few people not barred from entering with a full cup), which seemed insulated from the fevered street dramas now enacted on the Avenue. Some evenings I heard Dan Lyon on the KPFA news, bits of a speech he made before being arrested during a demonstration, then bits of another speech after his quick release. Angel was always on the scene giving a more reliable report of incidents than we could see on television, if we saw them at all. "Incidents" on Telegraph Avenue became too routine to be covered on TV or by the major daily papers.

I did join their table at the Med once, to ask Angel if he was planning to cover something I'd just seen while parking my car. "On that lot where those old houses used to be—"

"God, after this rain, you must be hub-deep in mud."

"When I got out of the car I noticed that someone had planted a bright red geranium right next to where I'd parked."

"That'll last about five minutes."

"It looked like it had been there a while. Like it was taking hold. Then I saw another one, bigger, between the ruts of other tire tracks. As if people are trying to park around the flowers, not crush them into the mud."

Daniel rolled his eyes. "Some Quaker out there making nice again."

"Hey, but wouldn't it be great—I think I'll try to get someone on my show, interview them." Angel's sweet smile lit up his face as he seemed to see an image in the air in front of him. "Imagine if everyone brought a plant and—"

Daniel stood up, pushing back his chair noisily, and

went off to distribute leaflets for a rally in support of the Third World Liberation Front.

What Angel imagined began to happen. Each time I glanced into the messy lot behind Telegraph I saw a single flower withering or ground under car tires, soon replaced by two more. Then another small space would be cleared of papers and garbage, and another little plant began putting out buds between parked cars. Another and another, more plants surviving as drivers tried to avoid grinding them under their tires. Within a month there was a little corner behind Jake's bookstore, the size of a parking space, sprouting a miniature garden.

Spring term classes started at the university, with the Third World Liberation Front pickets at the entrances to the campus. They staged sit-ins at classes and offices, and formed blockades demanding Ethnic Studies. Of course, their demonstrations spilled over into more riots on Telegraph Avenue, their ranks joined by what Fred Cody called, "a mixed bag of idealists, draft dodgers, drug pushers, hedonists, runaways from all over the U.S." (Perhaps for the first time, the Merritt College faculty was unanimously grateful that we already had started offering black studies classes.)

The university faculty showed none of the unity of support they had for the Free Speech Movement, only five years before. Many, like Marsha's husband, determinedly ignored the pickets, as did most science classes. (At lunch Marsha would describe each new explosion by Ivan—denouncing a speaker, or a rally, or a slogan chanted by strikers. I hardly had to wait for her account—the *Daily*

Cal enjoyed printing his long, outraged letters, casting him as the university's resident crank. Marsha complained that life at home was impossible.) A few professors—usually with easily portable class content, like literature—honored the strike, such as it was. They held their classes off campus, sometimes at local liberal churches (Father Mike, of course, opened the chapel basement for classes between the free meals). Some visiting lecturers like Denise Levertov and Alice Allen held classes in their apartments near campus.

The legendary Alice Allen had moved to San Francisco and started teaching at SF State just before I finished my MA. Everyone rushed to get into one of her classes, any one of her classes. I managed to get a place in her class on Expatriate Literature in the 1920s, and, after reading our first papers, she asked me to write reviews for a small literary magazine (soon defunct). After I left SF State, we met now and then at Jessica Mitford's famous parties at her Oakland home. At the most recent one, Alice had talked about rallying support for a Third World Strike at SF State—which ended dubiously, with Alice taking a leave and a temporary appointment teaching at UC. She'd called me to help her find a rental near the campus. She wanted to escape, if only for a few months, from the aftertaste of rancor and bitterness at SF State. Instead she had landed in the middle of another Third World Student Strike. There was no doubt about whose side Alice would take.

Alice let me interview her on KPFA, then invited me to drop in on the workshop that now met in her apartment. I took Harry with me. I'd already told her about him. As I'd hoped, she suggested he audit the workshop, and I told Harry he could skip my English 1B class on the days he was with Alice. I hoped he would find friends among UC students. Contact with them, as well as a renowned writer, might give him the push he needed to get on with his novel, and a push toward transferring to UC when the time came.

By the end of February, Telegraph Avenue was crowded with National Guardsmen ordered in by Governor Reagan to dampen disorder around the campus. (It had the opposite effect, of course.) Angel and Harry had sensibly decided to stay off Telegraph Avenue unless Angel was called by KPFA to cover a specific event. They went to a nearby house, where Angel now lived, and Angel gave Harry his first LSD tab, sitting up with him all night as it took effect.

I knew nothing about it for several days. I knew only that Harry hadn't come to my class, nor to any others at Merritt, nor to his job at Steadman's Used Books, nor even to Alice's workshop. I found Angel at Moe's Books and learned that Harry had had "a good trip" and "looked fine when he went home, at least, that's where he said he was going."

It had not occurred to me to look in the shed for him. I couldn't always tell when he was there. The shed's only window faced away from the house; I wouldn't necessarily see a light at night, or even hear his typewriter. I drove home and walked straight down the driveway, across the back yard to the shed. I knocked on the door more urgently than I meant to. It opened almost immediately. Harry looked as if he needed a shower, but otherwise seemed fine as he apologized for worrying me. "I dropped acid with Angel."

"I know."

He must have caught a look on my face. "You never did."

133

"No."

He smiled, then gave me the tolerant look I was used to seeing in the eyes of Angel. Harry had moved another step away from deferring to me as his teacher. Well, okay, I thought, that's probably good too.

"I'm fine. I'm sorry if I worried you."

Behind him I could see sheets of paper spread all over the table. I was curious. "Did your writing go better while you were—on a trip?"

"Yes. Well, no. I couldn't actually write—you can't do anything but—SEE—BE—everything becomes so completely REAL. You know what I mean?"

I shook my head, resisting my urge to ask him if LSD made him speak in capital letters.

"The first thing that happens is the light. You see the light that's in everything. Always there, everything is light, and I saw the light."

"You sound like Holy Hubert," I said, then wanted to bite my tongue. He was one of the characters who harangued students on Sprout Plaza. Harry looked annoyed. "Sorry. Go on, please." But Harry had dismissed me, frowning, tight-lipped. I nodded toward the papers on the table and said, apologetically. "I'm glad it helped you get back to working on your novel."

Harry smiled and forgave me. "Not my novel. A letter. A long one. To my mother. The first time I've written to her since I left Butte. Four years. She used to write to me, but I threw her letters away."

"Why?"

He laughed. "I don't know. I judged her. I blamed her for things she couldn't help. I was able to understand my mother, what happened to her, what really happened. I had it all wrong. I blamed her for looking at her chances and making a smart choice—this old Mafia guy that Nonnarina hated. I blamed her for doing what I might have done if I had been in her shoes. What any of us might have done. That's what I mean when I say I KNEW, I really UNDERSTOOD."

"Well, it's good that you wrote to your mother. Good for both of you. But if you can stop for a minute, come in and call Jake. Do it now. Call Alice too. They're both worried about you."

"Really?" He seemed pleased at their concern.

He followed me across the back yard and into the kitchen, where I handed him the phone. "And you better not mention the LSD to Alice."

He nodded vigorously. "She'd throw me out of her workshop. She's really old-fashioned about some things."

After speaking to Jake and Alice, he called Angel. I went up to my room to work, but I could hear him talking. Laughing. Then lowering his voice, except for an occasional, "Yeah!" or "Far out!" "Next Saturday?" Harry lowered his voice still more. They were setting up a date for another trip. It was none of my business.

A week later the white president of Merritt College was quoted in the *Oakland Tribune*, questioning the "wisdom of moving the college to a location inaccessible to so many of the people we serve." His office was invaded by a crowd of angry black students who accused him of serving "white people who want to keep blacks off *their* hills." The student invasion and sit-in was noisy but brief. They left after an hour. So did I, for once canceling my final class. Like the president of the college (who resigned soon afterward), I was tired of an argument I knew was long lost.

I ended up at Jake's store, where he nodded at my story. "Like when they moved SF State College and the academic high school, what's-its-name—"

"Lowell."

"Right. Moved them out to the sand dunes, as far away as possible from kids in the poor, black and brown parts of San Francisco. Pretty soon no one will remember when those schools stood right in the middle of town, where everyone could get to them."

Then he abruptly began to talk about his son, now in his senior year at Berkeley High. He frowned. Was there a problem? "I don't know. Something wrong between him and me."

I shrugged. "He's a teenager."

Jake shook his head. "More than that. Getting worse. I get the feeling he's really mad at me for—something. I don't know. It's like whatever we're doing, he's watching me and thinking something, it's on the tip of his tongue to tell me why he hates me. Yeah, really. Hates me."

"Maybe he just needs to get away from his parents. Is he going away to college?"

"He's been accepted here, but I want to get him out of Berkeley, soon as possible, like your daughter. He says, 'Berkeley is history in the making,' but I say, let someone else make it. I see too much stuff on the Avenue."

I had told Jake about the Freshman English anthology I was working on with Professor Person. He pressed several old books on me, refusing payment. "Check these out. You'll find a couple of great old ones—forgotten, but so contemporary it's uncanny."

I noticed that the aisles were filling up with stacks of books again. "Has Harry been coming to work?"

"More or less." Jake lit another cigar. "It's okay, whenever he wants to work. Business is so bad, I can't even keep myself busy."

"And you have Lisa when you really need help."

Jake exhaled, blowing out a long trail of horrible-smelling smoke. "No." So the affair with Lisa had ended without my noticing. Lisa had moved out of Jake's house, out of working in the bookstore, out of his life. "I like Harry." (Obviously, Jake didn't want to talk about Lisa; it was years before I learned any of the details of their breakup.) "Harry's a hard worker, and for a kid with his background, he knows books pretty well. I miss talking to him more than I miss his work."

"Angel has introduced him to LSD."

"Worried about him?"

"It's none of my business."

"It is if he's not doing the work for your class."

"It's spotty. Like his attendance. But he's keeping up. And—what do I know?"

"You never tried LSD?" I shook my head. "I did. Twice. The first time I felt illuminated, wise, creative as hell. But never did anything with it. Just remembered that feeling. So I tried again."

"Something happen that time?"

"Yeah. Got the scare of my life. It wiped out my memory for about a week. Totally. And I decided, hey, I've got a son to take care of. I can't afford to lose my mind, even if it comes back."

I stepped out of Jake's store and threaded my way through a dozen chanting, shivering white kids in gauzy orange robes, shuffling along, their bare, thin, goose-pimpled arms shaking tambourines. "Hare Krishna, Hare Krishna, Hare Krishna, Hare, Hare—" I still remember that moment as the first time I'd seen disciples of the sect that was soon to buy an old church and dozens of houses in my neighborhood. At the time they seemed just another oddity passing through Berkeley, not a preview of the 1970s.

It was after six, but a glazier was still working on replacing a broken shop window. Many of the merchants were simply leaving the plywood in place, expecting more breakage. (One had received a letter from a friend addressed to Plywood, California, plus the correct zip code, and had posted the envelope on his window, a forlorn joke.) At Dwight I turned toward the messy lot to get my car. There was more trash than ever blowing around, but since the rain had stopped, I wouldn't have to wade through mud. I was surprised to see that—it seemed overnight, but probably had been a couple of weeks—the zone of plantings had grown from Dwight to Haste. The informally spaced lines of parked cars now started at least fifteen feet from the back walls of all the stores. Three boys and two girls were chipping holes in the hard, dry clay soil, using only hand tools. As I walked past them I saw a nursery bucket containing a tiny lemon tree.

During the next two months, as the plantings increased, parking on the messy half-acre of dirt required skillful steering to avoid crushing plants or even people, always there digging and watering. More and more drivers gave up and found somewhere else to park. All this went on without anyone seeming to take notice. People's attention was focused on the seven men, familiar faces in Berkeley, on trial for conspiracy to incite riots six months before at the Democratic Convention. Or they talked about the increasing stream of young runaways coming in.

Occasionally, I volunteered at Father Mike's Kitchen, serving food to jaunty groups of kids arriving in vans and leaving again. More of them, however, began to look like Carol when she was coming down with a cold, and some were older men who looked like the tramps who came to the door begging when I was a child in the Great Depression. The rougher drifters rarely ate there; they had other ways of getting the food and dope they wanted. Once I served beans and corn to Bill Jackson, who insisted he was taking a meal only because he'd done an electrical job for Father Mike, who couldn't pay. He was also checking out the church basement so that he could help design a mural to be painted by the men who regularly ate there. He had to hurry because he had an appointment to photograph Gary Snyder and Ram Dass. I noticed that he was thin and that his shirt was not quite clean, like a man who has been living in his car.

"You haven't seen my latest mud flat photos."

Bill reached into a briefcase and brought out a dozen 8x10 photos taken through colored filters. I asked him if any were for sale, and he tried to look casual, even reluctant, saying he'd be happy to give me any that I wanted. I gave him twenty dollars for a garish image shot through a red filter—a huge hand, made of patches of plywood, reaching up out of the swampy tidelands, like the last sight of a giant drowning in a bloody sunset.

"City of Emeryville wants to put blowups of my photos in their City Hall." He shrugged. "I won't make a dime on it. My materials will cost more than they will pay me, but I don't care."

"That's wonderful, Bill." Was it?—a man whose photos were chosen for official display, but who had to eat in a soup kitchen?

139

When I left the soup kitchen, I stopped to show the photo to Jake. He nodded. "He's in trouble. He got into a fight with somebody on a building job, and no one will hire him. Why are you doing this?"

"Buying the photo? Just to help Bill a bit. Besides, it's a bit of history. When the new shoreline freeway comes through, all this stuff will be gone."

"I don't mean that. I mean why are you working in that crazy priest's soup kitchen?"

"Well. To do something. I can't stand political meetings, but once a week I can spend a couple of hours helping to feed people like Bill."

"I'm all for feeding Bill Jackson. But you're not feeding many like him. You're feeding drifters who come from towns that drive them out, or brats who want to punish their parents. They come here, eat at Father Mike's church, sleep and shit in my shop doorway, then after I clean up, sit there begging or dealing and driving away my business. And they're telling the others on the road—Berkeley's the place to come to, that's where the action is, that's where they'll feed us."

"What am I supposed to do, let them starve?"

"Tell Mike Rugo to set up a soup kitchen out in one of those empty warehouses near the Bay."

"Easier said than done."

"The university owns one, and they offered it for the homeless services."

That was news to me. I shrugged. "Father Mike says they won't go way out there."

"No! They want to be on Telegraph so they can hit up my customers for money, or steal books from Cody's and try to sell them to me, and be near the dealers who supply them!"

140

"You mean they're bad for business."

"Damned right. Lousy Capitalist Merchant? Is that what Dan Lyon calls me? Hiring Harry is what made me a capitalist, right? Is that so bad? I'm the villain? For providing you a place to browse? Or getting you some rare book you can't find? Are Fred and Pat Cody bad guys for juggling a low profit business to feed four kids? And taking the shit from the students and the street people and the agitators and police while they're trying to do what's right for everybody? If you think we merchants are such bad guys, don't worry. We'll all be driven off the Avenue in no time!"

Then, for the first time, he turned his back on me, strode to the back of the store, and started shelving books. I left quietly and stayed away for a couple of weeks. When I showed up again, he looked glad to see me. Neither of us mentioned his tirade, which had revealed the fresh outrage in the chronic sour temper I had learned not to take seriously.

Harry continued to turn in acceptable papers and to attend more than half of his classes at Merritt. According to Alice he never missed the workshop at her apartment, but had read aloud only once, from the early chapters of his novel, the ones I'd read.

Some time in the middle of April, on a day my classes ended early, I arrived at home before two. Angel called to ask if Harry was "all right."

"What do you mean, 'all right'?"

"Well, I mean—is he there?"

"I don't know. I haven't looked. You want to talk to him?"

"Yeah. No. I mean—look, Ruth, he had a bad trip

141

last night, left me about four in the morning, said he was going home. He looked—well, I just wanted to make sure he's all right."

I went out to the shed, knocked for a while, then called, then pushed the door open. Harry was coming out of the toilet, wearing only his shorts, drained of color, shivering, his long limbs unsteady. He looked like a huge baby, clinging to a door jam as he learned to walk. I picked up his shirt and threw it at him. "For God's sake, Harry, why didn't you answer my knocking? Angel called, worried about you, and when you didn't answer the door—"

He began poking his arms into his shirt, missing the sleeve openings, jabbing again and again. I watched, resisting the urge to help. "I thought if I didn't answer, you'd think I was out." His face suddenly looked concentrated, and he turned indecisively, then turned back to me, swallowed, nodded. I think he had been vomiting, and had fleetingly thought he might begin retching again.

"You're sick?" I reached up and put the back of my hand to his forehead—a motherly reflex I instantly regretted.

"I'm all right now. I'm sorry."

"I'm not running a drug house here. I'm not a nurse standing by to hold your head when you do something stupid. If you want to 'enlighten yourself' with drugs, don't come back here!" Harry seemed to be getting control of himself, but I certainly wasn't.

"No, Ruth. No more acid. I'll move out if you want, but that was my last trip." He picked up his jeans and struggled into them. They were a bit short for his long legs, and his bare, pale ankles looked thin and vulnerable, his feet white, with bluish toes. He looked so woebegone, so haunted, that I relented, waited while he put on his shoes. Then I threw his old Navy P-coat over his shoulders, and brought him shambling across the garden and into the house where I made hot tea. He sat warming his hands on the cup, but looking at it suspiciously. I saw his eyes widen in horror for a second.

"Harry!"

He shook his head, blinked, and mumbled, "Flashback," trying to smile at me. He shook his head again when I handed him a glass of warm milk, but took it and began to sip slowly. By the time he finished the milk, he had a little color.

"It was—I had—"

"Angel told me."

"The first few trips were wonderful. Beautiful. I was clear. There was nothing I couldn't see. And after a few hours, when I started coming down, the scenes would come. You know, like a movie in my head, those memories, scenes coming up, lost, then found." He sighed. "Then slipping away again before I could write anything down." He swallowed, took a deep breath, as if pulling together his strength to confront some horror. "Last night, it wasn't like that. It was—the Pit. First it was one of the mine shafts, and I was in the cage under the gallows frame, like—I think I remember, yeah, I think my father must have taken me down once when I was a baby. I was in the cage, alone, and the cable started screaming, and the cage dropped, down and down and down. Then I wasn't alone. Nonnarina was in the cage with me. And I could see other shafts, hundreds of shafts, with walls like glass, and cages shooting down the shafts, full of people, and it was the people who were screaming, and then there were no cages, no shafts, it was all open, and people raining down into the pit and screaming and clawing at the walls, at each other, at me.

"Angel tried to pull me out of it. Gave me valium,

then something else. Just made it worse. I kept falling and falling. I could hear Angel talking, and I tried to listen to his voice telling me I was going to be all right, but then I was falling again. I think I started screaming and trying to run away, escape, out the window, any way I could get out of that—and Angel stopped me, but then his girlfriend got really mad and threw us out because of the noise I was making. The fresh air helped. We walked and walked until it was light. And we were near Milton Street. So I told Angel to leave me. He had to go to work. I came in and lay down here. I think you were already gone to work. I couldn't sleep. Every time I closed my eyes, I started falling. Then I started throwing up.

"I'm really sorry. I'm going out now. To the gym. Take a shower. I can still make it to Alice's workshop. Don't tell her, please. It'll never happen again. Nothing stronger than pot, I swear, and I won't even smoke that here. Promise." He watched me, waiting until I nodded. Then he left.

Harry left his outline for his term paper in my mailbox on the due date, but I hardly ever saw him. I knew he faithfully attended Alice Allen's workshop, and that was what mattered. He returned to the shed so late at night that a whole month passed before I saw him in daylight—shirtless, digging in the old parking-lot-garden-patch now called People's Park. It was a Maoist slogan of the times—people's this and people's that—signifying something then believed to be done by and for ordinary people, often in defiance of some official policy (the opposite of what it meant in China, of course.)

The April 12 issue of the *Berkeley Barb* called for

action to make a park on the university-owned lot, which, "like the university, belongs rightly to The People, who will reclaim it." Of course, the gardening work had long been going on, but the Barb's vague declaration brought in more donated labor and materials: heavy equipment to plow up the impacted clay soil; hand tools from homes and local stores; flyers inviting everyone to come and work or to drop off a donated plant at Cody's Books.

The next time I approached the worksite, I saw Dan Lyon first, standing on a rented tractor, its scoop high in the air. I caught the last part of his speech, "—to dig out the foundations of housing destroyed by the university, lay in topsoil by the end of next week!" He then sat with his hands on the steering wheel, turned and lifted his head, paused, then climbed down and turned the machine over to the professional operator. That was when I noticed all the cameras. Lyon had been up there just long enough to be photographed.

Harry towered over most of the people hauling away debris by hand, lifting garbage, glass, chunks of concrete and throwing them into the backs of pickup trucks lining Haste Street. He dumped a full wheelbarrow into a truck, then began rolling the wheelbarrow back to where I was standing. He looked better coordinated than he ever had, his long limbs connected and working together. Several people looked to him for direction, as they did to a few other untitled "foremen." Working beside Harry was—yes—Alice Allen, over sixty (how far over, she would never admit) and weighing less than one hundred pounds. She was carefully made up, as always, her bluish-gray curls trickling over her forehead from under a sheer silk head scarf that perfectly matched her eyes and her work gloves. Alice might do anything—but she would do it in style. She had brought her entire writing workshop to help with the dirtiest work, clearing out the garbage.

"One of my students gave me these overalls," she said to me. "What do you think?"

"Made for you."

"Don't just stand there. Go home and get into some work clothes and pitch in. Harry'll show you what to do. He's the only one in my workshop who knows how to handle tools."

"Hi, Harry."

Harry gave me a huge smile. His face streamed sweat, streaking black earth down his cheeks, his neck, his chest—which was becoming ominously pink. His smile faded only slightly. "Going to miss your class again today."

"Just make sure you get your research paper in— May 20 deadline, no exceptions."

Alice nodded. "No exceptions. This is writers' work, writers' inspiration—not an excuse to neglect the writing." She spoke loudly enough that nearby students would be sure to hear. Then just as firmly to me, "Go home and change to overalls."

I didn't, not that day. But the next day and the next, after my classes, I wandered up to People's Park to check out the progress before going home. I mentioned the park to my students, but only a few showed any interest. Half of them had jobs after their classes. Others, envious of the students so privileged as to be at the university, were as resentful as Governor Reagan, who grumbled ominously about "outside agitators and permissive professors who incite students to violate trespass laws."

The following Monday I brought burritos and chips from the Mexican restaurant on the corner of Haste, passing them out as far as they would go. It was a beautiful day, and musicians were playing. On Wednesday, I picked up a

146

pair of work gloves from a pile, and helped load wheelbarrows until dark.

Now there were regular deliveries of food and bottled water from local restaurants. Portable toilets. Dan Lyon was always present, passing out leaflets, even grabbing a shovel and digging, now and then. I saw new faces every day, people so different from each other, they might not meet anywhere else in the normal course of their lives. It was as if an especially good day at the Med had been moved outdoors into the sun. Even Marsha showed up, passing out a plate of cookies. "I was supposed to take these to a faculty party, but I decided to play hooky." Her round, elfin face looked exalted. "He's left," she said. "I wrote a poem about it. My first in twenty years." I didn't know whether to congratulate her on the poem or on splitting up with Ivan Franklin, or both, or neither, so I only smiled and took a cookie. She moved on, turned once and waved, "Lunch next week." I nodded.

I called Carol on Friday and told her that if she was coming home for the weekend, I could promise her an interesting time. Yes, she had heard that people were making a park, and she was curious. She would come Saturday night and see People's Park on Sunday.

On that Sunday in May, Carol and I put on tattered jeans, stuffed a shopping cart with food, plants, and tools, and pushed it up to Telegraph Avenue. There were more police on the street than usual, quite a few ringing the park, just standing there, smiling at the people who were digging, shrugging when asked if they meant to enforce trespassing laws. The park was more crowded than ever.

Someone had set up a corner playground with swings and slides for the little kids and a sign-up schedule for volunteers to keep an eye on them. Three or four professional gardeners were supervising the raking of earth, the rolling out of lawn turf, the planting of shrubs and trees. Now and then they consulted huge drawings laid out on the plywood and sawhorse tables that had appeared. Whatever was needed somehow appeared, provided by workers, watchers, or anonymous donors who never came near the place. The layout of plantings and an irrigation system had become a class project in a landscape design class at the university.

Carol and I were assigned several shrubs in metal pots. "You dig a hole twice the height of each plant, wet the holes, scatter this plant food at the bottom, then put the plant in and fill it up. Pack it down good. Empty pots in that pile over there. Okay?" We nodded and went to work.

When we finished that job, there were no new directions, so we split up and went to help wherever each was needed. Musicians were playing from all four corners of the park, and people would stop working occasionally to break into a dance, joined by others, in a line or in a circle, or separately, weaving and waving at each other across some plants. One girl, about seventeen, wearing dangling beads and a bikini, grabbed my hand and pulled me into a waving, undulating line. A few minutes, then that dance stopped, and the shoveling and carrying started again. I saw Harry dancing, throwing his long legs around until a middle-aged black woman shook her head at him, grabbed him, and taught him jerks and stomps I hadn't seen since World War II.

Like the tunes from different bands, the smell of pot wafted over me from all directions. Lots of beer, public drinking laws ignored by the police. But I saw no sign of hard liquor or hard drugs. Or would I have known? Anyway, the atmosphere was benign, sweaty, kindly.

As the sun went down, the musicians went on playing. People loaded tools into the pickup trucks. Someone began

148

to sing. By the time I found Carol again, we were all singing "Blowing in the Wind," drifting out of the park, trailing down one street or another or getting into cars. Carol and I sang too and walked arm in arm, as we hadn't since she was thirteen. As soon as we reached the house, she showered and ran out to meet the friend who was already parked outside, honking his horn—her ride back to Davis.

During the next week came the final rush on term papers. Between classes, anxious students lined up in the hall outside my office, waiting to ask questions and get help they should have asked for weeks before. At night I stayed up reading the few early term papers that came in and preparing the final exam.

Whenever I was showering or dressing or cleaning up, I turned on KPFA. Angel's tape recorder had been busy. I heard the mayor, university spokesmen, and Governor Reagan issue stern warnings against trespassing. Their warnings alternated with defiant statements by Dan Lyon, or anonymous threats of violence that Angel read aloud from the *Berkeley Barb*. Then came moderate, mediating statements by clergy and, of course, by Fred Cody. "The hope that I nourish today is that society will take up this challenge and enter into a process that will transform our country by bringing to life the millions of the frustrated, the discarded, and the unused. It is that spirit that is going into People's Park. In digging there they somehow uncovered the conscience of a city." Fred ended that talk by announcing that there would be a "consecration" of the park at sunset—about 7:30. I went up to take a look.

I walked past the line of police and into the park, past half a dozen people setting up a wooden bulletin board. A hundred or so people were squatting on the newly rolled turf in concentric circles around Father Mike. Someone was strumming a guitar while the crowd hummed "Amazing Grace." I sat down at on the grass at the outer edge of the crowd—an older, more conventional group, university students, clergy, and odd residents like me. I couldn't hear much of what seemed to be a series of rituals from every tradition but the Judeo-Christian—from Hindu to Native American to Wicca. As the sky darkened, candles were passed among us, lighted—and re-lighted after cool gusts of wind repeatedly blew them out.

At a sign from Father Mike (his words inaudible) we stood and moved to follow him as he walked around the park sprinkling holy water. I noticed that on twiggy branches of some shrubs, people had hung tiny signs by slender threads. Some were photos, unnamed. Others were thin scraps of paper with a name scribbled —like "My Brother Johnny," or "Rosemary, My Love." I stopped for a moment when I saw a little sign, intricately painted red, white, and green, that read, "Casa Della Rina."

After one round, I was cold, and my candle had gone out again, so I left. I walked around the corner of Haste to Steadman's Used Books.

Jake was sitting alone behind his counter.

"Park looks pretty good," I said. Silence. Jake glared at me. "You don't think so." Here we go again, I thought.

Jake lit his cigar and scowled at it as he puffed up great clouds of foul smoke. "I think this whole 'People's Park' crap is the most phony, the most cynical thing I've seen in this town, and I've seen a lot of phonies and cynics here."

"Cynical?" I had expected him to say "futile" or "confused" but—

"That's right, cynical. Sentimental. Two sides of the same coin. An enormous effort not to see what's really going on. Did you know Fraser's is moving out? So am I. If I can find a sucker stupid enough to buy into this quicksand."

Cynical. Sentimental. Quicksand. What did it matter to me if an upscale furniture store moved? As for Jake, I didn't believe for a minute that he would ever leave Telegraph Avenue.

"I have papers to read," I told him, and I went home.

The next day was May 15. My telephone rang at four a.m. I grabbed the phone, with the usual mother's fear that Carol was suddenly ill or hurt. "Harry there?" I thought I recognized Dan Lyon's voice. Relieved and annoyed, I went out to the shed to get Harry. He staggered into the house, sleepily zipping up a pair of jeans. I handed the phone to him and stood there thinking, this had better be urgent.

Harry listened for a few moments, then said, "Okay, right, okay." He hung up and turned to me. "They're putting up a fence." I must have looked blank. "Around the park."

"Who is?"

"Some construction crew. With a hundred police around them."

"At four in the morning?"

"Okay if I call a few more people?"

I stumbled upstairs to bed and lay there listening to Harry make half a dozen calls. "Spread the word. Rally at Sproul Plaza. Yeah, right now." I heard Harry closing the back door, then, a few minutes later, hurrying along the gravel path to the street. I wondered if I should have offered to drive him. Then I dozed until sirens woke me. More sirens than usual on the streets? But there is a fire-house nearby—I couldn't be sure. I must have dozed again

151

until about six, then got up and prepared to go to work. I turned the radio on; nothing but the usual junk. I turned to KPFA, but that was before the station went on a twenty-four-hour schedule; they hadn't started their broadcast day yet.

I went to Merritt and taught my first class as usual. No one—faculty or students—knew anything about a fence or a rally. Impending finals were all they could think about. The morning was frantic with students begging for help or postponements.

It was not until after my noon class ended that word started reaching Merritt College. Something was happening in Berkeley—again. When I got back to my office, my office mate was listening to KPFA. I recognized Angel's voice, interrupted by gasping shouts, popping noises. "The police are shooting!" Then a sudden cut-off, followed by an announcer: "This was a recording made early this morning. We will air later developments as they come in. KPFA reporters remain on the scene." My office mate hunted for a commercial station that might give more news. At the end of another playing of Ed Hawkins "Oh, Happy Day," a disc jockey drawled in a bored voice, "Berkeley has exploded in violence again," then played "Raindrops Keep Falling on my Head." (Whenever I hear a scrap from either of those songs, I have a flash-back to standing in my office as my office mate spun the dial in a futile search for news.)

After my last class, I drove north on Grove Street. My car was passed by one, two, six military jeeps and an open truck full of grim, confused, very young boys in camouflage uniforms. They continued north as I turned off at Milton Street. The telephone was ringing as I came into the house.

"You're all right!" Those were the days before we

all had answering machines, so Carol could not have left a message asking me to call. All the lines at Merritt had been busy, and she had called here every half hour. "What is going on? On the radio it sounds like Berkeley is at war or something."

"I don't know any more than you do. At home here, it's quiet. Normal. I'll walk up to Telegraph and see—"

"Oh, don't, Mom, please! People have been shot. Don't go up there."

"Okay, okay." I promised that I would stay home until I knew more.

"And call me before you go anywhere. Call me anyway and let me know what's happening."

I made some phone calls: no answer at Steadman's Books or Cody's Books; busy signals on their home phones and on Marsha's. I went next door to ask if Mrs. Temple's nephew had told her anything. "He's been called in to work like all the others." She shook her head. "Black men finally get on the police force—for this?"

I turned on KPFA, left it on, and eventually got some facts. At four a.m. construction workers had started putting up a chain link fence around "the lot known as People's Park." Word had spread quickly, bringing a hundred or more people to the campus. As the sun rose they exited the campus on Bancroft and marched down Telegraph Avenue, joined by dozens, or scores, or hundreds (accounts of different witnesses varied) coming from side streets. The one hundred Berkeley policemen on the scene were soon outnumbered. Reinforcements came from the Alameda County Sheriff Deputies—men with shotguns. "At this time" (it was about four P.M.) "the rioting continues." At latest count, nearly sixty people had been wounded by buckshot, one of them blinded, and one man, standing on the roof of The Med, had been shot dead. "It is said that he had thrown Molotov cocktails at police." The windows of every police car on or near Telegraph had been smashed. The mayor had declared a state of emergency. Governor Reagan had called out the National Guard and declared a citywide curfew. Anyone on the street after sundown would be arrested. Then came Angel's voice: James Rector had been "only watching, not throwing anything from the roof of the Med." Angel was in tears. "I've never been so scared in all my life."

On Milton Street, only a mile away, everything was calm and quiet, except for the occasional passing siren. At midnight, I telephoned Carol, reported what I knew, then went to bed.

It was nearly two A.M. when Harry came crunching over the gravel under my bedroom window. I wasn't asleep—I suppose I'd been listening for him. I got up, put on a robe, and went out to the shed to hear Harry's version of what had happened. "By the time the sun was coming up, there were a couple of hundred of us at Sproul Plaza. I didn't know any of them. Daniel wasn't there. I didn't see him until—later. There were some speeches, I don't know, some student body officers, I didn't listen much. Then we started down Telegraph, just a march, a peaceful protest. But I saw some guys picking up rocks."

"Rocks on Telegraph? What rocks?"

"Little piles of them, chunks of concrete." Harry's eyes evaded mine for a moment, before he said, "I saw Dan, emptying a sack of them. Then someone yelled, 'Let's take the Park,' and everyone ran forward, started chanting, 'Take the Park, take the Park."

"What did they mean, 'take the Park.' "

Harry sighed. "I don't know. There was a lot of yelling. It was all confused. I was near the back of the

154

crowd. I couldn't hear what was going on up front. Until I heard the gunshots. I couldn't believe it. I tried to get off Telegraph, but this sheriff's car came by with an open window, a pepper-spray gun stuck out of it. All at once I was gagging, falling down. I couldn't see. My eyes burned like—I could hear people running back and forth. I thought I would be trampled to death. Then I heard a helicopter. It dropped a cloud of tear gas right over me. I was afraid to get up and breathe the gas, and afraid to stay down and get run over. I crawled to the gutter and just stayed there until I could see a little better.

"When I looked up, I didn't see anyone. I could still hear them, but the action was all up ahead, up Haste Street at the park. I thought, pretty soon the police will turn them back this way. A stampede. I was—so scared. I got up, tried to go down Haste, away from the park, but down there— more police cars, sheriff cars, waiting to pick up anyone who came west. So I couldn't come home. Maybe go uphill, east? That's where some older people were going, people who had been on their way to work, old women crying. I helped one of them. She kept saying, 'I just come to clean lady's house.' She took my arm, and we helped each other up Channing, past College, up toward Piedmont, the campus on our left, the Park on our right—like walking a tightrope between where the cops were gassing and shooting on either side. Maybe they didn't see me. Or maybe—and I thought of this, I hoped—they would leave me alone because I was helping this poor old Mexican woman who didn't know English, didn't know what was going on. I was so scared, I didn't care how I got away from there.

"I went up a couple more blocks with the old lady, left her at the house she was going to clean. Then I saw the bus that goes up to Grizzly Peak and took it up to Marsha's house. She let me stay there waiting for things to quiet down. I'm supposed to call her, no matter what time, let her know when I got back here."

"Better call her right away. She'll worry." I handed Harry the phone, and he made a brief call to Marsha, thanked her twice, hung up, then went back to telling me his story.

"Every hour or two I'd try to leave, but whenever I started down the hill, I saw more cops—cars, motorcycles, on foot. Sheriffs, National Guard, jerking their rifles around so it's a wonder they didn't all shoot each other. Then I'd go back inside and listen to the radio reports—curfew. In other words, I'd get shot or busted whether I left in daylight or at night. I still thought I'd have a better chance in the dark, so I waited. Then I worked my way downhill. Hiding in doorways, behind bushes, whenever I saw anyone. Guys are still out there, running in packs, throwing rocks. Cops hunting them. Whenever I heard anything, I hid, then went the other way." Harry sighed and turned away in shame. "Gutless."

"You think you should have joined them? Don't be stupid!"

"But I—"

"Harry, let's get some sleep. I don't want to argue with you."

I slept off and on until it was light, then turned on the radio. A commercial news announcer was saying that the violence had stopped about an hour before dawn. Berkeley was under martial law with after-dark curfew until further notice. The newscaster quoted a statement by an unnamed

Berkeley police officer. "We never took out our guns. The sheriff's deputies' shotguns saved our lives." (Later, Mrs. Temple told me her nephew said, "All the shooting was done by those cowboys. Those guys aren't trained, aren't even police, just moonlighting red-necks. If I hadn't been in uniform, they probably would have shot me first!")

That afternoon, I walked to Telegraph Avenue, turned up Dwight, and walked past the chain-link fence, past the frightened, angry young guardsmen who peered out through the fence, white-knuckled fists gripping their automatic rifles, fingers on the trigger. One of them looked me in the eye coldly. I crossed the street. I suppose my merely being in the area was, for him, proof of evil intention. I turned back down to Telegraph.

The smell of tear gas was still thick enough to burn my eyes. All the shops were closed, the Avenue itself closed to traffic. Garbage men with shovels and brooms were shoveling up rocks, sticks, chunks of concrete, tossing them up into the bed of a city maintenance truck. Police and national guardsmen swarmed all over the burned, blackened pavement, scowling suspiciously at everyone, though not stopping pedestrians from entering the street. A few more tense, accusing glares were enough for me. I turned off Telegraph at Parker to go back home. I stopped only for one amazed moment—to stare at a tank parked in the intersection of Parker and Ellsworth.

By the following day, Harry was more upbeat. "Dan's already out on bail. The Berkeley jail couldn't hold everyone. They had to let them go."

"He was arrested?"

Harry laughed. "He says the police are really in trouble now because they killed a man." Harry was pulling on a cap. "Dan says, it helps protect you a little if they use clubs."

"Where are you going?"

"Some people are taking over that strip up on Hearst—over the new subway tunnel?—start making another park."

"Harry, do you really think—" I stopped and sternly told myself, *None of your business, none of your business.*

A few days later a noon protest rally on campus brought out hordes of uniforms—police? National Guard? county sheriffs?—who surrounded the campus and inexplicably sealed in everyone while National Guard helicopters dropped tear gas over them. That afternoon, I was scheduled to read on KPFA from Turgenev's *Fathers and Sons,* the scene in which the fiery young Bazarov dismisses the liberalism of middle-aged Nikolai. When I climbed the long, steep steps up to the old studios on Shattuck, I found the halls full of women—faculty wives who had been caught on the campus while tear gas rained down on them. I don't think any of them had ever seen the grungy interior of the KPFA studios before, except Marsha, who must have brought the others.

"Ruth!" Marsha looked up at me, her wide blue eyes fierce with outrage. "We want to get on the air and tell what happened. The manager said we could if—"

"They want to pre-empt my reading? Sure." I was getting used to it.

"But there's no one here to interview us. Everybody

in the News Department is out on the streets."

That was how I happened to interview a half dozen furious faculty wives (all we could jam into the tiny sound studio) who'd been on their way to meet their husbands for lunch. One described struggling to push her baby's stroller beyond the gas. Another, who suffered from asthma, accused a uniformed man (she wasn't sure if he was campus police or Berkeley police or sheriff's deputy, or what) who'd stopped her from leaving to get her medication. Marsha was the last. She read "The Terror," a poem that she'd written on the spot. (I've always thought it was her best poem, written while her fear and anger were too raw to be brought under her usual control.) She concluded by saying, "My husband, Professor Ivan Franklin, has pointed out that 'Berkeley is the first city in the United States to be bombed from the air.' " (At our next lunch date she confirmed that they were back together. "How could I live if I left him? I'm pushing fifty, and the only career I ever had was pushing his!")

When I reached home that day, I heard from Mrs. Temple that her nephew was, if anything, even more furious than the faculty wives. "Like we needed THIS to make our job harder!" he had told her. He was on duty until further notice. Mrs. Temple was torn. She really did not approve of all this "agitating," and glared at Harry when she saw him, "Why you want to get mixed up with those trouble-makers." But what she heard from her nephew made her wonder if "that movie actor just wants to blow up Berkeley on TV so he can run for president." (At the time, I thought this was rather a far-fetched idea.)

That night I went to a meeting at the Codys' home. Nearly thirty people crowded into their little front room, people who were well over age thirty, except for three young clergy and a couple of UC students. After hours of talk, another meeting was scheduled, at which there was more talk, then another time was set for another meeting. That was the night before grades were due, and Professor Person and I had been given a deadline by our publisher. I called Pat and told her to call me if they had some specific job for me.

When Fred wasn't holding a meeting in their house, he was seeing the mayor, the chief of police, or any City Council member or university official who would talk to him, trying to convince them that the chain-link fence was a provocation. He spoke again on KPFA, repeating his hope that all this chaos would uncover "the conscience of the city." The governor made more speeches against "those who coddle lawless rioters," and Daniel Lyon announced a Memorial Day Demonstration to defy the university, the government, and any cowards who would try to placate them.

Harry brought home a stack of flyers Dan had given him. The flyers called for "people everywhere" to converge on Berkeley on Memorial Day.

"They're asking for trouble."

Harry nodded. "Dan says there'll be a blood bath."

"Is that what he wants? Is that what you want?"

Harry quieted down a little. "Dan just means if the police hurt any more people, it'll turn the majority in our favor."

"I think you've already got the majority. Yesterday, I interviewed some faculty wives on KPFA. Very conservative people, never set foot in the studio before, probably never listened to the station before this past year, let alone subscribed to it. You don't want to lose them."

But Harry was already out the door.

Within a couple of days, one of the meetings I didn't attend had formed what Fred Cody was calling the Peace Brigade, a nucleus of clergy, teachers, and students. They had been forced to focus on one simple goal—avoiding the "blood bath" on Memorial Day. Someone from the Brigade called me, and I accepted an assignment. Along with Lisa Lyon, I would spend a few hours a day at a designated freeway exit. We would display a banner welcoming incoming demonstrators, and would pass out information: where to get food, where to find lodging, and, most of all, when and where to attend classes in non-violent protest. The idea was to channel the energy of the expected kids, to get them into safe quarters, to give them some indoctrination in non-violence, and to give them a banner to carry instead of a club or a rock.

I volunteered to do the driving, an offer that came out of pure self-interest. Lisa was very near-sighted, too vain to wear her glasses, and too broke to get the brakes fixed on her old car, which she, therefore, drove very, very slowly, squinting at cross streets. Too often, I had watched her weaving at fifteen miles per hour through traffic before parking—that is, coming to rest five feet from the curb, like a wounded bird gliding to a stop.

I drove us down University Avenue toward the Bay and parked at the first legal space I could find near the University off-ramp. We agreed that I would stay in the car, holding out our sign: Welcome To Berkeley—Get Info Here. When a car full of kids came down the ramp and stopped, Lisa would get out of the car to talk to them and give them leaflets. She looked younger than I and dressed more as they did. She would try to persuade them to accept space in a supervised shelter and training in non-violence.

Lisa and I spent a few late afternoons in my car,

waiting and talking. She told me she had broken up with
Jake because he was "just too negative, too cynical. I
worked so hard in the store—and at home! You should have
seen that house. That's the way I always end up with a
man, working like a slave!" Lisa's teenage daughter Cheila
("Daniel named her after a twelfth-century Persian rebel")
had moved in too. At first, Lisa said, Jake had accepted
Cheila, but then had quarreled with her and with Lisa too.
"The son was the problem. Aaron stayed a couple of nights
every week, and didn't like us—just jealous, I guess. Aaron
and Cheila had a fight, a shouting match, you know, 'you
stupid queer,' and 'you stupid cunt' and we were out of
there." Lisa had insisted Jake pay her wages for the hours
she'd worked in the store, and the money had helped her
while she evicted her subletting tenant and got back into
her little house.

My hours in the car with Lisa became lessons in
how to live on almost nothing in Berkeley in 1969. Lisa had
an MA in English, but had "no intention of drudging over
illiterate papers instead of writing my poetry." Whenever
possible, she sublet her low-rent cottage and house-sat
for UC faculty on sabbatical or vacation, making a little
cash on both transactions. Her clothes came from thrift
shops or—very selectively—from those donated to Father
Mike's Kitchen. Clothes that would have been unaccept-
able at any regular job were high fashion in Berkeley, if you
knew how to assemble and wear them, and Lisa did. She
regularly dropped into Father Mike's Kitchen at the end
of the evening and took home leftovers from the meals he
served there. She received an SSI check every month for an
unspecified emotional disability. "An old boyfriend of mine
is a shrink—he signed the papers." I knew that, in addition,
she had a nest-egg deposited under a mutual friend's name,

but I didn't expect her to divulge that. (People in Berkeley gave graphic descriptions of their sexual adventures, but, I noticed, never revealed their monetary worth.) Occasionally Lisa took a temporary job for payment—in cash, of course, so as not to pay taxes or lose her SSI payments.

With virtually no visible income, Lisa qualified for free medical care and food stamps, and other poverty benefits I'd never heard of (nor, I suspect, had many of my truly poor students). She read books from the library and ushered at theater, concerts, opera, ballet—attending more events than I could find time for.

Most of Lisa's time was free for writing poetry. "Or an article for one of the underground papers now and then. They don't pay much, but it's fun."

"I didn't think they paid anything," I said.

"Depends," she said, but did not elaborate. "Say what you're thinking!" Lisa suddenly burst out. "Welfare cheat!"

"Not at all." I was stunned by her vehemence, her anger. "If our taxes can support a stupid war costing millions, we ought to be able to throw a few crumbs to poets." She looked dubious. "Lisa, I admire you—your courage. I could never—"

"Sure you could! Just quit that job."

"And do what?" I shook my head. "I'm not creative. You know what Shaw said, 'those who can, do, and those who can't—teach.' "

Then we spotted another car jammed full of kids, coming down the ramp. I raised the sign out the car window, and Lisa got out to greet them.

Demonstrations continued, day after day, but not

at People's Park, where young guardsmen stood clutching rifles in their ominously trembling hands. Dan Lyon had announced a new tactic, the "mill-in," inspired, he said, by Che Guevera. (Every dormitory room and student apartment of those days displayed the famous poster of Guevera.) A mill-in was a traveling demonstration that started with the sudden appearance of a few dozen people and could grow to a crowd of hundreds, stopping traffic and business, yet evaporating by the time police arrived, then flaring up like a brush fire somewhere else. It took a couple of weeks for the police to catch on and develop their own tactics of rapid movement and convergence on trouble spots.

I hadn't seen Harry for several days, but that wasn't unusual, since he often came to the shed very late and left very early. A few days before the Memorial Day holiday, I came home from work and found a note on my door: "Call me, Alice." I telephoned; no answer. I sat down to read final exam papers, calling her every hour. Still no answer. At about nine o'clock the phone rang.

"It's Alice. Did Harry get home?"

"No, I haven't seen him since yesterday."

"I think he's been arrested. The police haven't released names yet, but I'm pretty sure he was with two others in my workshop arrested downtown on Shattuck."

"When? What happened?"

"Late this afternoon there was one of those mill-ins. The police were waiting for them. They had Alameda County Sheriff's buses parked on the side streets near Shattuck. They blocked off the area, closed them in, beat them, dragged them onto the buses, and drove them out to Santa Rita. One of my students saw Harry looking out of the window as a bus drove past—or thought it was Harry. Jake is frantic—he can't locate Aaron, thinks he was taken too. I've been calling Santa Rita, but they're not giving out names." (Dan Lyon had not been arrested, had not been seen all day. Jake later insisted that he had been the informant—pursuing his longing for a "blood bath.")

"Can we drive out there and bail Harry out?"

"Fifty miles? This time of night? Legally the sheriffs have twenty-four hours before they're even required to notify anyone. Last time I called Santa Rita, they said lawyers can visit tomorrow, no one else until after arraignment. We can only wait and see. My lawyer thinks they'll all be let out tomorrow—how on earth could they keep all of them? As soon as my lawyer lets me know, I'll post bail. I'll call you when I know anything."

The next morning's headlines announced that over five hundred protesters had been bussed to the prison in Santa Rita. The photograph under the headline showed a long-haired white boy heaving a rock at a line of advancing officers—the kind of photo that, in those days, appeared so often that it might have been the same one used again and again. Between classes that day, I made phone calls: to Santa Rita, to Jake, to Alice—who finally had some news. Yes, her lawyer had confirmed that Harry was one of those arrested. They were being booked and interrogated, a long process because there were so many of them. Alice's lawyer assured her that she'd be able to bail out her students by tomorrow.

"I'm riding out there with Jake. We'll get his son and Harry and the other two. Want to come?"

"I have a final to give."

"No problem. We'll bring Harry back."

165

As I reached for the phone again, it rang. It was Carol, calling from Davis. "Hi, Mom, how are things in occupied territory?"

"The tanks are gone. Most of the National Guard too, just a line of them around People's Park. Harry's been arrested. Jake's son too. They should be out on bail by tomorrow. How are finals going?"

"All over but one, and that's a take-home. A few of us are planning to come down for the Memorial Day weekend." My heart sank. Yes, out by the freeway off-ramp, it had occurred to me that Carol could have been in one of the incoming cars. "Mom?"

"This might not be a good weekend to—"

"You couldn't keep me away. Or my dorm mates."

"Dorm mates."

"Just six or eight of us, maybe nine. We're coming down tomorrow night. On Friday, we'll join the demonstration, then we'll all go our separate ways, home for the summer." Not just Carol, but half a dozen friends? "Mom?"

"I don't know if—"

"When they found out my mother lives in Berkeley— well, I couldn't lie and say I wasn't coming down, and—well, do you think—is Harry still in the shed or could we stay there? Maybe in the yard? Everyone has a sleeping bag."

I took a deep breath. No point in wasting any of it telling them not to come. "They can lay their sleeping bags out on the living room floor. If I'm out when you come, you can help yourself to whatever's in the refrigerator. But no more than eight, you hear?"

"Oh, Mom. Great!"

"Wait a minute. There are conditions," which I listed as fast as I could think of them. "I don't want anything illegal in this house, no drugs, not even pot."

166

"Oh sure, no problem."

"And on Friday, if it looks like there's going to be trouble, you keep out of it, you get off the street and come back here. I don't want any parents calling me and asking me why I let their kids get arrested or hurt."

"Okay, sure."

"I want all of them to call and tell their parents. Now. Give them my phone number. The parents can call here if they want to reach them, but tell them I take absolutely no responsibility."

"Absolutely. I'll tell them to start calling home right now."

"And only those eight to stay here. There are a lot of strangers in town, and I don't want you or your friends bringing any of them back here."

"Promise. See you tomorrow." She hung up quickly before I could change my mind, which I wanted to do instantly. But what good would that do? I couldn't stop them from coming. I could only give them a safe place to sleep and eat. I sat down to read a couple of late term papers and to post numbers in the grade book. And I waited for the phone to ring. It didn't. Evidently the parents of Carol's friends had decided, as I had, that there was no point in trying to stop them.

At about four, I gathered up a box of books and papers and drove up the hill to Bernard Person's home. His wife would give us dinner while we sifted through the pared-down—but still too long—list of essays we were considering for inclusion in our anthology. We shuffled choices for hours, ate, shuffled, argued, drank, shifted a choice to another pile—until eleven, when we were both too exhausted to do any more.

When I got home, I found the refrigerator bare, the

sink covered with dirty glasses and dishes, and nine bodies in sleeping bags on the floor. I stepped over them carefully and went up to bed.

I lay there wishing I could just drive to Merritt in the morning, turn in my grades, then hop on the freeway and keep on going—up the coast, checking into a motel for the weekend, taking long walks, reading a book.

But, of course, I couldn't sit this one out. I would have to be somewhere in this march. During the past five years I had joined enough marches to learn the first law of demonstrations: the bigger and more varied the crowd, the more chance the demonstration would be peaceful and orderly and safe. It was always the protest of a few that turned ugly and violent, provoking police violence, escalating into a mess like Chicago in August. The best way for me to protect my daughter was to increase, even by one, the numbers of older, cooler heads on the street.

When I woke up Friday morning, it was after nine, and I was alone in the house. Carol had left a note saying they were off early to the starting point of the march, where rock bands would gather and play until the march began. Right after the march, they were all driving home for the summer. "I'll call you from Santa Barbara—Josie's parents invited me for the weekend." Probably they had decided this was the best way to get their daughter out of Berkeley as quickly as possible.

I telephoned Jake at the store—no answer. I reached him at home. He and Alice had put up bail for Harry and Aaron, dropped Harry off at my place, and taken Aaron to his mother. Jake started raving about suing the city, the

168

county, the university, for the treatment Aaron had suffered. He started to give me details on the telephone, then choked up and started swearing, the way some men do when they want to stop themselves from crying. He hung up.

I sat down to finish reading the *Chronicle*. On one of the inner pages I found a photo of Eldridge Cleaver, and a brief mention of his having surfaced in Cuba. I cut it out and walked out through the garden to the shed to give it to Harry. I knocked several times, but he didn't answer. He must have left early to cover the march with Angel. I tacked the clipping to the door and went back to the house.

I turned on the radio and started washing the dishes. Fred Cody was on KPFA again, his voice so hoarse he could hardly speak. He had brought in a Quaker organizer who took over the mike and called for a demonstration of "ten thousand flowers." Marchers should bring flowers from their gardens. The Quakers would distribute thousands of daisies. Everyone should carry at least one flower. Non-violent protest classes had been held throughout the night and would continue right up until the march to People's Park officially began—at eleven A. M. Someone else took over the mike and named the various starting points, linking up at Dwight Way, proceeding east to People's Park.

I left the house about noon, in bright, blinding sun, one of those blazing hot days we have in May just before the summer fog drifts in. I remembered to pluck a couple of geraniums from the front garden.

Walking north on Sacramento Street, I could see the slowly moving mass of people up ahead, moving east. At Dwight, I edged into the crowd filling the street, curb to curb, overflowing on both sidewalks, stretching east to west as far as I could see. People ambled along, waving flowers, pushing baby carriages, sharing water bottles, singing old civil rights songs that died off breathlessly in the sweaty heat. All along the sidewalks were young arm-banded monitors (the Quakers had done their job well) and a few Berkeley police, increasing in number after we crossed Shattuck Avenue. Not a sign of Oakland police or Highway Patrol, or Alameda County deputies. (Later Mrs. Temple said the Berkeley police chief had firmly told the mayor to "keep those cowboys out of sight unless we lose control of the situation.") The police were smiling, and when a monitor handed one of them a flower, he stuck it on his helmet. Every other person seemed to have a leaflet to distribute or a can for donations to a good cause.

One man was handing out free copies of an under-ground paper, its entire eight pages devoted to excerpts from the trial of the Chicago Seven, with the now-famous photo of Bobbie Seale chained and gagged in the courtroom. A girl handed me five mimeographed, stapled pages titled "King Alfred, Secret Government Plot To Put Dissenters in Concentration Camps."

"I already have this," I said, handing it back. "You know," I said to her, "this is the last chapter of a novel by John A. Williams. Fiction."

She stopped for just a moment, glared at me as if I were part of the plot, then walked away, continuing to pass it out.

As we neared Telegraph Avenue, thin, silvery streams arched over us. People were standing in front of their houses, holding garden hoses, sending sprays of cooling water, as we all turned our open mouths toward them. Some marchers began dancing around the sprays,

170

pulling off their shirts and whirling, in bare-breasted inno-
cence, boys and girls, in rhythm with the louder and louder
rock music playing up ahead.

There were some tense moments as we crossed
Telegraph Avenue and came alongside the park. The crowds
slowed, thickened, then stopped, people pressed together,
filling the three streets bordering the park. A line of monitors stood in front of the line of policemen facing out from
the chain link fence. Behind the fence stood a third line—
rigid, jaw-clenched young guardsmen holding automatic
weapons. I stood still, turning my head left and right. There
was no way I could move the rest of my body in any direction.

A chant started somewhere in the crowd. "Kill the
pigs. Kill the pigs!" A few voices joined. The chant grew
louder. "Kill the Pigs!" I turned my head, but couldn't see
who was chanting. Time to leave. Impossible to move. I
heard a whimper near me and felt a ripple of panic moving
toward me through the tightly-pressed bodies.

Then a girl's voice, a thin, reedy tone, cut through
the chanting. "Oh, beautiful for spacious skies, for amber
waves of grain. For—" A few monitors joined in, loudly,
waving their arms at us like ungainly, amateur orchestra
conductors. I got a glimpse of Angel, holding up his tape
recorder to catch the singing as others joined in. I tried to
see if Harry was with him, but there were too many heads
blocking my sight.

We sang, everybody sang in desperately loud, off-
key determination to drown out the chanters. Someone
threw a flower at the fence, and soon it was being pelted
with hundreds of daisies. My geraniums went too. Someone
laughed. The police started smiling again, broke their line,
and let people walk up to the fence to stick their flowers

through the wire links. A little girl beckoned one of the young guardsmen to come closer to the fence, waving a flower at him. He refused to move, but the third one she beckoned stepped forward and pushed his rifle up to the links. The girl pushed a long-stemmed daisy through the links and neatly into the barrel of his rifle. The young man stepped back from the fence again, allowed himself a slight smile, and stood at attention, rifle pointed upward, the flower sprouting from the barrel. (A photo taken of him appeared in newspapers the next day and is reprinted in most books about the sixties.)

Suddenly we were in one of those moments that cannot really be conveyed to people who believe the sixties were all about drugs and sex and self-indulgence. It is not true that "if you can remember the sixties, you weren't there." Many of us were sober, and can clearly remember moments like this one—a crowd united briefly by simple decency, a sense of wholeness like that described by religious mystics. The march on May 30, 1969 was not the last one I joined, but that moment, breaking weeks of fearful tension, was the last time a demonstration gave me that sense of sacred unity.

A cheer rose. More singing. The crowd loosened with the tension, thinning out slowly. Dripping sweat—my own and others'—I managed to work my way forward, uphill, past the park, past the makeshift platform where speeches were being shouted over bullhorns. People were dancing again, around the platform, rock bands clashing with one another in dissonant blasts, drowning out the speeches. Many of us—especially parents pushing strollers, or those faithful white-haired activist ladies—were edging away from both the music and the speeches. Everyone was smiling, all except a small group I passed. I recognized Dan

Lyon's voice, hidden in the center of it. "We fucking lost it. Fucking Quakers took over."

The rest of us tried to cling to our good feeling, already ebbing away. We exchanged congratulatory hugs with dancers, singers, children, and various other strangers. Why? We had not stopped the war in Vietnam, nor advanced civil rights, nor relieved poverty. We had not even won the right to use the university property as a park, nor was I sure we should assume that right. (Typical liberal ambivalence, or, as Dan Lyon would say, "Can't shit or get off the pot.") I wasn't even sure why the right to make a park had taken on such importance—because we had lost so many other good causes that we needed to create a smaller enemy (the university?)—and win one? What had we won? On that day, all we had managed to do was to avoid more violence. All right, I thought, resisting feeling down. That was something.

I smiled and hugged a man who was passing. He hugged me back, then looked startled. "Ruth?"

"Tom?" We had met in San Francisco just after my divorce and dated a few times before he went back for one last try at his sinking marriage, and I moved across the bay.

We turned on College Avenue to get out of the crowd, and walked south. At the first Chinese restaurant we passed, I said, "I'm starved," and we turned into the place.

We ate and talked, filling in the past five years, then walked across the street and into the Elmwood movie house, not even looking at the marquee. It was showing *2001:A Space Odyssey*. A heavy cloud of smoke hung over the kids who'd come in, like us, to get off their sore feet. We probably inhaled enough second hand pot to get a little high, sitting there dozing like weary children.

After we left the movie house, we walked to Tom's

car. On the street, army jeeps rumbled past, full of young guardsmen looking lost and grumpy.

"Let me take you away from all this," Tom laughed. So I spent the rest of the weekend in San Francisco, starting a rerun of the affair that again (unsurprisingly) fizzled out after a few months. Tom was not the first or the last of the men I met during those years, men who seemed, for a little while, possible, even likely. But that part of my life has nothing to do with Harry's story. I mention it only to explain why I never thought of Harry during the weekend the army rolled out of Berkeley and the curfew lifted.

On Monday evening, as I was reading the last late paper and averaging grades, Jake called.

"Harry didn't come in to work today. Is he okay?"

"Isn't he with Angel?"

"Angel says he hasn't seen him either—since before he was arrested."

"Let me try Alice."

I hung up and dialed. Alice hadn't seen him. "And today was the last meeting of my workshop. We had a party."

"Maybe Harry didn't know."

"I told him when Jake and I bailed him out. Did he say anything after we dropped him off?"

"I didn't talk to him, haven't seen him at all."

"He was quite traumatized by whatever they did to him at Santa Rita. Looked as if he hadn't slept for two days, filthy, smelled of vomit and, well, every bodily waste. Wouldn't talk at all. It was late when we dropped him off, after midnight. I suppose he didn't want to wake you. I've been hearing stories from the others who were arrested. I'm talking to some lawyers about bringing suit. Jake is too. Meanwhile, you keep watching for Harry. Ask him to call me."

I made a few more phone calls. Father Mike hadn't seen him. I got Dan Lyon's phone number from Lisa. After asking me a series of suspicious questions, he finally admitted he hadn't seen Harry either. I called a Merritt colleague whose class Harry was in. He hadn't shown up for the final.

I went to the shed. The clipping about Eldridge Cleaver was still tacked to the door. The hasp lock was not on, but Harry often left the door unlocked. I pushed it open, went inside. Books, school papers, clothes—all were piled in the usual disorder on and around the little table and chair. Harry's key, along with the hasp lock, lay on the table. A few things were missing. His sleeping bag. The Navy P-coat he wore on foggy days. The old portable typewriter. No duffel bag, no underwear, no Levi's, except for a filthy, disgusting pair (along with an equally smelly T-shirt) he had thrown on the floor.

Also on the floor near the door—as if thrown there or perhaps dropped accidentally as he was leaving—lay a blue envelope postmarked Butte, Montana. I remembered having pinned it to the door of the shed a month or two before, wondering if it was from his mother. I opened the envelope. Yes, that's what it was.

April 15, 1969

Dear Harry,

   I'm sorry it took me a while to answer your letter. Not that I wasn't thrilled to get it after all this

175

time. I'm not lying when I tell you that every night I went to bed wondering where you were and how you were. And then to find out you are just where I would hope. In California. In college. I have to admit I cried a little, for happiness.

Then I tried to write back an answer. But I would write and then tear up, write and then tear up. There were so many things you wrote about that happened and didn't happen between us, so many misunderstandings, so many regrets I had even before you wrote your letter full of love and forgiveness. Your letter lets me talk honestly. So that's what I'm trying to do in this letter.

First of all, there's one misunderstanding we have to clear up. Ettore—"Stiletto"—is not your father. I know there were rumors all over town about that because of all the things he gave me from the time I was a little girl. Rumors that he got me pregnant, then was paying off your father to marry me. That's not true. I never had anything to do with Stiletto that way until after your father was killed in the mine.

I'm not sorry you never knew your father. In high school he was handsome and funny and could have had any girl he wanted. But there was something wild about him even before he went into the service. He fought with all his family, and they wouldn't have anything to do with him—that's why you don't know any Lynches (of course, Nonnarina was just as happy not to know them, some trouble between her and his grandmother when they were young). And when he came home from the war, he was kind of crazy. He would have screaming nightmares when he was asleep, and screaming rages when he was awake. I

176

think he had seen some terrible things in the war. If he was kind of wild when he went into the service, by the time the war was over, he was unhinged. Violent, especially when you would cry a lot (you had colic the first few months), and he would shake your crib, and yell at you, then I would warn him to stop, and he would hit me. More than once I told him if he ever hurt you, I would kill him, and I think I would have. So things could have been worse if he'd lived.

I made up my mind then that I was not going to marry another miner and see him die slowly like my father or fast like your father. In fact, I didn't see anyone here I'd want to marry—the smart ones go away to college and never come back, or if they do, marry college girls. So I was going to be alone, but I was not going to struggle like my mother did and Nonnarina did.

Whatever you heard about Stiletto, most of it was fairy tales. He has always enjoyed the rumors about the Mafia and even being called "Stiletto," especially after The Godfather *became a best seller. I think it makes him feel important. But the truth is he never did anything but run errands for some gamblers—maybe some Mafia—when he was a kid in New York. Yes, he has a wife from Italy there, his age, and kids older than me, and then grandchildren, and there will never be a divorce because his wife is a devout Catholic. (And I don't want to marry him, anyway.) Early days in Butte, before Prohibition ended, he tells me, he made a good stake in boot-legging. That was when he got friendly with all the police, bought his first casino. The money from his casinos and saloons he sent back east, and his wife put it into real estate, put his kids through college, and so on. I'm not proud of our relationship, but he's good to me, and it suits both of us. You can't prove to me that it's worse than the marriage of my grandparents, Ghittara and Angelina, in Italy. Or worse than some pretty bad years between Nonnarina and Nonno Francesco—who was no angel just because he got killed in the mine fire. Just the same, I didn't blame you for feeling ashamed of me. I was glad you were close to Nonnarina so you'd have someone solid until you were old enough to understand. (By the way, she would be so proud of you, proud to say that one of us, her Enrico, finally made it to California.)*

Nonnarina was a wonderful, strong woman. But she was not perfect. I'm not talking about the fights we used to have about Stiletto, or about trying to get her to move down to the flats. That was all part of her strong will, and without her strong will, maybe I wouldn't have survived and neither would you.

No, the thing that makes me so sad, is not that she took my place as your mother, and got all your love, but that she pushed your grandmother aside and even became my mother. You never really got to know your Nonna Sara. I don't think I even really got to know her. I took my attitude from Nonnarina, who never, never forgot that Sara came from a bad family in the old country—bad in the old country and bad here. I think I knew that almost before I knew anything. Sara, my mother, was beaten up by her father, then ignored by Nonnarina, except when she thought of her as my father's mistake. But when I look back now I realize that your Nonno Joe and Nonna Sara really loved each other, that he was gentle to her (not like my Nonno Francesco, not like your father) and that she took care of my father, and worked to support us after he got sick, and put up with Nonnarina's disrespect of her, and with your father's craziness—she took care of Nonno Joe till the day he died. She deserved some love from us in return. But we never gave it. Between Nonnarina and I, she never could get near you, and she was terrified of your father. No wonder she left Butte and went to live with her brother in Idaho.

I started writing to her after Nonnarina died, sending her pictures of you. We patched things up a little bit. Now I'll be able to tell her you're in college. I think she's doing okay up there. She keeps the books for her nephew's garage, and her health is not too bad, considering she was a half-starved kid, never very strong, when your Nonno Joe married her. In her letters, she always asks when I'll come up to see her.

I've been thinking—this summer, when you're not in college, I might fly to Berkeley, then you and I could rent a car and drive up to Idaho for a week or two and you could meet your grandmother and your uncles and your cousins.

By August I should be able to travel. My health hasn't been too good, and I had to have surgery. (That's another reason it took me a while to answer.) But I had the best treatment available—yes, Ettore paid for it—and everything came out fine.

Of course, if you don't have time to take that little vacation with me, I'll understand. You have your own life, and it's going to be different from mine. I'm just so glad to know that. That's the best thing you could do for me, just to have a good life and not make the mistakes I did.

Your loving mother

I found nothing else in the shed, no clue as to where Harry might be or what had happened to him.

Should I call the police and report Harry missing? But if he had jumped bail, did I want to alert the police? I called Alice again.

"The preliminary hearing is day after tomorrow. Alameda County Courthouse in Oakland. He knows he has to be there or he's liable for arrest again." She didn't mention that if he didn't show up, she was out five hundred dollars bail. I told Alice I'd drive us to the hearing, and we'd both keep an eye out for Harry. Then I phoned Jake to see how his son was doing.

"Better. His mother's been letting him stay with me. I got him back to school yesterday."

"I'm going to pick Alice up to go to the hearing. Might as well pick up you and Aaron too, all go together."

"Good." Jake sounded tired, and grateful.

The county courthouse in Oakland is one of those massive white stone and marble-pillared monuments to justice built in the 1930s. The day of the hearing, it looked like a survivor amid bombed-out ruins. Just across the street was the recently cleared building site for the new Oakland Museum, and scattered all around loomed sooty old brick apartment buildings, naked in their dingy ugliness. On the steps in front of the court building, where a few

180

months before Black Panthers had waved Free Huey flags
during his trial, a few girls stood holding signs with slogans
like Liberate Victims Of Police Brutality. A steady stream
of quiet, neatly dressed people filed past them into the
building; however the defendants might have been dressed
during the "mill-in," they came to court—like Jake's son
Aaron—wearing suits, long hair cut off or pulled back into
neat pony tails. We followed the people to the biggest courtroom, and, although we were early, found no place to sit; half
of the seats were reserved for defendants, and (except for a
dozen in the front row occupied by men in Alameda County
Sheriff's uniforms) every seat for spectators already taken.
Aaron went to sit in the section reserved for defendants.
Someone recognized Alice and gave her his seat. Jake and I
were allowed to stand against the side wall. We managed to
get near the front, by the railing that separated the judge's
bench and attorney's tables from the public. From there we
could see the faces of the seated audience, and the people
coming in through the doors in the rear and on the sides.

While we waited for the judge, I slowly and system-
atically scanned every face among those seated or standing;
no Harry. Every time a door opened, I checked; no Harry. I
did see Marsha and Ivan Franklin come through one of the
doors, along with their friend on the Berkeley City Council,
but they stood on the other side of the hall, and Marsha told
me later that their interest was civic, not personal. Even
Ivan had been shocked and disgusted by the rumors of what
had happened to the arrested demonstrators at Santa Rita
Prison.

Clerks came and went, and finally one stepped up to
the microphone on the judge's bench and announced that
because of fire laws, no more spectators could be allowed
standing room. Only defendants would be admitted. Family

181

and friends could hear the proceedings piped out into the hall. She asked for volunteers to give up their seats to families of the defendants. No one moved. We waited while sound equipment was set up and the doors stopped opening and closing, letting defendants in. Still no Harry.

Finally the judge came in and sat down at the bench. "Remain seated," he growled into his microphone, looking grumpy. The clerk read off a number, and a man at a table near the judge stood. "The prosecutor," mumbled Jake. The man read a list of general charges: obstructing traffic, destruction of property, resisting arrest. Then he began reading from the list of defendants, each name, with itemized, separate charges.

The judge cut him off, waved a sheaf of papers at him. "That's all here, right?"

"Yes, your honor."

"And the defendants each have a copy of separate charges?"

"Yes, your honor."

"Then we can dispense with the reading and get on with it. Do you have anything else to say?"

"No, your honor."

The judge turned with a scowl to the next table, where several defense attorneys sat. "Who wants to go first?"

A tall, thin, white man stood. He had thinning gray hair and wore a dark brown three-piece suit, with an even darker bow tie. "Your honor, I have depositions from two hundred of the defendants. Instead of calling each of them as witnesses or reading all of these depositions aloud, I believe I can save the court time by summarizing the experiences of my client, experiences which are representative of those detailed in the depositions, and probably typical of all four hundred and eighty-two defendants. May I proceed?"

"Go ahead." The judge leaned back in his chair.

"My client stipulates that he stood in the inter-section of Shattuck Avenue and Center Street, waving a sign, obstructing traffic. And that he heard and ignored an order to disperse. He was then pushed and grabbed by a man in the uniform of the Berkeley Police Department, and hit on the head and shoulders with batons by two men, both wearing the uniform of the Alameda County Sheriff's Department. He was unable to get their badge numbers. He fell to the ground and was kicked repeatedly, while offer-ing no resistance. Half-conscious, he was pulled to his feet, thrown against the side of a car, and searched by officers who twisted his arm behind his back, continuing to kick him and shout at him. He was then pushed down Center Street. He fell and was dragged by his feet, then picked up and thrown into a bus marked Alameda County Sheriff's Department. Other arrestees on the bus helped him into a seat next to a man who was unconscious, his head and nose bleeding heavily onto a white medical coat he wore to signify that he was not joining in any action, but only standing by to give first aid if anyone were injured. I want to add that these especially severe injuries were typical of any man identifiable by a white coat as non-demonstrating medical support."

I turned to Jake and whispered, "Is that your lawyer?"

He shook his head and hissed at me, "Some labor lawyer. His son was busted too."

"No one was allowed, for any reason, to leave the bus, which sat on Center Street for more than two hours, until it was full. The bus was then driven to Santa Rita Prison in Pleasanton, a drive of approximately one hour and twenty minutes. After arriving at Santa Rita, arrestees were left to wait in the bus, doors and windows closed. The temperature in Pleasanton at one P.M. on that day was ninety-two degrees; in a closed bus it would have risen much higher. After one hour, my client and the other arrestees were ordered off the bus and onto an asphalt field, where they were made to lie face down. Like this."

Suddenly the lawyer threw himself down on the floor, prone, his next words muffled in the carpet. Then he rose to his knees, speaking slowly and clearly. "From that time until dark—from two P.M. until nine P.M.—for a full seven hours—my client and all other defendants in this case lay face down on asphalt, in the blazing sun." He threw himself face down again, as if to make sure we understood, then did a push-up and sat back on his heels. "By four P.M. the temperature—in the shade—had risen to 101 degrees. Sheriff's deputies walked among the men on the asphalt with batons, warning them not to move, not to speak, for any reason. If they moved a finger or made any sound, they were clubbed or kicked. Even when they did not move, they were clubbed or kicked. For seven hours."

Now the lawyer was back on his feet, his voice rising. "Some were singled out for special treatment. Face down, my client could not see, did not dare to turn his head and look, but he heard their screams. I have submitted depositions from those who suffered this special treatment. Alameda County Sheriff's Deputies stood them up. Tied them to the metal poles on the asphalt field. Tied them so that their heads were pressed against the poles. Then beat the poles with their batons, until the men stopped screaming and lost consciousness, when they were untied and allowed to fall to the ground. Not a mark on them, of course.

"Abruptly at nine P.M., the men on the ground were ordered to rise and run to nearby barracks. Run. Men who

184

had lain rigid for seven hours on hot asphalt? As the men staggered, crawled, limped, in the dark, they were beaten and kicked, yelled at, 'I told you to run, run!' all the way to the barracks, where they were ordered to use an open toilet—for the first time in ten hours—then to lie on a bare cot without moving until morning.

"As it often does in spring, the temperature dropped quickly after dark. Feeling cold after about an hour, my client got up and closed the window above his cot. Immediately a uniformed deputy entered, shouting, "Who closed that window?" When my client stated that he had closed it, he was dragged outside, where two uniformed officers gave him a prolonged beating—" now the lawyer was shouting, "—the results of which can be seen in these photographs." He picked up a stack of photos from the table. His hand shook as he set them on the judge's bench. The judge shuffled through the photos, expressionless, then put them down and silently nodded for the lawyer to go on.

"Throughout the night, the beatings continued. Every hour, a man was dragged outside, accused of some infraction the men inside could not quite hear. But they could hear the blows, the cries or groans of the man being beaten, then dragged in again and thrown on his cot. Needless to say, neither my client nor anyone else in those barracks slept that night."

At this point the prosecutor half-rose as if to make some objection, then changed his mind and sank back into his chair. I could see the sullen, set faces of the uniformed men in the first row. Gradually they began to look down into their laps and seemed almost to shrink under the stares of more and more spectators.

"In the morning my client was taken alone into an office for a pre-booking 'interview.' Each routine question

185

was followed by a threat—like, 'Don't move!' then the officer grabbing him by the hair, jerking back his head and screaming, 'I told you not to move!' After this twenty-minute 'interview' he was allowed to make his one telephone call, then sent back to the barracks, where he waited throughout the day, too sick and distraught to eat the only food—peanut butter sandwich—provided. Although I had arrived at Santa Rita even before he made the phone call, I waited until dark before I was allowed to post bail and obtain my client's release. I believe it was not until the following morning that the last of the 482 prisoners was released.

"In the ten days since his release, my client has been unable to sleep in a room without a light on. After dozing for a few minutes, he is awakened by nightmares. He is under treatment by a psychiatrist who states—" The lawyer picked up another sheet of paper and placed it on the judge's bench. "—that he displays many classic symptoms of torture victims." He turned, walked stiffly back to the defense table, and sat down.

There was a long, heavy silence before the judge cleared his throat and began to speak softly, casually, into his microphone, as if to cleanse the hall of drama. "I've already read the charges, including the detailed reports from the Sherriff's Department. And I've read a good sampling of the depositions filed by defendants. I don't think we need any oral testimony." He banged the gavel once. "All charges dismissed." Faces throughout the hall grinned and applause broke out. The judge smacked the gavel once and silenced the clapping. He turned, first to the prosecutor, then to the front row of uniformed officers. With a chilling calm, he said, "And I would strongly admonish the Alameda County Sheriff. The evidence points to a number of illegal acts by sheriff's deputies. I expect these matters will, as usual, be handled internally." Then, in a tone of cold anger more threatening than a furious shout, he said, "But if one hint of this kind of behavior reaches my court again, I'm going to demand that the prosecutor make formal charges, and believe me, I'll see that they go as high and as far as they can be pressed."

A cheer rose and swelled, and this time the judge didn't gavel it down. He stood and turned to leave. Then he stopped, turned toward the uniformed men in the front row, and roughly motioned them to follow him out through the side door, to save them from walking through the crowd. They quickly got to their feet and hurried after him, bunching up and stepping on each others' heels, as a few "boos" followed them.

Jake and Aaron went to talk to the still grim-faced defense lawyer, whose son—a long bruise visible across his left temple—was standing beside him. Both boys were pale but smiling as they shook hands. "You going to sue?" Jake asked, but the lawyer was trying to answer ten people at once, so I wasn't sure what he said to Jake.

We moved out with the crowd that was now cheerful, joking, celebrating as they lingered on the front steps. Reporters crowded around Alice, holding their microphones to her, print reporters taking down her every word. "The violence of this mass arrest was not a spontaneous and undisciplined 'police riot' like the one in Chicago during the Democratic National Convention last year. This one was planned. Its purpose was to use terror to stifle dissent. I know these tactics first hand. I was in Paris in 1942, when France fell to the Nazis. I saw only a little of what they did before I managed to escape, leaving friends I never saw alive again. Now I have seen these tactics again. In America. In Berkeley." Then Alice turned and walked away regally—Jake, Aaron and I scuttling after her.

When I went to Merritt to turn in my grades for the spring term, I posted a Withdrawal for Harry. I thought of him constantly, then frequently, then only occasionally, as in July, when Angel told me KPFA had received an audio tape just before Eldridge Cleaver was sent from Cuba to Algeria. The tape was never aired, perhaps, Angel admitted, because it was critical of Fidel Castro. "Critical in what way?" Angel wasn't sure.

Carol came home for the summer, with piles of things to store. So we cleaned up the shed, packing up Harry's belongings into three boxes we stored in a corner of the garage, finishing in time to sit in front of the TV and watch the astronauts land on the moon. The next week, when I walked up to KPFA, I found the narrow hall blocked by two men, noisily arguing with the news director, demanding that he declare the moon landing a TV hoax, faked to take public attention off the war. I edged past them to the studio and did my reading, a chapter from Hannah Arendt, comparing the fates of Jews in various European countries during World War II. (And I thought of Harry again, knowing he'd be pleased to learn that the Italians, even under Fascism, had done surprising well in saving their Jews, second only to Denmark.)

Then I went downstairs to eat lunch with Marsha, who had new worries. Her sons had both dropped out of college, one to enter a commune in Montana, the other wandering through parts unknown. Her daughter was at home, but small sums of money and a few small family heirlooms had gone missing—sold to buy drugs? Marsha was almost certain that she had backslid after her last stay on a detox ward.

August sped by. Bernard Person and I were close to final-final choices for inclusion in our anthology, choices that kept changing as we negotiated rights and permissions. Person would help write the introduction, but the tedious job of getting permissions was mine. Galleys had to go out for peer review by the end of the year, so that we could submit the finished collection for adoption by colleges.

I barely had time for anything but an occasional walk up to Telegraph, to buy a book at Cody's or Moe's or Shakespeare & Co., or have a brief visit with Jake and his son. Aaron was working in the store that summer.

During the time Aaron had stayed with Jake recovering from the Santa Rita ordeal, the Stonewall Riots had hit the news. Aaron and Jake were watching TV together and, perhaps shaken up and vulnerable, Aaron had turned to Jake and blurted, "I might be a homosexual" (the word gay was still an insult at the time).

"No shit," Jake had murmured. "Did you tell your mother?"

"Not yet."

"Better not wait too long. Look at that asshole!" (Nixon had come on the screen.)

Suddenly the tension, the "hatred" Jake had felt coming from Aaron was revealed to be fear of being rejected by his father. Aaron was so relieved at not being disowned that he wanted to spend more time with Jake. He had cheerfully tackled the job that always defeated Jake's helpers— getting the stock into some kind of order. Aaron's strenuous effort (also defeated) kept them both busy while Jake digested Aaron's revelation, and they both watched the early hopeful signs of opening closets and changing laws. I gave Aaron the names of a couple of my gay friends in San Francisco, long-time residents. "Bernie is ten years older than I, Al ten years younger. Both old men to you. But they were my best support when I was going through a divorce. Good people to know."

When I stopped at the Med for coffee, I saw that new signs had been posted on two walls, upstairs and down: Drug Dealers Not Welcome Here. The place was still crowded, but I saw few of the usual locals, the business folks and editors and poets and people like me who used to meet there. I was still working on some slow permissions when the fall term started, and I felt buried under papers without having had a moment of rest during the summer.

I remember the exact day on which I finally heard from Harry—November 15. I had gone to San Francisco to join 100,000 other people in one of the biggest Vietnam War protests yet. When I returned home I checked the mail and found a brief hand-written note from Harry wrapped around a postal order for fifty dollars, made out to Alice. "First installment on my bail money." No return address. A Butte postmark.

I dug out the letter from Harry's mother and mailed the postal order back to Harry at the return address on the envelope. I enclosed a note saying that the judge had returned all bail money, which Alice had donated to the fund to continue developing the Park. I included Alice's address in San Francisco, "in case you care to contact her yourself." Now that I knew Harry was safe, I was furious. He had simply walked away, leaving a lot of people worrying and, as far as he knew, costing Alice $500.

My note came back marked Not At This Address on December 6, the day of the Altamont disaster. What was supposed to be another mellow, outdoor, gloriously legend-making Woodstock concert disintegrated into chaos and violence, leaving four dead, hundreds hurt or sickened by drugs and alcohol. I was lucky—Carol was still taking finals at Davis. Marsha's daughter had been one of the rape victims. Jake's son, Aaron, also lucky, had arrived too late to get near the place. By the time he'd walked the near-mile from the parking area to the site of the concert, crowds of people were hurrying past him in the opposite direction, fleeing through the dry grass as if escaping ahead of a brush fire. Angel's tape recorder was one casualty. He gave his report live on KPFA the next day (pre-empting my reading of Kate Chopin), and told a confused story of moving masses of people and of how he had left the area on someone else's bike. He apologized to the owner—please to call him at KPFA and describe it, then claim it.

In early 1970 Marsha hosted a book party for the long-delayed publication of the Person/Carson *Spearhead Reader*. And there were more important celebrations that year, affecting more people: the acquittal of the Chicago Seven; the freeing of Huey Newton.

But these turned out to be brief moments of euphoria. More people saw an end to the hopeful sixties in the National Guard shooting protesting students at Kent State and Jackson State, or in the ominous splinter group, Weather Underground, whose first act was to accidentally blow up some of its own members. (Marsha was sure her older son had been one of those killed, and mourned silently until he surfaced two years later, tired of setting off bombs, ignored, except by people who cited them as proof of the violence of the anti-war movement.)

As the Vietnam War ground with deathly slowness to its end in 1975, it left hundreds of thousands of casualties, including indirect, quiet ones, like two of Carol's former classmates: one leaping out of the window of a dormitory three states away, one sitting in a ward at Napa State Hospital, after he failed to return from his first LSD trip. Marsha's daughter survived, in and out of detox. There were runaway parents too. The most memorable among those I knew personally were a long-married couple—older than I—ardent communists who became equally ardent Buddhist monks, entering a monastery after dumping their fifteen-year-old daughter on an elderly friend of ours. (You could say the girl avenged herself by becoming a well-known porn star.) A couple of fathers euphorically announced they were gay and abandoned even larger, younger families (a few years later their wives were grateful to have escaped AIDS). Some black/white marriages, begun in high idealism, were blown apart by Black Power separatism.

At Merritt College we began the move eastward and upward. There was sporadic picketing on the new hilltop campus by a few blacks who now saw the point of the college president they'd forced out: getting up that hill was virtually impossible for some of the people who needed the college most. The beating of a white instructor after he'd made critical remarks about the Black Panthers in one of the few classes left on Grove Street (soon to be renamed Martin Luther King Way) hastened the move up to the comparatively quiet hills, which were not entirely free of rumors. One was that the roof on one building of the new Merritt College was designed to be on a coordinate with the towers of Laney College, across town. One college (I can't remember which one) was to become a prison for black dissidents while the other housed gun turrets to guard it. But that story was a bit too fanciful for even the most paranoid, and it evaporated.

The gauzy-robed Hare Krishnas multiplied, rivaled by the Reverend Moon, Rajneesh, and dozens of other gurus who inexplicably attracted the sons and daughters of educated, liberal families (mocking our assumption that only right-wing, pro-war families were vulnerable). Even Alice Allen suffered a home invasion, takeover, and slapping around by a cult that four of her six children had joined. She fled to Berkeley again and wrote a book about her ordeal, while Bob Treuhaft (Jessica Mitford's lawyer husband) set in motion the legal machinery to clear them out of her house. But Alice never went back to live in San Francisco. She retired from SF State and moved to a little house in Berkeley slightly uphill from College Avenue.

I was luckier than many parents. Carol was attracted to Ram Dass, a Jewish Harvard professor who wrote benign, occasionally even wise exhortations to spirituality, but did not try to take people out of school and away from their families. She read his best-selling *Be Here Now,* and went to a series of weekend retreats. She came home early from the fifth one because, "I got bored," and started talking about law school.

Dozens of "enlightenment" systems adopted a more secular tone and required less time, though often quite a bit of money. In my usual way, I dipped a toe in, here and there. The last group I let Lisa introduce me to had one of the generic titles of those days—Mind-Expansion, or Unleashing Your Inner Genius or some such thing. It began with what I later learned was a standard exercise in such groups. We were to learn trust by standing in a cluster, then, one by one, closing our eyes, relaxing, letting go, and falling backwards to be caught by the others. I balked, pled a migraine, and left, while pitying glances followed me. Blind trust in complete strangers seemed a not very useful lesson to learn.

Interest in politics was far from dead in Berkeley, focused on national events like the legalization of abortion, or the publication of the Pentagon Papers, or Nixon ending the draft, increasing the bombing, stopping the bombing, then, best of all, writhing in the Watergate scandal. At parties we talked about global events like the final pullout from Vietnam or the election of a socialist president in Chile, or his death in a coup backed by the CIA and Anaconda Copper. (I thought briefly of Harry when it occurred to me that life in Butte must be affected by who governed Chile.)

"Think globally and act locally," became the popular slogan. In that spirit, we elected to our city council newcomers whose radical global outlook was impeccably pure, displacing long-time resident liberal black and white candidates who knew and cared more about local needs. Mrs. Temple reluctantly and briefly dipped back into local politics to support the recall of an especially destructive black official. He left town as suddenly as he had arrived, leaving a bitter residue and a wider gap between local politicians.

Dan Lyon's repeated assaults on the fence around People's Park were carried out by a shifting assortment of angry young people briefly in, then out of Berkeley. They knew nothing about the history of People's Park. They gathered long enough to disrupt traffic, to shatter windows of police cars, banks, and the Public Library, then scatter before they could be arrested. Most of them went back to their home state after a little excitement. But not before they managed, on Lyon's fifth or sixth try, to tear down the

194

fence around People's Park.

The university gave up, rented the park to the city for a dollar a year, and began to contribute a little money toward ongoing maintenance. It was now officially a park, but after the first month, I saw no families picnicking there, nor university students, nor Telegraph Avenue workers on lunch break. Only scruffy-looking men with backpacks, huddled under the now overgrown bushes we'd planted, sleeping off whatever drug they were on. When they woke, they often quarreled with one another, or with invisible presences haunting those who'd been thrown out of rapidly closing state mental hospitals—life on the streets being, it seemed, the "community care" we had all endorsed in the name of enlightened treatment of the mentally ill. Other men, alert and menacing, preyed on the drugged and delusional, and all of them drifted around the corner to Telegraph Avenue to beg from shoppers and students. After dark, they took over the street, but menaced no one but each other until after midnight when the last coffee houses shut down.

It wasn't exactly that everyone agreed to turn the park over to the outcasts (who often came on a bus ticket bought by the city that cast them out). It was that local people—except Father Mike and other good church folks—didn't have to think about them or the park. There were other places to shop, other coffee houses to meet friends. Venerable furniture and clothing stores, one by one, left Telegraph Avenue, as Jake had predicted, replaced by short-lived pizza joints, trash-trinket boutiques, and "head shops," closing, then opening, with more of the same. Bancroft Avenue became a narrow strip of shops hugging the south border of the campus and serving students (who made only quick forays beyond Bancroft, down to the used

bookstores, then hurried back). Even Alice, who still called
People's Park "sacred ground," usually held court in a new
coffee house a mile south on College Avenue. Some men from
Moe's Books opened Black Oak Books on north Shattuck,
which sold both used and new books, catering to many of
Ivan's colleagues who no longer wanted to walk even the
four blocks from the campus down Telegraph Avenue to
Cody's Books.

What had been the crossroads of Berkeley, where
students and residents and workers and visitors and—yes—
freaks and agitators of all ages and types brushed against
each other, was left to the university students forced to share
it with the castoffs and drug dealers. On weekends, street
vendors replaced students, their tables lining the curb,
selling tie-dye shirts and Fuck The Pigs bumper stickers
to visitors from suburbs twenty miles or 2,000 miles away,
who didn't look too closely into the deranged or cunning
eyes of the ragged, smelly, street people who begged, "spare
change," completing the furnishings of a 1960s theme park,
dirtier than Disneyland's Main Street USA, but no more
authentic.

I absentmindedly noted the changes (perhaps trying
not to think about them) until the day Pat Cody told me
that she and Fred had put the store on the market. They
had been struggling ever since the first riots in 1968. Their
final decision came suddenly on the day they were presented
with a letter signed by their dozen part-time workers (all
but Angel, who still took one late-night shift Fred was planning to cancel). The letter listed demands, the first being
that the "workers" be given "shares" in the store, which
they would take over and "manage collectively."

"What really hurts is thinking of the secret meetings
they must have had, drafting this—while I'm in the back

office trying to figure out which publishers will wait for their money so we can meet our payroll every week. My God, it's like lunatics trying to take over an asylum that's burning down!" When I asked Pat if she had a buyer, she looked at me as if I had joined the lunatics. "Are you kidding?"

In 1974 came what was probably the last "sixties-type" local event to become a major media event. Like the proposed takeover of Cody's Books, it was a parody of the sixties, but an even crazier, truly destructive parody. Newspaper heiress Patty Hearst was kidnapped, dragged from her apartment near the campus by people who called themselves the Symbionese Liberation Army.

I had heard of the SLA a few months before, when my KPFA reading of Simone Weil was pre-empted, replaced by a mysteriously delivered tape claiming "credit" for the killing of the first black superintendent of the Oakland schools. The sin of Marcus Foster, according to this strange rant against "the fascist insect," was his plan to issue student identity cards to help keep violent intruders out of the schools. "Who are these people, this SLA?" I asked Angel, but he didn't know. No one on the Left knew.

The newspapers called the motive for abducting the heiress "unclear." Thirty years later, the last fugitive member of the SLA, finally in custody after a generation lived in middle-class, white comfort, tearfully explained in an interview that the SLA needed a "symbolic blow against the rich" to erase public memory of their murder of Foster, a "strategic error." The Hearst caper worked—few people today remember Marcus Foster's name, let alone how he was gunned down. They remember only the sensation of the muddle-headed heiress photographed while robbing a bank with her kidnappers.

The Patty Hearst circus was finally pushed off the

front pages of newspapers by the resignation of President Nixon in 1975. A back page of the same newspaper featured a small photograph of Eldridge Cleaver surrendering to the FBI. Cleaver had gone from Cuba to Algeria to France. Along the way, Huey Newton had expelled him from the Black Panther Party, and his wife had taken their two children and left him (changes hardly noted in the press, which had completely lost interest in him). In Paris, he told reporters, he'd had a vision of Jesus in the moon. He no longer wanted to burn down the White House. With the help of the Right Wing evangelist in the photo beside him, he had made a deal to come home, yet stay out of prison. After that back-page news item, the major media forgot him again. *Soul on Ice* was quietly dropped from twelve classes at Merritt.

Of course, the news of Cleaver's conversion made me think again of Harry, made me wonder if Harry had read about his hero, and if so, what he thought. If I believed in telepathy, I'd believe my thoughts prompted a letter from Harry. It came on the day Patty Hearst was arrested.

September 15, 1975

Dear Ruth,

    It seems a lot longer than five years since I saw you. A dream of another world. Sorry I didn't write sooner to thank you for all that you did for me even if it was a waste of your time. One reason I didn't write was that I bounced around a few months before I came back to Butte. I couldn't face telling my mother I'd fucked up again. But when I got here, that didn't matter so much because there was worse news. She hadn't told me her surgery was for cancer and that it only bought her a little time. She didn't want me to know—wanted me to stay in college, stay in Berkeley. But she was glad to see me, and I told her I was just taking a break from school and promised I'd go back. She got good treatment (Stiletto paid) at the new cancer center—located right here, of course, because, wouldn't you know, the cancer rate in Butte is the highest in the state. I took care of her for about a year until she died.

Since then I've done a lot of things—mostly illegal—to get by. (not many legal jobs here) My final "criminal" job was working in an abandoned gold mine owned by two old guys on social security. They took plenty of gold out of that mine—but not ore. They hired me to tend the lights and water and air vents for fifteen hundred potted cannabis plants—three hundred feet underground. That was my best job, the easiest, and it more than covered my bar bill, which has been pretty high. Then the police raided the mine. The newspaper said they noticed high electric bills, but I suspect other reasons, like those old guys being too greedy or too stupid to give the police their cut. So that was the end of the only cash crop you can grow in Butte.

Luckily the police raided the mine on my day off. I decided to end my life of crime before my luck ran out. For the past two years I've been working in the only stable legal business in Butte, you guessed it, a saloon—Lynch's (no relation to my father). Minimum wage, tips, all the booze I want. I'm even going to marry the boss's daughter. Sandy got pregnant and won't have an abortion, so my boss is stuck with me for a son-in-law. He decided he'd better get me away

199

from the booze and send me to Montana Tech—on the west side of Mine Hill, where "Copper King" Daly waves me in, or warns me to stay out, depends on how you look at the upraised arm on that statue. I took a couple of courses there last year, and signed up for Expository Writing this year. That's how I ran across your name. A lot of courses are using "Person/Carson." That's what everyone here calls the Spearpoint Reader. *I recognized some of the essays you used to bring into class. Congratulations. I hope you make some royalties.*

They tell me that with some credits from Merritt and veteran's credits, I can get a BA in about two and a half years. If I can figure out a viable major. Montana Tech is big on math and engineering and science, but not very strong in literature, which is still the only thing I care about.

So that's what I'm doing here while Patty Hearst is robbing banks in California. I guess taking the fruits of other people's labor runs in her family.

Nothing else new here except that the ugliest town in America just got uglier. We lost our only green place. The Company thought there just might be something to dig for there. So Columbia Gardens became the Continental Pit. Nobody dared to oppose it—jobs, you know—so Butte never had a "People's Park" fight. But the Company didn't find anything worth digging out. Besides, once they got rid of Allende, they got the Chilean mines back, so why bother with Butte? (The only time the guys at Lynch's Saloon agreed with my "crazy Berkeley politics" was when Allende nationalized the mines in Chile, and Anaconda had to make more jobs in Butte.) So now we're back to normal. No jobs, and now, no Columbia Gardens, just another big hole in the ground.

The Berkeley Pit keeps growing. It looks like a moon crater. The Company wants to expand the Pit west, through all of the old Uptown. Of course they said the magic word again. Jobs. The new mayor is trying to move all the city offices down to the flats, build a new city hall near the mall. But, hard to believe, there's actually a tiny group fighting him—in the name of Historic Preservation. What's to preserve? The places where labor leaders were murdered, and miners blown up or buried alive or poisoned. Oh, and don't forget the places where they found comfort before dying—the saloons and the whore houses with the "prettiest whores in the west." Now that's worth fighting for. I'm serious. I'm all for this bunch of "oddballs" (and a lot worse things they're called). I prefer them to the town boosters who talk about the miracle of the "resilience" of Butte. That's the Butte word for survival another notch lower.

And, of course, they talk about the "spirit" of Butte, which I always defined as hot air. I didn't know how right I was. The spirit of Butte, the true spirit of Butte is fighting the preservationists with hot air. Literally. Real, burning hot air—fire. The fires started a few months ago, night after night. One at a time, the old Uptown buildings on mine hill started going up—and crashing down—the brick walls collapsing while the interiors burned. In Lynch's (one of the last viable businesses on mine hill) we hear the explosion, then the sirens. Around the bar, we make our bets on which building it is this time. Then we take our drinks outside so that we can see who won the bet. People have started driving up from the flats, following the fire engines. The crowds get bigger every night. The most exciting show in town, and free. Bring your own bottle, stand out under the stars and warm yourself at a good roaring fire. Last night the crowd cheered as each wall came crashing down. They booed the firemen who stood there helpless—low water pressure up here. Besides, the fires start suddenly and explode, so that by the time the fire trucks get here, there's not much to do but watch.

So far the count is thirty—thirty businesses destroyed, thirty businessmen collecting fire insurance and smiling all the way down to the mall on the flats. I guess the fun will stop soon because no insurance company will write policies in Butte anymore. The police have no clues, but a couple of them are driving new sports cars on their days off.

Harry

P.S. Sorry I left all that junk in the shed.
Just throw it in the garbage.
P.P.S. Enclosed another $100 for Alice.
Tell her I'll pay it all back within a year.

Berkeley was also suffering a series of arson fires at the time, but for different reasons. New three and four story apartment buildings caught fire while they were still in the framing stage—the work of anti-development protesters. A few decrepit old hotel buildings mysteriously caught fire too, not because they were worthless—quite the opposite.

New owners (said the rumors) wanted to drive the marginal people out of their untidy rooms and upgrade the property for more affluent tenants now coming to Berkeley.

I wrote back to Harry at Lynch's, Uptown, Butte, Montana. I congratulated him on his marriage, sent back his check, and asked him to keep in touch.

Jake read Harry's letter and said only, "Sounds like he was drunk when he wrote it." Alice read it, shook her head, and wrote to Harry. Like me, she received no answer.

Father Mike put Harry-at-Lynch's Saloon, Uptown-Butte, Montana on the mailing list for his *Streetwise Bulletin*, a two page sheet of inspirational reports on activities around Peoples' Park. Jake called it "Father Mike's Fairy Tales." If you only read *Streetwise Bulletin* and never came to Telegraph, you could imagine that the Avenue was still a destination for idealistic rebels, with a few guardian angels in rags on the street, blessing those who fed them until they were marvelously transformed and went back to practicing dentistry. (Every issue featured a true story of a return to affluence.) The monthly was written entirely by Father Mike and a young woman who assisted him, Ann Prester. There were rumors that they had three children kept out of sight in Ann's home in the exclusive suburb of Orinda. There were other rumors, that the Catholic Church had quietly removed Mike Ruga, that he was no longer a priest, though he wore his clerical collar above his sweatshirt. It was hard to tell these days, because bona fide priests might not wear the collar, and hard-working nuns had begun to run around in sweat suits.

I don't mean to call Father Mike a "phony," whatever that means. (Marsha did, but her attitude seemed to come out of a generalized Episcopalian hostility toward Catholics).

It's fair to say that Mike Ruga was just one of the less effective of folks from all the mainstream churches, temples, and mosques, who put money and energy into helping waves of runaways and drifters and lost souls wandering the streets of San Francisco and Berkeley.

The younger drifters became a flood in summer, most of them dressed to live the now fabled sixties—spiked green hair, black leather, and nose-rings added to their beads and tatters. They huddled in tight circles on curbs, looking confused and angry, like people who've missed their last train. They littered the streets with disappointment, rags, and human waste, until they tired of Father Mike's food, left, and were replaced by others.

As "Out of Vietnam" became a reality instead of a slogan, there were conversions as surprising as Eldridge Cleaver's. Some drop-outs of the sixties—bright, white, middle-class—dropped right in again, running for offices they'd called meaningless, or becoming professors at universities they'd once shut down. Fervent activists like Jerry Rubin and Bobby Seale became equally fervent businessmen. The sad changes were the suicides like Abbie Hoffman's, whose brilliantly manic stunts no longer touched nerves gone numb after more than a decade of war and shame. Or ironic horrors, like the shooting of lawyer Faye Stender, liberator of Huey Newton, by another black ex-convict.

I was willing to celebrate the transformation of Huey Newton into a Ph.D. candidate at UC Santa Cruz. As I told a UCSC professor at one of Marsha's dinner parties, I knew first-hand how brilliant he could be. After a moment of silence, the professor murmured to me, "He's in my seminar. I only hope I can pass him through and he gets out quickly—the man is terrifying."

It was a relief to point to one now-universally admired

204

hero, Mohammed Ali, the one whose rebellion had cost him the most. Reinstated in boxing, fighting again, vindicated, he had won the love even of those who'd called him a traitor.

On the day Ali won back his title, the mail brought me a clipping from the *Montana Standard*: "Butte City Hall To Stay Uptown." A few sentences detailed the vote of the Butte City Council not to move their municipal offices down from the old Mine Hill. That was all—no marks on the clipping, no date, no note, no return address. I could only assume and hope that Harry was celebrating a small victory.

The *Spearpoint Reader* was doing well. The publisher asked me to edit an anthology of writing by women, and the college asked me to design courses in women's literature. I was secure in a tenured job, with a trickle of book royalties to frost the cake.

But I was one of the lucky ones. The Vietnam War had removed the cushion of surplus doled out to the needy and the not-so-needy. Along with the highly visible losers on our streets, the less visible poor suffered more than ever. As for the "voluntarily poor" like Lisa and Angel, they could no longer count on cheap rent, freely dispensed food stamps and medical care, or dubious disability benefits. Suddenly there was intense competition for the part-time jobs that poets and activists with degrees could easily fall back on a few years before.

Angel settled into a thirty-hour week at Moe's Books, plus occasional shifts at Cody's and Shakespeare & Co., did less volunteer radio, and more drinking. It was disconcerting to see him losing hair and gaining a huge belly—no longer the angel on a sentimental Christmas card, yet too ailing and anxious to be Santa Claus. But at least he had a job he could count on. Lisa did not. She rented rooms in her now rent-controlled house. She gave massages, read auras and tea leaves and palms. She channeled. She taught sight without glasses, self-hypnosis to lose weight and cure writer's block. As one New Age self-development system became crowded, Lisa moved to another, always with a faith and optimism I had to admire.

One ripple effect of tighter money was the end of the underground press. Few people had time for unpaid work. *The Freedom Weekly* and *The Berkeley Barb* were long gone, replaced by *The Bridge,* a shoppers' weekly made up primarily of ads and entertainment listings. It occasionally printed some remarkably intelligent art and music reviews (by people who soon left for paying jobs), a few short letters to the editor, and one long lead article. The reviews, and sometimes the lead article, were the best things in the paper but not the most read.

That honor went to a political gossip column under the name "Bishop Berkeley," which resembled the sassy old underground press only as a reflection in a fun-house mirror might. Rumors, innuendoes, predictions, and interpretations of local politics touched only glancingly on facts. Whenever I had first-hand knowledge of an issue or incident, I was shocked at how Bishop Berkeley had distorted the reality. I pressed Angel, nagged at him to tell me who Bishop Berkeley was. He didn't know. I even accused him of writing the column. "Me! How could you think that I—" I believed him. Angel was too gentle, too decent, really, to throw around these attacks that got the facts wrong, attached them to real names, and injured real people.

"I hate his nasty, snide tone."

"Everyone does—but they open the paper first to Bishop Berkeley."

"Doesn't the editor worry about being sued?"

"Berkeley people don't sue, they write irate letters,

and that just adds to the fun."

Lisa told me she'd heard that Bishop Berkeley was the closely-guarded pseudonym of "a UC faculty wife, someone you know, Ruth." Marsha? I found that hard to believe. Marsha didn't know that much about off-campus politics—except what she heard from me at lunch, of course.

Despite her family troubles, Marsha's life had gained some satisfactions. One day at lunch she gave me *Scheherazade*, a short-lived journal of erotica by women—one of the more genteel rebellions of feminism in the late seventies. She proudly pointed to two stories she had written under the pseudonym Belinda Basket. One of her stories described the seduction of a professor's wife by a lesbian who bore a striking resemblance to me—even quoting things I remembered saying in class. (I took it as a tribute to the seductive power of education.) Her other story featured a satirical, unmistakable portrait of Ivan, with flashbacks to their highly erotic and combative young courtship. It was cruel but funny, even better than the poem she'd written about the tear gas attack on the campus.

"Really!"

"It shows a wicked wit I never suspected in you, Marsha. Has Ivan seen it?"

"Oh, no, he wouldn't bother to read it. And if he did, he'd never recognize himself. He's too egotistical."

"Isn't it likely one of his colleagues will?"

Marsha smiled, and changed the subject. Her marriage had reached a kind of truce, ceremonial, like the marriages of some politicians. She and Ivan, she told me, still worked together on university functions, public occasions, but they lived otherwise separate lives. The piece that skewered Ivan proved she was capable of a cutting wit, and was willing to hide behind a pseudonym. I asked what she thought of Bishop Berkeley. She answered vaguely, "in *The Bridge?* I hardly ever see it."

Southwest Berkeley had benefited from the generally rising cost of housing. Fewer white kids from middle America could afford their summer hippie adventure in a black neighborhood of Berkeley. And, despite Black Power separatists, we were becoming more integrated, especially after red-lining was outlawed, and black owners who'd moved to the suburbs were able to sell dilapidated houses—correction, "fixer-uppers"—to young white singles and couples who couldn't afford a house in San Francisco or on the East Bay hills. On weekends, Milton Street was filled with the sounds of sawing and hammering.

Only one of the houses—on Dante Street, directly behind me, with a common backyard fence—still housed a shifting group of transients who rented rooms from the owner, an old black man who lived in one room he no longer left. Mrs. Temple had known "old Mr. Horace" in his better days, "before he started drinking." She had once called the Health Department about the mess in Mr. Horace's yard, but had never made a direct complaint to the tenants: "Trash like that living next to you, you don't know what they might do." She suggested I get a dog, "a big one, with a doghouse near your back fence." (I followed her advice, went to the Animal Shelter, and adopted Pogo, a big white German shepherd found abandoned on the street after the last exodus of transients.) Mrs. Temple concluded that we'd just have to resign ourselves to waiting until "old Horace" died and the house was sold to "some nice young white or mixed couple." (Not Asians—Mrs. Temple had her own prejudices, bitter ones, based on her insistence that certain service departments at the university were run by "Filipino or Chinese, and they only hire their own.")

One night, when I looked down from my bedroom window onto what was either a fight or a party in the yard beyond my back fence, I thought I recognized Dan Lyon in the darkness. It was the first time I'd seen him this far from Telegraph Avenue, where he was conspicuously promoting the painting of a mural on the north wall of Jake's store. The one-story stucco wall ran nearly a hundred feet along Haste Street, to the edge of People's Park. Occasionally I stopped to watch the work. Invariably, Dan Lyon would call me by name and request a contribution to buy paint, the only time he ever gave a sign that he knew me. Sometimes he asked if I'd heard anything from Harry.

Dan had remained highly visible, regularly leading demonstrators to disrupt city council meetings whenever People's Park came up. His latest campaign had been his defense of the Free Box. Someone had built a huge wooden box and put it at the curb on Haste, alongside the Park, where Berkeleyans who now avoided walking on Telegraph Avenue could stop their cars, double-park, dump old clothes, then drive away "feeling noble," as Jake put it. They never stayed to watch the toughest drug addicts fighting each other for whatever was salable, then urinating on the leftovers to show their power over the weaker ones—the way an animal marks his territory. They did not see these toughs take the rags they claimed into the nearest shops and intimidate the clerks into "buying" them—a dollar here, a dollar there, until the dollars added up to a drug buy. These scenes were acted out every day next to the mural that merged heroic highlights of sixties activism: a male figure standing on top of a police car; gas-masked police shooting at children carrying plants, playing guitars, dancing, singing—or were those wide mouths screaming? and was that sunlight or fire behind them? and was that supposed to be Julia, the bubble-blowing street poet? Mario Savio on top of the car? Huey Newton with the spear? People come and go in Berkeley; fewer and fewer of the students and shoppers knew or cared what the mural depicted.

As the problems on Telegraph Avenue increased, the overflow drained off to Shattuck Avenue, then even further west into the neighborhoods. These folks tended to be more orderly and sane, attempting invisibility. One of them was Cole—the only name I knew him by—who lived in his van with a dozen whippets, tiny dogs like miniature greyhounds. Cole moved about during the day, avoiding places where drugged or violent drifters congregated. After dark he usually parked alongside a grassy field, where he exercised his whippets, before he bedded down for the night with them in the van.

I met Cole one night as I was walking Pogo, and then our meetings became a regular ritual. Pogo would see Cole's tiny dogs running and leaping around the weedy lot, and would gallop awkwardly into their midst, where he stood like an indulgent old grandfather, happily wagging his tail as they leaped on and over him. I would stop to chat with Cole, a gentle, ruddy white man who could not have been over thirty. Cole told me that he raised whippets, then sold them somewhere out of state. That's all he ever told me about himself. From time to time he would disappear, then appear again with another batch of tiny dogs. He was a good neighbor, a kind of unofficial watchman after dark.

Almost everyone I knew who lived or worked in the flatlands had adopted one or two well-mannered street people who became familiar residents, as "permanent" as most people in Berkeley. I could hardly imagine the self-discipline with which they politely accepted church-sponsored handouts of food, clothing, showers, shelter, and medications, remaining invisible until I might realize that a certain man with a backpack—sitting in the library, or at a bus stop, or outside a church—had become a familiar face. Then he might disappear, and I would hope he had found his way back to a safer life. Even Jake had his regulars who, near the end of the month when their disability checks ran out, showed up with a worthless book salvaged from a garbage can. Jake always gave the sober, non-aggressive ones a dollar or two, but never would have admitted it if I hadn't caught him at it. I asked if Bill Jackson had been around with more photographs of mud-sculpture. Jake shook his head. "Last time he came in, the whole side of his skull was flattened. Said he'd had brain surgery. I gave him a few bucks, told him I wanted to order one of his photos. He looked at me like he didn't know what I was talking about. Probably dead by now." (Like Bill, the whimsical sculptures he photographed had disappeared, pulled out by highway workers, or buried by the new freeway.)

Jake, like Pat and Fred Cody, was still waiting for a buyer who never came. I couldn't imagine Steadman's Used Books without Jake, though I dropped in less frequently, and I rarely went into the Med. The place was too quiet. A few people sat alone at fewer and fewer widely spaced marble tables (were the table and chairs wearing out and not being replaced?). The lone sitters looked vaguely familiar, aged survivors of the crowds that had disappeared. On the rare occasions that I did go into the Med, I still searched the tables for a sign of Bill. One day, sweeping my eyes across the room, I stopped and stared at a lone man at the table in the corner window.

It was—no—yes, unmistakably, Eldridge Cleaver.

Soon I was seeing him in coffee houses all over Berkeley, wandering from one to another, like a ghost—a

gray-haired, paunchy, arthritic ghost—searching in vain for
visibility. I never saw a sign of recognition from anyone.

His second book *Soul on Fire* had come out, detailing
his disillusionment with the Left, with the countries that
had briefly accepted him—Cuba, Algeria, France. It ended
with his Christian conversion and his return to America in
1976, grateful to be home again, to have "found the bridge
between me and God," and to be speaking at "fifty universities and scores of churches." I don't know where he was
speaking—not around here. Nor had anyone I knew read
his new book. Cody's Books had stocked only one copy, and
Fred Cody gave me a weary, grateful smile when I took it
off his hands. "I'll give you a discount. Couldn't give the
thing away in this town." Then he told me that he and Pat
had finally found a buyer with energy and money enough
to take over the store. "You'll like Andy Ross. He's going to
improve the stock, computerize it."

I wasn't surprised to find *Soul on Fire* poorly
written—lacking the help of Beverly and the now-scattered
Ramparts staff. What caught me was the surprising naïveté
of this rapist/convict turned political hero. He had been
genuinely shocked to find that in the socialist dictatorships
that (briefly) welcomed him, no Beverly Axelrod, no radical
press could advocate for prisoners, let alone publish any of
the enraged challenges that became *Soul on Ice*. He had
known little of the world but a prison cell and books sent
to him by the sympathetic radicals who won his release. He
had left the United States—innocent as Candide, and his
confusion, his sense of betrayal by the Left, the emotional
crisis leading to his conversion made me, for the first time,
pity him. Incidentally, *Soul on Fire* confirmed the rumor
Bentley had carried to me ten years before. Cleaver truly
had plotted to collect arms, to have the Panthers and street

kids shoot it out with police from the tower of old Merritt College. Huey Newton, Cleaver wrote, had vetoed the plan.

By the time I saw Cleaver, his born-again speaking engagements and his book royalties must have declined. Jake told me Cleaver had made the rounds of bookstores, looking for work. ("Who could hire him? Haven't we got enough troubles?") I began seeing him at street fairs and flea markets, sitting at a table with his self-published poetry, sneering at people who looked through him as they passed. Or, I would see his panel truck stop outside my house before daylight, picking up papers and bottles intended for the city recycling project, just as the street people with nothing but stolen shopping carts did. He showed up at a friend's cloth-ing store, peddling his line of jeans that featured a "Cleaver Sleeve"—a garishly colored sac for male sex organs. (How did this go over with his supporters on the Christian Right?) Most disconcerting of all, he began to show up at neighborhood meetings, conspicuously setting out a tape recorder, whenever he heard of a group opposing our new City Council. I was stunned when he sat down next to me at Mrs. Temple's church—where we were drafting a letter opposing a bizarre plan by these "progressives" to build public housing in school yards in our neighborhood.

The next week, for the first time, I was mentioned in the Bishop Berkeley column as a "white gentrifier joining born-again right-winger Eldridge Cleaver in opposing housing for the poor." Throughout one sleepless night, I wracked my brain: who was at that meeting? But it needn't have been anyone there. I'd talked endlessly against the crazy scheme to anyone who would listen. (Usually they listened silently, then remarked that they just loved our mayor for visiting Cuba.)

Fortunately, I had happier things to think about.

Carol had passed the bar, become pregnant, and married boyfriend Steve, in that order. She and Steve arranged their own simple, private wedding, then threw a party at Sigmund Stern Grove for family and friends from Chicago to Seattle (Steve's home). They settled in San Francisco. By mid-1978 I had a grand-daughter Judith (named after my mother), and Steve had a job in the office of the SF District Attorney.

That's how he happened to be in City Hall on the day a San Francisco supervisor shot down the mayor and the first openly gay supervisor. Whenever I think about that first year of Judith's life, I remember holding her while Steve and Carol endlessly discussed the inside story of the surreal politics behind the assassinations and the trial.

Jake was affected more personally by that crisis. After Aaron finished college, he had moved to the Castro. Sensing the coming boom in that run-down area, Jake had refinanced his building on Telegraph to help Aaron buy an old storefront. Aaron opened a gay bookstore and lived in an apartment above it. He was at the center of the horror and grief at Harvey Milk's death, followed by the ordeal of the trial. When the assassin got off with a light sentence, Civic Center exploded in riots, police cars were burned. Police retaliated with a raid on the Castro, perhaps, as they said, in pursuit of the rioters. They chased men into Aaron's store, smashing windows, destroying stock, and dragging Aaron into the paddy wagon along with the others.

It was People's Park all over again: arrests, bail, hearings, trials, depositions describing police beating Aaron and the other men. Again the charges were dismissed, but, with the expense of replacing Aaron's uninsured windows and helping pay publishers for ruined stock, Jake was even deeper in debt. He was working on a deal to sell his building and take a long-term lease on the store. "That way I can hold out for someone who agrees to just buy the stock and rent the space. And I can get out."

"Aaron's okay now?"

Jake shrugged. Aaron had had enough of the book business. "Rents in the Castro have shot up so high, he can make more money just renting out the space—a bar, a restaurant, a bath house—Aaron figures he can make just enough to live on and write full time. He's already been published in the gay press. He's working on a book. He's really good, Ruth, not just that he's my son."

My father died suddenly in May. I spent the last week of May in Chicago, then came back home long enough to finish up the term at Merritt, before returning to Chicago for what was to become at least a month every summer with my lonely, also failing mother.

I arrived back in Berkeley on the day the front page of the *San Francisco Chronicle* was nearly covered by its first color photo: the Jonestown massacre, all those bodies in ordinary T-shirts and jeans, face down on the ground in the lush green rain forest, hundreds of terrified people meekly swallowing poisoned Kool-aid as ordered by their mad leader. My first thought was of Mrs. Temple, who had stopped talking about "rich white kids in cults" when her cousin's daughter suddenly joined the Jim Jones Temple, and a few months later followed him, with her four children, to the settlement in Guyana. At the time, Mrs.

Temple had said, "I don't understand this business of going to the jungle to live like a sharecropper, but I have to give that man credit, he got her off drugs." When I reached the house, I dropped my suitcase, then went next door to sit with her until it became clear that definite news would not come to her cousin for days. After a couple of hours, I went home, sorted through the mail, and found another letter from Harry.

June 7, 1979

Dear Ruth,

I guess you wonder if you're going to hear from me only every four or five years, or when I'm ready with another disaster report. It's not all bad news. The good news is that I did get my B.A. And better news—I have a beautiful daughter who's starting to look like a photo I have of Nonnarina, taken in Turin almost a hundred years ago.

The bad news is that my wife divorced me. Not her fault, mine. Her new husband is a good man, Walter Boyd. An old friend of mine from school, part Crow Indian. I still remember the day we cut school and hitchhiked all the way to Custer Park to see his cousins put up a grave marker for one of his ancestors. Walter made good—got an athletic scholarship to Montana Tech and became a chemical engineer. He teaches a few months a year at Tech and the rest of the year travels as a mining consultant all over the world. I guess that means I'll see my daughter only during the spring, when he comes back here to teach. That's for the best. Butte is no place to raise a child, if you can help it.

It was Walter who kept telling me to get out of literature and try engineering or geology, something that could relate to mining in other countries, where Tech places a lot of its graduates as consultants. (Chile is big again, now that they have a dictator who "disappears" people who bother The Company.) Or chemistry—toxic waste. Congress is getting ready to vote money for cleanup, and Butte will be number one in line for it. That's right, for a hundred years the money was made by poisoning this town. Now the money will come out of cleaning up the mess.

I took a couple of courses, but toxic waste couldn't compete with Keats. Sandy tried to laugh and make the best of it, but what's the best you can make of an unemployable husband with an English major from a tech college? She was right to throw me out. Walter to the rescue again. He knows the equations, but words are something else. He hired me to work on his articles, then his book, then got me some other work. So I'm a technical writer. It's not literature, and it's boring, but it's almost a living, along with some part time work at the Montana Tech Bookstore when I'm short of cash.

I still try to write fiction. I've tried to write stories about Butte. But who wants to read about Butte?—least of all here in Butte. Here the smart ones read technical books so they can get out of Butte, and the others don't read much of anything. Last night I had a great dream. I dreamed I was sitting in your shed writing a poem, a brilliant, beautiful poem. Is my unconscious telling me that in Berkeley I'd be able to write, to breathe? Everything about the atmosphere here is suffocating me. Well, I had my chance at a different kind of air. "No second acts in American life." Who said that?

The address on this envelope is where I am now, a one-room abandoned miner's shack in Walkerville (unincorporated northwest summit of Butte). Walkerville has the distinction of being the most polluted neighborhood of Butte, waste left from about sixty mines sunk here in the old days. I got title to the shack for almost nothing, and I have a view of the Historic Uptown, through a gallows frame not twenty feet away from my window. The rest of my view? To the north, a little higher up, is the Yankee Doodle Tailings Pond—a sink of solid sludge. Farther east is the Horseshoe Bend River. From here it's a thin, curved, greenish stream—you have to get closer before you see the crud in it. Yes, from my one little window (well, no, I have to step outside to get the full view) I can see the biggest toxic waste site in America, number one in line for Superfund cleanup.

I'm a few minutes' walk, between mounds of black slag, to the half-sunk gallows frame where my great-grandparents died. Nonno Francesco is still buried deep in the old Granite Mountain Mine. (Nonnarina is down at the Holy Cross Cemetery.) The worst hardrock mining disaster in history, yet you'd never know it happened here—not a marker, not a stone, nothing. I'm beginning to understand how Walter felt about putting up something for his ancestors who died along with Custer's men. I met a couple of people at the library who are trying to raise money to put something up there—some kind of grave marker, at least. ARCO (new owners of Mine Hill) and the Butte Boosters want to put in new topsoil and finally make something grow up here. But the Granite Memorial group at the library says, "No, let's keep the rusty, dead gravel—the last thing men saw before they went down the shaft."

They're having trouble raising any money for such a "negative" project. Not inspiring, "not in the spirit of Butte," as one old drunk said to me last night. He donated to a fund for—you won't believe this—a statue of the Virgin Mary. (It's not like this guy has seen the inside of a church for forty years.) This statue started out as sincere holy bribery. A man promised the Virgin he'd build a little statue to her, if his wife didn't die during surgery. She didn't. Somehow this statue idea got out of hand—turned into a fund-raising campaign (are you ready for this?) to raise a ninety-foot sheet metal Virgin Mary on top of a ridge above Butte. I was stupid enough to tell that guy in the saloon that I couldn't understand why anyone would want to build an idol to preside over the corpse of this town, instead of a memorial to the reality of—that's as far as I got. The bartender threw me out, probably saved my life.

Even the group at the library told me to just shut up. They're going ahead with their little memorial project, collecting nickels and dimes, which they said they won't get by showing disrespect toward folks who mean well.

Their other project is the Butte Archives. They finally got permission to use an old firehouse on Quartz Street. I volunteered to help carry the piles of stuff from the basement of City Hall. Whatever wasn't junked or burned has been sitting there for *years, rotting. I'll help with sorting and cataloging what we can salvage. Maybe I'll find Nonnarina's name somewhere in that mess of old newspapers and municipal records. Maybe not. Keeps me out of the saloons anyway.*

Not many fires in the Uptown now. Most of the shops have made their move to the mall, leaving mostly boarded up shells, shabby hotels for winos, drug treatment centers, and a few state and city offices hanging on. I heard someone at the library say that with rents so cheap in the Uptown, he could even afford to open a bookstore. The only operating businesses from the old days are (guess what?) the saloons, and some of them say they're part of "historic preservation" too, and should be funded. There's some talk of keeping offices for Superfund scientists and bureaucrats up here—if the money ever comes through.

Of course, there's always the hope that ARCO will bring back some prosperity. Though I don't know why anyone should hope—no other corporation has left anything but poison when they pulled out with the money.

I just read this over, and it sounds pretty sad. I'm really not that bad off—better than I was when I first wrote to you. I'm drinking less and writing more, writing about some things I had tried to drown in the bottle. Maybe you wouldn't mind looking at something?

Harry

Two days later I received a large, slim envelope from Harry, containing a short story and a note asking for my comments. It was the story of his arrest ten years before, the ordeal at Santa Rita—essentially the same story that the defense lawyer had dramatized in court. The difference was that, like many victims of rape and torture, the protagonist of Harry's story felt ashamed, dishonored, subhuman. The first-person narrator "Herb" blamed only himself for his panic, his fear, his uncontrollable shaking and sobbing, and most of all for his thoughts—that he would do anything, say anything, if only the guards would torture someone else, not him. The story ended with "Herb" judging himself not worth the "second chance" he had been given, convinced that his friends and teachers in "Athena" would forever view him with loathing—like the disgust on the face of the guard who pushed him, still stinking of his own vomit, out the gate, and pointed toward the road, where he stood until a car picked him up. The driver was going to Reno. "From Reno to Spokane to Coeur d'Alene, to Poisonville, where drunks and failures like me are as common as widows and saloonkeepers." The only way the story differed from Harry's experience was that "Herb" had not been picked up and driven back to Berkeley.

I treated the story as a work of fiction although I knew he had offered it to me partly as an explanation of his disappearance. I wrote "good!" in the margins as often as I could, marked a couple of awkward transitions. Then I wrote a note saying that the self-loathing of the narrator was especially effective in showing the psychic wounds suffered by a victim, but that a subtle word or phrase here and there were needed to heighten the difference between the protagonist's shame

221

and the reality of his victimhood. (In other words, Harry, you have nothing to be ashamed of, get it?) I suggested he rewrite it, then submit it to some little magazines. Unfortunately, I didn't have any contacts that could help, but I was sure Alice did. He should send her his revised version. She'd be glad to hear from him in any case.

I sent the story and my notes back to him. I heard nothing more, and neither did Alice.

During the early 1980s I heard from Harry now and then, short letters that seemed prompted by some national or international incident. He wrote to me when John Lennon was killed, when Ronald Reagan was elected president, when Reagan was shot, when the Pope was shot. Occasionally he would add a note about another local loss in Butte: another retail business, another mine, the only major airline into Butte.

I saw no need to send Harry bad news from here, but perhaps I should have mentioned, for instance, the first murder in People's Park. Instead I wrote him about our "Writers' Campus Sit-in" for divestment in apartheid South Africa (Jessica Mitford insisted on including me even though I'd written no more than an editor's introduction and a few book reviews). I sent him a photo of my grand-daughter, but I never sent the *Daily Cal* photo of two middle-aged "progressive" city council members grinning in fierce defiance into the camera, middle fingers raised at constituents (including me and my neighbors) who had defeated another of their misbegotten schemes.

In 1982 I spent much of the summer in Chicago with my mother, who was suffering a second or third illness in the decline that began with my father's death. I sent Harry only a picture postcard of a new Calder street sculpture, but he must have intuited how I felt from the few words I scrawled on the back of the card. When I got back to Berkeley, I found in my mailbox another story Harry'd written much earlier, in the voice of a twenty-something alcoholic talking to his dying mother, reciting all the things he wishes he had understood when he was young, regretting lost time he could have been close to her, confessing his own failure to make the most of far better chances than she had. The note he inserted with the story said, "Don't bother to comment. This one was just therapy. If it's any comfort, you won't have the same regrets as the guy in this story."

Then in 1983, came the death of Fred Cody. During the five or six years since the sale of Cody's Books, Pat had thrown herself into women's health issues, starting what has become an international organization. Fred wrote, published, broadcasted—but with less and less of the fire-in-the-eye that had never left him even during the worst crises. He had lost his base, the book-lined forum where he had stood at the center of what so many of us had hoped would be a world-changing drama. Like an embodiment of our hopes, Fred seemed to visibly fade. On the day Pat insisted he see a doctor, he confessed that he'd been coughing up blood for months.

There was a good crowd at Fred's memorial. The mayor spoke, as did other "progressive" community leaders who'd stopped listening to Fred after he helped get them elected. Old moderate politicians, who'd considered him "radical," spoke of him with more respect. A few gray-haired former activists (who no longer spoke to each other) flew in from corporate jobs, unrecognizable in cropped hair and three-piece suits. One told whimsical stories of being busted in front of Cody's Books, as if nostalgically describing a football game. Some Free Speech Movement protesters were better. Now respected teachers, social advocates, a judge, they came to speak of themselves as hot-heads offered a model of purpose and focus by Fred.

It was a middle-aged crowd. In the five or six years since the store was sold, a whole generation of students had swept in and out of Berkeley. Those who'd replaced them knew nothing about the namesake for Cody's Books—some thought the store was named after Buffalo Bill Cody.

The only young person I recognized was the ever-more-handsome Aaron, who'd come along with Jake. When the memorial was over, he stopped outside to greet me.

"Jake tells me you're getting articles published all over the gay press."

Aaron frowned, suddenly looking like a slim, young, intensely furious Jake. "I think my newspaper career is over—certainly in the gay press."

"What's the trouble?"

Aaron shrugged. "I picked the wrong subject."

"Your article on health problems in the Castro? It was very good. The blurb said you're working on a book on the same subject?"

Aaron shook his head. "I got a lot of hate mail. So I wrote another article, with more statistics on this new gay cancer. Nobody would print it. All six gay papers called it anti-gay."

"Did you try the *Chron*?"

He nodded. "Science editor gave me a run-around. Privately admitted to a friend of mine that it would offend gay readers and bore straight readers, who couldn't care less if all gays dropped dead tomorrow."

"So just get back to your book. You're always going to offend some people if you—"

"No thanks! I'm through with writing. It's not worth it. There's no money in it, and if the people you're writing for turn against you for telling the truth —"

"You tell it anyway!" I insisted. "Remember Ernest in *The Way of All Flesh*? He knew he was likely to write something that his best friend wouldn't like, but even if he had to lose that friend, he knew he had to write the—"

Aaron was looking over my shoulder, waving at someone he recognized. Then he drifted off, too polite to tell me to stop preaching and mind my own business.

When I got home, I found a letter from Harry in the mailbox.

June 20, 1983

Dear Ruth,

    Six months ago ARCO "suspended" mining in the Berkeley Pit. Translation: they shut down. By using the word "suspended," they slipped out of the severance pay clause in their contracts with the unions.

    Now we're finding out that the only thing worse than spreading the Pit is shutting it down. And not only because more jobs are gone.

    About noon, Walter (you know, my old friend,

my daughter's step-father—they're here for the spring semester) took me into the Pit to show me what's happening down there. I'd never gotten really close to it before because when it was operating, the guards got ugly if you weren't authorized, and the rock and dust kicked up by the blasting and hauling were even more ugly, and dangerous too. Since it closed, fences and guards keep cars off the road the trucks used, but Walter knew a place where we could walk in.

A few dimensions: the Berkeley Pit is a mile wide, over a mile long, 600 feet deep. A hole that reeks of sulfur from gouged-out walls—terraces—of rusty rock. Terraces about forty feet wide, forty feet apart—a spiral road down the walls of the Pit. 170-ton trucks used to rumble and bounce down that road into the quarter-mile hole—then load up and haul the blasted rocks from the bottom, grinding gears and roaring all the way to the top. Up and down, all day and part of the night. The earth vibrated all through mine hill, all the way up to my shack in Walkerville. Now the Pit is eerie, quiet as the grave, as they say—a mass grave for those promises of "50 years more mining."

Walter and I climbed down the east wall. That's where Meaderville used to be. Walter's done it before, so he could help me find footholds and hand-holds down each forty-foot wall from one terrace-road to another. The sixth drop was really steep, with narrow footholds far apart, and pieces of rock suddenly crumbling under my weight. Tell you the truth, I was glad when Walter decided we better not try to go any deeper. We walked to the edge of that terrace and looked down. The sun was high, so we could see all the way to the bottom. "What do you see?" There was something dark covering the bottom. I just made a guess, "Water?"

"That's right, Harry. Water. Leeching out sulfur from the rock. Presto—sulfuric acid."

And what is that acid doing? Dissolving metals, every kind of metal, some that occur naturally in the rock, some put there—a hundred years worth—to get the ore out. When ARCO shut down the Berkeley Pit, it shut down the pumps that kept it dry. Now ground water is seeping up into the Pit. And Horsehoe Bend River is dumping two or three millions of gallons a day into it. Plus runoff from ordinary rain and snow.

The water's already about sixty feet deep. Rising, Walter estimates, about 200 feet a year. That means in twenty or thirty years it will reach the level of the alluvial soil, permeate it, seep through and poison the aquifer. From there it's on to the streams and rivers and—that's unless an earthquake comes first and cracks the walls of the Pit. In which case, that chemical soup will pour through the cracks and come down in waves over the flats of Butte—where most people live now. I asked Walter what was being done about it. He shrugged. "They say they're working on it." In other words, no one knows what in hell to do.

I was offered a tech-writing job for one of the companies pitching its method of solving The Problem. Like half a dozen other companies, they're after Superfund money. They told me if their proposal is accepted, I'd have a steady job, high pay (compared to what I usually get), benefits. But Walter calls their research proposal pure fantasy, (our tax dollars at work!) and after seeing what's happening in the Pit, I knew I couldn't do it. Compared to working on their science fiction, growing pot in the gold mine was a service to mankind.

So I'm sticking with the free-lance tech-writing, plus a few hours in the college bookstore. And one other hustle: I get a few days work (summer and fall) down the valley, working as a guide for vacationing businessmen from Texas or New York who come to fish the "pristine streams" of the state they're starting to call "the last best place." Needless to say, they do not visit Butte, and I don't tell them what's flowing into those streams from my hometown. They sit around the campfire and make plans to buy a "ranch"—that's what the rich ones are doing now, buying up the state. Walter says I could do worse than becoming a caretaker for one of these huge spreads the owners only visit in the summer. "And you'd have plenty of time to write all winter."

I haven't been writing at all for quite a while. I don't know how many starts I've made on my Butte Novel. How many notes. How much historical research. But there's something missing. Always something missing. Like maybe talent.

But I'm glad you didn't throw away the stuff I wrote in Berkeley. Scraps of family history, if nothing else, something to pass on to my daughter. Jennifer doesn't care about it now (I didn't either when I was ten), but some day she might. She's a smart kid, and in a few years her mother and Walt will send her to college somewhere and I'll see even less of her than I do now. Some day, she'll be curious, and want to ask questions, and I might not be around to answer them, but the stuff I wrote will be. No, don't send any of it here yet. I have to fix some leaks before I can find a corner to store it in. I might ask the folks at the Butte Archives if they plan to store any junk like that.

I think a lot about what I have—don't have—to leave to Jennifer. (I sound like I'm near 80 instead of pushing 40.) All I've got is books. I still love to read, love the smell of books, new books, old books. I guess that's why I like helping at the Butte Archives, that smell of old print. I found my great-grandfather's application for citizenship in a box of city records dated 1915. Nonnarina is mentioned on the papers, getting citizenship through him. But I haven't found her citizenship papers. She used to tell me that she took out her own papers, as soon as women could, sometime in the twenties, I think. She used to say, "I wanted my own citizenship. I have my own papers. Ask me about the 9th Amendment—you don't know? I'll tell you." Some day I'll find her papers too, if they didn't go up in one of the fires.

Harry

P.S. I seem to have fallen off Father Mike's mailing list. Or did he give up the newsletter? I enjoyed reading about the Avenue. Brings back some interesting memories.

I answered Harry, suggesting that he write an article on the Berkeley Pit. Maybe he could sell it to one of the new environmental magazines. I told him I'd ask my daughter, who was starting to do environmental advocacy; she might have some ideas. Carol sent him a list of environmental journals and contact names, but didn't hear from him.

The next time I heard from Harry was three years later, a picture postcard of a white statue standing on top of a mountain pass. It was an aerial photo, distantly showing a featureless, rear view of a white robed figure resembling the tiny plaster Virgins some of my students glued to the dashboards of their cars. Below the mountain-top figure was a blurred landscape of houses and bare spaces, surrounded by scrub-covered hills. On the back of the postcard was the postmark, Butte Feb 18, 1986, and a printed caption:

> Our Lady Of The Rockies
> 90 Feet Tall, 51 Tons Of Steel,
> 8,510 Above Sea Level
> Overlooking Butte And
> The Berkeley Pit.

Below this caption, Harry had scrawled,

> *Hoisted in pieces by army helicopter—nearly crashed. Note our two tourist attractions—(1) our very own Golden Calf worshipped above our genuine poison (2) River Styx. (okay, lake) No comment. No signature. Some Butte Booster postal worker might gather a lynch mob if I write what I think and sign it.*

I showed Jake the postcard photo of *Our Lady*. I expected Jewish outrage at this Catholic symbol hovering

230

over a whole town (whose best writer, he maintained, had been a homosexual Jew). But, as usual, Jake surprised me. "Like the AIDS Quilt."

"What?"

"A community in denial sinking in disaster. Deny the disaster and comfort yourself creatively, with a giant statue, or a giant quilt with embroidered, bejeweled names of the dead. The only difference between Harry's town and this one is we have more intellectuals, and that just means more elegant, intricate forms of denial." In the three years since Aaron's health articles had been rejected, gay men had been dying in large numbers from the new disease that now had a name, an identified virus, and a recognized, long, symptomless incubation period. Jake, of course, was worried sick.

I quoted Jake in the letter I sent Harry in answer to his card. Then I forgot to send it. I was distracted by a crazy neighborhood mess.

Old Mr. Horace had finally died. We expected that some energetic young folks would buy the old wreck, evict the shifting assortment of dubious tenants, and fix the place up. We waited. And waited. But the place only got worse—more people, more noise, more disorder, more filth. Neighbors on Dante Street—one after another—tried to identify and talk to Mr. Horace's official tenant, getting only curses or silence in response. "Can't you give me the name on the rental agreement?" I insisted to a drunk or drugged man draped over my back fence. He shrugged. "Who pays the rent?" The man looked at me and laughed, then threw up.

One night Mrs. Temple counted twenty-eight men,

231

two women, and four children coming and going, half of them sleeping on the ground in the back yard. Gradually, counts by neighbors revealed fewer women, no children—the noise, the fights—obviously the place was too dangerous for women and children. The numbers hovered at around thirty, never the same thirty. Some nights, another thirty or so might wander through before leaving noisily. More garbage was strewn around the back yard, liquor bottles and syringes thrown over the fence into my yard or others on either side of the house.

We called the health department, the police, our district council member, the mayor, whose aide said he would be back from North Korea next week. Mrs. Temple had a friend who worked at the city attorney's office. She looked up the records and found that Old Horace had refinanced the house with Wellington Bank, but had stopped paying on his new mortgage more than a year ago. Carol and Steve told me, "Foreclosure should be pretty cut and dried: the bank notifies heirs, if any, puts the house up for bid." Another neighbor called Wellington Bank and was passed from one person to another. No one would even admit that the bank now owned the house. Finally the bank manager said the foreclosure had been turned over to a loan agency. We called the loan agency. No one there knew anything. They would call us back. They didn't. We wrote letters. No answers. We called the Health Department, which said that for two years all complaints had been forwarded to Wellington Bank. We started the rounds again.

Cars cruised all night, obviously buying and delivering drugs. After many phone calls, we persuaded a police car to drive by every hour, and for a while the street quieted down a little. The day after the police car stopped its drive-by, there were more cars than ever. Screaming sirens regularly announced emergency medics from the fire department to rescue the overdosed.

One day I saw Dan Lyon over the back yard fence, his hair longer than ever, thin, transparent silver streaming in fringes circling a bald crown. "Dan!" I held up a shovel full of syringes, garbage, rags, bottles, even feces. Dan looked, nodded. "Yeah, I'll tell 'em to keep it cleaner." But nothing changed. I continued to complain to anyone I saw, a different man every time (there were no women now). Their responses ranged from sullen indifference to obscenities, threats, and more garbage tossed over the fence. An anonymous note appeared in my mail box. "You call the police again, you better watch your back." I sent the note to the police, along with a letter signed by those few neighbors not afraid to sign—and received a form letter acknowledging our complaint.

Most of my friends outside the neighborhood fell silent when I mentioned the problem, then murmured phrases with terms like "housing crisis," "homelessness," "nimbyism," and "gentrification." This last label referred to the fact that our block now had a few more white people living on it. "You mean what we used to call integration? Remember?" Silence. "Or does gentrification mean when a white owner paints his house?" They looked irritated and changed the subject to the mayor's laudable stance on Nicaragua. I went to a City Council meeting where officials I'd voted for called me a racist. Next time I went along with Mrs. Temple, and half a dozen other black neighbors; no one called them racist, but no one did anything. We got a new mayor, who seemed disposed at least to listen, but we were drowned out by the Dan Lyon crowd, always there when we managed to get our problem on the agenda. Mrs. Temple refused to go to another Council Meeting.

I stopped going after the time Eldridge Cleaver showed up and sat down next to me. In that week's issue of *The Bridge,* Bishop Berkeley's column mentioned "Eldridge Cleaver, born again right-wing agitator, accompanied a long-time Merritt College instructor relentlessly trying to turn the City Council against the Dante Street Homeless Collective."

I saw familiar faces on the street who didn't return my wave or nod. Maybe they just hadn't seen me. If they had—I raged about them to Jake. "It's bad enough that this Bishop Berkeley, whoever he is, should pick on me, but that people who know me should believe this crap, without even asking me—!"

Jake eyed me coolly. "You've been living in this town about twenty years now. But you never noticed the gaps between rhetoric and reality until you fell into one."

One good thing was happening: in an endless series of block meetings—neighbors were getting to know each other better. Most shared the same complaints: break-ins and purse snatchings, mail stolen from mailboxes. After several times finding my mailbox strangely empty except for advertising, I put a lock on it. (Later Harry told me he had written to me twice and received no answer.) When a break-in on Dante Street included a rape as well as robbery, the police officer who attended our meeting agreed that someone passing through 1629 Dante Street was likely the rapist.

"How many complaints have been called in about the house?"

"Forty-two."

"And what have you done about them?"

The officer cleared his throat. "We need an official eviction order from the City. And the City needs an order from the owner. You need to contact these people." One of the neighbors held up the thick file of letters we'd been writing. The officer sighed.

"And what about the dogs? Do we need an official eviction order from the City to get rid of their dogs?" The biggest one, said Mr. Moses, from Dante Street, sat on the front porch of the house during the day, growling, attacking small dogs and mail carriers, and once even Mr. Moses himself. "I was watering my front yard—turned that hose on the dog and just about managed to get in my door!"

We won a small victory on that dog, calling Animal Control to haul the dog away, but our victory was hollow. After that incident, the dogs were kept in the back yard— closer to me—where, day and night, they barked and fought each other. I had to keep Pogo inside the house except when I took him on walks—the growling, barking dogs throwing themselves against our back fence drove him crazy. The foul smell wafting over our back yard fences grew stronger. We all telephoned, wrote letters. Police pinned citations to the front door no one would open.

Mrs. Temple's nephew told her the police couldn't move on the place ("and, believe me, Auntie, we'd love to") without specific legal orders in place—notices, warnings— that the bank kept putting off, as if denying authority, even ownership. Another friend of Mrs. Temple, a woman in real estate, told her the bank had quietly put the house up for auction. "But it'll be a hard sell, even at a bargain foreclosure price," because the new owner would be faced with the problem of evicting all those people. This real estate agent had managed to learn the name of the original tenant, "long gone, she's a lawyer too, old friend of Dan Lyon. She left Berkeley a long time ago, just handed over the key to someone else, who handed it to someone else, and so on—then that Daniel Lyon got into it, and—well—"

The last straw—what a silly expression! there never seemed to be a last straw—was the lead article Angel wrote for *The Bridge* in January 1987. Angel began it as an interview with his old friend, "activist Daniel Lyon," who stated that he had moved into the Dante Street Collective "to support this new approach to housing poor people who reject the humiliating dependency of homeless shelters in church basements." Dan introduced Angel to six of his house mates, and explained that "the new model was a sweat-equity collective that would take over abandoned buildings and work to maintain and improve them."

Angel did not challenge Dan's calling the house an "abandoned" building. Instead he wrote about its inhabitants as if they were modern versions of Thoreau, rejecting the "consumerism, conformity, capitalism" of their hostile "yuppie neighbors." The most critical thing Angel wrote was that the house was "pretty messy," but that Dan had posted a new list of assigned household chores. Then Angel reminisced for a paragraph or so about the chaotic but loving, utopian commune where he'd lived twenty years ago. (I would have thought that Angel wrote the piece while drunk, if I did not know that he was now living with an ex-lesbian Buddhist who monitored his drinking, cooked organic vegetarian food, grew medicinal herbs, and kept an immaculate house on a quiet, lawn-trimmed street in Albany.) The article ended with an overview of Dan Lyon's years of activism and his ringing statement that "the new war is here, the victim is the poor, and I know whose side I'm on!"

236

I was so furious that I marched up to Moe's Books, found Angel shelving books on the third floor, and shook my copy of *The Bridge* at him—sputtering incoherently, I'm sure. Angel was stricken, as he always was when he offended anyone. "I didn't realize you lived right there. Maybe you should talk about it on KPFA."

"I read literature on KPFA, remember?" I sputtered. "I don't do my personal political agenda!"

Angel gulped and invited me to be interviewed on his KPFA talk show, but the first open slot he had was several weeks off. I answered that I hoped the problem would be solved by then, no thanks to him. "I'll put you down anyway," Angel said, "and you can cancel a few days before."

The Bridge printed some letters written by my neighbors, listing the ugly realities of living with the "homeless sweat-equity collective." Mr. Moses wrote that the only time anyone in the "collective sweated was when he couldn't get any drugs." Mrs. Temple's letter concluded that Angel's article showed "what happens when you're so open-minded that your brains fall out!" Of course, these letters attracted counter-letters repeating the usual indictments of anti-poor-yuppie-nimbys. Bishop Berkeley took a sarcastic shot at our "nimby" letters too, and I wondered if maybe Dan Lyon was Bishop Berkeley. No, I'd seen two of his three-page manifestos, enough to know he couldn't put words together into anything but slogans—at most he might be feeding material to the writer.

The weeks passed, but the problem did not, and I ended up going on Angel's radio show to read a list of complaints on a petition signed by neighbors all the way around the block. When I finished, the phone lines all lit up. In those days KPFA did not screen these listener calls, as other radio stations did, and the calls that came were abusive name-calling, some of it by voices I recognized—not only Dan Lyon's, but a couple of old (former?) friends, members of the fraying coalition that had elected some city officials like the ones photographed giving all of us the finger. I kept my answers brief, and when one caller referred to attacks on the "helpless homeless," I answered by reading the anonymous note telling me, "watch your back," then described my most recent find in my backyard, a page from an old Merritt College class schedule, with a cut that looked like a knife stab, outlined in blood-red ink, through the listing of my Women's Studies course.

It didn't help that Eldridge Cleaver showed up the following week on Dante Street, leading half a dozen people carrying signs like Property Owners United, and Impeach the Rent Board. The picketing went on only for a day (reported with gleeful sarcasm in B.B.'s column) because that night Cleaver was arrested for drug possession and burglary. He pled police harassment, and—in what seemed to be compassion for his ineptitude and decrepitude—he was given probation and soon was dozing again, alone, in various coffee houses.

Busy at too many meetings and writing too many irate, futile letters, I hadn't seen Jake for a long time. When I did walk up to Steadman's Used Books, I found him looking especially glum.

"I sold the business."

"And you're not celebrating?" Neither was I. I went to Telegraph Avenue less and less, but I couldn't help wishing that Jake would always be there, glum but surviving.

"The buyer is Harry Lynch." I must have looked stupefied. "Yeah, our Harry Lynch. Your student? Worked here a little? Remember? Twenty years ago?"

I calculated. "Eighteen years ago. I don't understand.

It can't be—I haven't even heard from him for—"

"Cash offer for the stock, assume the lease on the building. I grabbed it. It was the only nibble from anyone who could swing it—anyone who has the money takes one look at the Avenue and puts it into a bookstore somewhere else. I didn't realize—Enrico Carlo Cardone Lynch? At first I didn't make the connection. When I did, I told my agent I wanted to warn Harry before the deal went through, make sure he knew what he was getting into. The agent had a fit, threatened to sue me if I messed up a deal that he put so much time into, 'trying to find somebody on whom to hang this albatross'." Jake shook his head. "Every damned real estate agent in Berkeley majored in literature. So I didn't argue with him, but I did write to Harry anyway."

"In Montana?"

"I would have called him, but he doesn't have a phone. Got his address from Mike Ruga. He's been sending him that fairy tale newsletter of his? I wrote Harry that maybe he should just come out and take a look, talk to some people before making a final decision. I told him, sure, someone could make a go of this place, near the university, same block as Moe's and Cody's and Shakespeare. There's money—a sort of a living anyhow—to be made here. But there's a lot of grief too, things have changed, it would have to be someone with plenty of savvy, with some reserves, preferably a couple, each working a shift, not meeting a payroll."

"I don't understand where Harry got the money. The last time I heard from him he was broke. You say he paid cash for the stock?"

Jake rummaged in a box on a shelf behind the counter. "Here's the letter he wrote back to me. He still calls Ruga 'Father Mike' as if the Church didn't boot him out for having that woman and his three children—in Orinda? Then she booted him out too. You know she's another one who sells real estate?"

I nodded. I had read the soap opera of the ongoing Mike/Anne battles, a running joke in the Bishop Berkeley column. For a change, the B.B. account checked out with what I'd heard from other sources, to whom Anne Prester spoke freely and often, cursing Mike Ruga, for reasons that were not clear—and didn't interest me.

Harry's letter was dated only three weeks before. He had inherited some money around the same time that Mike Ruga's newsletter mentioned in his chatty "On the Avenue" column, that Jake Steadman was contemplating retirement. Harry had written back to Mike, who'd referred him to Anne, who'd called Jake's agent. "Don't worry, Jake," Harry had written. "You don't have to tell me that Berkeley can get pretty wild. But if I think too much, I might not do it, and then I'd probably start drinking again, and spend all the money anyway." Harry's letter ended by asking if Jake would work in the store part time for a while, to ease the transition.

"Are you going to stay and work with Harry?"

"I don't want to stay in this place five minutes longer than I have to!" Jake stuck the dead stump of a cigar into his mouth. "But the poor bastard will need me, I guess."

When I got home I found my own letter from Harry. If I'd been made uneasy by what Jake told me, I was appalled by the news Harry had written me.

February 4, 1987

Dear Ruth,

By the time you get this letter, I'll be driving

my old VW van westward, the back packed with a couple thousand books I've accumulated. I'm sure Jake has already told you that I'm taking over his bookstore.

I once told you that Berkeley had given me a second chance, and I'd failed. Now I've been given a third chance by—of all people—my mother's old boyfriend Stiletto, whose real name (I never knew before) was Ettore Italo Cappodonico. That's the name on the papers from the lawyers handling his estate. The old guy moved to New York after my mother died, and that was the last I heard of him. I almost felt friendly toward him by the time she died—he got her the best of care, and at her funeral, the way that old tough guy cried was something I never expected to see. I thought he was long dead by now—he was at least 25 years older than my mother. But it seems he died just two years ago, and left me some money "in memory of Maria and La Donna Rina." A fraction of his estate, but a lot of money for me. Probate took over a year. I put some of it into a trust fund for my daughter, to get her through college.

What about the rest of it? No question: I could stop working and write. So I started another novel. And another. I took a class. I tried short stories. I had this idea I'd produce something really impressive, publish it some place like the New Yorker—*and then I'd tell you I was writing again. Well, I never sent anything to the* New Yorker—*or anywhere else. As soon as that dream became possible, it evaporated. I'm forty-three. If I were a writer (aside from the tech stuff) I'd be writing somehow, the way real writers do, even when they're working longer hours than I do.*

They may mess up the rest of their lives—and other people's lives too—but one way or another, they write. Loving books doesn't mean you can write them. Or should. Or should want to.

Loving books, that's what I'm good at. Being around books, and around people who care for books. Oh, I know there's more to it than customers coming in and talking about the classics. I've done it—hauling boxes, shelving, paper work, talking to those paranoids Orwell said gravitate toward used book stores. I looked around here, thought about all those empty store fronts and cheap rent. But someone beat me to it. There's a new (three-year-old) bookstore just barely getting by. No point in starting another one and putting us both out of business.

When I gave up that idea, I started waking up in the middle of the night telling myself, get used to it, you're going to spend the rest of your life with that white specter looking down on you from the mountain—they light up Our Lady *at night now—while you watch the acid water rising in The Pit.*

Then a couple of things happened. The first was a flock of migrating snow geese that made the mistake of landing on that lake. I went to see them. Hundreds of floating white bundles of feathers, dead the minute they hit that chemical soup. For a while, there was more traffic driving up this hill than we've had for years—people driving up to the Pit to look at them. A quiet crowd. They don't cheer the way they used to when they drove up to see the old Uptown buildings in flames. As I stood looking at them, I got this terrible taste in my mouth, this burning all down my throat, to my gut, like I was one of those dead birds.

The second thing was the mail that came the very next day—Father Mike's newsletter with one line about Jake retiring. I think that settled it. I thought—I don't have to stay here and watch the Pit fill up with poison and dead bodies and wonder what happens next. I had to say it aloud to myself: I don't have to stay in Butte. A third chance. Stiletto, the old crook, has given me a third chance. I can go back to the only work I ever loved in the only town I ever loved. I called Anne Prester (you know, Father Mike's girlfriend) and she gave me the name of Jake's agent. I didn't want to write to anyone else until I was sure I could swing it—just the stock and assume the lease. I can do that.

When it looked like the deal was going through, I was going to call you and ask if you knew of a place for me to live. But then I heard from Anne Prester again. She had a foreclosure, less than half the price the cheapest house in Berkeley goes for now, and guess where! On Dante, near you. She said I'd have to act fast because some others were interested, and it sounded like an auction coming up. If I could just come up with a down payment; she had a friend at the bank who would arrange for me to take over the mortgage. Eviction is under way; Anne says the place should be empty by the time I get there. If not, she said, I could always rent a room with Lisa Lyon, still in her same little old house.

I've been trying to sell my Walkerville shack, to give me a little more cash, but you can't sell anything on Mine Hill, can't even get an agent to handle it. But I can't wait any longer. We're between snow storms, and the sun is out, but that won't last. I'm on my way.

243

I'll call you from the store or from Lisa's house.
     Love,

                              Harry

Now I understood the cryptic item I had read in Bishop Berkeley's column the day before. "What Orinda real estate agent has pulled off a colossal practical joke on an old friend of her hated holy ex? Is her revenge complete? Stay tuned."

The next day I read from Zola's *Germinal* on KPFA, then met Marsha for lunch, and told her about Harry's impending return. "The tone of his letter—it made me think of a modern-day Rip Van Winkle, coming back to Berkeley after almost twenty years, thinking everything was just the same."

"Well," Marsha said, rather sharply, "he hasn't been on Mars. I assume they get newspapers and TV in Montana." Marsha ordered a glass of wine, which she never did at lunch. I guessed that one of her children was in trouble again, but when I asked, she shook her head.

"Something's bothering you. What is it?"

"Ivan's on the rampage again. He finally read that piece in *Scheherazade*. He said everyone knew I wrote it, and that I'd made a fool of him, wrecked his career."

"How so?"

"He was passed over to head the department. He's bitter. So he blames me."

"Could your story really have anything to do with it—with his not getting the position?"

"Of course not! Campus politics are so—but it's easier to blame me. Anything I do that isn't directly focused on advancing or at least protecting *his* career must be destroying it. Thank God he's off at a conference in Phoenix. Peace and quiet for a few days. Maybe I can even start a poem before he gets back."

That night about eight o'clock, there was a knock at my front door. It was Mrs. Temple, wearing her warm coat. "Marsha's daughter just called. It's her father."

"Isn't he in Phoenix?"

She nodded. "He dropped dead. Right on the stage, reading a paper. Heart, I guess. They're not sure yet." I was pulling on my coat. "My car's out." I followed her to her car, and she drove up the hill.

Marsha seemed quite composed, offered us coffee, then sat silently while her daughter made phone calls. As we sat on either side of her, Marsha reached out and put her hand on Mrs. Temple's hand, leaving it limp in Mrs. Temple's firm grasp.

I got up several times to answer the door, let in a couple of neighbors, Marsha's son (the one who'd refused to go to college and had become quite a good plumber), Marsha's younger sister. Marsha greeted each one with a polite smile, stiffly endured their embraces, then fell into her numb silence again.

About midnight Mrs. Temple took Marsha upstairs and got her to bed. "She wants me to stay."

Marsha's son drove me home, speaking only once on the way. "My father really liked you."

Two weeks later, Ivan Franklin was given a splendid memorial at the university, where the colleague who had led the move to block Ivan's appointment praised his "unparalleled accomplishments." Later, at Marsha's home, old friends talked about sharing adventures in Democratic politics, or in the PTA, or during one crisis or another at her church (which Ivan had never attended). All of Marsha's friends ended their remarks with a tribute to the long, close, "ideal marriage" of Ivan and Marsha. The polite, wan smile on Marsha's face never changed. Totally opaque, it was unreadable.

During the next few days I glanced over the backyard fence, saw another new man with Dan Lyon, then another and another, but none of them was Harry. I could hear sawing, hammering. Under the direction of Dan Lyon, men were building something in the back yard.

When Harry telephoned, I knew his voice at once. "I would have called sooner, but I've been at it day and night, trying to sort through—well, you know what the place is like. Jake has been a big help. He stopped me from throwing out a couple of valuable old books. That part is almost done. I finished painting the walls. Almost finished redoing Jake's old counter. Coffee machine comes in tomorrow. How are you?"

"Fine. I'm glad to hear from you, Harry." I didn't know what else to say. I certainly wasn't going to ask any of the questions whirling in my head.

"Actually I called to ask a favor."

"Sure, if I can do it."

"I'm having a big re-opening party after we get cleaned up. About two weeks from now? March 15." He laughed. "The Ides of March, oh well. I wanted to have some local writers do short readings, say twenty minutes, all day long. Alice Allen has already agreed to come. Lisa says you know Jessica Mitford?"

"Right, I'll call Decca."

"Great! Oh, and tell her to read something autobiographical."

"Maybe from her first book, about her crazy family?"

"Perfect. I have to get back to work. If you have time, drop by and see how the place is shaping up."

"I will."

Two weeks later *The Bridge* carried an item in Bishop Berkeley's column, noting the "transformation of Steadman's Used Books into the haven of the solipsistic, in tune with our times." As usual—except when Bishop Berkeley was in full attack—it was hard to tell from the tone of amused superiority whether the writer was praising or damning the "transformation." I concluded that the item was favorable, calculated to create curiosity and bring customers.

I walked up to Telegraph Avenue. The plum trees on the street were already dropping their February blooms, and the sidewalks were covered in purple-pink flecks. The air was fresh, the little flatland cottages sitting in their untidy green flood of plants, with unpruned trees to duck under, root-broken sidewalks to trip over, spring growth overflowing all borders, except for the occasional austere and symmetrical Japanese garden. Not for the first time, I thought of how lucky I was to live in a town where I could walk everywhere—through year-round greenery, at that.

I was in a good mood by the time I reached Telegraph. Even an aggressive young beggar in front of Cody's Books didn't faze me. I gave him only my guiltless smile (I paid monthly conscience money into the project that had taken over and expanded Father Mike's Kitchen). As I crossed Telegraph, I saw that Jake's old sign had been taken down. In the window of what used to be Steadman's Used Books, a large sheet of white paper had been taped. At the curb, I could just read the hand-lettering on it:

> *Grand Opening March 15*
> *GET A LIFE*
> *Biography, Autobiography, Letters*
> *New And Used*

In smaller letters below was list of local authors who would give readings during the all-day opening festivities. The alphabetical list started with Alice Allen and ended with Al Young, with Jessica Mitford at dead center.

I stepped around a saw-horse barrier, over drop cloths, then through the partially opened doorway. Lisa was there, standing at a row of new shelves, pinning a label on one. "Ruth! Hi! What do you think of my sign? I couldn't get Bob Hass or Ishmael, they're going to be traveling. Luckily I scheduled Alice and Decca hours apart. I didn't realize—Decca's made Alice's enemies list after all these years—getting to be a long list! I hope we don't run head-on into any other feuds. And I still haven't got a Native American. You know one?"

"Ask Malcolm Margolin; he'd know."

"Oh, right, of course!" Lisa tossed back her thick black—just a bit too black—hair. How old was she now? Surely my age, mid-fifties, perhaps older. But from across the room, she looked thirty, still thin and slight; still dressed in odd pieces from some thrift shop, assembled with

248

her flawless, lawless style; still moving in quick, impulsive jerks. Only up close did you see the web of wrinkles around her eyes—still without glasses as she squinted at the title of a book she held almost to her nose.

Jake's store had been cleared out and painted white. New shelves lined the walls. Free-standing shelves stood in long lines through the center of the building, from front to back. They were about half filled. Boxes of books covered the floors of the aisles between. The broad counter near the window, where Jake had sat reading or playing chess, had been rebuilt as a coffee counter. "No espresso yet," said Lisa. "Harry can't afford to hire someone to work the machine. Just help-yourself coffee, tea, and cookies—honor system, coins in the box."

"Jake would never let anyone even carry a cup of coffee in," I said, "for fear of spilling it on some rare book."

Lisa laughed. "All the newer bookstores have coffee bars now. Good money-makers. Encourages people to hang out." The place looked so much bigger that I wondered if Harry had knocked out a wall somewhere. "No, it's just the way Jake piled stuff up all over, you felt walled in. Harry moved some shelves, got rid of a lot of junk. Made Jake stay away after he'd identified a few rare books. He couldn't stand to see the rest hauled away."

"Where to?"

"Most to the dump. Angel's doing it. He's not charging Harry for the hauling because he gets to keep whatever he can get selling a few things to Moe's or Shakespeare."

"Are you working for Harry?"

"He pays me for this." She nodded toward the shelves. "Shelving and shit work. But the authors' reading—I did that volunteer. And I want to set up a regular series of workshops. I'm going to do a poetry translation workshop.

249

It would be wonderful if you'd do—whatever—some kind of writing workshop. Or a reading group? You decide what you want to charge. Harry won't take any of it—he just wants to bring people in. Alice plans to do her next birthday party here, you know, the benefit for UNESCO."

Lisa led me to the rear of the store, where a large space had been cleared. "I got someone to donate this old couch, some chairs. I need a couple of tables. Got any old tables?" This space would be for browsing, reading, talking, and some of the workshops. "Harry says he wants to have something going on here every night. We need folding chairs. I still haven't found a good price on folding chairs."

At that moment Harry came through a narrow door from the closet-sized office and bathroom in the back corner. He still moved in the old loose-limbed, awkward way. His blonde hair had thinned, he wore glasses, and was not quite so lanky. His face was still smooth, but deep lines had creased the corners of his mouth, as though the clenched-jaw tension of his youth had settled into a brooding, defensive disappointment. He saw me, broke into a huge smile, and he was suddenly the young Harry again, still tense but hopeful. He rushed to hug me briefly, then dropped his arms awkwardly. "It's great to see you. What do you think?"

Harry walked me around and between the shelves, pointing to each one and telling what it would contain. "Biography means anything from new bios, here, to used ones, here, this shelf for self-published memoirs, letters here. The new celebrity biographies should help pay the bills, while some unknown bio of a farmer can sit on the shelf until the right buyer comes along. Someone came in yesterday asking if I'd stock unbound letters and unpublished memoirs in manuscript. I don't know. This isn't a library, but maybe we could have readings of unpublished things?"

He picked up one old faded book after another, the kinds of books that always made me feel a bit sad, wondering what dead, forgotten authors had poured their lives into them. Harry laughed. "I could fill up a whole shelf with self-published memoirs by pre-1900 midwives in places like Turkey or Alaska."

"Lisa tells me you're planning to have readings, workshops, classes."

"The only way to get people out of those new big chain stores. And I don't want to compete with general used bookstores like Moe's and Shakespeare & Company. I'll be featuring stuff they wouldn't bother to stock—don't even have room for—and they don't want to bother with readings. And I'm not competing with Cody's for the new book trade. The best-known authors will still prefer to read at Cody's, but there are plenty of others that can't even get on the Cody's series. I think I can get all kinds of people into the store, writing about their families, their little adventures. Historians from the university too. I just had a windfall—a sale to the Bancroft Library, an old California memoir no one ever heard of. Even Jake just forgot it, at the bottom of one of those piles of books he hadn't disturbed for twenty years." As Harry talked, he turned an occasional uncertain, inquiring look at me, as if hoping for approval, and the anxiety lines around his mouth would appear. "Oh, forgot to show you!" He reached into his pocket and pulled out his wallet, opening it to the color photo of a teenage girl, fair like him, with his blond, straight hair, worn long with a little tuck behind one ear and a carefully twisted strand over one eye. "Jennifer!"

"Your daughter. How old is she?"

"Fourteen. Beautiful, huh? See, right next to her, this is Nonnarina. Check out the resemblance." It was the

251

first time I'd seen a photo of the great-grandmother he'd written about, a faded, sepia print from a century before. Harry's daughter did resemble her, except for the severely drawn-back hair and the determined mouth of the young Onorina. Whatever teenage insecurities Jennifer faced, they were nothing like the hardships the eyes in that century-old print had seen at her age.

I handed the wallet back to Harry and followed him to the front of the store, where he stood looking out the window onto Telegraph Avenue. We both watched a sullen girl quarreling with a much older man—his clothes, hair, his backpack, and his anger as ugly as hers and more threatening. As they weaved past the window, Harry must have seen my expression. He groaned, "Not you too, please. Jake gave me the whole doom and gloom thing—business down, crime up." Harry laughed. "But the bookstores haven't gone out of business. Because the university isn't going out of business. The students will be back every fall. They buy books. The professors too. Cody's is still the best new-book store in the Bay Area. Maybe a store like Get A Life will even bring people like you back to the Avenue for more than just the occasional author reading at Cody's."

I wanted Harry to be right. I even stayed and shelved books with Lisa for a couple of hours. Then Harry took me to the Med for a coffee break. Lisa smiled and waved us out. She'd watch the store. We threaded our way among the street people sitting at the tables that had been put outside the Med when no-smoking laws were passed.

Inside, the Med was almost empty, as usual. Someone had added a few heavy, ugly chairs with high backs covered in dingy red plush. Three old men sat alone at separate tables, each of them vaguely familiar, someone I'd seen there years ago. "Isn't that Bill Jackson?" asked Harry. I looked more closely, then shook my head. We got our coffee and sat down. I began to feel like one of the ghosts I sensed or imagined all around at the empty tables. Harry read my expression and smiled broadly.

"Dead, huh. People are just going to have to go next door to Get a Life, for their coffee. I'll manage to get an espresso machine soon." Harry laughed. "You're not going to discourage me."

"No, Harry, I'm not. But there's something else, another problem I have to tell you—about that house you bought."

He rolled his eyes, then nodded. "You don't have to tell me. Anne Prester's revenge. I guess any friend of Father Mike is an enemy of hers. Jake showed me the item in *The Bridge.* A gossip columnist called "Bishop Berkeley"—only in Berkeley! Do you think maybe Anne Prester writes that column? It has to be someone who knows a lot about Berkeley. Or do people just send in gossip for revenge? Why does Anne suddenly hate Father Mike so much?"

"Harry, the important question is what are you going to do about the house?"

"Go through the eviction procedure—owner occupancy, the law's on my side, cut and dried. I know, I know, in Berkeley that could mean a couple of months, maybe three or four. Lisa says I can stay. I don't think you have any idea what a little house like yours costs in Berkeley now. Even if they can delay me for six months, I'll be way ahead on my investment. Did you know Dan Lyon is living there?"

I nodded.

"I haven't had a chance to talk to him yet, but I'm sure we can work something out. Now. Would you consider doing a workshop on writing family history?"

"If you'll help me kick it off."

"You mean read something? Me?" He shook his head.

"Just your poem? 'The Berkeley Pit.' I still have a copy of it in my garage with your other papers." Harry was still shaking his head. "People will love it, if only for the title, and you could talk about the historical connections between Berkeley and Butte."

"You decide how much you want to charge."

"This one's on me, Harry, ten sessions, just for the fun of it. If you'll read your poem to start it off."

"Okay, it's a deal." Harry clinked his cup against mine. The sound echoed in the nearly empty room.

The grand opening of Get A Life took place two weeks later. The books weren't all shelved yet, but no one minded stepping around the boxes. The refinishing of the old counter was only half done, showing the contrast between the layers of muddy paint we were used to, and the wood revealed by Harry's patient sanding. Someone was always lifting the protective cover under the food and drinks to show the fine walnut grain that had been hidden for years. The readings began at noon, and would go on every half hour until midnight. Most writers rushed in to read and then left, but Alice Allen was there long before I was, vowing to stay to the end. I hadn't seen her for quite a while, not since her 80th birthday benefit. She was as elegant as ever, perhaps thinner if that were possible, and in great good humor. Her eyes turned misty every time she looked at Harry. "He was nearly destroyed at Santa Rita," she said. "We finally talked about it, while he was squatting on the floor, sanding that old counter. That's what Get A Life is. Against all odds, that's what Harry has done. What a title for a story."

"You going to write it?"

"Oh, I don't write fiction anymore. Just letters." Yes, Alice's letters of denunciation were all over the place, addressed not only to former friends who, as Lisa put it, had made her enemies list. They were more general denunciations, scattered like blasts of buckshot, always printed because of her famous name. Unfortunately, like buckshot, they were not always on target. She had written one of them in support of the Homeless Collective on Dante Street. But at least she had not joined the small group of my ex-friends at the party who pretended not to see me. Or maybe Alice had forgotten I was one of those nimby neighbors she had denounced. Suddenly, she broke into a delighted smile, and I realized she was looking over my shoulder. I glanced around and saw that Mike Ruga was standing behind me.

Father Mike—his thick, wavy hair now white—was more handsome than he had been twenty years ago, and thinner, his smile benevolently spiritual. He had been standing near the front door since noon, a small can in one hand. I wasn't sure what he was collecting donations for this time. He had started many programs for street people over the years, but all of them had been taken out of his hands either by funded professionals or by church volunteers from all over town. More than one of them had told me, "He's crazy. He's full of good ideas, but he turns them into chaos. No one will let him do anything in their churches anymore. The Catholics kicked him out, told him to go and marry the mother of his children. But now she won't have him either." The newsletter that had brought Harry back to Berkeley was gone too. His funders had backed off, and the Quakers had begun putting out a monthly written by street people.

Mike always wore his clerical collar now, and I had seen him in the midst of a prayer circle one day at People's

Park—a half dozen men standing with him while others stood drinking from paper-swathed bottles and quarreling over rags in the free box. He had led another prayer vigil in front of the Dante Street house on the day Animal Control took the dogs away. And he was always insisting on getting arrested with people pulled out of illegal camp sites in the park. Embarrassed policemen would go through a casual arrest, admonishing him and sending him away. I wasn't sure if he was a candidate for the madhouse or for sainthood. Alice put a twenty dollar bill into his can. I suspected his donation can might be feeding him as well as street people, so I put in a five.

"God love ya," said Mike. "Isn't it wonderful, Harry coming back and taking over Jake's store? And buying a house near you? He's going to move into the collective, like old times."

"Did Harry tell you that?"

Mike ignored my question. "We're a real community here in Berkeley. We hate to lose anyone. It's a blessing, Harry's return." He moved back to the doorway, to catch incomers with his collection can.

"I wouldn't mind losing a few like him," growled a voice behind me, Jake, of course, leaning against his old, half-renewed counter. Jake was in his seventies now, and every time I saw him I was newly surprised to see him looking stooped and tired and—well, old. "You remember Aaron."

Aaron wore a gleaming white tank-top that showed his tanned muscles. The shirt was tucked neatly into his pants over his enviably flat belly. (I reminded myself again that I really ought to start going to the gym again.) He was in his mid-thirties now, but his age showed only in lines around his eyes, and their expression—suddenly bleak.

"You're still living in San Francisco?"

"Looking for a place over here," he said quietly. "It's just too depressing there. All I do is go to funerals."

"I hope—" During those years, as AIDS deaths reached their height, we were all attending too many funerals. "I hope you're—okay."

"I tested negative so far. I was lucky. For a long time, I was with a man who'd never gotten into the bath scene. Since we broke up—" His voice trailed off uneasily.

"And what are you doing now?"

"Oh—" A wry smile, almost sheepish. "I started writing again. Finished a book."

"That's wonderful!" I laughed. "So you couldn't stop even if you wanted to."

"At least I think it's done. I'm not sure what to do with it. A memoir. Growing up gay."

"Sounds like something that would sell."

Aaron shook his head. "It's not your standard How-I-Survived-Being-Disowned-And-Found-True-Love." Aaron laughed. "I tell my father he deprived me of material by not giving me a hard time. I don't know where to send it."

I wrote down the name of my agent, warning him, "She does mostly textbooks, anthologies. But she might be able to give you the name of another agent who can help you."

I kept moving toward the door, stopping every few steps to talk to someone I hadn't seen on the Avenue for a long time. I stopped to talk to Marsha before she edged out the door, then to Pat Cody, who was noncommittal about Harry's effort, which meant she was not optimistic.

People kept coming and going. A few of them even bought a book off the shelf or out of a box, handing money to Lisa, who made change from her pocket because "the new cash register hasn't come yet." I thought I recognized one man from the university, Professor Lyford, the "Joe" I'd seen, but not met, back in 1968, at that first party at Marsha's house. His *Berkeley Archipelago* had been published about five years before. I introduced myself and told him I'd found his view of Berkeley politics interesting and smart. He sighed and shook his head. "It sank like a stone. Except for the few who sent me hate mail, calling me a right-wing extremist." He looked around squinting through his glasses. "I seem to be the only person here from my little island of Academia."

"Marsha Franklin just left."

He nodded and moved away, standing in stoop-shouldered but alert silence behind one group or another, listening for a minute, then moving on till he reached the door and was gone.

Street people had been drifting in from the beginning, at first one or two, then a steady stream, in and out. By eight o'clock all the wine had drifted out with them; in one instance, jug and all had disappeared as soon as Harry put it out. I guess no one had told him that Cody's Books no longer put out a jug of wine at readings. Jake stopped Harry from going out to get more. "They know about it now, all over the Avenue and the park. We won't miss it—or them. They'll disappear now the wine is gone."

Just before I left, there was one more arrival I almost missed. Tony Russo had once recruited me to leaflet with him against the Vietnam War outside the oil refinery where he worked. (He didn't mention that he used women as shields between him and guards with clubs. Perhaps I should have been flattered by having "chicks up front" applied to me, a pretty old chick even then.) Tony was one of the people who hadn't spoken to me since Angel's article on the "Homeless Collective" appeared. He strode across the room looking fiercely indignant. I braced myself. "Is that who I think it is? There, sitting in the corner!"

I didn't have to look before I nodded. Yes, it was Eldridge Cleaver against the wall, his straight chair tipped back. He sipped what looked like a glass of water as his narrowed eyes traveled around the room (no dark glasses now; I guess his night vision had dimmed with age). His growing paunch protruded through his open black leather jacket, and his gray hair was sparse. He sat alone—within a magic circle of silence. Nearly everyone going and coming in this crowd knew him, had once defended him, cheered him. He sneered as they looked, made their eyes blank, then walked past as if he were invisible.

"He's got his hand on a gun, there, look, on the table!"

"No, Tony," I said. "It's a tape recorder. He has it with him all the time."

"So now he works for the FBI!"

I laughed. "Somehow, Tony, I doubt that."

"Somebody ought to throw the bum out." Tony scowled at me, waiting for a response. Then, as if remembering that he wasn't speaking to me, he turned away.

On my way out, I passed Dan Lyon coming in— pretending not to see me as he brushed past. That didn't matter. What mattered was that he had come, that he and Harry might have renewed their friendship, that he might be ready to turn the Dante Street house over to Harry.

I had a June deadline on an anthology of plays by women, and I hardly left home except to teach my classes or, on weekends, to spend a day in San Francisco with Judith, who was nearly ten, that precious age before the storm of puberty. I met my deadline, finished the term at Merritt, then took off for my fifth summer in Chicago with my mother. Every summer, I begged her to move to Berkeley, but every summer, her decreasing powers still included a stubborn—or brave—refusal to leave her home. This time Judith went with me for two weeks, saying solemnly that this might be her last chance to see her namesake great-grandmother alive. Judith's presence cheered us both up as I dealt with the latest problems of my mother's health and her house.

A week after Judith flew home, my mother suffered her second stroke. I spent the rest of the summer at the hospital and the nursing home I found when it became clear even to my mother that she could never live in her own house again. I stopped arguing with her about finding a place close to me when she discovered an old high school friend in the nursing home. "Just let me share a room with her, not a stranger." By then it was late August, too late to make definitive decisions about her house. I rented it for a year, as is, to a visiting professor from Nigeria. Next summer I could decide what to do about it.

Back at home, the first thing I noticed was the view from my bedroom window. There were now half a dozen wooden and scrap metal shanties in the back yard beyond my fence, housing a dozen? two dozen? men. They sounded like even more when their noise woke me at night. Mrs. Temple sighed, "I been calling the police all month. They come, they go, and those men keep coming and going." I called the city code enforcement office. They promised to send someone.

I was far from rested and ready to start teaching, but I managed to settle into my classes, which were becoming less and less "remedial." All the colleges charged fees now, even Merritt, and the fees at the university were so high that many well-prepared students chose to take their lower division work at a community college. They were easier to teach, but left me with haunting questions, like, what was happening to the needy, confused people who used to fill my classroom? Weren't they the students I was hired to help?

As soon as I had some breathing space, I took a walk, and, like a migratory bird stuck in old flight paths, headed toward Telegraph Avenue. A new wooden sign urged, Get A Life, over the door of Harry's store. I went in and found him behind the counter pricing books. His stock seemed to be getting ahead of sales. Stacks of books covered the floor, as they had when Jake owned the store. And I began to notice that while he talked to me, Harry's eyes darted nervously around the store, following the few customers who came in.

"Some losses," he muttered. "Not even sure how much. Jake said I put the register at the wrong end of the counter, too far from the door. I shifted it, but the quick ones can still—someone even got into the glass cabinet where I keep the valuable books. I don't know how. The lock was okay, but a book went missing. Lisa put a new lock on."

"Cody's Books has one of those electronic things at the door."

Harry sighed. "I'd have to put a strip in all the books. Besides the time involved, there's the money."

"Are you all alone here?"

He looked at his watch. "Lisa should be here in about half an hour. She's been great, spends a lot of her own time here. I can't expect her to go on this way, but I can't pay her any more than I do. Did you see the list of events? That's

261

mostly her doing."

I nodded. "Good turnout?"

"Fair."

I chattered about books, teaching, my mother, anything at all, until I finally mentioned the increased population in the shanties over my back fence.

Harry nodded. "I got this today," and showed me a notice that he, as owner of the house at 1629 Dante Street, was in violation of several building code laws and must remove "illegal construction." All I had accomplished by calling Code Enforcement was to bring on another order that Harry was powerless to obey.

"But I talked to Dan, and there's good news. The city is going to give the Collective another house, down on 13th Street. Sometime this fall. They're working out the permits and getting approval for the housing grant. Another couple of months, maybe three, or—" Harry's voice trailed off as his eyes followed another man wandering among the shelves. "Luckily I can stay at Lisa's as long as I want, but paying rent and my mortgage for the house and the lease here—"

I hadn't the heart to ask if he could really imagine that any city, even Berkeley, would turn over any house, anywhere, to the shifting crowd of transients on Dante Street.

In October, I started an eight-week workshop in family history at Get A Life. Twenty-three people (some my former students, now at the university, or now teachers themselves) showed up the first night. Harry started it off with his twenty-year-old poem. The others were fascinated. Their questions about "The Berkeley Pit," and all the more recent history and politics of the now toxic menace went on for so long that we had time for only one more short reading—an old man describing his beloved sister's death from diphtheria in the days before inoculation, when so many children died. After answering questions, he said, "I never knew that a family loss was part of 'history.'" I could not do a better summing up of the value of the workshop. "Next Tuesday again; bring a friend." Harry happily sold a couple of books, and then it was closing time.

Marsha came to the next meeting, bringing with her some university faculty wives and widows like herself. I hadn't seen any of her writing since Ivan died; at lunch we talked mostly about her attempts to get her poems published. She had brought some poems to read.

I expected some of the incisive, even wicked satire she'd brought to my class or the passion of her furious poem about the tear-gassing on the campus. Instead Marsha read three poems about her loss of a husband I couldn't recognize as Ivan. Nor did I recognize the blandly harmonious marriage she mourned. The women who came with her applauded enthusiastically, tears in their eyes. Others in the workshop were silent, in respect for the grieving widow. I gently pointed out only one of the string of flabby clichés she'd written. Marsha listened to my suggestions, her sad smile fixed like armor. Then she announced that the three poems would be in a collection to be published by a new small press.

The next morning she telephoned to say she might not be coming again, "—but not because you didn't like my poems."

"I didn't say—"

"I just don't like to go there after dark."

"Telegraph? I think it's safe, plenty of people on the street."

"It's when I turn off Telegraph. I keep looking over my shoulder. I stay away from doorways or bushes, keep my car keys ready, lock all the car doors as soon as I get in."

"So do I," I laughed. "Modern urban life." But then I thought, what if I insisted she'd be safe and one of those transients slouching against the store windows after dark was watching for an older woman to follow and rob? Most of them were harmless, but it only took one.

Aaron appeared at my next workshop and read the first few pages from the manuscript of his memoir—a child-hood scene, sitting cross-legged on top of the old counter among piles of dusty old books, Jake teaching him to play chess. Jake had come, and sat there listening, squirming, looking down at the floor in the futile hope that no one would notice his tears of pride. His pride was justified; Aaron was good, very good. At the end of the reading, Aaron announced that his agent (not the one I'd sent him to) had found a publisher. The book should come out in the winter of 1988-89.

Marsha had come to that session, without her friends. After that she stopped coming. Others began to drop off, saying "If you ever do a workshop in the daytime or somewhere else—" At the final meeting, there were only three left.

I'd have thought the fault was mine if it hadn't been for Alice Allen's Friday night workshop, scheduled more like a class, and starting off with twenty she chose from a crowd willing to pay a large non-refundable contribu-tion to the ACLU. After a couple of weeks, the same thing happened; some of them began to drop off and others asked for a change of location. Alice wouldn't hear of it, scolding a woman who'd asked for some kind of escort to her car. "If you can't be near people who look different from you, you'll never be a writer. I walk at least three blocks from here to my car, and take a short-cut right through People's Park!"

That was more than I would do after dark. Alice was old and thin and frail-looking, but she strode ram-rod straight on the dark side streets and through the darker park, handing out smiles and coins. What she did not know was that she had an inconspicuous bodyguard following her to her car—Cole.

Cole had joined the group after I met him parked near my house with a new batch of tiny whippets. He asked if it was true that the famous Alice Allen was teaching writing in a bookstore on Telegraph.

"Yes, why do you ask?"

He shuffled and grinned, then said he'd been thinking about writing down some things about his life. "But she wouldn't want me there."

"Oh, yes, she would. She'd love you to be there." In fact, I could imagine her delight at confronting the more squeamish women with a street person.

Alice had refused to take any money from Cole, but he said he could not attend unless he could give something in return. Finally he and Harry found a solution. The losses in the store had been getting worse. "Cole, if you want to just hang around here, off and on, afternoon or evening, between the shelves. Watch for—do you think you could spot a book thief?" Cole only smiled.

Cole began to slip into Get A Life at odd times, as anonymously grubby as any other street person. He might stand in a shadow behind a shelf, eyes seemingly fixed on an open book he held. Sometimes he crouched, sitting on his heels near a low shelf or a pile of books on the floor. He was helpful from the start, explaining to Harry some methods of theft and suggesting simple precautions that cost nothing. He knew as much as an expert shoplifter, which he might once have been. It didn't seem polite to ask. Nor did Alice

learn anything about him. He came every week to her workshop and left promising to write something to read "next
time" but never did. He listened attentively, made intelligent, encouraging comments on the writings of others.
He began escorting all the women to their cars, refusing
any money they offered him, always maintaining his silent
privacy when they began to ask him friendly questions.

Unfortunately, Cole did not escort the men to their
cars. One man in Alice's workshop came back the next
morning and told Harry that, while turning off the Avenue,
he'd handed a quarter to a beggar, "some kid" who then
followed him, demanded his wallet, knocked him down,
and walked away as others watched. The man sputtered,
"Where in hell are the police?" and never came back. Cole
was slumped silently between shelves at the time. When the
man left, he stuck out his head and suggested gently that
Friday night was not a good night for Alice's workshop. "A lot
of rough kids BART in from all over, looking for trouble."

Against Jake's advice, Harry went to a City Council
meeting to ask for more police presence. No one from the
Avenue would come along to support Harry—no customers,
certainly no other merchants. Jake reluctantly went along
to see Harry heckled and shouted down by "the usual gang
that shows up to support the so-called homeless." Harry
spent the next week cleaning graffiti from his outside walls.
"You were lucky they didn't break a window."

Only three people showed up for Lisa's Tuesday night
workshop on translation. I did a four-week afternoon workshop, which went well, but it took more energy than I had
to give after teaching at Merritt and spending hours on the
phone with my mother or her doctors. I told Harry I needed a
break before trying another one. The workshop idea seemed
to be slowly dying. Readings continued at Get A Life, mostly

266

attended by a few supportive friends of each writer. Well-known authors still drew an audience at Cody's, made up of people who drove in, then out again, not hanging out for coffee as they had twenty years before. At the other end of town, readings at Black Oak were always well-attended, especially, I began to notice, by older people.

The only famous (infamous? ex-famous?) author who asked Harry to schedule a reading was Eldridge Cleaver. (Cody's and Black Oak had been able to turn him down—with relief—because his book wasn't new.) Cleaver showed up once or twice a week in the afternoon, to sit at Harry's and sip coffee and doze on the couch at the rear of the store. (Cole assured Harry that Cleaver wasn't stealing anything.) I never asked Harry his feelings about the reappearance of his hero in his dreary transformation, and Harry never volunteered a comment. I think it was too painful a subject. I gathered that Cleaver came and went without either of them acknowledging the other, until Cleaver approached Harry at the counter, a copy of his second book in his hand.

"He wants to read from *Soul on Fire*," Harry told me, "the book about finding God and leaving The Left."

"What did you tell him?"

Harry shrugged. "What could I tell him? The book fits our criteria—autobiographical, new or old. I put him on the schedule. I've already had three letters protesting his appearance. The one from Tony Russo is almost threatening."

Tony Russo's letter also appeared in the *Bridge*, though Cleaver's upcoming appearance went unmentioned in the Bishop Berkeley column. "No one will come," I said, hoping, for Harry's sake, that I was right. I wasn't. A fairly large and unfriendly crowd came, but Harry got lucky. Cleaver didn't show up. Tony Russo and his friends sat waiting and arguing with an old Free Speech Movement veteran who defended Harry's right to schedule even Eldridge Cleaver. After an hour Tony and his friends announced victory and left. Two days later the *San Francisco Chronicle* devoted an inch on a back page to Cleaver's whereabouts that night; he had been found wandering, disoriented, down the middle of a boulevard in Oakland, and put into a detox center for a couple of days.

1988 was a difficult year for me—teaching, broken by three flights to Chicago. Then a summer of setting my mother's house in order and trying—unsuccessfully—to persuade her to sell it. In August I rented the house again, and flew home in time for my classes, hoping some magical solution had removed the mess beyond my back fence. But no miracle had removed it. As often as possible I tried to escape it, spending weekends driving up the coast—often with Judith. She enjoyed the scenery, I enjoyed her, and Carol and Steve enjoyed a child-free weekend.

When I next saw Harry, he had lost weight, looked stringy and slightly stooped—tired. I didn't mention the Dante Street house—he did, with a sigh of weary apology. Yes, he told me, he knew about the latest problems. We'd had some cold nights, and the newest back-yard squatters had begun lighting bonfires outside, and even inside their shanties. One of the fires had scorched our common fence, almost setting it on fire. We called the fire department. Mrs. Temple called the police. Both the police and fire departments posted more notices on the front door no one would open.

"They don't answer when I go there either," said Harry. "Daniel won't talk to me anymore. That stuff about the city giving them another house? It was a lie. Now he

268

has filed some protest with the Planning Commission under the condo conversion law—condo conversion! Just because Mr. Horace kept a separate room and bath at the back for himself? I went to the hearing. Daniel didn't even show up. The board said he had no case. But that ate up another two months. I'm behind on my mortgage payments. Dan's smart, he probably knows the bank will foreclose. Then the house will be in limbo again, back on the market, no buyer, the bank doing nothing. Maybe I should just give it up."

"How far behind are you?"

"A few months."

"Maybe if you could just pay something on it, any little bit, the interest."

"Even the interest is beyond me at this point. With the eight hundred room rent at Lisa's house, I'm—"

"Eight hundred! For that tiny room? Lisa's paying half that for the whole house!"

Harry paled. "You're mistaken. You can't rent anything in Berkeley for—"

"It's under rent control, stuck at the 1980 rent, plus minor rises. I know because Lisa got in trouble with the rent board once already when she sub-let it for more than the rent ceiling. She was reported by her tenant."

"Oh, I could never do that to Lisa," Harry said.

"It wouldn't matter if you did. The rent control law applies only to owners and their renters who sublet the whole house. As long as Lisa is living in the house, there's no limit on what she can charge for renting a room."

"Are you sure?"

"Ask her. She should know. I think she was still with Dan when he helped draft the rent control laws."

Harry shrugged. "Lisa's just barely surviving. Has no income. And she works so hard at the store, a lot more hours

269

than I can pay her for. She probably figures I owe her."

I didn't know what to say. "Come to dinner Saturday? You close early on Saturdays now?"

Harry gave me a subdued, elderly smile, and said he could come at eight.

But he didn't. He called to say there were some problems and he needed to stay at the store overnight. The next day I searched through the *Chronicle* and found another routine story worth two inches on a back page: someone had smashed a window at Moe's Books, then overdosed in People's Park, dead man's name unknown.

Then came the grotesque "dumping" on Dante Street. Mrs. Temple had gotten another petition signed, this one sent to the Health Department, reporting the filth accumulating in the back yard where more and more men spent the night—there was no telling how many slept inside the house. Her nephew promised that somehow he'd get someone to come out that day with citations and stronger threats. Someone must have come; we saw trash being thrown out of windows and men raking up piles of it in the back yard. "There's a truck out in front on Dante," said Mrs. Temple, "to haul that stuff away."

I could hardly believe she'd gotten results. We watched from her back porch as the huge truck, piled high, drove off at sundown.

Two days later at five a.m., my phone rang. It was the block captain of the Dante Street Association. Her husband, who drove a public transit bus, had gotten up early to go to work. As he left the house, the same hauling truck, piled high with tons of trash, lumbered down the street, stopped in front of

1629 Dante Street, and dumped. When the driver saw the open-mouthed man standing on his front steps, he yelled, "Those fucking assholes wrote me a bad check!" and drove off.

As soon as business hours began, all of us picked up our phones and called every city office we could think of. People from all over the neighborhood came to look at the stinking mountain of trash in the middle of the street. Someone must have called Harry too, but by the time he showed up, it was noon, and three city garbage trucks had appeared to begin loading and hauling away the mess. A crowd stood watching. A few shook their heads, smiling. When I saw Harry, I went to stand beside him, so he wouldn't think we blamed him. He turned to me and said, in a numb voice, "Like the people in Butte, coming up the hill to see the buildings burning down."

At the end of the month Harry got a bill from the city: $486 for trash collection. He telephoned me. "I can't pay it. I keep waiting for the bank to foreclose, take the damned house, but they don't. The bank even paid the utilities before I bought the place. Now the utility bills are coming to me. The gas and electric bill is over $800 a month. I think they run extensions, plug electric heaters in, all over, inside and out."

"You haven't paid any of them!"

"Of course not. How could I? Pink notices, final notices. Everything, the water too, is going to be shut off."

"Maybe that will drive them out," I said, hopefully.

The following week, standing at my bedroom window, I saw Dan Lyon instructing a crew of men with shovels. Mrs. Temple was watching from her back porch. She saw me at the window, and called out, "When you see Harry, you can tell him there's going to be a new Berkeley Pit. They're digging a hole in the backyard for their garbage and toilet." We made phone calls, wrote more letters—to the police, the fire department, the health department, the mayor, and so on—and on.

It was June before Harry was able to get away from the store to have dinner with me. He brought a half-empty jug of wine. From his flushed face and the smell of his breath, I guessed he was the one who'd half-emptied the jug. We ate, drank some wine, talked about the current drought, floods in Brazil, the Fatwa against Salman Rushdie, Iraq gassing Kurds, everything but the mess just beyond my back yard fence.

Finally Harry sighed and said, "You might want to see the latest." He pulled a wad of papers out of his coat pocket, then spread three closely-typed pages on the table. "I got this from the city yesterday. It's a list of safety, building code, plumbing, electrical violations—compiled by Dan Lyon, 'copy filed with Board of Adjustments, Rent Control, health department.'" He nodded his head in the direction of the backyard. "This page is a letter addressed to me signed by Dan, 'for the Dante Homeless Collective.' Cites a law that tenants can withhold rent if the landlord refuses to make necessary repairs."

"But they've never paid you any rent."

"That doesn't seem to matter. This sets in motion some new process, according to another regulation: repairs have to be made before tenants can be evicted for any reason." He shrugged. "Aside from the leaky roof, it's all

272

small stuff—probably damage they caused. I think I can do it all myself."

"There are a few tools in the shed. Ladders. You're welcome to use whatever you need."

"Thanks. I'll work on it early in the morning before I open the store."

Silence. "Can they really make you—have you tried calling the Rent Board?"

Harry nodded, then laughed, a gruff, sad, scratchy sound. "A couple of them used to live in Angel's Haste Street commune back in the sixties. Now they're on the Rent Board. To them I'm a scumbag slumlord." Harry sighed. "They've kept the faith, and I'm the one who's changed."

"There must be someone you can—"

"It's quicker just to make the repairs than to protest it."

"But Lyon will only find another way of delaying—"

That nasty laugh grated in Harry's throat again. "He always could. God, how I used to admire the way he could—I don't think he's even living in the house anymore, is he? Have you seen him?"

"Not lately. But I try not to look over there if I can help it."

"I heard he's with a woman who lives in the Oakland hills. He just does stuff like this for squatters." Harry held up one of the sheets of paper. "Legal advice. Strategy." Harry drained his glass, looked moodily at the empty jug, then stood up to leave.

"Wait, Harry. I'll probably be in Chicago most of the summer. I'd appreciate it if you'd house-sit for me. I don't like leaving the place empty with all those—it might be convenient for you while you're working on your house." I didn't add that he'd save the money he was paying to Lisa. "Here. Here's a key to the house and to the shed."

273

Harry hesitated, then nodded, and took them. "Thanks."

The first thing my mother said when I arrived at the nursing home was, "You put your old dog down, didn't you? Why can't they do the same for me?" (She had remembered my sad mention of Pogo's death two months before, while I had to repeat immediate, important facts to her again and again.) Her room mate had died. She was ready to let me sell her house. That meant sorting through her accumulated possessions to decide what to keep, what to give away, and to whom. Every day, it seemed, I wept over some old forgotten trinket or photo I found tucked away in boxes. Every day I sat with my now silent mother, who did not respond to any of the anti-depressants her doctor prescribed. I remember calling Carol at one point and ordering her to have another child before it was too late. "Don't make Judith an only child and have to deal with this alone! You'll know when it comes to be your turn!" Stupid things like that. Then backtracking, trying to reassure Carol that I was all right, "no, don't worry, no, you can't drop your work and come here now. And there's nothing for you to do."

I telephoned Harry every week, got curt answers to my questions. Yes, everything was okay. No, he hadn't made any repairs on Dante Street. No one would let him in to do the work.

I listed my mother's house with an agent and booked a flight for September 1, barely in time to start the new term at Merritt. I called Harry.

"I'll get out next week."

274

"Back to Lisa's house?"

"No!" I waited for more, but got only silence.

"Where will you stay?"

"At the store I guess. There's a toilet, a cot where I can use my sleeping bag."

"But Harry, you can stay at my place as long as you like. No need to camp out at the store."

"To tell the truth, it's better than looking out the back at that mess." We were cut off—by accident, or because Harry hung up.

I started teaching the day after I got home, but never seemed to climb up out of jet lag. Carol insisted that my exhaustion was made worse by the sights and smells beyond my back fence. "Come here on weekends. You can correct papers just as well over here, and the nursing home has our number too, just in case—"

The call came on Christmas Day. We all four got seats on a half-empty plane to Chicago, where my mother lay in a coma for a few days, then slipped away. Carol and Steve made the funeral arrangements. My job, with Judith's help, was to telephone relatives and the few still-living friends listed in my mother's address book. The funeral was held a week later, right after New Year's Day.

More family came than I expected, perhaps because many had time off from work and school during the holidays. The reception in the church social hall was cheerful, like a family reunion, far-flung cousins I hadn't seen since childhood, introducing their children and grandchildren to each other.

"Ruthie? I'm Will," a cousin I hadn't seen since his

wedding in 1950, when he moved to a suburb of Cleveland—
or was it a suburb of Raleigh, or a suburb of Dallas, or—
"Meet my son, George, my youngest son. He's a lawyer
like your Carol. I think he works for one of the companies
your daughter is always suing." He laughed. "George, this
is cousin Ruth, I told you about her, the smart one." Will
moved away, leaving me with George, a thirtyish man, trim
and tan, his impeccably tailored dark suit fitting him with
an ease that comes only at high cost.

"Ruth," said George appraising me with a friendly
smile. "You're the Ruth from Berzerkeley?" His eyes widened
mockingly, as he waited for my response to his original
sense of humor. "And your daughter lives in San Francisco?
I just got back from a conference in Frisco." He shook his
head. "Must have been a beautiful city once. All those filthy
beggars. You wouldn't believe what we saw while we were
waiting to get on a cable car. Oh, I guess you would. You see
it all the time." He waited, blinked at me.

"Yes."

"But The Castro was worse, in a way. We took a tour
bus up there and—" He shuddered. "Men walking around
holding hands. Where I live, they'd get themselves killed."
He looked at me expectantly again, then shrugged. "Well,
that problem is solving itself. They're dying like flies. You
know where AIDS comes from—sex with monkeys." Again
he waited for me to respond. "Did you know that?"

"No."

He nodded. "We only spent one day in Berkeley. The
beggars were even worse there. Aren't you afraid to walk
down the street?" I shook my head. "You've got a strong
stomach. Our police run them out, put them on the first
bus." He waited.

I took a deep breath. "Yes. I know."

276

"Don't know how you can stand it."

I smiled. "Well, we just do the best we can with the problems you dump on us." Judith had come up beside me in time to hear my answer. She took my hand, gave it a little apprehensive jerk.

George went on as if he hadn't heard me. "I guess it's that li-ber-al city council." He laughed. "The People's Republic of Berkeley." Another laugh. "They have their own foreign policy, but can't get the human garbage off their own streets. You still have that nigger mayor who is always going off to—?" He reached up into his falsetto voice. "Oh, dear me!" He resumed his normal voice. "I'm sure you don't use THAT word in Berkeley."

"No, we don't."

"Don't dare say 'nigger' or don't have that mayor anymore?"

"Both—neither."

"Don't you ever think about moving out?"

I hesitated, then admitted, "Yes, sometimes I do."

"Well, I'm just glad I don't live there."

"So am I."

That time he heard me. "Grandma," Judith whispered. She tightened her grip on my hand and tried to pull me away. I put one arm around her shoulders and stood firm, glaring at him, my anger rising like a wave of new energy. For the first time in weeks, I was enjoying myself.

George's eyes narrowed. Then he grinned and focused as I imagine he would have eyed a hostile, but not overly bright witness. His voice was softer as he said, "Dad didn't mention that you'd become one of those Berkzerkeley radicals yourself."

"Oh, didn't he?"

"I thought you didn't swallow all that stuff."

"I don't."

"Then I wonder how you can stay there."

"I used to wonder too—until now."

He hissed through clenched teeth, "Don't think there aren't plenty of people like me around Berkeley, right in Berkeley."

"I know," I hissed back at him. "But whenever we catch one on the street, we put him on the first bus to your town." Then I let Judith pull me away.

Carol and Steve stayed to clean up more of the details, and Judith insisted on staying with them. "You're through, Grandma. We'll do the rest." The three of them put me on a plane that night, and, gaining three hours, I was home by midnight. On the kitchen table I found the set of keys I'd given Harry, a bottle of good wine and a note thanking me for letting him stay.

The next morning I woke up with a headache and fever, the usual flu that hits me after a period of stress, knocking me out for at least a week. Luckily, my final exams were ready. One of my colleagues came to pick them up. He promised to meet my classes, give the exams, and bring the papers back to me. I collapsed in bed, dozed for a couple of hours, then sat up and began sorting through the mail. Aside from a pile of advertising, there were just three bills and some complimentary copies of new books.

One of them was *Heartwounds*, the collection of poems containing the three by Marsha. I reread them, hoping she'd sharpened them. She hadn't. She could have written about the honest love/hate passion between her and Ivan. Why hadn't she? The other poems in the anthology were well-crafted, if not exciting, three by fairly well-known local academics. The blurbs on the back cover were more impressive, carefully phrased compliments from Ivan's colleagues and a kind phrase from a famous poet, long-gone from Berkeley, but once a playmate of Marsha's children. There was a statement of thanks "for a generous grant" from a foundation on whose board Ivan had served. I looked at the verso page again. Redwood Peak Press? It looked as if Marsha had started her own press—and done it capably— even handsomely. I put Marsha's book aside and picked up a thicker book bag.

It was Aaron's book *Survivor,* published a couple of months before. Inside the book was the usual note from the publisher praising the promising young author who had given my name as someone who might help launch the book with a review.

I turned to the first page and began. The chess scene was there to start off the story: Jake and little Aaron, sitting in Steadman's Used Books, "a Berkeley institution that made me so proud of my father."

Then the narrative described the shadows of secret confusion, fear, and shame coming over that childhood as Aaron slowly confronted his sexuality. The account of his People's Park arrest became somewhat confused with his Castro riots arrest ten years later, both punctuated by too many sexual encounters and too few political details to make the period clear to readers not familiar with the Bay Area.

But Aaron hit his stride again with the story of his struggles—only six years before—to publish his articles on the deepening but denied health crisis among gay men. "That was when I tried to give up, tried to stop writing. My friends were dropping dead around me, or frozen in fear, yet when I tried to name the fear and urge some precautionary changes in our behavior, they turned on me. I did stop writing for nearly eight months, getting more and more depressed. Then I ran into an old friend of my father's, Ruth Carson. She reminded me that if I was afraid of offending my friends, I was no friend worth having." (So he *had* been listening—but gave me too much credit.)

He ended with an unpretentious, simple, but very moving statement of what he had learned—not about the sins of others, but about "the fear, in all of us, of facing a humiliating or threatening truth. If I want to face and destroy this fear, I know I have to start with myself." Another twenty or thirty pages of appendices were made up of nine of his unpublished articles, accompanied by samples of hate mail he had received.

I telephoned Jake. "I just finished Aaron's book. It's really fine. Congratulate him for me."

"He's not exactly celebrating. Taking a lot of flak. I told him what would happen if he included those appendices."

"Oh. The gay press again? But at this stage, they can't say he—"

"Yes, they can. Crucified him. For 'kicking his gay brothers when they're down,' for saying 'I-told-you-so.' "

"Oh, no, the book doesn't have that tone at all, it's really—"

"Two people threatened to sue over his printing their letters—even though they'd signed permissions! He had his phone disconnected after death threats from some nuts who call themselves the Gay Gladiators. He's still scheduled to read at Get A Life—he wanted to give Harry the business—but that's all Harry needs now is the Gay Gladiators showing up. What with that house full of squatters and the latest mess at the store."

"What's that?"

"Ask Harry. I haven't kept up on it. I don't go up to the Avenue, don't even want to know what's happening up there."

I hung up and called Harry at the store, but reached only the answering machine.

Lying in bed, I began reading the final exams and late term papers my colleague brought to me.

It had started raining, breaking a year-long drought with what seemed like a deluge. The rain went on, day after day, breaking all records. Flooding was bad along rivers in the north counties. But the Bay Area had its own problems, including mud slides on the hills. On the television news I saw a woman standing on a narrow road beside yellow wooden barriers, where her house had stood before it slid down with the mud. With a shock I recognized the site, next to Marsha's house, still safe on its promontory of solid rock. Less attention was given to the flooding in West and South Berkeley, where aged, inadequate sewers carried water and mud down from the hills. A few of my neighbors had some basement flooding and ran sump pumps day and night. Perhaps because of the rain, there were more men than ever in the house behind mine. But they huddled inside the house itself or in their back yard shanties. At least the nights were quiet. I tried not to think about what might be overflowing the pit in the midst of those shanties.

Over a week passed before I felt able to drive up to Merritt and turn in my final grades. That night I went to a neighborhood meeting. Mrs. Temple gave her usual report from her nephew. Police had come in response to complaints four times since the rains started, but in all four cases, the person who called had refused to sign a complaint. Two of them said they had already been threatened.

Harry had come to two meetings held while I was gone, telling the group he had not made a mortgage payment to Wellington Savings for eight months, but that, as far as he knew, foreclosure proceedings had not started. A neighbor who worked at a bank said, "If they foreclose, they're responsible again."

The following week I drove to KPFA through more driving rain to do my scheduled reading from Orwell's *Homage to Catalonia*. The head of the Drama and Literature Department asked me to stop afterward and talk to her. That was when she told me that I'd been pre-empted permanently, so to speak. Nothing personal, she said in low, depressed tones. Nearly all literature, drama, art, and classical music programs were being dropped in favor of "more politically relevant programming" which might halt the steadily declining numbers of listeners. (The purge didn't work. It would take years, another internal eruption, the attack on New York, and a war to bring back listeners.) I shook her hand and wished her luck with her gutted department.

When I joined Marsha at the Thai restaurant, the first thing she asked was, "Have you had time to look at *Heartwounds*?"

I complimented Marsha on the handsome design of the book and asked if Redwood Peak Press were her invention. She nodded, and I asked more questions, hoping not to be pressed for my opinion of her poems. She was having fun and planned to continue, publishing at least one collection of poetry annually. "Manuscripts are already pouring in." Abruptly she changed the subject. "I'm working on grant applications to the Jerwold Foundation. You know the Jerwold family?"

"Not really. I taught one of the Jerwold kids years ago in San Francisco."

"But he might remember your name, if—"

"I haven't talked to the man since he was sixteen."

"Well, he'd remember you, I'm sure!" Marsha's innocent smile was hardening.

"No, I couldn't do that."

Marsha looked away from me and dropped her glance. That was a sign, the only sign, ever, that she was very angry. I thought again of the rumor Lisa had passed on, that Marsha wrote Bishop Berkeley. I knew her unfailing composure could hide anger that came out slashing on paper. But her political outlook ran completely counter to Bishop Berkeley—didn't it? Yet, when I'd seen her functioning as a faculty wife, I'd realized it was almost impossible ever to know what she was really thinking.

When Marsha looked up again, her smile was firm. "I was hoping for a little blurb from you about this book, so that I could mention you on the grant application."

I nodded. I'd managed some kind words for weaker books. "Sure, I can do that."

"And I'd was hoping you'd be able to schedule a reading of *Heartwounds* on KPFA."

I was almost relieved to tell her that I had just been canceled, along with a couple of dozen other people who did literary readings.

"Oh, but that's awful! Did you tell them what you thought of them?"

I laughed. "No, no, it's routine. When I started doing

this twenty years ago, I vowed that when the time came, I wouldn't leave KPFA the way everyone does—stomping and cursing the ingrates and slamming the door. Enough ego around there without adding my own."

But my ego must have been a bit bruised because my stomach started churning when Marsha tried to amuse me with a story about her two nieces, recent high school graduates from an affluent South Carolina suburb, who'd stayed with her throughout October. "They spent all their days in People's Park, then took the bus back up to tell me their wild adventures before going to sleep."

Instead of smiling with her, I lashed out. "In other words, you let them stay safely at night with you—so they can roll down the hill to act out their hippie fantasies in my neighborhood—and in a park you won't go near anymore. But I go near it. Lots of people—like Harry—have to be near it. All day! Every day! And now that your nieces are tired of adding to our problems, they're back home telling about their adventures in Berzerkeley!" Our lunch ended soon after my tirade, without our scheduling another.

The next day the sun came out, and the spring term began. After meeting my new classes, I drove home, then walked up to Telegraph to see how Harry was doing. I walked along streets covered with twigs, leaves, whole branches from evergreens, pavement slick with thousands of petals washed from the plum trees as soon as they put out their first sign of pink. At least the streets were clean, even on the Avenue. A few street people were back in their chairs outside the Med. I made my way around them, stepping over the usual legs outstretched and blocking my way.

My role in this game was to pretend not to notice that they were pretending not to notice me.

I found Harry in the store waiting on a customer. Wandering along an aisle between bookshelves, I approached the couch in the rear, where—yes—Eldridge Cleaver was dozing, a copy of a book open on his lap. I walked back to the counter and waited for Harry to finish his sale. I picked up a flyer, glancing over it now and then at Harry's haggard face. The flyer listed events at Get A Life for the next two months. Aaron's reading was scheduled for late March. Only two other readings were listed; I didn't recognize the names of the authors. A line at the bottom of the page read, "coming—a one day workshop by Alice Allen, April date to be announced." Indomitable Alice would never desert Harry.

"Welcome back," Harry said, after his one customer left. Harry's eyes shifted to a man who'd come in quietly and was now invisible behind a back shelf.

"Thanks for watching the house while I was gone. You're sleeping here now?" Harry nodded, then moved away from the counter. Did he want me to go? He shifted some books from here to there, then came back. "I'm surprised Lisa didn't give you a month or two free rent. She had already collected quite a bit of money from you."

"Quite a bit?" Suddenly Harry leaned over the counter, head down, as if collapsing in hysterical laughter at a wildly funny joke. After he stopped laughing, he raised his head and looked at me. "Yeah, quite a bit. Remember I told you we'd had a lot of losses? Even some of the books I'd kept locked up? I couldn't figure out how someone got into that glass case without breaking it. Well, it's easy if you have a key." I must have gasped. "When Cole told me, I couldn't believe it either—so he said, 'Okay, next time, can I stop her at the door and open her backpack? Okay with you?' So that's what he did."

Harry described Cole pulling the first edition of *Land of Little Rain* out of Lisa's backpack, and Lisa accusing Cole of planting it there, and why would she bother to steal "any of your pathetic books, and after all the cheap labor you've squeezed out of me, all the people I've brought to your amateurish little attempt to Get A Life!"

"And so on, screaming as she stormed out. Gave me an earful about you too."

"About me?"

"About your contempt for her? Your superiority?"

"Me?"

"Not only you. Half a dozen poets. Shook me up, the way she kept screaming till she got out. I guess that's what she wanted to do so I wouldn't get a chance to ask her how many books she took. I went to Moe's and to Shakespeare, and they said she'd sold books there regularly. They figured she was scouting garage sales and flea markets the way they do. No valuable first editions—they'd have remembered and been suspicious. Probably she took those over to San Francisco. Cole had been watching her for a while, to make sure before he told me." Harry shrugged and smiled ironically. I wished he would pound his fist and yell and—anything but that smile. "I had some trouble getting my things back. I owed her a month's rent, you know. My clothes weren't worth much, but there was a radio, my sleeping bag—stuff like that. Angel went over there to get them for me. Lisa told him she was suing me for sexual harassment, and said she'd burn my clothes before she'd give anything back to me. But that night she must have dumped all my stuff in front of the store. When I got here in the morning, most of it was still there, except the radio. I guess someone on the street took that. The next day some guy came in and

286

sold me my good pants for a couple of dollars."

"I'm so sorry, Harry."

He shrugged. "I was stupid. Jake warned me that she held him up for a lot of money before they broke up, but I didn't want to hear about it. Not when I was living in her house. Not when she did so much, was so generous. She was even nice to Jake whenever he came into the store. But, you know, doing so many good things for people seemed to make her—so bitter, furious. She just kept saying I owed her."

There was a sound at the back of the store. Cleaver got to his feet and shuffled to the front, slowing down as he passed us, as if using the only power left to him, his power to prolong our silence until he was out the front door.

"You don't have to sleep here, you can come back to—"

"It's okay. I have my sleeping bag now. Not a bad idea to have someone here all night."

"Don't tell me you take a shower at one church and meals at another one, along with the other homeless! Please, Harry, come and stay in the shed. You still have a key, don't you?"

He just looked at me, and I remembered the view he would have from the shed.

I bought a couple of books I didn't need, then left and went across to Cody's to see if they had a new novel just reviewed that day. The sidewalk was littered with young bodies—pale, pierced, bare-chested, blue-lipped and sullen. Their huge dogs growled at me as I stepped over them to enter the store. Andy told me the novel was on order, arriving any day; he'd hold one for me. He looked pale and harassed, but, unlike Harry, angry and energetic enough to shout at one of the street people as I left. "I told you to get your dog out of the doorway or I'll call the police again." I walked among the obscene jeers that rose from the sidewalk, stepped over blankets, dog droppings and trash, then turned the corner and went down Haste Street. At the first newsstand, I bought a *Chronicle* and read a back-page report on demonstrations during "the latest attempt by the Berkeley City Council to consider an anti-panhandling law." Dan Lyon, of course, was quoted on "continuing persecution of homeless, throwaway kids." Kids? The only creatures under twenty I'd seen sprawled in front of Cody's were the dogs.

The Bridge carried a short item in Bishop Berkeley's column that week. "Does everyone know that the slumlord threatening the Dante Street Homeless Collective is none other than the proprietor of Get A Life bookstore?"

That turned out to be the first of a series of barbs aimed at Harry, week after week:

"Few care to hang out at Get A Life and share the couch with the owner's buddy, born-again right winger, Eldridge Cleaver. You'll recall that Cleaver led a group in support of slumlord Lynch in front of the Dante Street Homeless Collective."

"Get A Life owner Harry Lynch is the same Harry Lynch arrested among People's Park protesters nearly twenty years ago, who jumped bail put up by Alice Allen. Seems he returned to scenes of his earlier exploits, fat with inherited money and values to go with it."

"Staunch advocate of the down-and-out, the beloved Father Mike led twenty of the homeless in picketing Get A Life bookstore last Friday. 'We love Harry,' said Father Mike, 'but we must remind him that housing is a human right, even for the less fortunate.' "

I had no doubts left about who wrote Bishop Berkeley, remembering that, of course, it had been Lisa who told me the "rumor" that pointed to Marsha.

I tried to go to Harry's store every week or two. Often I was the only browser there, but occasionally someone came in looking for a specific old book, or with a vague question about a forgotten war or plague, and Harry usually found something for them.

Two weeks later Harry told me, "Aaron's not going to do his reading here. There was a cancellation at Black Oak, so they had an empty slot. Tell you the truth, it's a relief. I got a couple of weird phone calls warning me against having a reading by an 'anti-gay gay.'"

I shared Harry's relief—until the following week, when Jake called to ask me if I'd seen the current *Bridge.*

"No, I've been busy with work." Actually I'd avoided picking up *The Bridge* for a couple of weeks.

"Shall I read you the item in Bishop Berkeley's column?" Jake didn't wait for my answer. "'Seems that as soon as Get A Life owner Harry Lynch got a peek at the gay themes in Aaron Steadman's first book, he told Steadman he wasn't welcome, then fired Lisa Lyon, who'd scheduled the reading. Aaron was welcomed at Black Oak Books, where, we trust, Eldridge Cleaver will *not* be in the audience.'"

"But it was Aaron's idea to go to Black Oak."

Jake was silent for a moment. "Lisa's out for blood now. Gotta be her. But never a word against Dan Lyon—in fact she's like a mouthpiece for him. That's what threw me off—she hates him."

"She told me once that she often asked him for

289

money for their daughter. Now that Cheila's living in Paris, she probably needs even more. Someone ought to call Aaron and tell him to send in a correction right away."

"He already called *The Bridge*."

But it was too late for a correction to matter, as I learned when I walked up to Telegraph Avenue to see Harry again. "I just talked to Aaron. He called *The Bridge* about that stupid B.B. column."

Harry silently reached under the counter and handed me four or five sheets of paper. Letters. One was from Alice Allen, canceling her scheduled workshop. Another was from Jessica Mitford, signed by half a dozen other writers, protesting the censoring of gay writers. We'd all been arrested together only a few months ago at our "Writers' Sit In For UC Divestment" from apartheid South Africa. If only they had asked me to sign this letter, I could have told them— but maybe they didn't ask me because they'd read about me as a hostile neighbor of Harry's tenants? There were two more letters from lesbian advocacy groups—protesting the book itself as "self-hating anti-gay."

"But this is crazy! Some people are protesting the reading of an 'anti-gay' book, and some are protesting the cancellation of the reading!"

Harry smiled wanly. "Damned if I do, damned if I don't."

"Didn't any of these people even come in to talk to you first?" Harry shook his head. "Not even Alice?" He shook his head again. "Well, at least I can call Alice and Decca and tell them they're off base."

"Don't bother. Reporters from the *Chronicle* and the *Tribune* were here already. They all got copies of the letters. I told them, look, here's a list of other gay writers I've had here. 'Then why did you cancel him?' I didn't cancel him,

I said. 'Didn't you fire Lisa Lyon for scheduling the book?' No. 'Why, then?' What am I supposed to do, call her a thief? What proof do I have? Cole? He was gone the minute he saw the reporters; who knows when or if he'll turn up again. I did call the editor of *The Bridge* and asked him to hold back the letters until I could talk to Alice—he said the paper was already at the printer. It'll be out tomorrow. He suggested I write a letter, and he'd print it in next week's issue."

"Are you going to?"

"Why bother? It just keeps the whole stupid mess going."

I hated to say he was probably right. "Come to dinner tonight? Late as you like. We'll talk, and try to think of something."

Harry shook his head. "I'm almost afraid to leave this place. Two mornings now, I've had to clean some stuff off the windows. Someone needs to be here, in case—"

"Look, Harry, if there's something I can do, please call me."

"Okay."

"Really, Harry, anything at all that I can do." As I left, I crossed the street to stay clear of a scuffle that had broken out in front of the Med.

The phone was ringing as I walked into the house. It was Harry. "I just got a phone call from my ex-wife. About Jennifer."

"Jennifer?"

"My daughter. She's run away. She and her mother have been having problems—well, you know, she's fifteen. I haven't seen her for over a year, but I call her every week since they got back from Brazil. Walter got a Superfund grant to check out another proposal to clean up the Berkeley Pit, and they were going to be in Butte until summer. Well, Jennifer and her mother had a fight, over some restriction, ending with the usual complaint. 'Daddy wouldn't treat me this way. He's open-minded.' Up to her room, slam the door. The usual, except—next morning, she was gone, along with some clothes and whatever cash was in the house. Her mother thinks she may be coming to Berkeley. The last time I saw her I vaguely promised she could visit me as soon as I got settled." There was a pause. "When I think of those guys at People's Park just waiting for the summer girls to show up and—Ruth, I'd end up killing someone if—this is my fault, the way I talked about the sixties in Berkeley—all my rosy memories—she has no idea of the reality, no preparation, no—"

"How can I help?"

"Well—this is asking a lot."

"Ask."

"I don't—I don't have—a place for her to stay."

"How long? A week? Two?"

"Less than two. Her mother will come and get her. Maybe she could stay in the shed."

"No. Jennifer—if she does show up—stays in Carol's old room, and you stay in the shed. I don't want her to turn that shed into a crash pad for anyone off the street. If she stays right inside the house, she wouldn't dare, not when I'm home, sleeping in the next room. Except I won't be here this weekend. I'll be in San Francisco. I want you on the premises at night."

"You're a good friend, Ruth. I won't forget this."

292

Two days later, Harry telephoned about eight P.M. to say Jennifer had arrived. She must have been standing beside him as he spoke; his voice was artificially cheerful. "I'll come by and introduce her to you."

They showed up an hour later. Jennifer was a healthy-looking fifteen-year-old, but the sweet smile in the photograph in Harry's wallet was gone for the present, replaced with a sullen pout. She had Harry's light hair and skin, a paleness so fragile it seemed dangerous to expose it to the sun. We said nothing about why she was here, only chattered awkwardly as she spread her brooding silence over us.

"Jennifer, your room is upstairs on the right. Want to take your things up there?"

She silently picked up her backpack and the shopping bag of toilet articles Harry had bought her, turned away, and went up the stairway.

As soon as she was out of earshot, Harry said quietly, "I called her mother, gave her your phone number too. Hope you don't mind." I nodded. "She's driving out—take her two or three days."

"Did she talk to Jennifer?"

Harry shook his head. "Jennifer wouldn't talk to her, and now she's mad at me for calling her." I poured Harry a glass of wine. We both stood in silence as we heard Jennifer coming back down the stairs.

"I want to go to bed now. Okay if I take a shower?"

"You'll find towels in the bathroom cabinet." She turned silently and started up. "Oh, Jennifer! " She stopped. "Tomorrow's Saturday, and I think your dad has a long day at the store. I'm going to spend the day with my grand-daughter in San Francisco. She's younger than you, but fun and friendly. The two of us could show you the city."

293

Jennifer smiled before she could stop herself. Then she remembered to frown, mumbling, "Okay."

"Okay then. Good-night."

"Good-night sweetheart." Harry moved toward the stairway to kiss her, but Jennifer ran up and disappeared before he could. We waited silently until we heard the shower running.

Then I turned to Harry. "You can't keep her off Telegraph Avenue, but after she's been around the city, she may find half an hour of Telegraph is enough. We'll run her all over San Francisco, then put her on BART. You pick her up at the Ashby Station, and she's all yours till I get home Sunday."

"I think I'll close the store for a couple of days. Sunday is Easter. I'll put up a sign, Closed for Spring Break."

"But that's a busy time, isn't it? Kids—like your daughter—coming for Spring Break."

"I don't think it'll be busy for me. Today someone was out there—someone who lives in the house, I think—" Harry's head jerked sideways toward the back yard. "—with a sign, Boycott Anti-gay Slumlord."

"Did it really keep people out?"

"Hard to tell. Business hasn't been great on the Avenue for anyone. Not books, anyway. The worst part of it was—that sign was the first thing Jennifer saw when she showed up. She walked in with a flyer in her hand, there were quotes from Bishop Berkeley on it. She looked at me like—I tried to explain, but—" Harry shook his head. "I'll close the store Sunday and just spend all my time with her until her mother comes." Harry stood and picked up his old duffel bag. I handed him to key to the shed. He looked at it and said, in funereal tones, "Like old times." Then he went out the back door.

294

During the night I heard some noises coming from beyond the fence. Usually I just rolled over and tried to ignore them. This time I got up in the dark and looked through the window. Someone had lit a fire between the tents and shanties. Two men stood on either side of it, their faces obscured by smoke, then lit for a moment by the flickering orange light of fire, then clouded again. They were shouting at each other across the fire, waving their arms. Then I saw Harry. He was standing outside the shed, leaning on the fence, looking over it at them, unnoticed by the two men. After a while, they and their fire sank down and disappeared. Harry stayed there, looking over the fence. I went back to bed.

In the morning I came downstairs to find Harry had already made coffee. He and I made small talk until almost ten.

"You have to go and open the store."

Harry looked at his watch and nodded. "I thought she'd be up by now."

"She's probably tired. How did she get here?"

"Some hitchhiking, some Greyhound."

"She slept on the bus?"

Harry shrugged. "She wouldn't tell me anything, hardly said a word."

"You go on to the store. As soon as she's up, I'll drive her to the city."

Harry had hardly left when I heard Jennifer on the stairway, as if she had been listening and waiting for her father to go. She ate cereal, fruit, a scone, drank the rest of the coffee.

"You're my dad's old English teacher?"

"That's right."

"You're the Carson who edited *Poems of Exile*?" I nodded. "My father sent me a copy. I write poetry."

"Maybe you'd like to show me some?" I was relieved when she said she hadn't brought any poems with her. "Your father wrote a poem about Butte once. Did he ever show it to you?"

"No. He writes poetry? Really?"

"One poem anyway. About the Berkeley Pit. And he started a novel about his great-grandmother."

"Oh, his Nonnarina."

"I have his first version in the garage somewhere in a box. Maybe you'd like to read it while you're here."

Jennifer yawned. "Dad says I look like her." She stood.

"Ready to go?"

"I'll get my stuff."

"Better bring a sweater. It'll be foggy over there."

When Jennifer came downstairs, I wrote down all our addresses and phone numbers for her. "Just in case." She started to stuff the paper in her backpack. "No, put them in your jeans pocket, to make sure. And here's a key to the house just in case—but your father'll pick you up at the Ashby BART Station. And some change. For the phone, in case something goes wrong. No, not in your backpack, in your pocket. Any money, anything valuable, don't carry it in the backpack. People can reach into it and pull stuff out before you know it." Jennifer gave me a wilting look.

As we drove over the Bay Bridge, she talked about her favorite sport, skiing. "That was what I hated about Brazil. No snow."

"But there was swimming, surfing, wasn't there, in Brazil?"

She shook her head. "Not where we were, inland, a little dried-up village near a big pit mine." She shuddered. "Nothing else. Worse than Butte. We only got to Rio every month or so." Then she was silent, looking at the bay.

I picked up Judith on Potrero Hill. She had written an itinerary. "First Twin Peaks, just to give you a panoramic view. Then out through Golden Gate Park, up the Great Highway, Golden Gate Bridge, Marin Headlands, back over the Bridge, Fisherman's Wharf, North Beach, down through Chinatown, cross Market, down to the Mission, dinner at that Mexican restaurant you like, Grandma." She smiled, proudly efficient. "How does that sound?"

"Perfect," I said. "After dinner I'll put you on BART at 16th Street, okay Jennifer?"

"Okay!" Jennifer smiled at Judith, who chattered on like the tourist guide she too was learning to be whenever relatives showed up from parts east. I didn't have to say another word all day. I just drove. Jennifer forgot herself and chattered with Judith, who answered her questions with statistics I didn't even know. Judith is, after all, a native San Franciscan, the first in the family.

At nine o'clock I called Harry. "We just put her on BART. She should be at the Ashby Station at nine-thirty-eight."

"How did it go?"

"I think she had a good time. Judith did all the talking, but I'm wiped out."

"I won't forget this, Ruth. Thanks."

I drove back to Carol and Steve's house on Potrero Hill, where Judith and I went straight to bed.

The phone rang about ten-thirty. Carol put her head in. "For you, Mom." It was Harry, still at the Ashby Station. Two more trains had come in since the one Jennifer was supposed to be on. Could she have taken the wrong train? Had I remembered to tell her about changing trains at 12th Street after seven o'clock? Even as Harry recited the whole sequence—waiting while two more trains arrived, having Jennifer paged at every station—we knew. Just before midnight, Harry called us for the last time. He had gone to my house, checked the spare room. There was nothing of Jennifer's, not even her toothbrush. She had left with no intention of coming back, not tonight anyway.

Harry agonized over whether to call the police. No, not yet. Whether to stay in the store tonight. Yes, in case she showed up there. "They're closing the BART station now. I have to get out. I'll be back at the store in fifteen minutes, so call me there if you hear from her—no, make it forty-five minutes—I think I'd better check People's Park."

"In the dark?" I said stupidly, then tried to make up for it with even more stupid reassurances. "She'll be all right, Harry. She'll show up tomorrow or the next day, satisfied that she's given you a scare." He hung up.

Three weeks went by. Whenever I called Harry at the store, I heard only the answering machine, reciting the

298

business hours and saying "leave a message." I did, several times, but Harry didn't call me back.

The only news of Harry came in the relentless attacks by Bishop Berkeley. In the May 5 issue of *The Bridge*, B.B. wrote that "despite censorship at Get A Life, Aaron Steadman, the gay writer made unwelcome by slum-lord Harry Lynch, had presented a reading at Black Oak, attended by literary luminaries, like Alice Allen, pleased to see that Eldridge Cleaver was not present." (Evidently the Gay Gladiators weren't there either.) Again in the May 12 column, Harry was mentioned as the "anti-gay slumlord who has taken to harassing homeless youth in People's Park. On the eve of the twenty-year-anniversary celebration of People's Park, Mr. Lynch is still trying to Get A Life, haunting the Park at night and—according to one source—stalking young girls, thereby giving credence to earlier hints of sexual harassment by a former employee."

The next week I went up to Telegraph Avenue. The window of Get A Life was nearly covered by a huge hand-lettered sign:

Going Out Of Business Sale

Taped on the edges of the big sign, as if to mock it, were a dozen flyers:

20th Anniversary People's Park
Friday, May 19
Documentary Films From 1969
Poetry Reading, Street Fair,

Crafts, Music
Starting 4 P.M.

As I stood in front of Get A Life, I saw Dan Lyon stapling more flyers on a telephone pole, reaching up as high as he could, eyes turned skyward. With his wrinkled, gaunt face, his thin silvery hair shining in the sun, his eyes nearly closed against the glare, he reminded me of those renaissance paintings of a saint absorbed in prayer.

As I walked through the doorway, Harry looked up from the counter where he was making smaller signs. "I tried to call you. Jennifer's back. She's all right. I think. I hope."

Her mother Sandy had been staying at the Durant Hotel ever since she arrived, nagging the police in four counties while Harry wandered, going repeatedly to every place where young people gathered. Even to the coffee house up on College and Ashby, where, since Get A Life was often closed, Eldridge Cleaver had been seen telling cop-shoot-out stories to a little circle of young, awed white girls. But that tip had been a false lead—Cleaver was back in detox.

Harry had gone to People's Park at least three times a day, passing out dollar bills and showing a photo of Jennifer, asking if anyone had seen her. No, no, no, no—yes (for two dollars to an old black man with an eye patch, new to the park, Harry thought). "She left with that guy they call Big Buster." Harry passed on this information to the police, who grimly said they knew Big Buster very well. It might take a few days. Buster was elusive, wise to the ways of the police.

Then, suddenly, night before last, about midnight, Harry heard scratching and faint knocking on the door of Get A Life. When he opened the door, he found Jennifer crouching against it. Harry called Sandy, and they took her to a hospital. The emergency room doctors found bruises and abrasions, signs of gonorrhea, no apparent sign of drugs, though she might have taken something that had already passed through her system. She was released, with various prescriptions, to her mother, who took her to the hotel, stripped her, bathed her, put her to bed, then threw all her clothes into the hotel incinerator, and walked down Bancroft to buy her new panties, socks, shoes, jeans and sweat shirt. The next day they were gone, on their way back to Butte.

"Did Jennifer talk to you about it?"

"Not a word. Not a word to her mother either."

"Sounds as if she learned something—and was lucky."

"Just pray the HIV test comes up negative. Sandy blames me—for 'filling her head with fairy tales about this disgusting place.' She's right. It's my fault."

"Harry, Jennifer isn't the first rebellious teenager to run away to Berkeley."

"Yeah, I guess." Harry went on making the little signs: Half Off; $1; 50¢.

I said the obvious, "You're closing the store."

He nodded. The owner had sent him a final notice for back rent; his insurance on the stock had been canceled last week for nonpayment of premiums. "The owner's giving me almost a month—mid-June—to get out. I'll sell off whatever I can, split it with him for some of the back rent, and keep half to tide me over until—" His voice trailed off.

"What about the house?"

"I've long since given up on—I try not to think about —let the bank—" He decisively slammed an old book shut and threw it into a box marked Free. "The people at Black Oak Books offered me a job. I think they felt bad—caught

301

in the middle of that mess with Aaron's book. That's what Jake says I should do. Work at Black Oak for a while, until maybe something else turns up." Harry laughed. "Jake says what's wrong with Berkeley is that as soon as anyone loses their stupid illusions—they leave. He may be right." Harry shook his head as his words hung there again. "I'd like to get away for a couple of weeks and think. I could use some of the money to drive up and visit my grandmother in Idaho. That's what my mother and I were going to do, before she—" Harry reached into his pocket, pulled out the key to the shed, and handed it to me.

I refused it. "You might decide you want to sleep there some night."

He hesitated, then nodded. "Maybe Friday." Harry's crooked smile was more than ironic. "You know, twenty-year celebration of People's Park. Most of the shops are closing up early."

On Friday I spent the day in San Francisco. It was one of those fogless spring days at Ocean Beach. Judith and I slogged through the sand from the zoo to the Cliff House, then had fish dinner, and picked up two of her girlfriends for a movie. By the time I got everyone home and got myself back to Berkeley, it was midnight. I fell into bed, thinking, I'm getting too old for this. Oh, well, next time, Judith won't want me along when she goes out with friends.

Sirens whined in and out of my dreams. I live only two blocks from a firehouse, and usually I sleep through the sirens. More of them than usual. I looked at the clock: one A.M., closed my eyes, turned over onto my back, and heard another, fainter noise. Footsteps on gravel? Someone walking along the side of the house to the back yard? Probably only Harry, come to sleep in the shed. I got up and looked out the window, to make sure. Yes, it was Harry, his back to me, his tall frame a barely visible shadow. He stood near the back fence, looking over it. I went back to bed.

Just as I was dozing off, I was startled awake by a louder noise. Men shouting—another drunken quarrel at the Dante Street house? I pulled my pillow over my head to dampen the noise. Another siren screamed, louder and louder, coming close, suddenly stopping. Someone on Dante Street must have called police. Maybe things would quiet down now. I burrowed my head under the pillow.

Getting light. No. Yes. Dawn seemed to flicker through the lid of my right eye, not quite covered by the pillow. What time is it now? As I pulled the pillow off my head, I drowsily took in several things: the clock telling me it was only three A.M.; another siren; a huge blast from one of those fire engine horns; the flickering orange glow that was not dawn.

I rolled out of bed and staggered to the window. Fire. The shed? Harry? No, it looked as if one of those fires they were always lighting had gotten out of control again. The back of the Dante Street house was on fire. Maybe my fence too. Still looking out the window, I started pulling on a sweat suit and shoes. I could see three or four uniformed men. Firemen? No, police. In my back yard. Down the path, leaving by the front gate. They seemed to be taking someone with them. Why through my back yard? Now I could see the yard beyond the back fence filled with fire fighters, and beyond them, on Dante Street, the red and blue flashing of police car lights.

I hurried downstairs and out the front door to see my Milton Street neighbors, dressed in whatever came to hand, walking up the street and around the corner. I caught up with Mrs. Temple and turned the corner with her. She wore a coat over bright-flowered pants—as carefully dressed and coifed as always. She turned to me. "You see the police take Harry from your backyard?"

"Harry? Are you sure?"

"It was Harry, all right. The police came through the Dante Street yard, jumped the fence, and grabbed him. Three of them. All those thugs yelling and pointing at him, Harry just standing there. The police took him down the path, walked him down your driveway and out your front gate. Then around the corner, I guess. You didn't hear?"

"I heard, but I thought it was just the usual—I was trying not to hear." As we turned the corner of Dante Street, we saw it full of neighbors with coats hastily thrown over night clothes. One police car. No fire trucks. I was surprised. "There's still a lot of smoke. Why did the fire truck leave?"

"Probably went back up on Telegraph Avenue."

"Something happening on Telegraph?"

"Where you been?" asked Mrs. Temple. "Didn't you watch the news?"

"I got home late. Oh. The People's Park celebration. It got out of hand?"

"My nephew's been up there since nine o'clock. Every policeman in Berkeley. And fireman. Leah—that's my nephew's wife—she called to let me know he's all right. He says it's quieting down there now, and he should be home in an hour or two. He told her two fire trucks got burned up, store windows broken. Those people just broke the windows and went in to steal. Throwing fire bombs at the fire trucks, at the police, at my nephew, and him with strict orders not to draw his gun! A lot of policemen hurt. My nephew got a sprained wrist, thank God. Maybe they have to give him a few days off."

By that time we were in front of 1629 Dante Street. A policeman stood taking notes while four men from the house waved their arms and shouted at him.

"Threw a bomb just like a—"

"—whole tent went up. If I hadn't—"

"—backside of the house."

"A guy's dead in there, the smoke I guess." There was a pause while the policeman asked him questions. "No, I don't know his name. But I know he's dead, that crazy mother-fucker killed him, tried to kill us all."

One of the Dante Street neighbors touched my arm. "It's Harry. You know it's Harry?" She pointed to the police car. "See him, sitting in the police car. He did it from your yard. Over your fence."

"Did what?"

"Threw a fire bomb into the yard. That's what they're all saying." She swept her arm through the air toward the men who were shouting at the police. Then she smiled. "Just since I've been standing here, I've seen a dozen men come out of there, with duffel bags, blanket over their heads to hide their face. Don't want to talk to the police, uh-uh— probably know the police very well. They just want to disappear. There goes another one. Harry ought to get a medal."

She stopped smiling as an ambulance, siren screaming, drove up and stopped. We all watched silently as four medics jumped out of it, went into the house carrying a stretcher, then quickly came out again carrying a bagged body, put it into the ambulance, and drove away quietly, no siren, no hurry. I walked over to the police car. A policeman stood beside it, watching me. I could see Harry sitting alone in the back seat, head down, torso tilted forward, handcuffs pinning his arms behind him. The windows were closed. I tapped on one of them. "Harry." He made no sign that he heard or saw me.

"You know this man?" asked the policeman.

"Yes. Harry Lynch."

"A friend of yours? A relative?"

"A friend. I live in the house behind this one." I pointed toward my house. "Why are you arresting him?"

"These men say he fire bombed their house. So does he. 'I did it.' That's all he would say, just, 'I did it.' I'd like to have your name, please. The inspector might want to talk to you."

I watched him add my name to the list he was making. "Where are you taking him?"

"Berkeley City Jail. He'll be there until he's arraigned—a day or two. Then, probably Santa Rita." It all sounded like an uncanny re-enactment of what Harry had been through twenty years before. Except that this time Harry was in real trouble, and alone.

"He'll need a lawyer."

"Looks like it."

"Can I see him tomorrow?"

The cop turned to me. "I doubt it. Just his lawyer until he's arraigned."

I turned to the car window again. "Harry, we're going to get you a lawyer. I'll call Jake, Alice—" No, not Alice, she wouldn't help him this time. When I'd tried to explain the silly misunderstanding about Aaron's book, she'd hung up on me. "I'll come to see you as soon as they let me." Harry didn't move, didn't show any sign of having heard me. The other cop came, and both of them got into the car. As they drove off, a couple of Dante Street neighbors slapped the side of the police car, shouting at the window, "You take care, Harry, hang in there, Harry." Harry gave no sign that he had heard them.

We stood around for another hour as one neighbor after another gave his or her version of what had happened. We fell silent whenever a man emerged from the house and shuffled off into the dark. "Still plenty more in there," someone said. We went on repeating our stories of what we had seen and thought and done, until we were tired enough and, one by one, just as the sky began to fade, went back to our houses.

I slept late on Saturday. Then I put on coffee and brought in *The Chronicle*. Yes, Berkeley was back on the front page for the first time since Patty Hearst days. The headlines read "Berkeley Rampage: Telegraph Avenue In Flames." Below them was a photo of Dan Lyon glaring into the camera as two policeman cuffed his hands behind his back. According to the report, the trouble on Telegraph Avenue had begun about nine P.M. when a movie was projected onto "the backside of a building adjacent to People's Park." The crowd watching the movie grew, then spilled into the street, blocking traffic. When police arrived to clear the street, the growing crowd began setting bonfires in the middle of the street. By the time the fire trucks arrived, they were breaking store windows, stealing merchandise, setting more fires. The second page carried a large photo of a tall, lithe young man jumping down from a shattered display window, his arms full of clothing.

"By eleven P.M. the crowd had grown to seven hundred, mostly juveniles, smashing windows and looting up and down the Avenue. Police were forced to retreat for their own safety and wait for back-up from off-duty, university, and reserve officers.

"At 11:30 the first fire bombs appeared, thrown into fire trucks and into a bookstore. Rioters grabbed hoses away from fire fighters, and before they could regain control of them, the store was gutted and two fire trucks severely damaged.

"Near midnight, the crowd—attracted perhaps by television coverage—had grown to more than one thousand, some with cans of gasoline they poured on fires in trash cans, dumpsters, and on one large bonfire set earlier at the corner of Durant and Telegraph. A line of one hundred police officers swept down the Avenue, sustaining some minor injuries while driving away part of the crowd. Twenty minutes later, a second sweep by police resulted in about a dozen arrests, including long-time Berkeley activist, Daniel Lyon, one of the organizers of the celebration, who allegedly had been pouring gasoline on fires and obstructing fire fighters.

"By one A.M. the crowd began to thin. An hour later order was restored, and public work crews had moved in to board up vandalized shops."

On the fourth page of the *Chronicle* I found a large photo of a young woman identified as manager of a shop (it looked like the jeans and t-shirt shop shown being looted in the other photo) who had been working late when the rioting started. She had hidden, crouched under a stairway, as shouting looters roamed through the shop, taking what they wanted. "I thought I was going to die, I thought they would rape and kill me." She had been rescued and escorted out by a homeless man she called "Cole," who had disappeared as soon as police arrived.

I went through the whole paper before I found a short paragraph on the last page, next to the obituaries, headlined "Owner Torches House."

"An unidentified man died, apparently of smoke inhalation, during a fire that did minor damage to a house at 1629 Dante Street. The owner, who admitted tossing a fire bomb into the backyard of the house, was identified as Harry Lynch, who owns and operates a bookstore on Telegraph Avenue. The incident does not appear to be connected with the riots that swept through Telegraph Avenue a few hours earlier."

I went to the phone. Jake already knew about Harry, had called his lawyer an hour before. "See you at the arraignment."

That afternoon I walked up to Telegraph Avenue. There were quite a few of us walking up and down the Avenue, watched by pairs of cops standing in front of shops where workmen were putting up the last plywood sheets. Some of the plywood had already been smeared with graffiti, the largest one reading PEACE. The last shop to be boarded up, the most heavily damaged, was Get A Life. The brick walls were still intact, but, just before the last sheet of plywood went up, I could see, through the open window frames, the black mounds of smoldering books. Harry's stake, to "tide him over" was gone. Painted in red on the sidewalk in front of the store, were the words Bigot, Gay Hater, Slumlord, Kill Yuppie Scum.

I looked up from the splotches on the sidewalk to see Lisa standing there, looking at the store, tears running down her face. She saw me and looked panicky. She shook her head. "I didn't mean to—I didn't really think that—" she mouthed. Then, as I went on staring silently at her, she turned away and hurried down the street.

When I got home, I called the City Jail and got the date of Harry's arraignment, two days off, Thursday. "All arraignments are set for one P.M. at 2120 Martin Luther King, next to old City Hall. Arraignments in room 203."

During the next couple of days, I looked for follow-up articles and photos of the Telegraph Avenue riots. There was a small photo of Dan Lyon, holding up a triumphant clenched fist after being cited and released. There was nothing about the fire and the death at the Dante Street house. The destruction on Telegraph was reduced to a few columns on a back page. Front page headlines concentrated on the riots in China, the Tiananmen Square massacre, most of the page covered by the image of a young man standing alone, confronting a tank.

On Thursday, I hurried home after giving my first final exam. Mrs. Temple and I walked the few blocks up Martin Luther King Way, past old city hall, to a low green building I'd never noticed—2120, Superior Court Building. It looked like one of the cheap two-story office buildings thrown up after World War II. "My nephew says there's a tunnel connects it with the jail around the corner." The inside walls were green too, relieved at intervals by double doors of pale wood, with room numbers stamped above them.

Room 203 was shaped like a shallow but wide classroom, with only four long rows of fixed, padded seats. A railing separated these seats from an elevated platform strewn with Formica-topped tables and metal-legged chairs. At the center and slightly above this scatter of furniture stood a massive carved wooden judge's bench, like something ripped out of an older building and set down into this tacky clutter. Jake was already there. So was Marsha. We hadn't seen each other since that abruptly terminated lunch, and I think we were both glad to have the silence broken. She gave Mrs. Temple a hug, then me. I guess I looked surprised that she had come.

"I saw it in the paper and called the jail."

I looked at my watch. It was after two o'clock. We waited in silence, like people in church or like a theater audience after the house lights go down.

To our right there was a glass partition, and through it I could see a metal door with heavy levers and locks around its edges. That must be the door used by a prisoner to enter the little glass square of space. I had seen shackled prisoners in orange jump suits being arraigned on television news. I wondered if Harry would be wearing one of those garish uniforms, his hands and feet hobbled by chains that made the most powerful young men move like shambling, stumbling ancients. Would Harry be on television?

At that moment, my question was answered. A ruddy man with a camera perched on one shoulder entered from the outside hall, while at the same time a thin black woman wearing a brilliant blue dress came through a side door carrying folders she began to set out on the tables and on the judge's bench. She turned, glanced at the man with the camera, and said, "No television here, you know better. Take that camera out of here." The man shrugged and left. After a few minutes, he was back without the camera.

Jake was looking old and ill, his face sallow and elongated with sudden weight loss. Only his voice seemed to have his old growling, rough strength. "Harry refused to see my lawyer. That means he'll get a public defender, whether he wants a lawyer or not." We both silently turned our faces forward. The silence deepened. No longer like a theater or a church—more like a funeral.

Another twenty minutes passed. The clerk came and went. Other women and men came from the side door to the tables below the judge's bench. They spoke familiarly to one another, almost every comment ending with a laugh. They left, came back, exchanged cryptic references we spectators were obviously not meant to understand. Then they laughed some more, like old friends. These professionals—the clerk, bailiff, lawyers in dark suits—spoke a language full of unfinished sentences, like characters in a novel by Henry James.

A couple came in from the hallway and sat as far as they could from us in such a small room. Then a single young man entered and sat down on the other side, apart from them and from us.

One of the Henry James characters shuffling papers on the tables around the judge's bench, a small Asian woman, stepped down to the rail and scanned the room. Her long padded-shoulder brown suit coat almost reached her mini-skirt hem line. "You here for Harry Lynch?" We nodded. "Relatives?" We shook our heads. "I'll ask for a continuance until I can get an autopsy and a psychiatrist. That should keep him here a few more days before Santa Rita." She turned away again and went back to her papers.

Another half hour passed as people walked in and out through the side door. Only the clerk stayed in her place beside the judge's seat, behind the bench. No sign of a judge. Finally the half-dozen men and women settled into chairs hunched over the Formica tables facing the judge's bench.

"You need not rise," intoned the clerk, without a glance at us, then named the robed judge as she entered, a white woman with attractive white streaks running diagonally across her gray hair. As we waited, I wondered how to find out where she got such an elegant dye job. No, I decided, I'd have to lose fifteen pounds and upgrade my wardrobe to go with it. The judge mouthed questions at the people facing her from the tables, then sideways at her clerk, none of which I could understand. She shifted papers. Asked more questions. Nodded at brief answers, half-swallowed, key words blurred, like a circle of old friends at a large party, excluding eavesdroppers from their private gossip. She shifted another paper to another pile. I gathered that some cases were being put off or had already been settled.

Suddenly there was a loud grating of metal on metal, or metal dragged across concrete, or—I couldn't tell exactly what made the ugly noise echoing from behind the wall. Then the visible metal door opened just wide enough for a guard to squeeze through, followed by one prisoner, the two of them now side by side in the glass enclosure. The door quietly shut again. I was relieved to see that the prisoner— an Hispanic man, stout and sleepy, or just confused—was dressed in an ordinary plaid shirt and jeans. He kept his cuffed wrists low, hidden behind the wooden frame holding the glass, until he had to raise them to hold the papers the clerk handed to him. "Mr. (inaudible) you are charged with—" The judge mumbled and slurred the next words as if she didn't want to embarrass him. A man—the prosecutor?—rattled off several incomprehensible sentences, almost whispered at the judge. Then the public defender said, "Mr. (inaudible) stipulates—" and the rest was lost in another mumble. Everyone looked at everyone else and nodded. The judge asked the prisoner if he understood, and he nodded. Then he was led out again through the metal door, and, after it closed, I heard that hollow metal scraping sound again. I imagined some terrible cage he was being put into, but I knew the noise was probably made by an old gate, with rusted-out hinges, dragged across a concrete floor.

The judge left her bench again, going through a side doorway left open for all the comings and goings. Mrs. Temple glanced sideways at Jake and then at Marsha as if to ask, what now? another half hour? But the judge was back again in five minutes, shuffling through papers the clerk handed to her. While the prosecutor and the public defender mumbled answers to the judge's questions, I could hear the grating sound of metal dragged across concrete. Then a pause, then the narrow opening of the visible metal door. A guard came through followed by Harry, wearing a T-shirt and jeans, not his own, a bit loose, and I felt sure, if we could have seen his legs, a bit short. His eyes moved once around the room, but he gave no sign that he saw us. He stood unnaturally erect, rigid, expressionless, silently obeying the directions of the guard. Then he swayed slightly, touching his cuffed hands to the glass to steady himself. The guard leaned toward him solicitously. Harry shook his head, let his hands drop, and stood more firmly.

Papers were being passed back and forth, but when they were passed to Harry, he didn't take them until the guard spoke to him again. Then he took and held the papers without looking at them. The judge asked him a question quietly, then more loudly, "Mr. Lynch, do you understand?" Harry hesitated, looked around, then nodded slightly, then dropped the papers. The public defender and the prosecutor murmured a few sentences, out of which I picked up "continuance" and "psychiatric evaluation." The judge nodded. "We seem to be in agreement on this. Okay." The little metal door opened a crack, the guard turned Harry around, and he was gone.

So was the judge, out through the side door again, but not before she gave the slightest nod and smile in our direction. I looked at Marsha, who was giving the same nod and slight smile. When she saw me watching her, Marsha said, "Bunny. We were in third grade together at Hillside School."

The public defender leaned over the railing and flicked her fingers toward the door in the back of the room. We four got up and went out to the hallway, the defender following us. We huddled around her as she looked up at us and stated briskly, "So we got a continuance. The autopsy can take anywhere from a couple of days to a couple of weeks. By postponing arraignment till we have the report, we keep him here where you can visit him more easily than at Santa Rita. At least here he's got a private cell. That's policy in a murder case. Suicide watch."

"Is his mental state that bad?"

She shrugged. "I'm not a doctor. He's withdrawn. Won't talk to anyone. Maybe if you come and visit, you can get him talking."

"Are you going to plead insanity?" Marsha asked.

"That's pretty hard—ever since Hinkle got an insanity verdict after shooting President Reagan. The public was outraged—even though Hinkle had a long history. What about Mr. Lynch? Does he have a history of mental instability?" She was looking at me.

"Not that I know of."

"You've known him a long time?"

"Yes and no. He's from Montana. He was my student about twenty years ago. Then went back to Montana,

315

returned to Berkeley a couple of years ago. I know he had a difficult childhood—he wrote about it in my class."

"Abused?" she asked hopefully.

"No."

"So, how does it look?" Jake asked.

The defender paused, flicked a bit of lint off her suit, then shook her head. "Objectively, not good. There's a history of conflict between him and his tenants. Clear evidence of premeditation—home-made fire bomb carried there in his van. He admitted throwing it."

"But did he admit making it?" Marsha asked. The public defender looked impatient, and I wasn't sure what Marsha was getting at. "I'm sure he didn't mean to kill anyone."

"You throw a Molotov cocktail at a house and—"

"Into the back yard," Jake corrected.

"—at three in the morning, where people are sleeping, and it becomes hard to make a case for lack of intent to harm. A man died as a result of an act of arson. That's special circumstances, first degree murder."

"Harry? Murder? That's absurd," I said.

She glared up at me, then sighed. "I am explaining how the justice system works."

"Justice!" Mrs. Temple exploded. "Justice! You'd be ready to throw a bomb too! Justice? Harry trying to earn a living on a street they let that same trash take over. My nephew could have got himself killed up there the night this happened. That young man can't get into his own house because it's full of rotten no-goods we been trying to get out of there for two years. Two years. We call the police, we call the mayor, we call the rent board, we call the bank. Nobody will do anything. You call that justice?"

Silence. The public defender sighed again.

316

Marsha asked, gently, blandly, persistently, "What if Harry didn't make the fire-bomb? Would that change anything?"

Jake caught on. "What if he picked it up on the street the night of the riots?"

Mrs. Temple was nodding vigorously. "While he was watching his store burning, everything he had—going up—"

"Yes," I said. "What if he picked it up, and in his distraught state, drove back to his house and—would that still be premeditation?" We were all four nodding at what seemed to be the obvious explanation.

Even the public defender slowly began to nod. "I can try. Let's see what the psychiatrist says. If I can't get a strong enough diminished-capacity defense, I can try for second degree murder. I have to go back in now."

On our way out, we talked about ways to help Harry.

Jake would go to the Telegraph Avenue Association, try to get some merchants behind Harry while the riots were still fresh in everyone's mind. "Meanwhile, the burned-out store will sit there as is, to remind them." I saw Jake's eyes glisten before he turned away. It had been Jake's store too, his home, really, for twenty-five years. When he turned back to us, he said, in his usual rough voice. "Don't expect much—the others don't want to get their windows smashed again."

Mrs. Temple would work on the neighbors. I would write yet another letter giving the history of the house on Dante Street, and send copies everywhere I could think of. Mrs. Temple would get one copy of it signed as a petition to present at the City Council. "I'll get some neighbors to go with me. Maybe they're not so scared now." Mrs. Temple turned to Marsha. "You say you know that judge?"

Marsha nodded, but then we all shook our heads. Nothing should look like trying to influence the court. "But

317

I do know someone who can make sure we get Lillybee on the City Council agenda before Harry's trial. And I'll go along with you."

I called Angel, ready to bully him to put us on his morning show on KPFA. But even Angel had been bumped off KPFA, despite the fact that he had cut down on his drinking and was beginning to do a better morning show than he had in years. He gave me the name of the woman who had taken over his two-hour slot, but she never returned my calls.

The next day Dan Lyon's lawyer filed suit against Harry for $100,000—wrongful death of "John Doe," the still unidentified man, plus pain and suffering of the other inhabitants of the house and yard, also unnamed and uncounted. *The Bridge* printed an article on the third page with a photo of dejected men standing among charred ruins of their backyard shanties, mourning the lost "improvements" they had made in the house. I turned the page to read what Bishop Berkeley had to say. Nothing. The column was missing. (It never appeared again, and *The Bridge* itself folded a few months later.)

I called the jail, to arrange to visit Harry and tell him about our efforts, but the guard told me that Harry still refused to see anyone.

We finally got some good press, an article in a weekly that had been around for years, but that I rarely saw because it was distributed free only in more affluent neighborhoods. A young student/reporter new to Berkeley had interviewed our neighbors, summarized the house's history, then interviewed a few of the men still in the house, describing them as "alcoholic and disoriented." The young man's clear listing of facts was picked up by the *San Francisco Chronicle* and the *Oakland Tribune*.

And suddenly, really good news: the autopsy report revealed no trace of smoke in the lungs of John Doe. He had stopped breathing many hours before the fire bomb was tossed, and he had lain there unnoticed, a victim of drug overdose. The charges against Harry were reduced to arson and assault with a deadly weapon.

This must have shaken Dan Lyon's lawyer, who made a sudden offer to settle his clients' "pain and suffering" case for $80,000, part of the deal being to allow the district attorney to drop all charges against Harry. The *San Francisco Chronicle* carried a curt comment by the Berkeley District Attorney that "attorney for those suing the defendant in this case is not a Berkeley City official with authority to settle a criminal case."

There was only one further mention of Harry in any newspaper as he awaited trial. It was an editorial in the *Daily Cal*, titled "Injustice For Homeless." It mourned the "tragedy" that a judge intended to let Harry out on bail, "set loose to commit further acts of violence" because the judge "considers homeless people to be somehow less than fully human. In that regard, she has something in common with arsonist Harry Lynch." The writer needn't have bothered. Harry refused to post the bail money Marsha put up. But he did agree to let me visit him.

It was the first time I'd ever visited anyone in the Berkeley City Jail, which was on an upper floor of the police station, but felt and looked like an underground, gray concrete bunker. I was taken to a narrow, backless, plastic seat in front of a small window with a telephone hanging on the wall beside it.

319

After a few minutes Harry appeared and sat on the other side of the window. He looked pale and depressed, but not as stunned as he had looked during the arraignment. We each pulled a telephone off the wall and began a strangely near/far conversation—our faces only inches apart on either side of clear glass, speaking in voices that sounded far away.

During that first visit he asked me to thank everyone for trying to help. "Tell them the reason I couldn't see anyone at first was—when I thought I killed someone I— Jesus, I've been unable to—to ACT—all my life, and then— when I finally do something—then I lose it—and I'm a killer. How could I face any of you? I couldn't face myself." Then he explained why he still preferred to stay in jail rather than post bail. "Where would I stay? With you? Bring down a crowd of TV cameras? Not to mention pickets."

"We could find some other place. More private. Maybe Marsha or Jake know—"

"Some place to hide me?" He shook his head. "I might as well stay here. It's only a few days, maybe a week, they say, until some kind of hearing. Then we'll see. There's a chance I won't have to serve much time."

And time was up.

Harry's case disappeared from the news as headlines proclaimed "Huey Newton Shot Dead." It was the first time I'd seen his name in a headline in years. Newton had died on the street in a quarrel with a drug dealer. There was a huge memorial service. Others who also had once been in the headlines flew in to eulogize him. Within two days of printing the eulogies, newspapers were printing articles written by men and women "afraid until now" to mention threats, embezzlement, torture, and murder ordered or actually committed by Newton. Then came letters denouncing these writers, not denying the specific charges they made, but attributing all illegal acts to FBI undercover agents. A couple more letters scoffed at that view. Then silence.

On my next visit, I asked Harry if he'd made any plans for the future, after—whatever was decided.

"I can't stay in Berkeley."

"What about Black Oak? They haven't gone back on their offer?"

Harry shook his head. "But they'd be crazy to hire me. A killer? Okay, so the guy was already dead. But I could have—any customer walks into any store here will recognize me. If I owned Black Oak, I wouldn't hire me. No more than they would hire Eldridge Cleaver. I don't blame them."

"Where will you go? What about your grandmother in Idaho? Was it in the papers there?"

Harry nodded. "A Berzerkely story. Didn't make any connection with my relatives there, but I'm sure they saw it. I thought of maybe writing to one of my uncles, ask if I can just visit my grandmother—then go back to—there's still my shack in Walkerville. I wrote to Nonna Sara once after my mother died, then sent a photo of Jennifer when she was born, but hell, she could have died already. I'll have to find out. I'd like to see her before I—" Then a guard loomed behind him, and he hung up the phone.

On my third visit, Harry told me he had a hearing date three days off. He was more talkative—though he spoke into the telephone as if he were talking to himself, puzzled, even guilty about "failing Butte, missing the point," not "asking the right questions." When I asked him what the right questions would have been, he rambled a bit about the toxic, murderous Butte of Nonnarina's time being somehow a time of strong, even satisfying community. Was it adversity? Hope? Just another immigrant illusion? No, Nonnarina had been too down-to-earth for such illusions. Did the present-day Butte have any of that old down-to-earth strength? Had he just failed to see it? "If I was to start that novel again, I think I'd come at it from—" Suddenly Harry stopped, then nodded as if remembering something. "*The Auditor!*"

"What?"

"I kept trying to remember. It just came to me. "The Auditor," that's what they call him. This old wild dog, no one knows how old. I thought he'd be dead by now, but Jennifer told me people still see him wandering around the Berkeley Pit. Won't leave it. Wanders over mounds of acid rock that'll eat the soles off your boots. Up and down the ledges—a miracle he hasn't fallen into that acid water and dissolved. All you can see is a mass of dirty-gray, matted, mangy, tangled hair so long it drags on the ground, covers his eyes so he's blind. He's all alone, and he's mean, won't let anyone near him—except for one time he let an old miner cut the hair covering his eyes so he could see. People go up there and put out food for him. I used to do it too, before I left. Never got anything but a growl out of him. The guy who cut his hair built him a little dog house, for the winter, but no one ever sees him use it. Every winter they think he'll die, think they'll find his body after the snow melts.

But, come spring, he's back again, mean and mangy, still there."

Harry shook his head and hung up before I could tell him I was finishing up final grades, and wouldn't be able to see him before the hearing.

When I drove to Merritt to post my grades I found students already submitting designs for a mural to commemorate the Black Panthers—on top of that hill, so far from where Newton had lived and died. When I got home, the phone was ringing.

It was Jake. "I just talked to the public defender: Harry'll plead no contest and waive trial.

"Will he have to go to jail?"

"She's trying for a fine and probation. Keep your fingers crossed—and bring everyone you can."

The following day Mrs. Temple's nephew led a squad of police to evict the sixteen men left at 1629 Dante, taking some of them to jail for outstanding warrants. Neighbors came out to watch as the cops boarded up the house and told us to call them immediately if even one person tried to move back in; they now had clear authority to stop them.

Harry's hearing took even less time than his arraignment, and this time our neighbors and a few of Marsha's overflowed the little courtroom into the hall outside. Harry

323

got three years probation and a $10,000 fine, to be taken out of the equity of his rapidly appreciating house, after the bank had completed the foreclosure sale. People smiled and nodded, but no one applauded as we had after the People's Park hearing. We were glad to be rid of the squatters, but the way it had to happen, and the cost to Harry, were nothing to celebrate.

People stood near the door, shaking Harry's hand as Jake and I took him out of the building and put him into my car. Jake sat in back with him, Mrs. Temple up front with me. Just before we pulled out from the curb, Marsha reached in and pressed a wad of cash into Harry's hand. "Somebody took up a collection. To help tide you over."

No one spoke as we rode home, where I had some soup waiting. I put out some wine, and Jake raised his glass in a silent toast. The wine didn't loosen our tongues either. Finally Harry raised his glass and said, simply, "Thank you."

After a few more awkward attempts at conversation, Harry said, "I've got a rotten headache. Guess I'm tired. Maybe I could lie down in the shed?"

In the house, I insisted, but he shook his head and said, "Please," as if pleading for mercy from all our good intentions.

I left him in the shed, rolling out his sleeping bag. "Call me if you need anything."

Harry nodded. "I just want to sleep. I think I could sleep for a week."

When I got back into the house, Jake and Mrs. Temple had cleared the table and were ready to leave.

That night I slept straight through. It had finally sunken in that we were free from shouted obscenities, fights, fires, and filth.

The next morning, I stepped outside to get the morning paper, and noticed that Harry's van, parked in front of my house since his arrest, was gone. I went out to the shed. It was empty. I wasn't surprised.

That month I turned sixty. I had always planned to teach until at least sixty-five, longer if my health lasted. But thoughts of Harry hung over me like a dark, enervating, choking smog. As September came closer, I felt a terrible weariness—and guilt. I dreaded facing a group of new students and—I knew this was irrational—and doing them some unintentional, terrible injury. When I told the new president of the college that I had decided to retire, he made a long face and mumbled the obligatory phrases about my retirement being a loss to the college. But I could see in his lively eyes that he was calculating how much money he'd save by replacing me with a series of young part-timers on hourly pay, no benefits, no tenure, like migrant farm workers.

More than a decade has passed since Harry left. I've never heard from him. The Probation Department said his location is confidential, especially since the term of probation has expired, with, apparently no other trouble. Even the bank (citing "client confidentiality") refused to divulge where they had sent the few thousand dollars left to Harry after they foreclosed and paid his fine. The house at 1629 Dante Street was bought by a young inter-racial gay couple who gutted, repaired, and restored the house to a condition better than it had ever been—a turquoise, gold-trimmed little jewel.

After the 1991 Oakland hills fire, Alice, who hadn't spoken to me since the trouble at Harry's store, moved to a nursing home across the Bay, where I understand Father Mike visited her and converted her to Catholicism before she died.

Sometime that same year, I walked through one of the huge new shopping malls beside the shoreline freeway, and found myself at the newly built Emeryville City Hall. On impulse, I walked in and asked if the Bill Jackson photos of mud flat sculpture were still on display in the old City Hall Museum next door. Photos? Mud flats? No one knew what I was talking about. Finally an older woman remembered that there had been some huge photos on the walls of the little old council chamber, years ago. "They were stored in some warehouse when they built the new city hall." She knew of no plans to hang them anywhere again.

I don't remember exactly when I realized that Eldridge Cleaver had become truly invisible, no longer haunting local coffee houses. After nearly a quarter of a century in Berkeley, longer than he had lived anywhere else outside of prison, fewer and fewer people had to pretend not to see him. Not many recognized him or remembered why anyone should. In 1997 a couple of inches on the *Chronicle* obit page announced his death in Southern California. His "family" (so he had been reunited with his children?) refused to give a cause of death; no one cared enough to verify or refute the rumors of suicide. Cleaver was mentioned once more, the following year, in Beverly Axelrod's obituary, which told me something new. Years ago Beverly had quietly and persistently sued him for her share of royalties, as stipulated in the contract for *Soul on Ice,* but never paid by Cleaver. She had collected a regular if modest payment from the publishers. When I mentioned that interesting fact to people, they only looked confused; no one remembers Beverly either.

Nor any of the figures depicted on the Haste Street mural, regularly freshened up with new paint by the artist's friends, led by Dan Lyon. At the most recent touchup, an instantly recognizable figure was added in the lower right corner, a beggar with his hand out. Teenagers who come to buy and sell recordings in the store have no clue of its long sleepy history as Steadman's Used Books or its short, turbulent history as Get A Life.

The university continues its attempts (with regular payments for landscaping and regular demands on the city government for better policing) to make People's Park less of an open-air flop house for the lost, the lunatic, and the lawless. The volleyball court was given up after someone added broken glass to the sand where some UC students played barefoot. The asphalt basketball court is doing better, frequented by mostly black kids dreaming of athletic stardom. Church folk still gather in prayer circles and dole out food. (But I seldom see Father Mike, who, according to Angel, suffers from Alzheimer's and gets lost if he leaves the apartment where his children take turns watching over him.) Surly men still growl threats around the free box, robbing, then driving off the weaker lost souls.

Only at the southwest corner can you see anything like what we hoped for when we defended the park. It is a small, carefully laid-out patch of plantings that burst into colorful blooms every spring. Very early one morning I discovered Angel tending it. He was sober and slim, with the quiet dignity of a white-bearded sage. I stopped to praise his efforts. He smiled. "It's my church, I guess." He devotes what used to be his radio time to cultivating his garden, "keeping the dream alive in one little corner." He had started the work when his health began to fail; now he, and that corner of the park, are looking much better.

A few yards north of Angel's flower garden stands the platform built when the park was first finished, intended for revolutionary music, dancing, and speeches. It usually stands empty all year until May, when Dan Lyon convenes the annual celebration of People's Park.

The last one I walked through was quiet and poorly attended—by a few dozen middle-aged people (not quite old enough to have been among those who helped create the park). Half of them had stripped naked (which I never saw anyone do during the actual beginnings of the park) displaying sagging, sun-burning bodies, ignored by police and passers by. On one table, faded and blurred photos were displayed, captioned Building People's Park; at another table a man my age distributed literature urging resurrection of the Peace and Freedom Party and copies of an annual Black Panther Party Commemorative newspaper. Its contents were the same as previous years—quotations from Huey Newton's 1965 speeches— with one new feature: a full page ad bought by the remnants of the Gay Gladiators, denying that the HIV virus causes AIDS. (Aaron tells me that they still try to sneak into his e-mail with a virus that will disable his computer.) On the platform, speakers denounced the present war to the few who were listening. (Well-attended anti-war protests, featuring well-known speakers, take place in some other part of town.)

I asked, at one table after another, if I could leave a few flyers advertising the Public Library Literacy Project, where I began volunteering a few years ago. One table finally granted a bit of space for my flyers. On the speakers' stand, a man had grabbed the microphone and was furiously groaning into it, "I just put my backpack down, and someone stole it. Man, I had everything in it—everything—"

I stepped outside the park, drawn by shouts of excitement. On Haste Street, daredevil skate boarders, who seemed oblivious of the occasion for which the street had been closed, careened up and flew off the edges of wooden ramps, their landings even more graceful than their flight, then ran back for another try. I stopped beside one teenager who sat on the curb catching his breath. His eyes brightened as he watched other boys spinning into the air. Then he sprang up and ran toward the highest ramp.

Some years are worse than others on Telegraph Avenue, especially in the summer, when the streets are full of pierced, dyed, drugged, sick, surly, older-than-ever "youth" lying between their huge dogs. It is a routine invasion, hardly mentioned in the newspapers, except when reporters relish a Berzerkeley story. Like the summer the street squatters accepted free twenty-pound sacks of dog food offered by the local churches, but refused "infringement of animal sexual freedom" in the form of free sterilization of animals (then left dozens more sick, starving puppies to be euthenized at the animal shelter). Or the time the City Council debated the distinction between the right to sit on the street and the right to lie down, and tried to fix a legally allowed number of dogs to each human being. Their deliberations were drowned out, of course, by protesters brought to the meeting by Dan Lyon, who seems to be immortal, like some aged symphony orchestra conductors. It must be all that arm waving—good for the heart?

Sometimes Lyon loses a round, like the time the

squatters painted swastikas in front of Cody's Books to show what they thought of Andy Ross yelling at them to "clear the doorway!" That was a serious blunder, and Andy made the most of it. He called the newspapers and the television channels, who gave good coverage to this expression of neo-Nazi anti-Semitism. The City Council passed a resolution. The mayor called for a rally in front of Cody's Books.

Hundreds of people who had hardly set foot on Telegraph Avenue for years showed up. Even Jake, who could hardly stand anymore, came and sat on a chair Angel dragged out of Cody's Books. Together we all cheered the mayor's proclamation and the speeches by every politician who could manage to grab the microphone. After the rally, the mayor sent out the Green Machine, steaming, spraying, brushing and flushing the streets with (despite Dan Lyon's accusations of caustic chemicals) plain hot water.

The squatters never knew quite what hit them. Jake maintained that they didn't even know exactly what a swastika was or what "Nazi" meant, let alone that the owner of Cody's Books is a Jew. "And the funniest part of it," Jake said, "is that Andy knows they don't know, all of us know they don't know. But we do know our lines, we all played our parts perfectly in this farce." And, I must say, with considerable zest.

The effect was magic. It was amazing how little was needed to make these confused people pick up their dope and blankets and dogs, and leave. Until next summer.

Not long after that rally, just before the 2001 attack on New York, Jake died of his second or third heart attack. The *San Francisco Chronicle* printed a nice obituary, mentioning something Jake had never told me, that as a very young man he'd been an actor in New York, in Off-Broadway productions of comedies by Noel Coward.

Remembering how dramatically handsome he was when we were both substitute teachers in San Francisco, I could believe it. Aaron arranged the outdoor memorial service for a Saturday afternoon. Telegraph Avenue was closed between Dwight and Haste, and Cody's Books provided a microphone and a few folding chairs turned to face the record, tape and CD store that used to be Steadman's Used Books.

I spoke first because I'd known Jake as a teacher in San Francisco. His ex-wife talked about Jake's first store near Sather Gate. A retired professor told about early days, sitting for hours and playing chess with Jake. Pat Cody spoke about selling books on the Avenue in the sixties. Angel told about a brief period when he worked for Jake, who had paid for expensive dental work Angel needed. Father Mike wandered around the seated people with a confused look until Aaron took his arm gently, inviting him to say a few words about Jake. Father Mike smiled, took the microphone, and then, in a moment of convincing clarity, named Jake as the most generous of any of the merchants in supporting the soup kitchen. Even I was surprised at that, remembering the way Jake railed—right to the end—against locating these services near the campus. But then, I had no idea whether Father Mike was telling the truth or weaving another fantasy.

Aaron—looking thin but still fairly well—gave the longest speech, mentioning his third book, coming out in the fall, a detailed indictment of our health care system. He credited Jake with inspiring this interest from childhood, taking him to science fairs, buying him books. Aaron got a good laugh when he imitated Jake's gruff remark on learning Aaron had tested HIV positive. "Well, damn it, you'd better outlive me or I'll kill you!" Aaron has become

331

an impressive writer, and I'm trying to interest him in co-writing a how-to book on health advocacy with Pat Cody.

Mrs. Temple didn't come. She uses a walker now and rarely leaves the house. But she sent her son (now a Kaiser doctor on the verge of retirement). Bobby Temple told the crowd that he was one of the children to whom Jake had given books their parents could not afford.

Lisa had not been invited to speak, but she asked Aaron if she could read a poem about Jake. She looked, and was, mortally ill, her face corpse-like against her unnaturally black hair. (She died a few months later.) The poem wasn't bad. I remember the first two lines: "If you called Jake a just man/He'd throw a book at your head." Lisa concluded by announcing that the poem would be published in the tenth anniversary issue of the annual *Redwood Peak Review*.

Marsha has made a great success of the series. Famous names appear above their minor poems, along with better verse and stories by a few unknowns. She even printed a few poems by my students from the Library Literacy Program (and won for Redwood Peak Press yet another handsome foundation grant, this time for "outreach to the deprived"). Her children are all doing better now; two of them work for her in the publishing house. A new poem by Marsha appears in each issue, her trademark poem of loss and yearning. The latest versions have become so standardized that they read like an unconscious parody of the first one she wrote after Ivan's death. But I'm apparently the only person who sees them that way. (She now denies that she ever wrote under the name Belinda Basket, and the last time she visited my house, my old copy of that book went missing.)

When Lisa finished reading her poem, Angel started moving the chairs back into Cody's, and one of those over–amplified electronic trios Jake hated began playing. As I stood there, Angel stopped for a moment and put one arm around my shoulders. "You know, Ruth, I didn't tell my favorite story about Jake."

"What was that? Maybe I know it."

Angel shook his head. "I don't think you do. It was in sixty-nine, seventy? People's Park was still going on, but Harry was gone already. We were sitting at the Med—you and Jake and me—when Dan came and sat down, started talking. After a few minutes you had to go, "papers to read," as usual. Danny watched you leave, then looked at me and said, 'I don't understand how you can be so friendly with a woman who's so nonpolitical.'

"Jake exploded. 'Nonpolitical? Because she's not out there with you throwing rocks at the police?' Jake started thumping on the table. 'Because she's too busy showing up every morning, to face the *people* you're always going to save—making them read the books that will show them who's screwing them—making them put a thought on paper. And when the first thing they write is that she's a privileged, elitist, racist bitch for pushing them so hard—she corrects their spelling and suggests a stronger adjective!' By then Jake was standing. Everyone was watching. 'Ruth is more political on a bad teaching day than you ever will be in your whole life!' And then he marched out."

Angel started laughing—and suddenly I was stupidly sobbing on his shoulder. He patted my shoulder awkwardly, embarrassed. I blew my nose in a wad of tissues he handed me. Then I let him go back to folding up the chairs.

As I stood there wiping my eyes and watching people who were drifting past, I saw a very tall, pale man in his fifties, standing on the edge of the crowd, staring at the store that had been Steadman's Used Books, then Get A Life. He looked like Harry, so much like Harry that I stood up and walked toward him. But it wasn't Harry.

That was my first "sighting" of Harry. Since then I imagine that I catch a glimpse of him in various places: on the UC campus, in Sproul Plaza or near the Hearst School Of Mines; on the street that used to be called Grove in front of the building that used to be Merritt College; in a photo in the newspaper, like that street scene after the attack on the World Trade Center; in a photograph of war protesters or strikers near docks or mines; even, God forbid, on a TV news video of arrests at one of those "survivalist militia" camps in Montana.

In my more optimistic moods I remember Harry's story of the tough mongrel dog hanging on near the Berkeley Pit. I imagine Harry, too, hanging on back in Butte. Maybe his daughter visits him from New York or Texas or wherever she settled after finishing college, and has even brought a grandchild to sit on his lap. Maybe he married again and has more children. Maybe he is again doing technical writing for Superfund scientists, and working part time in a historic saloon—where he is now accepted, having won the respect of the old customers, as the bomber of those "Berzerkeley communist hippies." Maybe they tell him old mining stories and confide secret griefs and undying hopes, knowing he may write them down, but trusting him to give voice to their pain and their pride. Maybe at the end of his shift behind the bar he goes back to his old miner's shack in Walkerville, where, looking over the orange moonscape of mine hill toward the head frame where his Nonnarina died, he feels inspired to make another try at her story. I'll bet he is getting it right this time, and one day, a manuscript will thud through my mail slot, with a note asking for my comments.

Twice a year, the mail does bring me some news from Butte. When Get A Life was burned out, Harry's mail came here for a while. Somehow my address was never taken off the mailing list for *Pit Watch*, a one-page newsprint publication, reporting on the status of the Berkeley Pit, published with the help of Superfund money.

The front of the current issue pictures the Butte High School students most recently awarded prizes for studying and writing about the Pit. Every issue of *Pit Watch* opens up into a double-page, cross-section diagram of the Berkeley Pit. Lines and labels clearly mark, define, and explain terms like bedrock, contact point, alluvium. Within the stratified, labeled walls of the pit, a delicate baby-blue tint depicts the rising liquid.

Across the bottom of the page runs a timeline, starting from 1982, the year the Pit was abandoned and began to fill, and extending to 2021, the date originally projected as the year of Critical Water Level: the year when the toxic liquid would rise high enough to poison the alluvial soil. Like every previous issue I've received, this one adjusts the Year of Critical Water Level, bringing it closer. The toxic liquid continues to rise faster than expected, while all attempts to reduce it, to purify it, to extract the poisons, have failed.

But this latest *Pit Watch* offers hope. A recent analysis of the rising chemical soup has isolated a previously unknown bacteria. This new bacteria not only survives in the waters of the Berkeley Pit, it feeds on the toxic chemicals in it. The brief article concludes that a new life form may be evolving and multiplying to absorb, assimilate, and neutralize the toxic chemicals, rendering the rising waters harmless, even drinkable.

Design and Production Notes

Just as I have always insisted the frames on my paintings reflect the thought, care, and effort that went into the works themselves, at Clark City Press we feel the same way about the production values of the books we publish. Obviously, fine paper, proper binding, and a handsome cover can do nothing to help poorly crafted writing. However, we go to great lengths never to publish such, and therefore, do everything possible to dignify our books, as exemplified by *The Berkeley Pit.*

Not only do we put considerable effort into design, typography, and the selection of materials, but we also keep our authors completely inside the loop with every decision. For instance, I first envisioned the cover for this book as the Campanile on the Berkeley campus, superimposed somehow with a gallus frame on the Butte Hill. However, no matter how many months I struggled with this, I finally had to tell Dorothy I could not make it work.

What about this then?" she said. "Some white feathers on oddly colored water, symbolizing the flock of birds that all died right after landing in the Pit." And that was it. I saw it immediately as a perfect concept. So, I turned to Cody Redmon, our technological staff of one, and tried to explain what I saw in my mind based on Dorothy's suggestion. A month later, he handed us two dozen digital photographs, all of which were approximately correct, but one was extraordinary beyond my highest hopes, and we were done; a cover which reaches out for the reader's attention like Muhammed Ali's left jab.

The text is set in Century Schoolbook, and the titles in Centaur. R.C.